I have never told anyone this before.

The worst was long over, of course. Intense shame had faded and the knowledge of having made the greatest possible fool of myself. Forty years and more had done their work there . . . I had done my best never to think about it, to blot it all out, never to permit to ring on my inward ear Mrs. Thorn's words: "How dare you say such a thing! How dare you be so disgusting! At your age, a child, you must be sick in your mind."

The memory, never completely exorcised, still had the power to punish the adult for the child's mistake.

Until today . . .

—*from "The Orchard Walls" by Ruth Rendell*

MORE MYSTERIES FROM THE
BERKLEY PUBLISHING GROUP . . .

THE HERON CARVIC MISS SEETON MYSTERIES: Retired art teacher Miss Seeton steps in where Scotland Yard stumbles. "A most beguiling protagonist!"
—*New York Times*

by Heron Carvic
MISS SEETON SINGS
MISS SEETON DRAWS THE LINE
WITCH MISS SEETON
PICTURE MISS SEETON
ODDS ON MISS SEETON

by Hamilton Crane
HANDS UP, MISS SEETON
MISS SEETON CRACKS THE CASE
MISS SEETON PAINTS THE TOWN
MISS SEETON BY MOONLIGHT
MISS SEETON ROCKS THE CRADLE
MISS SEETON GOES TO BAT
MISS SEETON PLANTS SUSPICION
STARRING MISS SEETON
MISS SEETON UNDERCOVER
MISS SEETON RULES
SOLD TO MISS SEETON

by Hampton Charles
ADVANTAGE MISS SEETON
MISS SEETON AT THE HELM
MISS SEETON, BY APPOINTMENT

SISTERS IN CRIME: Criminally entertaining short stories from the top women of mystery and suspense. "Excellent!" —*Newsweek*

edited by Marilyn Wallace
SISTERS IN CRIME
SISTERS IN CRIME 2
SISTERS IN CRIME 3

SISTERS IN CRIME 4
SISTERS IN CRIME 5

KATE SHUGAK MYSTERIES: A former D.A. solves crimes in the far Alaska north . . .

by Dana Stabenow
A COLD DAY FOR MURDER
DEAD IN THE WATER
A FATAL THAW

A COLD-BLOODED BUSINESS
PLAY WITH FIRE

INSPECTOR BANKS MYSTERIES: Award-winning British detective fiction at its finest . . . "Robinson's novels are habit-forming!" —*West Coast Review of Books*

by Peter Robinson
THE HANGING VALLEY
WEDNESDAY'S CHILD

PAST REASON HATED
FINAL ACCOUNT

CASS JAMESON MYSTERIES: Lawyer Cass Jameson seeks justice in the criminal courts of New York City in this highly acclaimed series . . . "A witty, gritty heroine."
—*New York Post*

by Carolyn Wheat
FRESH KILLS

DEAD MAN'S THOUGHTS

SCOTLAND YARD MYSTERIES: Featuring Detective Superintendent Duncan Kincaid and his partner, Sergeant Gemma James . . . "Charming!"
—*New York Times Book Review*

by Deborah Crombie
A SHARE IN DEATH

ALL SHALL BE WELL

WOMEN OF MYSTERY: Stories of suspense from today's top female mystery writers!

edited by Cynthia Manson
WOMEN OF MYSTERY

WOMEN OF MYSTERY II

WOMEN OF MYSTERY II

Stories from *Ellery Queen's Mystery Magazine*
and *Alfred Hitchcock Mystery Magazine*

EDITED BY
CYNTHIA MANSON

BERKLEY PRIME CRIME, NEW YORK

WOMEN OF MYSTERY II

A Berkley Prime Crime Book / published by arrangement with Carroll & Graf Publishers, Inc.

PRINTING HISTORY
Carroll & Graf hardcover edition / September 1994
Berkley Prime Crime edition / November 1995

ISBN: 0-425-15054-2

Berkley Prime Crime Books are published
by The Berkley Publishing Group,
200 Madison Avenue, New York, NY 10016.
The name BERKLEY PRIME CRIME and the BERKLEY PRIME CRIME
design are trademarks belonging to Berkley Publishing Corporation.

PRINTED IN THE UNITED STATES OF AMERICA

10 9 8 7 6 5 4 3 2 1

Contents

Introduction

The success of the first anthology *Women of Mystery* prompted us to turn to the pages of *Alfred Hitchcock Mystery Magazine* and *Ellery Queen's Mystery Magazine* once again to gather stories that feature private detectives, amateur sleuths, cops, journalists, and spies, all of them having one thing in common: they are all women. Many of these leading ladies of crime, suspense, and mystery are the creation of well-established, award-winning authors and they are complemented by the work of emerging new writers.

Most of the stories in this anthology reflect issues women today face in their everyday lives, yet the writers do not allow their political views to overshadow their suspenseful narrative and well-crafted plots. To illustrate this point, I call attention to "The General's Task Force" by Pearl G. Aldrich, in which the tables are turned on the men in the U.S. military when a female-led task force fights for equal rights in the army's barracks. The military "boys' club" policies are challenged even as this clever thriller unfolds.

Another excellent thriller is "Match Point in Berlin" by Patricia McGerr, in which her well-known character Selena

Mead spends a terrifying evening in Berlin during the Cold War. Other familiar series characters include Antonia Fraser's Jemima Shore, Amanda Cross's Kate Fansler, and Gillian Roberts's Amanda Pepper.

Two new female detectives who were introduced for the first time in *Alfred Hitchcock Mystery Magazine* are D. L. Richardson's Cassie Dillon in "Emerald Hookers and Gold Shields," who searches for her ex-partner's gold shield in the seedy side of Miami's backstreets, and S. J. Rozan's Lydia Chin in "Body English," a Chinese-American private investigator who fights cross-cultural barriers in order to prevent a murder.

These are well-developed characters who pound the streets as equals to their male counterparts. Building on the theme of strong characters we introduce Anne Wingate's Lorene Taylor in the story "Evelyn Lying There," a powerful story of a demoted policewoman who saves the life of her ex-partner, a man at the mercy of his wife's revenge.

Worthy of special mention are Ruth Rendell's "The Orchard Walls," a psychological thriller with a classic twist ending, and Joyce Harrington's "Cop Groupie," a harrowing tale of an undercover policewoman who "sets up" a serial killer. This collection would be incomplete without stories by Margaret Maron, Marcia Muller, Joan Hess, and Sharyn McCrumb, all of whom are included in this anthology.

We invite you to join these women of mystery as they continue their exciting adventures in *Women of Mystery II*.

—Cynthia Manson

WOMEN OF MYSTERY II

EMERALD HOOKERS AND GOLD SHIELDS

by D. L. Richardson

Why couldn't Dixon keep his problems to himself? And if he couldn't keep them to himself, why did he have to come to me for help? All I wanted was to get on with my life, run a great little restaurant, forget the ambush that put an end to my career as a cop.

So far I'd been doing a pretty good job. Just ask Tad, my friend and half owner of Dillon's. Then Dixon showed up. An unwelcome blast from the past ruining a perfectly good Tuesday.

In the first place, he should have known better. In the second place, he was a cop. He could have handled it himself and been faster about it. All that information just a computer entry code away.

"But you're a woman, Dillon," he protested.

"And here I thought all this time you had never noticed."

"You know what I mean." He looked around at the servers, who were giving us a wide berth while they finished their pre-opening chores. "You'll be discreet."

1

"You should have considered discreet before you picked up a hooker."

"I told you. I was after information."

"Most cops use a twenty dollar bill. Budget cuts got you guys offering your—uh—services? Must have been one surprised hooker."

"Ah, come on, Cassie. Cut me some slack. This is serious."

It certainly was. Cops usually lost their gold shields through suspension or dismissal. Sometimes an officer-down situation resulted in a stolen shield. But this—at the very least this would get Dixon an official reprimand, which would just about negate any chances for promotion. Not that the beefy, sandy-haired cop was necessarily headed for bigger and better things. At the worst—well, a gold shield in the hands of the wrong person could cause all kinds of PR nightmares for a profession constantly fighting for favorable press even on good days.

I didn't like to consider what crimes could be committed with the aid of Dixon's detective shield, what crimes could have already been committed. What was I thinking about? I was a private citizen now, had been for nearly two years. What did I care?

"Why me, Dixon? You could do it yourself or get one of your buddies to help."

"I can't go to work without my shield." He leaned over the table for two next to the bar. "I have to be in court all day Thursday and maybe part of Friday. I'm taking the rest of the week as vacation."

"I repeat. Why me?"

"I told you. You'll be discreet." His green gaze was intent. "I can trust you."

Trust. There was a word I no longer used in the same sentence with police department.

"You never went in for all the juvenile razzing," he continued. "You knew when to keep your mouth shut. What happened two years ago—"

"Is old news," I snapped. "It has nothing to do with now."

Which was a lie. It had everything to do with now, with who and what I was.

"I'd be asking the same favor if you were still on the force." He hurried on. "Besides, you know this kid. It's Emerald."

Chronologically, Emerald could be considered a kid. But at nineteen, she'd already been on the street for four years, hooking for three and a half of that. Old beyond her years. A runaway that got away. A kid I couldn't reach.

"Find her yourself."

"What do you think I've been trying to do since Saturday night?" He realized his raised voice had filled the customerless dining room. "I've looked everywhere I know to look. She's disappeared."

"Does her disappearance have anything to do with the information you were trying to get from her?"

"Yes, but I can't tell you anything about that. It's police business."

"Dixon, how am I supposed to find her if I don't know why she's hiding?"

"Does this mean you'll do it? You'll find Emerald and get my shield back?" No beaver was ever more eager.

I looked around the still quiet restaurant. Coping with the lunch crowd would be no problem. One of the servers could double as hostess. But there was still plenty to do, once the noon rush was over, to get ready for our regular Tuesday Little Italy Night. I did some quick calculations and thought about my failure with Emerald. Then I gave myself a mental kick.

"I'll try."

Since my separation from the police department—that was their euphemism for my decision to take the disability pay and split—I didn't go into the city any more than absolutely necessary. At one time I expected to remain there until retirement. The city was a source of energy, excitement, stimulation. The country girl had found a new home.

But all that had changed in the course of one steamy evening in a trash-filled alley with thunder rumbling in from the Gulf. The alley had erupted with the sound of small arms fire, and the only thing that had given either of us any kind of chance was someone's nervous trigger finger spasmed by the thought of ambushing two cops. Even so, when the shooting was silenced by approaching sirens, my partner lay dead, and I was so near death the paramedics never expected me to make it to the hospital. They might not have given it much effort if it hadn't been for Dixon, who had shouted at them, "Just keep that thing on my bumper! I'll get you there!"

His voice had seemed to come from the far end of a long, dark tunnel, but some part of me—that part that was refusing to let go of life even as the blood poured from my body—had wanted desperately to scream in return, "Damn right! I'm alive. I intend to stay that way!"

Maybe that was why I was going back on my promise to myself to stay as far away from police and police work as possible. I owed Dixon, owed him for being one of the few who hadn't turned their backs on me and my partner when word leaked out we were working for Internal Affairs.

I pushed the bitter memories away and turned onto Parker Avenue. I was helping Dixon because he was a decent person, even if he wasn't always too bright a cop, and because, like it or not, I couldn't spend the rest of my life doing a one-person version of isolationism.

Nothing had changed in the Harbor District in the last two years. Surprise, surprise. Urban renewal would be a waste of time and money. Some dynamite and an army of bulldozers would be the best bet. But even they would only send the denizens of the area scurrying elsewhere to create another Harbor District under a different name. Talk about your black humor. I had a mental image of destruction crews following hookers and pimps and dealers around the city aboard giant tanks, waving fistfuls of dynamite, with new buildings springing up in their wake.

I parked and locked the Camaro. Even on the inland edge of the District, the scent of the Gulf mingled with the odors of diesel and garbage and errant lives. I checked my watch and headed for the Harbor Bar. In the heat of the afternoon, most of the hookers retreated to the shade, in this case various bars dotting the waterfront area, looking to pick up a stray seaman or a dock worker playing hookey. At night the street corners would be a fashion parade to make Blackwell shudder.

I was looking for one particular hooker. A tall, slender black woman who called herself Cherry Cola. Believe me when I say you don't want to know why. It took a couple of minutes to spot her, through dim light and last night's cigarette haze, sitting alone at the far end of the bar.

"Taking a break, Cherry?" I perched on the stool next to her. Cherry usually sat close to the door, "so they can see the fine stuff right off."

"Thinking about takin' the rest of the damn day. Maybe go to the beach. Drive out in my Bee Em Double U."

The bartender snickered and let the water out of his counter sink. It left under loud protest.

"Sold the Jag, huh?"

She really looked at me then, through the forest of false eyelashes. "Why, if it ain't the Sheriff, as I live and breathe. Where you been hidin', girl?"

Having Dillon as a last name had earned me more nicknames than I cared to remember. Sheriff was one of the benign ones.

"Around," I answered.

The bartender sighed, his big belly getting to me about two minutes before the rest of him. "I guess you'll be wanting something like white wine."

"Watch your mouth, Joe," Cherry snapped. "You're talkin' to a stand-up cop. Ain't too many of them around."

"Ex-cop, Cherry. I'll have a beer. Whatever's cold. And bring one for Cherry."

He snorted and turned away.

"I heard about what happened, sugar." Cherry lowered her voice in reference to the shooting. "Bad business. Heard they never caught the guys."

Officially, it was still an open case. Unofficially . . .

"Nope."

Joe set two bottles in front of us.

Cherry frowned at him. "What happened to all them glasses you just washed?"

"The bottle is fine," I said.

"Girl, you don't know where that bottle's been."

"Like a lot of things around here," the bartender muttered before retreating under her barrage of obscenities.

Cherry made a big show of wiping the mouth of the bottle. "Word on the street was all your cop buddies suddenly had a bad case of we're-busy-call-later's."

"Crime is on the rise."

"Everywhere," she said wisely, downing another swig of the tepid beer. "Hear you're living up in Sunset Beach now, running a restaurant."

The street system of communication could put AT&T to shame. She probably knew how many people came into the place on a good night.

"You ever want to get out of the business, I'll give you a job."

"I'll keep that in mind."

She knew I was serious, and we both knew she'd already been in the business too long.

"So, girl, what brings you back to the armpit of the city?"

"Emerald."

"Ain't you give up on that skinny little white thing yet? Some people don't want to be saved."

"Is she still tricking for Big Ed?"

"That sleazoid done found himself on the wrong side of

the wrong person. Fished his body out of the water two, three months ago."

A lot of people on the street called Emerald's pimp Big *Bad* Ed. Definitely meaner than a junkyard dog if crossed. "Must have been some kind of heavy-weight wrong person."

"Ain't nobody down here talking much about it." She swigged and shrugged. "Probably drugs. The whole world's goin' to hell on a cocaine highway."

"Does Emerald have a new pimp?"

"She's been freelancin'. Don't see much of her." Cherry studied her beer a little too intently.

The bartender wandered over and pointed a stubby index finger at my untouched beer. "You gonna drink that or just admire it?"

"I'm letting it breathe, and you're polluting the air."

He held up both fat hands in surrender and backed away. When he reached the other end of the bar and started wiping the counter, I returned my attention to Cherry in time to see the last of a grin.

"You ain't lost your touch, Sheriff," she said. "Still know how to nail 'em with a look. Never knew gray eyes could be so mean."

"Cherry, I need to find Emerald. It's important."

The long red fingernails of her right hand gently scratched up and down the amber bottle. I'd seen her use the ploy on potential johns. It was designed to be just sensuous enough to keep their interest while she sized up their wallets and their temperaments. It was one of the reasons she had survived as long as she had with as few injuries as she'd had. Now she was stalling for a different reason.

"I haven't seen much of her lately." She read my look. "I'm a busy woman. Got a business to maintain, problems of my own. I ain't got time to listen to no skinny white girl whine about her problems."

"What kind of problems does she have?"

She hesitated just long enough to give the impression that

she had decided, against her better judgment, to tell the truth. "She had some trouble with a cop. One of your old buddies. He thought he could get a freebie. She thought she was grabbing his wallet. When she realized she'd grabbed his I.D. and shield, she freaked. Been hiding ever since. I ain't seen her since Sunday."

It was an old trick. Tell just enough of the truth to make it all sound like the truth. Something was definitely up, something big. Dixon's losing his gold shield should have been a source of great amusement. Cherry should have been laughing, making bad jokes, finagling a way to arrange the return of the I.D. in exchange for a finder's fee. Instead, she was lying and not doing a very good job of it.

I made sure the bartender was still out of earshot. "Look, Dixon wants his shield and his I.D. back. That's all. No questions, no recriminations."

"That's what the cops say."

"You know me better than that, Cherry," I snapped. Then, remembering what life was like for her, I reined in the anger. "You're forgetting I'm not a cop anymore. I'm down here doing a favor for a friend. If Emerald won't deal with me directly, that's fine. All I want is that shield." I paused, thinking about a skinny sixteen-year-old with two black eyes and the defense mechanisms of a seasoned warrior. "If Emerald is in trouble, maybe I can help. Maybe Dixon can help."

She snorted. "He's the one got her into this."

"By asking her questions?"

"What do you know about that?"

"What do you know?" I countered.

"All I know is, that's one scared little girl. She's been skittish ever since Big Ed got killed, but now she's just plain terrified. Won't say nothin' to nobody."

"Where is she, Cherry?"

"If she's that scared, I don't want no part of it. Life's no picnic even on a good day without going around invitin' trouble."

"Where is she, Cherry?"

"I done told that cop friend of yours I didn't know where she was."

"You don't owe Dixon. You do owe me. Where's Emerald?"

"I guess it was that stubbornness that kept you alive when ever'body else done give up on you." She sighed. "She's been staying with a friend of mine over on Nieland. Wilkins Arms, Apartment 3C. But she may be gone by now. She was as nervous as a junkie without a dime to his name and talkin' about gettin' out of town."

I pushed my untouched beer toward her. "Thanks, Cherry." I pulled one of the restaurant's business cards from my purse. "Any time you want a job." I put money for the beers on the counter. Exact change. No tip.

"I already got a job," Cherry said. Then, as I reached the door, she called, "But when I get the Jag out of the shop, we'll do lunch." Her breezy laughter followed me into the Florida heat.

Geographically, the Wilkins Arms was two blocks from the Harbor District proper. Attitude-wise, it was a lot closer. Wearing that same air of fatalism, the building looked as though it had resigned itself to a life of steady decline. If the two women sprawled on the shaded stoop were any indication, the residents were willing to bear silent witness to its demise.

I stepped over the younger one's outstretched legs and entered the dim foyer. As I climbed the stairs, cooking smells assaulted my nose, a raucous ethnic mixture strongly flavored with the odor of cooked cabbage. On the second floor landing a Latin youngster stared at me with huge brown eyes and then pedaled off down the hallway on her battered tricycle. I continued to the third floor, glad that I at least didn't have to pick my way over garbage and rats.

Rock music almost covered the sound of voices behind 3A. A board creaked underfoot, and by the time I was even with 3B, an eye peered at me from the tiny crack between the door and the frame. I smiled. The eye disappeared like a frightened bird, and the door closed. I stopped in front of 3C, noting three more apartments beyond, and knocked.

"Who is it?" a scratchy voice cried out almost immediately.

"My name is Cass Dillon," I shouted. "Cherry Cola sent me."

In a moment the door opened the width of the safety chain, and a gnome of a woman studied me with a suspicious frown. "How do you know Cherry?"

"I've arrested her more times than either she or I would care to remember."

The frown relaxed a centimeter. "You the one she calls the Marshal?"

It was a test. "Sheriff. I never could convince her that Matt Dillon was a marshal, not a sheriff."

The frown disappeared, as did the gnome while the door was freed of its restraint. "Can't be too careful," she said, swinging the door wide to admit me.

"No, ma'am."

The apartment didn't belong somewhere like the Wilkins Arms. The walls looked freshly painted, and the rug underfoot was Oriental. The real thing, unless I was badly mistaken. Furniture filled the room, the far end of which was a kitchen, but everything was so neat and tidy, you didn't notice. I spotted two obvious antiques, a walnut breakfront china cabinet and an old-fashioned pie safe, before I realized that most, if not all, of the furnishings were antiques. Genuine, well-cared-for antiques. A small fortune's worth.

Then I realized that the gnome of a woman who could have been somebody's grandmother in her blue floral print dress was the infamous Lady Jane Gray. A madam with a reputation for taking good care of her girls as well as her often influential clients. A woman who they said could be as intimidating as any six foot, two hundred pound pimp. I had never met her while I was on the force. She had already retired—at age seventy—and Cherry had already been on her own on the streets for a couple of years.

"Please, sit down."

"Thank you, Miss Gray." I settled onto a Queen Anne chair.

She smiled, her face a becoming maze of wrinkles. "Cherry said you were a smart one. Said it wouldn't take you long to figure out who I was." She sat in another Queen Anne chair, her feet barely brushing the floor.

"I guess she also told you why I'm here."

Lady Jane nodded. "Emerald." She shook her snow-white head morosely. "The business just isn't what it used to be."

I had to agree, reluctantly. As bad as prostitution was, at least with people like Lady Jane young girls had been protected, had even had a shot at something better. Today's pimps were into profit and the power trip that comes with degrading another human being.

"Is Emerald here?" I gestured toward the open doorway of the bedroom, where a fan pulled in cool air generated by the soft hum of an air conditioner.

"Left about an hour ago. Said she couldn't stand being cooped up a minute more. I told her being cooped up in here was a lot more pleasant than being cooped up in a coffin."

"Did she tell you what kind of trouble she's in? Who she's so afraid of?"

"She told me about taking that cop's shield, even showed it to me. But that's not what has her so scared. Whatever it is, she wouldn't tell me."

"You have any ideas?"

Her laughter was surprisingly youthful, and I could imagine the younger Lady Jane charming a roomful of men with a laugh, a touch of the hand. "Old habits die hard, don't they?" Her dark eyes sparkled. "I stayed in my old stomping ground even though I have more than enough money to move into one of those fancy condominiums on the beach. You still think and ask questions like a cop." Sadness touched her warm smile. "Some things can never be taken away from us." Before I could respond, she continued. "If I were guessing, I'd say it had something to do with her pimp's murder."

"Big Ed?"

Lady Jane nodded twice. "The street's been quiet about that one. Too quiet. At first I thought it was because somebody new was moving in, somebody with the kind of weight nobody wanted to cross."

"What changed your mind?"

"If you're going to move in on somebody's territory, you do it quick while the memory is fresh. That didn't happen."

"What about Ed's girls?"

"Scattered. A few are still independent, but most of them started working for someone else."

"But no one pimp profited more than the others?"

She shook her head. "Johnny the Razor picked up three, but that was the biggest group."

None of this cleared the mystery. Even if she had witnessed the murder, which is what Lady Jane was implying, Emerald wouldn't necessarily be in danger. Not in the Harbor District where nobody ever saw anything even if it happened under their noses and where identities and names were changed with regularity. Unless—

I looked up to see Lady Jane smiling at me, her eyes twinkling. She was right. Old habits did die hard. Big Ed's killer was the police department's problem. Mine was finding Emerald and getting Dixon's shield.

"Do you think Emerald will be back?"

"She had the look of a scared rabbit. And she was carrying that big purse of hers."

The oversized denim purse was as much a part of Emerald's signature as her green miniskirts. She carried her most prized possessions in it, always ready for what she called "the possibility of a lifetime."

I stood. "Thank you, Lady Jane."

"Only wish I could have held on to her longer." She followed me to the door. "You might try the bus station."

"Did she have any money?"

"Said she did, but I'm not sure how much." She saw my glance around the room. "Nothing's missing, and if it were, she'd be welcome to it."

I paused in the open doorway. "Cherry didn't tell me how Big Ed was killed."

Lady Jane's hesitation was brief. "He'd been stabbed in the gut and then had his throat slit."

Her dark eyes met mine evenly. We were thinking the same thing. Among Emerald's possessions in the oversized purse was a wicked looking switchblade, a switchblade that Big Ed had once taken away from her and used to cut her.

The bus pulled out with the usual diesel roar and black belch. Fumes stagnated the air. I had watched four buses depart in the last half hour. According to the schedule board, the next one left in twenty minutes. Destinations meant nothing. A scared, nineteen-year-old hooker with limited funds didn't care where she was going as long as she was going.

Twenty minutes was enough time to search the terminal. Emerald would probably hide out somewhere original, like a restroom. I pushed into the coolness of the terminal. That is, if she hadn't already left and if she was even going by bus instead of by thumb. But she was here. I could almost feel her, or maybe it was her fear I felt.

Vinnie called it my "seventh sense." All good cops had a sixth sense, he said, gut reactions, hunches, intuitions. "But you, Dillon girl, have a seventh sense that goes beyond hunches. It's downright spooky, but you ought to listen to it more." Then he had grinned and said, "You wouldn't happen to know how the Dolphins are gonna do this weekend, would you?"

Vinnie, with his handsome smiling face and his good cop's sixth sense. We had made one hell of a team. Maybe if I'd paid closer attention to that seventh sense that day—

I sidestepped a maintenance person with a push broom. Stop it, Cassandra Dillon. We've been over this territory so many times there are ruts in the landscape. Vinnie's dead. Emerald isn't. Not yet, anyway.

The city was determined the three-year-old terminal was not going to end up like its seedy predecessor. Janitorial personnel were highly visible, as were signs regarding smoking and littering and loitering. A security guard gently hustled a drunk out a side door. I gave the coffee shop a quick scan. I checked between the rows of rental lockers and let my eyes sweep the lounge areas on my way to the women's restroom.

A female attendant left, a spray bottle in one hand, a sponge in the other. The blonde preening in the mirror stiffened.

"Hello, Emerald." I stood with my back to the door. "How long have you been a blonde?"

She shrugged and went back to combing her hair. "A while." She slid the comb into the huge denim purse.

"Funny. Dixon didn't say anything about the hair color change."

She smoothed the tattered jeans and knotted the large Bon Jovi T-shirt over one hip. "Who?"

"No games, Emerald. I don't have the time or the patience. Give me Dixon's shield, and I can go back to my restaurant and you can go wherever you're going."

"I heard you owned a restaurant now. Doing real good, too." She got a grip on the purse, wrapping the long shoulder strap around her hand twice. "I like your hair long, down on your shoulders like that. Real becoming. Ever think about going a couple of shades lighter?"

"I like it dark brown. Dixon's shield."

She rolled her eyes and took a couple of steps toward me. "You still got that cop's one-track mind, dontcha?" And she swung the purse.

I was ready and ducked. The weight and momentum of

the swinging purse gave me the extra seconds I needed. Before she could recover, I grabbed her arm and twisted it up behind her back.

"How many times to I have to tell you, Emerald?" I disentangled the purse from her grip. "Swing for the legs."

"You're hurting me," she protested.

"Quit being such a crybaby." I pushed her against the wall and worked to change my one-handed grip on the purse so I could turn it upside down. "I want Dixon's shield."

"Hey, Dillon! That's my stuff!" she cried when the contents began to spill on the floor. "You can't do that! I know my rights!"

"You're forgetting I'm not a cop anymore. Your rights don't mean spit to me." I shook the purse again. The switchblade clattered to the floor next to the clothes, the cosmetics, the shoes, who knew what else. Still keeping a firm grip on her arm, I used my foot to push through the junk. "Where's the shield, Emerald?"

"What shield?"

"Cut the crap!"

"I don't have it!" she shouted back.

"Where is it?"

"I sold it."

"You what?"

"I needed the money."

Then she started to cry.

I chose the park because it was quiet and public. The inability to escape one's past and its habits was being thrown up in my face at every turn today. The bench where we sat commanded a shaded view of the Gulf, while at the same time making it easy for me to keep an eye on the rest of the park.

The fact that Emerald was too scared to care if I knew it or to care if I saw her cry was enough to make me nervous. From our first meeting, she'd been a tough cookie, daring anyone to take his best shot, openly defiant of attempts to help her change her life. The walls she had thrown up to protect the little girl inside were virtually impenetrable.

She finished the hamburger and washed it down with icy Mountain Dew. "Thanks, Dillon."

Our two-person parade through the bus terminal had turned a few heads, but only because it was a break from the monotony. Once her sobs subsided, I had pulled into a gas station and stood guard while she got rid of the streaked makeup. When she emerged from the restroom, you could have mistaken her for any college freshman. Until you looked into her hard green eyes.

"What happened with Dixon?" I asked, gathering our trash and stuffing it in a paper sack.

"He wanted a freebie. I thought I was getting his wallet." She wasn't meeting my eyes. "Damn cops arrest you a few times they think they own you."

"Okay, that's the story you and/or Cherry concocted. Now, what really happened?" I asked it gently.

She almost smiled. "You still don't give an inch." She sighed and gazed out at the Gulf, the breeze toying with her platinum hair. "He caught me at the hotel." She knew I would know which one she meant. "The john had just left, and I was on my way out. I'd already told him half a dozen times I didn't want to talk to him."

"Dixon can be a nuisance when he wants to be." Any chance I had of getting information out of her was dependent upon my ability to keep our conversation just that—a conversation.

"He's a nuisance all right. I figured it was a setup, so I made him empty his pockets on the bed and then I made him take off his jacket and shirt."

"Why did you think he was wired?"

"Cops do that. They get down on tape and then they close in for the kill."

"What could you know that's worth a wire?"

She chewed on her thumb and scuffed at the sandy dirt. "I know who killed Big Ed." Her voice was quiet.

"So why didn't you just tell him?"

"You know better than that. How long do you think I'd last on the street if people thought I was a squeal? Besides, he already knew. He just wanted me to testify."

"Is that why you ran?"

"I thought I was grabbing his wallet. Honest to God. I got no use for a cop's shield or the trouble it brings."

"You found a way to make a profit from it," I pointed out.

"Yeah, well, I told you. I needed the money."

I thought about the bus ticket in my pocket. "To go to Atlanta."

"To go anywhere. To get out of here, man." Some of the old defiance was creeping back. "I can't make a living with the cops on my case."

"Testify. Get this murderer off the streets." Mentally I added, *And in jail with his own kind.*

"Nobody's gonna take the word of a hooker. He'd never see a day in jail, and where would I be? How long before they fished me out of the Gulf?" She flung her arm toward the broad blue expanse.

A little alarm was starting to go off in a recess of my brain. "Dixon knows better than to build a case on the testimony of a hooker. I'm sure your testimony is just part of the package."

"Then why is he so determined that I testify? Tell me that."

"An eyewitness account is the last nail in the coffin."

"Only it's my coffin," she muttered, brushing angrily at a stray tear.

The alarm was growing louder. "Why all the paranoia? Seems to me the police are the least of your worries."

She didn't answer, just swiped at another tear and chewed her lower lip.

There was a five-alarm fire in my head now. "Who killed Big Ed? Who's got you afraid of your own shadow?"

She looked away from me, toward the park. The breeze bore the scent of salt and a snatch of laughter.

"Cynthia." I used her real name gently. "Who killed Big Ed?"

She took a deep breath, expelled it, and then looked at me. Her platinum hair struggled in the wind. I knew before she uttered the words that it was trouble.

"A cop." I could barely hear her. "A cop killed Big Ed."

"Dammit, Dixon! You should have told me!"

I had run the bookkeeper out of the restaurant's small office in order to yell at Dixon in private. The dining room was empty except for a four-top of businessmen in earnest discussion and the servers working to transform the room into an Italian cafe. Emerald was ensconced in the kitchen under Tad's watchful eyes, a huge piece of Mert's pecan pie in front of her. Calorie City.

I hadn't wanted her to see Dixon arrive. She was convinced she was in a no-win situation. Maybe Dixon was drawing her into the open with the promise of protection so the only witness to Big Ed's murder could become another Harbor District statistic. If he was on the level, her testimony could still get her killed, because like it or not, she had a valid point. Who was going to take the word of a hooker over that of a cop? And just what were Dixon's intentions?

He opened his mouth, and I flung a finger in his face. "And don't give me that crap about police business."

"What would you have done differently if I'd told you?"

"I would have watched my tail, for one thing. What if someone followed you here and then followed me? Emerald's butt wouldn't have been the only one in a sling. I wasn't even carrying a gun."

"Nobody followed me. And even if they did, big deal. I was just visiting an old friend, making arrangements for a special family outing. I swear, Cass, if I had thought there was any danger I would have told you."

He seemed sincere. Hell, Dixon had always been a lousy

liar, a real washout at good-cop-bad-cop. I expelled a lungful of air and a mountain of tension with it.

"Does he know he's under suspicion?"

"Who?"

"The cop who killed Big Ed."

"It's been almost three months. He probably thinks he's free and clear." Dixon ran his fingers through his thick sandy hair. "He's been walking a straight line since then. Don't know how long that'll last."

I sat in the chair behind the desk. "Who is it?" I didn't really want to know. The department's garbage was its problem. But if I was going to be looking over my shoulder, I wanted to know whom to look for.

"Tierzog."

"So ol' Sammy finally screwed up and did something stupid. Why am I not surprised? You working through Internal Affairs?"

"After what happened to you and Vinnie?" A definitive headshake punctuated the sentence. "Until I've got a solid case to take to the D.A., it's just me and the captain in on this one."

I wondered about the logistics of that and then promptly dismissed it. I had other things to worry about. Namely a scared hooker in my kitchen.

"Emerald doesn't have your shield. She sold it for bus fare to Atlanta."

"She what?" Dixon jumped out of his chair.

"Don't go having a heart attack yet. I'm pretty sure I can get it back."

He dropped into the chair. "Pretty sure," he moaned and wiped his face with his hand. "Who'd she sell it to?"

"You don't want to know."

"My career is going down the toilet," he groaned. "What about Emerald?"

"For now, she's my problem. Once I get your shield back . . ." I shrugged. "I may put her on a bus myself."

"Come on, Cass. Without her I got no case."

"If she's all you have, then even *with* her you don't have a case and you know it." I forestalled any further protests. "Get out of here. Bring your family back for Little Italy Night. Seven thirty's a good time. Great food. Great company. Might be something special served with your dessert."

"And maybe the Tooth Fairy will pay for my kid's college education," he mumbled.

I don't know which bothered me more—watching over my shoulder for a dirty cop looking to cover his ass or trying to get Dixon's shield from Johnny the Razor, who hadn't gotten his nickname from a box of Cracker Jacks.

It would have been nice to be able to say that the quirks of the judicial system had disillusioned Tierzog, had so shattered his idealism that he had fallen into taking bribes and looking the other way at choreographed moments. But the truth was, Sammy Tierzog had been a rotten apple from Day One.

Every once in a while, one slips through the cracks of all the testing and evaluation. Tierzog had slithered his way onto the force and up the ladder to sergeant, where he would stay until he stopped a bullet, retired, or got caught. He was cagy enough to keep himself miles away from any life-threatening situations and smart enough to elude Internal Affairs for all these years. One scared hooker would be little more than a pebble in the road. The thought of his drawing a pension made me sick. I hoped Dixon could nail him.

Johnny Carmenetti's sadistic fondness for a straight razor made him one of the most feared pimps on the street. If you were one of his hookers, you didn't hold out on him unless you enjoyed collecting scars. He had been in and out of jail so many times since the age of twelve that they might as well have kept a designated cell for him. He and I had clashed twice—once when Emerald first hit the streets and then again when one of his hookers, out of desperation and terror, had come to me for help. Ironically, that same terror had driven her back to Johnny, and a week later her body had turned up in an alley. No new slashes. Just recent needle tracks.

As I crossed the park toward the meeting site, I decided that Dixon might indeed have better luck getting the Tooth Fairy to cough up college tuition than I would have getting his shield back from Johnny the Razor. To say there was no love lost between us was like saying Imelda Marcos *liked* shoes. After not being able to connect him to the hooker's death, I had spent three months making his "professional" life miserable. In fact, that harassment had started the chain of events leading to the ambush in the alley.

I spotted Johnny's strongarm help, a body builder with a shoulder-length ponytail, standing some twenty-five yards away next to a car. The muscle was for any males foolish enough to cause trouble. Johnny liked to handle feminine problems himself. Johnny and his trusty straight razor. I had often wondered if he was still carrying the same one he used to slice up his mother when he was fourteen. You know, for sentimental reasons or as a good luck charm. But I doubted Johnny even knew the word "sentimental" existed, and as far as luck went, he was probably only interested in profiting from other people's bad luck.

"Business must be pretty good, Johnny." I gestured toward the silver BMW.

He lounged back against the shaded picnic table and looked at me from behind a pair of dark Ray-Bans. "Times have changed since you've been away, Dillon. Diversification is the name of the game now."

"Give me a break, Carmenetti. You can't even spell the word."

"M-O-N-E-Y." It came out slowly, around the edges of a grin.

It wasn't hard to see how the young girls, many of them runaways, fell under his spell. Dark complexioned with long, curly black hair, he had a ready smile, gorgeous and gleaming. Always a snappy dresser, his clothes fit his slender frame with just the right combination of snugness and drape. Today it was chinos and an open-collared shirt with the sleeves casually rolled to the elbows. But his dark eyes, when you could see them, were as glacial and glittering as any snake's.

"I hear you changed careers, Dillon."

I leaned against the tree shading the picnic table. Both Johnny and his bodyguard were well within my field of sight. "I meet a better class of people."

"Me, too, Dillon. All the way around." The grin was slyer.

I just had time to wonder what he meant by that before he continued.

"So, Dillon, to what do I owe this honor?"

"I just thought we'd shoot the breeze a while."

He laughed. "Okay, okay. Can't blame a man for trying. It's not every day the cops come to me for help."

"I'm not a cop."

"But Dixon is. And from where I sit, he looks to be in a lot of trouble." He eased off the sunglasses and inspected the lenses. "Now, I seem to be in a position to do him a big favor." Johnny eyed me. "That would put him in a position to do *me* a favor."

"You're dreaming. Dixon would turn himself in before he'd do any favors for you. And if he didn't, *I'd* turn him in."

"You've been away too long, Dillon. You've forgotten the rules of the game."

"You're the one with the short memory. I never played your game, and the only rules were my rules."

"It's a whole other world now, Dillon."

"Pond scum is pond scum, whether it drives a beatup Caddy or a shiny new BMW."

His jaw tightened, and his eyes narrowed before the smirk was back in place. "Why should I help a cop?"

"What are you into now, Johnny? Gambling? Porno? Drugs?"

He shrugged. "I like to think of myself as an entrepreneur."

"A true entrepreneur always donates to humanitarian causes, charities."

"Charities are for assholes."

"Well, then, you'd fit right in."

He straightened and pointed a finger at me. "You know, Dillon, that mouth of yours was always trouble. You don't have a badge to hide behind now, so I'd be watching what I said if I were you."

I took some satisfaction in knowing I could still push his buttons. "You gave Emerald fifty dollars for the shield and I.D. A hundred dollars buys them back and buys you anonymity."

"A hundred dollars? It's worth a lot more than that."

"It's a fairer offer than the one you made Emerald."

"She's a dumb little hooker. I was feeling generous."

"So am I."

He looked around the park and then shook his head. "I'm doing all the giving and getting nothing in return. That's bad for business."

"You're getting fifty dollars. I realize that probably won't cover your gas for a week, but it is a profit. If it'll make you feel any better, think of it as completing your entrepreneurial image."

He thought about it, glancing over his shoulder at his bodyguard, then looking out over the short expanse of sunny grass. He returned his attention to me. "What if I consider it a favor to you?"

"What if you drop dead?"

He grinned. "You're so predictable, Dillon. I tell you what. You tell me where to find Emerald, I'll give you what you want, and we'll call it even."

"Why do you want Emerald?"

"Hey. Don't go getting that mother hen look. You had your shot at getting her off the street. She didn't want your help. I could use another pretty young thing. All I want to do is talk to her. Just talk. I told you, Dillon. Things have changed."

The wrapping had been prettied up, but the contents of the package were as rotten as ever. What I wanted to know was why he hadn't told me to get lost. And if he wanted Emerald, why hadn't he taken her when he had the chance, when she was trading Dixon's shield for bus fare? Something sure as hell was going on.

"I don't suppose you have it with you?" I asked.

"Too much crime on the streets. It's in a safe place." He consulted his Rolex. "I have another appointment. What if I meet you back here in two hours?"

"Just you and the muscle. Everybody in the same spots as now."

"Ooooh, Dillon. Getting paranoid in your old age."

"Humor me."

He stood and slid on his sunglasses. "Consider yourself humored."

He strolled in the direction of the BMW, and I had a sudden chill. Not only was something going on, but I was smackdab in the middle of it. Thanks a lot, Dixon.

"You didn't tell him where I was, did you?"

I started to say yes, he was waiting in the dining room, until I saw the genuine panic on Emerald's face.

"Even if he knew you were here, he knows better than to show his face, much less try to force you to go with him."

"Yeah, but . . ." She stopped and inspected her finger-nails.

"But what?"

"Nothing."

"Is Carmenetti connected to Big Ed's death?"

"You know who killed Ed."

"That's not what I asked."

"What difference does it make?" Her chin lifted in her characteristic I-don't-give-a-damn pose.

"Dammit, Emerald!" I resisted the urge to pound my

desk. Barely. "I'm trying to keep you alive. Dixon is trying to keep you alive. But you're so busy trying to prove how tough you are that you're hindering more than helping."

"How do you figure Dixon is trying to keep me alive? He got me into this mess."

"He didn't turn you out on the streets. He didn't force you to refuse all the help you were offered. He didn't make you associate with sleazeballs like Big Ed and Johnny the Razor." I realized I was shouting and took a deep breath. "Dixon could have used official channels to find you. He didn't. He came to me, even knowing how I feel about the department, because it was the safest way to find you. Not the safest for him, but the safest for you."

Her gaze dropped to the floor. "Yeah, well, I didn't ask to witness a murder," she mumbled.

It would have been useless to point out that that was exactly what she had asked for when she chose to be a prostitute.

I spoke quietly. "You weren't too scared to go to Carmenetti to sell Dixon's shield, but now you don't want him to know where you are. He had the perfect chance to talk you into working for him, but for some reason wants to have that conversation now. Explain."

"There's nothing to explain."

"Have it your way."

I pushed up from the desk and left the office. I checked all the tables in the dining room, spotted a soiled tablecloth, replaced it with a clean one, and redid the place settings. The blue-checked cloths gave the room a festive air which would be heightened by the arrival of the fresh flowers. I consulted my watch. It was about time for the delivery.

I moved to the bar and found that work on the candles had been interrupted. The customers loved the corny wax-dripped wine bottles with their stubby candles. I used a blue taper to drip wax on a bottle that had lost part of its coat and then replaced any dripless white candles that looked as though they wouldn't last the evening. I was working the tables closest to the bar when Emerald walked in, hands shoved in jeans pockets, chin less defiant.

"Can I do something to help?"

"There are some short bud vases in a box under this end of the bar. You could get them out, wipe them off, and fill them with water."

When the last of the candles were on the tables, I returned to the bar where Emerald was seemingly engrossed in her task. Just then Tad came in from the kitchen, a bucket of flowers in his hand. He spotted Emerald and raised an eyebrow in my direction. At my slight shrug, he set the bucket on the bar, smiled when Emerald looked up, and then returned to the kitchen. I set to work on the flowers, daisies, zinnias, marigolds, calendulas, lovingly tended by the residents of a home for the mentally handicapped with the assistance and guidance of a group of senior citizens.

"He's cute," Emerald said. "Is he your boyfriend?"

"He owns half of the restaurant. We've been good friends for a long time." I cut stems and stripped lower leaves.

"That's a pretty one."

I considered the red and white candy-striped zinnia in my hand. "They're my favorites."

"I like the daisies." She began filing the vases. "I went to Johnny because I knew he'd give me the best price. I didn't call ahead or anything. I just showed up at this bar where he does a lot of his business. He was real surprised to see me. Do these look okay?" She indicated the three vases she had filled with flowers, biting her lip as she waited for my answer.

"Very nice. You have a good eye for color. Each table gets a vase."

With a pleased smile on her face, she disappeared into the dining room. Tad stuck his head in from the kitchen.

"Need any help?"

"We're doing fine."

He winked and disappeared.

So Emerald had caught Carmenetti unawares. That still didn't explain why he had let her go.

Emerald returned from the dining room and resumed her work and her explanation. "I told Johnny I needed gas money so I could drive down to Naples with a friend, spend a few days. He seemed real pleased when he saw Dixon's I.D."

Yet when all things had been weighed, Johnny had considered knowing where Emerald was more important than possessing Dixon's I.D. Why? "He didn't try to talk you into working for him?" My fingers smelled like marigolds.

"He mentioned it. I said I'd think about it while I was gone." She combined variegated marigolds with daisies. "He sent me to the bar for some matches, but I still managed to overhear him tell that deltoid sleazoid of his to call The Man."

"The Man as in cop?"

"I didn't wait to find out. I had my money, so I got out of there." She used one of the bar's round serving trays to carry six filled vases into the dining room.

When she returned, I said, "Johnny was driving a BMW and wearing a Rolex."

"The watch is a fake, but he's real proud of that car. He's into a lot more than prostitution now." She fussed with a combination of daisies and calendulas.

"So he said. How long has that been going on?"

She shrugged. "A year or so. I'm not sure. I stay as far away from him as possible. He's crazy. Thinks he's indestructible now. Hasn't done a day of time in over a year. Brags about it."

"Can you finish these up? I need to make a phone call."

"Sure." A smile crossed her face, and she looked like sixteen-year-old Cynthia before she got off the bus.

In my office I dialed Dixon's home number and was glad he answered the phone.

"Dixon, this is Cass. Can you connect Johnny Carmenetti to Tierzog?"

"What does Johnny the Razor have to do with this?" he asked after a brief pause to shift gears from whatever he'd been doing to my abrupt question.

"Just answer."

"Circumstantially. Never hold up in court. He's got his tracks covered pretty good. Better than Tierzog. Why?"

"Curiosity. See you at dinner tonight." I hung up in the middle of his protests, knowing the rest of his afternoon would be plagued by questions and worst-case scenarios. Served him right.

When I returned to the dining room, Emerald was basking in Tad's praise.

He turned to me, his blue eyes sparkling. "The dining room looks great, doesn't it?"

"Does this mean it hasn't looked great on other Tuesday nights?"

"I didn't say that." He looked at Emerald. "Did I say that? Don't go putting words in my mouth, Dillon. She's always putting words in my mouth. She didn't get temperamental until we put her name over the door. I knew we should have called the place The Blue Duck."

Emerald giggled. I slipped my arm through his.

"Tad loves playing to an audience," I said to Emerald. Then I asked him, "Do you think you could find some other work for Emerald? She could use the extra money."

"Around a restaurant there's always something to be done. Hey, how are you at busing tables?"

"Well, okay, I guess. It's been a while."

"It's like riding a bicycle. You never forget."

She considered her jeans and Bon Jovi T-shirt. "I don't have a uniform or anything."

"No problem. We can come up with something. You finish the flowers, and then I'll show you the ropes."

She questioned me with a look and when I nodded hurried back to the bar.

I hugged Tad's arm close to me. "Thanks."

He dropped his voice. "She's a good kid."

I kissed his cheek. "And you're a good friend."

"What are you going to be doing in the meantime?"

"Hopefully, making it so she can get on that bus to Atlanta without looking over her shoulder." He was frowning. "Don't worry. I'll be back in time for the dinner rush."

"If you aren't, I'm changing the name to The Blue Duck." He headed back toward the kitchen and then paused. "Take your gun."

I opened my mouth to reply, but he was gone.

It was Tad who had convinced me that I should be an active partner in the restaurant and that I could rebuild my life just interstate minutes from the place where it had been destroyed and never know the difference. He had also urged me to take advantage of the privilege to continue carrying a concealed weapon. His father had been a cop, and Tad knew what a police officer's firearm meant to him or her.

"And no matter what has happened or what you say, deep down you still are and always will be a cop," he had said.

One of those rare moments when the intensely serious Tad came to the surface, it had also been the last time the gun or my dedication to my previous career had been discussed. So whatever information he'd been able to glean from Emerald during my first meeting with Johnny had been enough to make him mention the gun he knew I kept but hadn't carried for six months.

I locked the Camaro, pocketed the keys, and surveyed the area. Then I slung the strap of my shoulder purse across my chest like a bandolier and checked the length of the strap. The purse rested at hip level, and I could easily slide my hand in and curl my fingers around the butt of the Ruger 9mm. The guys on the force had made fun of me, but I had always pointed out that they were just jealous because they had to wear jackets in the hot Florida summers to conceal their weapons. One day I had come back to my desk to find two leather thongs attached to the bottom of a fabric purse so "you can tie down your holster like any self-respecting gunslinger."

Smiling in spite of myself at the memory, I crossed the street and began scouting the area surrounding the ten acre city park where I would be meeting Johnny. The heat of the day was trapped between its apex and its descent into the coolness of the night. Sweat slid down my back. I checked cars, looked down alleys, searched for familiar faces.

My captain had been the one to make arrangements necessary to keep my handguns legal. But only after he'd done everything he could to try to convince me to return to the force. He understood my refusal, recognized the bureaucratic thinking behind the department's offer of disability pay, put a stranglehold on his own feelings about the situation. He'd already had his say, at several departmental levels and at various volume levels. Nothing to be gained by pressing it further.

"Dammit, Dillon, carry the gun," he had snapped, his face red. "There are plenty of creeps on the street who would still like to take a shot at you."

I approached the park cautiously and began reconnoitering its perimeter. What I hadn't told the captain, or anyone, for that matter, was that I fully intended to carry a gun, legally or not. In fact, a snubnose .38 had been in the purse next to my chair in his office that day. The desk sergeant hadn't asked to search my purse, and I hadn't offered.

The BMW was parked exactly where it had been earlier, almost as if it had never moved. The bodyguard, chinos and T-shirt straining to contain his muscles, stood next to the right front tire. I glanced at my watch. From my position I couldn't see the picnic table, but I knew Johnny was there. I was almost ten minutes late, but I had something he wanted, and he would wait while I satisfied myself he was being true to his end of the bargain.

He was consulting his watch for the third time since I'd spotted him when I approached the picnic table from the same direction as earlier in the day. He adjusted the open collar of his shirt and stood. "You're late, Dillon."

"Actually I was early."

"You're really into this paranoia thing, aren't you?"

"I'm just picky about whom I choose to trust."

He shouted over his shoulder. "Lewis! Open up the car!" When the four doors stood agape and the trunk lid was raised to the sky, he said, "Johnny Carmenetti is a man of his word." He did a slow turn, hands away from his body, and then lifted each pantleg. "And I'm not carrying a gun."

"What about Lewis?"

"Lewis! Put your gun on top of the car."

"And," I prompted.

"And step away!"

Lewis obeyed. Johnny grinned. "See? We're two professionals conducting a business transaction." He made a sweeping gesture. "In a picturesque park in sunny Florida. Yuppie heaven."

"Let's not get carried away." Was he stalling for time, or was he just nervous? I could think of two reasons for him to be nervous. Either he was going to try to doublecross me or someone else was waiting in the wings. Maybe it was both. If he was stalling, I had already obliged him long enough. "I have a restaurant to run. Where's the shield?"

"Right here," he smiled, taking the leather billfold from his shirt pocket. "Good as new." He handed it over.

Everything was in order. The gold shield shone from one half of the leather wallet and Dixon's picture I.D. glared from the other side. I guess some law of nature makes mugshots and I.D. photos interchangeable. I slipped the leather case into my purse and handed Johnny an envelope.

"What's this?" he asked.

"One hundred dollars. As promised."

"I told you we'd call it even if you told me where I could find Emerald."

"Yeah, well, there's a small problem there."

"What do you mean?" The charming smile was replaced by a frown.

"When I caught up with Emerald, she was just about to board a bus for Atlanta. She coughed up your name in exchange for my letting her get on."

"We had a deal, Dillon." His voice timbre had dropped two threatening notches.

"Technically, I kept my end. You wanted to know where to find Emerald. I just told you. On a bus to Atlanta. The problem is that bus must make two dozen or more stops between here and Atlanta. You know how flighty Emerald is. She could be anywhere."

"Nobody welshes on a deal with Johnny Carmenetti." His hand slipped inside his pants pocket as he took a menacing step toward me.

Taking a corresponding step backward, I slid my hand easily into the purse. "I only paid five dollars for this purse at Wal-Mart, Johnny. Blowing a hole in it won't bother me one bit."

He stopped.

"Stay away from that gun, Lewis!" I shouted, keeping him in my peripheral vision while holding my eyes on Carmenetti.

Johnny raised a halting hand in the bodyguard's direction. After ten long seconds, he relaxed somewhat. "You were leaving yourself wide open there, Dillon, letting that cheap little hooker get on that bus before you checked out her story."

"Yours wasn't the first name she gave me." I shrugged. "Besides, she wouldn't have had that much of a head start on me. I could have caught up with her by now."

He seemed to be at a loss, caught somewhere between the desire to retaliate and protect his image and the common sense of simply walking away. Complicating matters was a third party, someone with strong motivation for finding Emerald. He turned, started away from me, then whirled.

"You know, Dillon, in the old days, you would never have gotten away with this."

"It's like you said, Johnny. Times change. Of course, Sammy Tierzog might not consider that an acceptable explanation."

"What does ol' Flatfoot Sammy have to do with this?" It was too casual.

"You tell me."

A lazy grin that would have made a teenager's heart flip-flop spread over his face. "Rumor has it ol' Sammy may be about to get his hand slapped for getting caught in the cookie jar."

"What do you know about it?"

He shrugged. "I hear things. I guess you could say I have my finger on the pulse of the city."

"Or in the same cookie jar with Tierzog?" I probed.

"Most people would say that having a cop for a business partner was pretty risky. Maybe even downright stupid."

"What do you say?"

He consulted his watch. "I say that you have a restaurant to run and I have appointments to keep." He tossed the envelope containing the hundred dollars onto the picnic table. "Keep your money, Dillon."

"No favors, Johnny," I warned.

"The way I figure it, Dillon, things work out, I could end up owing *you* a favor or two." He winked and then slid on his Ray-Bans. "Be seeing you, Dillon." He paused before getting into the BMW and called across to me. "Next time you talk to Emerald tell her Johnny C. sends a big kiss."

The bodyguard closed all the doors, and in under a minute the silver car glided off down the street and around the corner, almost as if it had never existed.

"I can't believe Carmenetti gave up so easily." Dixon's skepticism showed.

"I think he decided it was in his best interest to forget about Emerald."

I knotted the scarf at one hip and adjusted the triangle over the other hip. The vibrant blues, greens, and pinks contrasted nicely with the slim black skirt, which, along with a long-sleeved white blouse, I kept in the office closet for emergencies. Little Italy Night had been well on its way to full swing by the time I got back to the restaurant. I had just buttoned my blouse when Dixon had come barging in.

"How would he figure that?" Dixon had slipped the leather billfold into his hip pocket and his hand kept straying to it.

I pulled a mirror from a drawer, propped it up on the desktop, and began putting my hair up. "Maybe he's tired of being in business with Tierzog. He practically admitted to not trusting him." Under the circumstances, a simple ponytail was the best I could manage. "Maybe he already has everything he wants out of the partnership." I pulled eye shadow, mascara, blush, and lipstick from another drawer.

"Whatever the reason, he seems perfectly content to let the police department dissolve the partnership for him."

"Kind of risky, isn't it? I mean, Tierzog won't go down quietly."

"You said yourself that Johnny had his tracks covered. He didn't act like a man worried about his future."

"He's probably going to manage to turn a profit from this. I wonder what kind of plan he has up his sleeve," Dixon mused.

I applied lipstick and gave my face one last check before returning all the paraphernalia to the desk drawer. "I have no idea, and frankly, I don't care." I closed the drawer deliberately.

Dixon stopped his mental meandering. "I know I said it before, but thanks, Cass. I owe you big time for this."

I came around the desk and slid my feet into one-inch black heels. "As far as I'm concerned, I owed you for one hell of an ambulance ride. Just consider us even."

He became quiet, and I knew each of us was reliving personal memories of that day. The air felt weighted.

Then Dixon whistled. "You never would have been able to chase perps dressed like that, Dillon. I didn't know you had such good-looking legs."

"Better not let your wife hear you say that." I ushered him out of the office and paused in the bar long enough to give it a quick check. Only laughter and pleasant conversation.

"What about Emerald?" Dixon asked.

"After we close, I'm driving her up the coast to stay with a couple I know. They've had some success working with girls like her. She's promised to stick around if you need her." I shrugged. "Other than that, who knows?"

"You really think she can turn it around, start over?"

"If she wants to. I just don't know if she wants to badly enough."

"It won't be easy."

"No, it won't."

Leaving the street was never easy. Habits acquired from ugly survival lessons died hard, especially when some of the behavior on the streets was also present in the "civilized world," only in the more acceptable guises of society.

I could feel the old police cynicism slipping over me. Shaking it off, I put my arm through Dixon's, and we started toward the table where his wife and two children waited.

"You know, Cass, you're good at this," Dixon said.

"Why do I get the feeling you're not talking about the restaurant business?"

"I know this guy who has a problem. Seems someone in his company is selling company secrets. We're not talking IBM here, of course, but it's still costing him money."

"Forget it, Dixon. The one-time-offer-only has expired."

"It's in your blood, Dillon."

"I kicked the habit. Order the fettucini, but leave room for dessert. Mert promised something spectacularly sinful tonight."

"You can run, but you can't hide."

"Watch me."

ONE BEAUTIFUL BODY

=======================================

by Gillian Roberts

English teachers do not have power lunches.

It took a while to get this concept across to Ivy Jean Hoffman, but then, we moved in different circles.

I was surprised to find Ivy Jean still in Philadelphia. I had thought she'd moved on as literally as she had figuratively. I was still more surprised to find her in my neighborhood, and I was stupefied to find her in a supermarket, since she and food have been at war longer than the Arabs and the Israelis. Then I noticed that her cart contained nothing to chew or slurp or gnaw. It was piled high with non-edibles. A dozen boxes of designer facial tissues, an industrial-sized aluminum foil, bundles of soap, three colors of toilet paper, and five boxes of plastic wrap. I wondered what leftovers she wrapped in the plastic and foil.

"Amanda Pepper!" she chirped. "I don't believe it!" Which gives you an idea of her sincerity. She knew my center-city address and she also knew that, unlike her, I ate, so why shouldn't she believe I'd forage for food in my own neighborhood?

We sent make-believe kisses across our carts. Ivy's face barely moved. Way back when we were both eleven years old, she mastered the starlet's wide-eyed amazed stare to avoid building future wrinkles.

"I live right across the square now," she said.

I was not going to join Welcome Wagon.

"Finished redoing our condo this morning."

Maybe that's what she'd encase in plastic wrap.

"You have to see it. Must be time for our annual lunch, anyway." She pulled an organizer out of an alligator bag and flipped pages, looking for a window of opportunity in which to fit me. "Oh, dear," she murmured, "no wonder I'm stressed out."

I explained why I, too, would have difficulty making a date. With five sections of English, one study hall, one yearbook meeting, and sporadic lunch duty, I didn't "lunch." Furthermore, my school's definition of an hour was as skimpy as a psychiatrist's, though less well paid.

Ivy Jean Hoffman responded to the facts of my life with incredulity. "I can't believe you stand for being treated like a *slave*!" Her outrage made it clear, as it was intended to, that she was treated and paid extremely well and I was a mere lackey. "But we *have* to get together," she wailed. "Isn't there any time at all?"

We both knew weeks had more than five days, but we also knew that Saturday and Sunday were for fun, not for each other. "I have a free period after lunch Thursdays," I said. If I didn't prepare lesson plans or meet with disgruntled students, I could extract an hour and a half midday.

"But Thursday's perfect! This coming one I'm having the reunion committee to lunch. Nikki and I are co-chairs." Nikki was another high-school acquaintance and Ivy's business partner. "You zip over, you hear?" Sometimes Ivy played Southern Belle, although the high school she was reuniting had been just slightly west of Philadelphia.

"I really don't want to work on the reunion committee," I said.

"I hear you. Come anyway, Mandy. It'll be fun!"

I doubted that. Ivy Jean was a legacy. Our mothers had been close friends and so desperately wanted us to follow suit that the fact that we disliked each other from conception on didn't matter. Year after year, Ivy and I shared celebrations: we sat next to each other at *The Nutcracker* each December at the Academy of Music; we watched our dads burn burgers on July Fourth; we rode the waves at Beach Haven and even shared a high-school graduation party.

And still and all, Ivy — to me — was selfish, shallow, and stupid, and I was — to her — bookish, unstylish, and boring.

But when we were finally, happily separated in college, Ivy's mother died in a terrible automobile crash. Embarrassingly soon after, her father married a creature who kept forgetting there was such a person as Ivy and, somehow, Ivy's father's memory also failed. Ivy's bed was donated to Goodwill and the room quickly filled with cribs for newborn twin boys. That's about when Ivy began using me as a touchstone, proof that she did indeed exist.

She was obnoxious, self-obsessed, and unreliable, but she was also truly unmoored and lost. She gave a new meaning to the word insecure. It seemed little enough to shore her up, give her a personal history fix, prove that somebody remembered her. I was her past. And that is why, once a year, two women who didn't like each other nonetheless "did" lunch. Our table talk was always the same. First we validated the past with a round of nostalgia in which celebrations remembered were infinitely more pleasurable than they'd been when actually lived. Then we validated her present. We did Ivy — Ivy's face, Ivy's body, Ivy's food, Ivy's problems, Ivy's business, and Ivy's husband, all of which topics were basically interchangeable.

Ivy had been an unpopular child. She was convinced this had been due to her having been plain and pudgy.

I thought her obsessive concern with her appearance would subside once she snared Mitchell and married him, but I'd been wrong. Their marriage wasn't the answer to anything. Body size was. Ivy knew the caloric count of every menu listing in North America and the details of every get-thin-quick scam. I have "lunched" with her when she ate only red meat, only bananas, only protein, only carbohydrates, only beans and rice, only fruit, only fruit juice, only water. I listened to details of spas visited, diet gurus consulted, wraps and massages attempted, and lipo suctioned.

I listened and nodded. Now and then I said she would kill herself dieting. "You'll be a beautiful corpse," I'd say. An old joke, but she never laughed.

In the gospel according to Ivy Jean, goodness equaled thinness. Virtue equaled trimness, success equaled freedom from cellulite. Her single measure of man—or woman—was the span of the waist, hips, and thighs. Evil was "letting yourself go."

Five years ago, Ivy Jean turned her private obsession into public cash. She co-created "The You Within," or TYW to the initiated, a high-priced diet boutique that promised not only to unveil the thin woman smothered inside your flab, but to outfit her, style her hair, and set her free.

A ripe and timely idea. Ivy and Nikki now had three clinics and a fourth due to open. There was talk of nationwide franchising.

I bent over my grocery cart and camouflaged my half gallon of ice cream with a low-cal TV dinner. "Sounds like things are going wonderfully for you."

She rolled her eyes. Eyeballs never wrinkled, so she was fairly free with hers. "There's a reason I stock up on aspirin." And indeed, an economy-size bottle of extra-strength headache pills contained the only ingestible items in her basket. "Just between us," she said, "I haven't been too brilliant about picking partners. I'm talking business and marriage."

I knew her anxiety was sincere because she scowled, activating muscles and risking lines. "I wouldn't tell anybody but you," she continued, "because you're practically family, but Nikki makes me so *nervous* the way she fights over every penny the business needs—and I *eat* when I'm nervous and I'm becoming a *pig*—and what will that do to my *business?* Nothing *fits* and I have a TV spot for TYW to shoot next week! An *ad!* She's *destroying* me, and if she—" She stopped herself, looking momentarily confused. Once off the topic of herself, she was on unsteady ground. "And you?" she finally said with an air or discovery. "What's new?"

"Nothing much. Still teaching."

"And men?"

"Kind of." I didn't think she could understand the allure of my now and then, mostly now, thing with a homicide cop like C. K. Mackenzie. After all, it was my opinion that Ivy's husband Mitchell could be replaced by a boa constrictor—as long as the snake was rich—and nobody, most of all Ivy, would notice.

There was talk that Ivy Jean craved husbands—anybody's—the way other women lusted for chocolate. She had even once computed how many calories were burned at an assignation.

"Hmmm," Ivy said, spotting the Rocky Road in my cart. "Ice cream. Sixty percent fat. You know my saying: a minute on the lips, a lifetime on the hips." She seemed much cheerier, buoyed like a missionary who'd stumbled across a native worshiping tree roots. "I have a wonderful chart of fat percentages I want to share with you on Thursday," she said. "And don't worry. Lunch will be simple. I'll make something light."

The elevator deposited me in the foyer of Ivy's condo. The others were already there—partner Nikki and five other former classmates, all contemplating Ivy's locked door. We rang, knocked, chitted and chatted, but by twelve-fifteen, I was hungry and edgy.

"She does this all the time," Nikki grumbled. "Most unreliable—"

"I'm going downstairs," I said. "The lobby has chairs. And a phone. I'll call her. Maybe she fell asleep. Anybody want to join me?"

We all packed into the small elevator and descended. The lobby was not much larger than Ivy's foyer and it had a total of three chairs. We became excessively polite and democratic, which meant that none of us used the chairs. We all stood in a clump near a woman in a glow-in-the-dark lime outfit. She guarded a large carton filled with plastic foam containers. "Mrs. Hoffman expected me half an hour ago," she whispered harshly at the guard. "I'm her *caterer*."

"But, ma'am, I buzzed her apartment. She isn't home." He wore a cranberry uniform trimmed smartly in gold braid, but he looked defeated, as if he'd been drummed out of the corps but allowed to keep the costume.

"You don't understand! She wanted me out before her— she's expecting—" She finally noticed us, did a quick count, added one for the missing hostess, and her shoulders sagged. She lowered her voice, but we could all still hear her. "She didn't want her guests to know I'm doing the—"

So the simple and light thing Ivy made was a telephone call. It didn't really surprise me. Ivy was afraid of touching food, as if calories could be absorbed through the fingertips.

"Couldn't I set up and leave?" The caterer was frantic. "Now my next order's late, too. I'm going to lose every client I have! *Please?*"

The guard considered her, her carton, and the unscary seven of us. "Well," he said, "she did tell me about this little party of hers. I have the guest list, so I could double-check your names, ladies, I don't see why I couldn't let you into Mrs. Hoffman's." Slowly, slowly, demanding driver's licenses and a major credit card for I.D., he went through the list.

While the first of our group went through the guard's routine, Nikki seemed to lose it, but quietly. "Damn Ivy. Completely inconsiderate and self-centered. She probably forgot. Found something more exciting, like aerobics in bed. A nooner. With whoever."

"Whomever," I murmured.

"You shouldn't say that, Nikki!" For a second, I thought I had an ally, but Barby White wasn't talking grammar. I could see her eyes moisten.

"Sorry!" Nikki snapped. "I didn't say *who*, did I?"

Whom, I said, but silently.

Barby White sniffled.

"Well, then," Nikki said, "if the shoe fits, wear it."

Bad grammar and excessive use of clichés. It was obvious that Nikki was no good.

"You're so mean!" Barby wailed.

"Come on," Nikki said. "Grow up. Sometimes the truth hurts, but knowledge is power. You'll get over it, and so will he. He'll come back. Ivy has a short attention span."

The guard called Nikki's name.

Barby stood to my right, by herself. Her skin flushed, then drained, pale to beet-borscht red to pasty bloodlessness.

I was almost as stunned as she. Zoological images filled my brain. Nikki was a snake, a cat, a cur, a rat. The rest of the reunion committee seemed to agree. I heard a whispered chorus of reactions on my left.

"That was way, way below the belt."

"But Barby must have known, don't you think? I mean if *we* did, surely she must!"

"It was obvious that she knew. Why else would she react that way? But all the same . . ."

"I don't think she did. The wife's always last. Besides, would Barby be on Ivy's committee if she knew?"

The guard decided that Nikki was who she was and called Barby. Looking loose and flabby, like one who had definitely Let Herself Go, Barby turned to nobody in particular and said, "My husband wouldn't sleep with that broomstick." But she walked to the guard like someone drugged.

"Neither will Ivy's husband," somebody said. "His girl-friends tend to be voluptuous."

One by one we were okayed by the guard and then finally admitted into the absolute splendor of Ivy Jean Hoffman's abode. Muted, exquisite colors were on the glazed walls, oversized paintings, bleached and waxed floors, rich fabrics, fresh flowers in oversized vases. It was, in short, your generic incredibly rich person's living room.

We whispered, as if in a museum, running reverent light hands over smooth woods and exquisite accessories, and then we sank into downy sofas and waited.

And waited some more. Half my break time and all my patience were now completely gone. "I'm going to have to leave," I said.

"Me, too," another woman said. "Do you think I could take a peek around before I go?"

"Might as well while you can," Nikki said. Her mood seemed permanently soured ever since the altercation with Barby. "The creditors will probably be up to repossess it before the next reunion committee meeting."

She greeted our shocked expressions with a shrug. "It's no big secret. Ivy's uncontrolled spending on this place has Mitchell near bankruptcy. He's always saying so."

"He must be using hyperbole," I suggested.

"I don't know who he's using," Nikki said. "But I know he probably couldn't afford anybody too expensive anymore."

"Exaggerating," I said. "Using a figure of speech."

Nikki raised an eyebrow. "I know Ivy and her spending, so I doubt that he's hyper anything."

Maybe because our curiosity was the only thing we could feed, we began investigating, heading for the kitchen first, perhaps hoping for a stray grape or cracker. Instead, we found a twenty-first-century laboratory, a prototype of a space station, with not an alien microbe in sight. Except for what the harried caterer had forgotten to remove. A plastic foam container and two salad dressing lids lay on the black granite counter. I personally thought plastic pollutants were a wonderful touch, and very much in keeping with the futuristic theme, but somebody joked about how angry Ivy would be. On behalf of the caterer's future, I tidied up. It took a while to find the compactor and when I did, it was filled to the brim with more plastic foam boxes floating atop a sea of plastic wrap, but I shoved my trash in, slammed the gizmo shut, and pushed the button to squeeze it all in. Ivy's kitchen was now the way she liked things—devoid of any sign of life.

We moved on, stomachs growling in the lettuce-colored dining room where the bread sticks and salads the caterer had put out looked as good as the baronial decor. We toured Mitchell's paneled lair, admiring its "manly" color scheme and aroma, both dark, both tobacco, and the ornately carved racks—one for pipes, the other displaying antique, expensive pistols. We moved to the media center, electronics swaddled in fine cabinetry that silently opened at the push of a hidden control panel. We murmured through Ivy Jean's Art Deco home office, and in the mirrored state-of-the-art gymnasium we stared at our non-state-of-the-art reflections.

And then we reached the master bedroom.

Nikki had been right. Ivy Jean was in bed. But she'd been wrong about the rest. Ivy was alone and she wasn't doing aerobics because she wasn't doing breathing. There was a large and ugly hole in the center of her chest and an ivory-handled gun in her hand on the bloodstained spread.

I don't know who screamed first, but the whole group backed up. Some, gagging, rushed off to bathrooms. Barby, skin now parchment hue, shook her head, over and over, and Nikki exhaled loudly, the way you do when a hard job is finished.

I stared, horrified and immeasurably sad for Ivy and the dead body she'd never enjoyed. I looked at the wisp on the bed, all bones and no conviction, a heartbreaking waste, and wished for another chance at lunch with her, another chance to convince her that she did, indeed, exist.

"Don't touch anything," I whispered to whichever committee members were still in the room. It was a foolish thing to utter, even in a whisper, because we'd already fondled and stroked most of the apartment. "I'll call the police," I added. At least that made sense.

A gaggle of specialists appeared. Some headed for the bedroom to inspect, identify, and label, and others questioned the reunion committee.

"Why on earth are you keeping us?" I asked Mackenzie. I was being interrogated in a flowery, wickery guest bedroom. "I have to leave or my tenth graders will never know 'The Rime of the Ancient Mariner.'"

"Movin' fast as we can," he said. Whatever our relationship, when push comes to shove, what matters is that he's a cop. Especially at a crime scene. I was given permission to use the guest room telephone to call my school. The brief and painful conversation that ensued gave me a brain ache. My principal has remarkably low tolerance for staff involvements in murders.

"An entire classroom of kids who'll never thrill to 'Water, water everywhere, and not a drop to drink.' And I'm in big trouble, too."

"I'll write you an excuse," Mackenzie said. "Now, tell me everythin' about Ivy Jean Hoffman."

I did just that, back to communal *Nutcracker* outings and forward through today's gossip. "And that's it. And none of it explains why she'd kill herself," I concluded.

"She didn't."

"But—the gun, I saw, we all saw—"

"Somebody wanted you to think she did. For starters, she shouldn't have been holdin' it. Gun shoots out of the hand of a real suicide. And if she'd fired it, powder burns would be on the front and back of her hand, not just the palm, like they are. There's even somethin' peculiar, somethin' wrong about the bullet hole itself. . . ."

"Murdered," I said. "Murdered. But by whom?"

"From what you said, there was enough money and sex and cheatin' and anger right in the committee for a whole passel of murders."

"That was only talk. Besides, none of us was in here until after she was dead."

He lifted an eyebrow. "How 'bout somebody comin' up earlier? Ivy'd let any one of you in and then, bang, she'd be dead and you could leave. Later, you come back and look innocent. That's why we're checkin' y'all for powder burns."

"That's ridiculous. How do you think we arranged for her to undress, lie down, and be shot?"

Mackenzie paced the small room. "I need to work on that part."

"Furthermore, the front door was locked."

"Door locks automatically when you close it."

"The guard," I said. "He knows who came up here."

"This one's shift started at noon and he says the mornin' guy's the building owner's nephew. He flunked out of drug rehab and tends to sleep on the job when he isn't drinkin'. Didn't log a single visitor to the building all mornin', let alone the last hour. Frankly, I think the tenants could save a lot of money by replacin' him with a photo of a guard. Be just as effective."

"Why'd you single out the last hour as important for visitors?" I asked.

"That's when she was killed. Her temperature's still normal, so figure it out yourself. A body drops a degree and a half an hour, more or less. And a skinny thing like her with no body fat would cool down fast. No insulation."

"She thought she was fat," I murmured.

"Rigor's movin' fast, but she's pretty muscular," he said. "A weird thing—the body's salty. Must've worked out and not showered. Lay down for a nap, maybe?"

"Sweaty? On her brand-new spread?" But before I could further explain domestic niceties, there was an explosion of male sounds outside. Mitchell Hoffman was back in his castle. We went out to watch.

"Why would Ivy do such a terrible thing?" he wailed. "Why?" He put his hand to his face as if hoping there were tears there. There were not. He dropped his hand. He was a rotten actor and obviously had no idea of how grief felt.

After he'd been taken aside and informed that it was murder, he erupted. "Where's goddamned security? What are we paying for? I'll have their heads, by God, I'll—"

No horror, no sorrow, no tears, no surprise, no questions, especially the ones about who would do such a terrible thing or why anyone would consider it. My money was on Mitchell, and after Mackenzie had finished questioning him, I said so.

The detective sighed. "He has motive, sure. In over his head and couldn't afford a divorce. It's his gun, too. But he also has an alibi. He's been, since nine A.M., in a corporate strategy meeting—don't ask what that means—and he has one dozen witnesses for every minute of it. Includin' trips to the men's room, he says. So, Cherchez la femme. Or les femmes, perhaps?"

Abiding and abetting Mackenzie's suspicions, neither Nikki nor Barby had decent alibis. Nikki claimed to have worked alone at home all morning and Barby had been in and out of stores, killing time, not Ivy. Unfortunately, she'd bought nothing and no salesperson was likely to remember her.

They found no powder burns on any of us, but we'd had lots of time to wash or chemically treat our hands or do whatever killers did to hide evidence.

"Why aren't you thinking about a lover?" I demanded. Mackenzie and I had relocated to a corner of the living room, where we were eyed suspiciously by my former high-school classmates, as if we were forming a clique and snobbishly excluding them. "Somebody with a key who didn't even talk to the guard," I said. "Because if it wasn't a lover, why was she lying naked on top of the bedspread?"

"No signs of sex so far. Could she have sweat enough in anticipation to make herself salty? Or maybe the caterer . . ." Mackenzie mused. "Maybe she was already up here first and—"

"If you'd seen the woman, heard her, you'd know how far-fetched that is. She called Ivy 'Mrs. Hoffman' and she was scared to death of losing her as a customer." Mention of the caterer triggered thoughts of her work, of the wilting salads. "That food's going to spoil." I couldn't even repackage it, since I'd crushed all the containers in that gizmo. "Should I wrap and refrigerate it?" I asked, hoping to snag a lettuce leaf. I was exceedingly hungry, even though it was probably inappropriate to feel such mundane urges at this time. "You don't need it as evidence. She wasn't poisoned, after all."

"Don't touch anything, okay?" Mackenzie said.

Something nagged at me besides hunger. Something I'd already said echoed, but too distantly to catch.

"She really thought she was fat?" Mackenzie asked.

I nodded. "Obsessed. You've seen her at her worst, though. With clothes on, she didn't look that scrawny." It was a shame she'd died naked. As soon as they allowed, I'd dress her as a last act of decency.

More mental nagging. Bits and pieces of the day bumped and clumped in my mind, like magnetic shavings. I sifted through them. Ivy, Ivy, of course. The Ancient Mariner. Water, water. Obsession. Sex. Salt. The incompetent guard. Salty bedspread. Mitchell and money. Perfection. Mitchell and other women. Ivy and other men. Quick rigor mortis. Water, water.

Now I was not only hungry, but thirsty. I wondered if I could disturb the scene of the crime, or at least the water faucet. I'd wear gloves and leave no fingerprints. But even so, a human touching anything in that pristine house was an intrusion. Ivy appeared to have been as fanatical about her house as she'd been about her body.

Pathetic Ivy. So driven and frightened and obnoxious and needy. So *hungry*.

Anorexic Ivy complaining last Friday that she was too fat, that a TV commercial for TYW would be ruined.

Ivy shopping for nonfood. Five boxes of plastic wrap and not a leftover to cling to.

The compactor. Plastic foam floating on a sea of—"Mackenzie," I said. "I have it."

"I've known that for a while now."

"I'm talking about Ivy's murder."

He raised an eyebrow.

"Could body temperature be a wrong estimate of time of death?" I asked.

He shrugged. "Sure, if, say, the victim had a fever when she died and the coroner didn't know it, or if the temperature of the room was real high or low. Things like that."

"Or a thing like the corpse had been done up like a mummy in plastic wrap?"

"What's that? A kinky sex trick?"

"A kinky diet trick. To sweat off pounds. Instant sauna."

"You're kidding."

"Dangerous. It can raise your core temperature." I'd read that warning in a fitness magazine. I read about diet and exercise a lot, trusting my muscles to acknowledge my good intentions and firm and tone themselves.

"Well, well, well," he drawled. "Her core temperature was up and she was sweating. The Case of the Salty Corpse. Amanda Pepper does it again."

"Yards of plastic wrap in the compactor," I said. "I assumed the caterer put it there, but she used plastic foam containers. Ivy put it there."

"Correction: Amanda Pepper almost does it again. Ivy's murderer put the plastic wrap in there. She was shot while she was wrapped. Pretty much point-blank, but it wouldn't seem logical to imply that a woman had wrapped herself in plastic before shooting herself, would it? That's why the wound looked odd. I'll bet the lab finds melted or fused plastic wrap in it, but even so, they'd never have guessed why."

"So you think the killer saw that she was wrapped up and fairly immobile—certainly couldn't jump up and trot away easily—shot her and unwrapped her—"

"And put the gun into her hand," Mackenzie added, "and—"

"—left for a corporate strategy session." We smiled at each other. For once, the most logical suspect was the most logical suspect. "And sober, stoned, or not, the guard didn't log anybody coming up here because nobody did. The mister left for work, that's all."

"So maybe," Mackenzie said slowly, "instead of givin' you a note for your principal, we should give you a police citation."

"I'd settle for a late lunch."

"How do cheeseburgers with fries sound?"

"Here? In this house? Pornographic. Sacrilegious. Depraved. But I want onion rings, too. And Rocky Road and Oreos afterward." I would exorcise the diet devil who had possessed Ivy Jean until only bones, obsession, and plastic wrap were left.

Poor lost Ivy. Rest in peace.

I hoped she could, but I doubted it. What, after all, would she do for all eternity with no body of her own or others to criticize and desperately try to improve?

In order to tackle such a metaphysical puzzler, my brain required feeding. And so began my first annual Ivy Jean Hoffman Memorial Lunch.

In the end, out of respect, I told them to hold the onion rings.

NOT ALL BRIDES
ARE BEAUTIFUL

==================================

by Sharyn McCrumb

They say that all brides are supposed to be beautiful, but I
didn't like the look of this one. She came into the prison
reception area wearing a lavender suit and a little black hat
with a veil. Her figure was okay, but when she went up to
Tracer and that other photographer from the wire service,
there was a hard look about her, despite that spun-sugar
smile. I knew it would be easy to get an interview—she'd
insist on it—but that didn't mean I was going to enjoy
talking to her.

"Is it true you're going to marry Kenny Budrell?" I called
out.

She redirected her smile at me, and her dark eyes lit up
like miner's lamps.

"You're here for the wedding, honey?" she purred. "Have
you got something I could borrow? I already have something old, and new, and blue."

Just a regular old folksy wedding. I was about to tell her
what I'd like to lend her when I felt a nudge in my side.
Tracer—reminding me that good reporters get stories any

way they can. I managed a faint smile. "Sure, I'll see what I can find. Why don't we go into the ladies room and get acquainted?"

She smiled back. "This is my day to get acquainted."

"That's right," said Tracer. "You've never met the groom, have you?"

Kenny Budrell had been a newsroom byword since before I joined the paper. By the time he was eighteen, his clip-file in the newspaper morgue was an inch thick: car theft, assault and battery, attempted murder. He did some time in the state penitentiary about the same time I was at the university, and it seems we both graduated with honors. The next news of Kenny was that he'd robbed a local convenience store and taken the female clerk hostage. Tracer was the photographer on assignment when they found her body; he says it's one of the few times he's been sick on duty. It took three more robberies, each followed by the brutal murder of a hostage, before the police finally caught up with Kenny. He didn't make it through the roadblock and took a bullet in the shoulder trying to shoot his way past.

The trial took a couple of weeks. The paper sent Rudy Carr, a much more seasoned reporter than I, to cover it, but I followed the coverage and listened to the office gossip. The defense had rounded up a psychologist who said Kenny must have been temporarily insane, and he never did confess to the killings, but the jury had been looking at that cold, dead face of Kenny's for two weeks and they didn't buy it. They found him guilty in record time, and the judge obliged with a death sentence.

After that, the only clippings added to Kenny's file were routine one-column stories about his appeal to the State Supreme Court, and then to Washington. That route having failed, it was official: in six weeks Kenny Budrell would go to the electric chair.

That's when *she* turned up.

Varnee Sumner—sometime journalist and activist, full-time opportunist. In between her ecological-feminist poetry readings and her grant proposals, Varnee had found time to strike up a correspondence with Kenny. The first we heard of it was when the warden sent out a press release saying that Kenny Budrell had been granted permission to get married two weeks before his execution.

It shouldn't have come as a surprise to me that Varnee Sumner wanted to be pals—that's probably what my city editor was counting on when he assigned me to cover the story.

"What's your name?" she asked me as she applied a fuchsia shade of lipstick to her small, tight mouth.

"Lillian Robillard. Tell me—are you nervous?" I decided against taking notes. That might make her more careful about what she said.

She smoothed her hair. "Nervous? Why should I be nervous? It's true I've never met Kenny, but we've become real close through our letters—I've come to know his soul."

I winced. Kenny Budrell's soul should come with a Surgeon General's warning. Maybe *she* wasn't nervous about marrying a mass murderer, but I would have been.

My thoughts must have been obvious, because she said, "Besides, they're not going to let him come near me, you know. Even during the wedding ceremony he'll be on one side of a wire screen and we'll be on the other."

"Will they let you spend time alone with him?"

That question did faze her. "Lord, I hope—" I'd swear she was going to say *not*, but she caught herself and said, "Perhaps we'll have a quiet talk through the screen. —Honey, would you like to be my maid of honor?"

"I'd love to," I said. "And would you like to give me an exclusive pre-wedding interview?"

"I wish I could," she said, "but I've promised the story to *Personal World* for ten thousand dollars." She straightened her skirt and edged past me and out the door.

I didn't think it was possible, but I was beginning to feel sorry for Kenny Budrell.

"You looked real good out there as maid of honor," Tracer told me as we left the prison. "I got a good shot of you and the warden congratulating the bride."

"Well, if I looked happy for them pictures *do* lie." The television crews had arrived just as we were leaving and Varnee was granting interviews right and left, talking about Kenny's beautiful soul and how she was going to write to the President about his case. "You know why she's doing this, don't you?"

Tracer gave me a sad smile. "Well, I ruled out love early on."

"It's a con game. She stays married to him for two weeks, after which the State conveniently executes him, and she's a widow who stands to make a fortune on movie rights and book contracts. *I Was a Killer's Bride!*"

"Maybe they deserve each other," said Tracer mildly. "Kenny Budrell is no choirboy."

I pulled open the outside door fiercely. "He grew up poor and tough, and for all I know he *may* not be in his right mind. But there's nothing circumstantial about what she's doing!"

Tracer grinned at me. "I can see you're going to have a tough time trying to write up this wedding announcement."

He was right. It took me two hours to get the acid out of my copy. But I managed. I wanted to stay assigned to the story.

I didn't see the new Mrs. Budrell for the next two weeks, but I kept track of her. She went to Washington and gave a couple of speeches about the injustices of the American penal system. She tried to get in to see the Vice President and a couple of Supreme Court justices, but that didn't pan out. She managed to get plenty of newspaper space, though, and even made the cover of a supermarket newspaper. They ran a picture of her with the caption: Courageous Bride Fights for Husband's Life.

Because of the tearjerker angle, her efforts on Kenny's behalf received far more publicity than those of the court-appointed attorney assigned to the case. Allen Linden, a quiet, plodding type just out of law school, had been filing stacks of appeals and doing everything he could do, but nobody paid any attention. He wasn't newsworthy, and he shied away from the media blitz. He hadn't attended Budrell's wedding and he declined all interviews to discuss the newlyweds. I know, because I tried to talk with him three times—the last time he'd brushed past me in the hall outside his office, murmuring, "I'm doing the best I can for him, which is more than I can say for—"

He swallowed the rest but I knew what he had been about to say. Varnee wasn't doing a thing to really help her husband's case, although she'd been on two national talk shows and a campus lecture tour, and there was talk of a major book contract. Varnee was doing just fine—for herself.

The whole sideshow was due to end on April third, the date of Kenny's execution. The editor was sending Rudy Carr to cover that and I was going along to do a sidebar on the widow-to-be. I wondered how she was going to play her part—grieving bride or impassioned activist?

"I'm glad to see it's raining," said Tracer, hunched down in the back seat with his camera equipment. "That ought to keep the demonstrators away."

Rudy, at the wheel, glanced at him in the rearview mirror and scowled. He had hardly spoken since we started.

I watched the windshield wipers slapping the rain. "It won't keep *her* away," I said, feeling the chill, glad I'd worn my sheepskin coat.

"You've got to give the woman credit, though," Tracer said. "She's been using this case to say a lot of things that need saying about capital punishment."

I sighed. If you gave Tracer a sack of manure, he'd spend two hours looking for the pony.

"She's getting rich off this," I pointed out. "Did you know that Kenny Budrell has a mother and sisters?"

"And so did two of the victims," added Rudy with such quiet intensity that it shut both Tracer and me up for the rest of the trip.

The prison reception room was far more crowded for the execution than it had been for the wedding. By now Varnee had received so much publicity she was a national news item, and when we arrived she was three-deep in reporters. She was wearing a black designer suit and the same hat she'd worn for the wedding. I knew she wouldn't give me the time of day with all the bigger fish waving microphones and cameras in her face, but I did get a photocopy of her speech on capital punishment from a stack of copies she'd brought with her.

"You'd better talk to her now," Tracer said. "In a few minutes they're taking the witnesses in to view the execution and you're not cleared for that."

I stared at him. "You mean she's going to watch?"

"Oh, yeah. They agreed on that from the start."

I might have gone over and talked with her then, but I noticed Allen Linden, Kenny's attorney, sitting on a bench by himself, sipping coffee. He looked tired, and his gray suit might have been slept in for all its wrinkles.

He looked up warily as I approached.

"You don't have to talk to me if you don't want," I said.

He managed a wan smile. "Have I seen you somewhere before?"

I introduced myself. "You've dodged me in the hall outside your office a few times," I admitted. "But I didn't come over here to give you a hard time. Honest."

He let out a long sigh. "This is my first capital murder case," he said in a weary voice. "It's hard to know what to do."

"I'm sure you did your best." He was very young and I

wasn't sure how good his best was, but he seemed badly in need of solace.

"Kenny Budrell isn't a very nice person," he mused.

I was puzzled. I thought lawyers always spoke up for their clients. "You don't think he's innocent?"

"He never claimed to be," said Linden. "At one point he expressed surprise at all the fuss being made over a couple of broads, as he put it. No, he's not a very nice person. But he was entitled to the best defense he could get. To every effort I could make."

I guess it's inevitable for a lawyer to feel guilty if his client is about to die. He must wonder if there is something else he could have done. "I'm sure you did everything you could," I said. "And if Varnee couldn't get him a stay of execution, it must have been hopeless."

He grimaced at the sound of her name. "She's not a very nice person, either, is she?"

I hesitated. "How does Kenny Budrell feel about her?"

"Very flattered," smiled Linden. "Here is a minor celebrity making his case a prime-time issue. He has a huge scrapbook of her—he keeps her letters under his pillow. He said to me once: 'She loves me, so I must be a hero. I've worried a lot about that.'"

There was a stir in the crowd and the warden, flanked by two guards, came into the room. I stiffened, dreading the next deliberate hour.

"It will be over soon," I whispered.

"I know. I hope I've done the right thing."

"Are you going to watch the execution?"

Linden shut his eyes. "There isn't going to be one. I found an irregularity in the police procedure and got the case overturned. I've just made Kenny Budrell a free man."

"But he's guilty!" I protested.

"But he's still entitled to due process, same as anyone else, and it's my job to take advantage of anything that will benefit my client." He shook his head. "I can't even take credit for it. It just fell into my lap."

"What happened?"

"Remember when they captured Kenny at the road-block?"

"Yes. He was wounded in the shootout."

"Right. Well, in all the excitement nobody remembered to read him his rights. Later in the hospital, when he was questioned, the police assumed it had already been done. One of the state troopers got to thinking about the case and came forward to tell me he thought there had been a slip-up. I checked, and he was right: Kenny wasn't mirandized, so the law says there's no case. The trooper told me he came forward because of all this business with Varnee. He said maybe the guy deserved a break, after all."

Tracer got a first-class series of pictures of the warden telling Varnee that her new husband was now a free man until death do them part, and of Varnee eventually starting to scream right there in front of the TV cameras. As far as I'm concerned, they deserve a Pulitzer.

EVELYN LYING THERE

==

by Anne Wingate

When you see an FBI agent and two detectives coming in the door of the police station, you figure they're working on something.

At least, I did, and I said, "Hi, Steve."

For a minute he looked as if he didn't even recognize me—no wonder, in this dumb uniform, and after all, I knew he was here but he didn't know I was here. He'd had no reason to know. But it had only been seven months, and after a moment his eyes focused on me and he said, "Lorene?"

Then he stopped, so suddenly one of the detectives bumped into him, and said, "Are you working here now?"

I started to say yes, but before I quite got the words out one of the detectives growled, "Come on, Hallett," which didn't sound too friendly to me, and Steve and the detectives went on.

I headed for the master room to sort out my paperwork, angry tears stinging the back of my eyes. Seven months ago I could have said, "What've you got?" and he'd have told me and we'd have talked it over. Or, more likely, he'd have said, "Lorene, come help me with this, would you?"

It wasn't fair, it wasn't fair, and no use reminding myself that life isn't usually. Then I'd been a detective myself, four hundred miles away, but Allen had been transferred, and after all, I was Allen's wife even if I was beginning, off and on, to wonder if I really wanted to be. So I'd come here, too, and started over as a rookie in this two-bit department, doing routine door-shaking and writing parking tickets, because I was the first female officer this small town had had and they didn't know what to do with me, never mind that it had been eight years since I'd written a parking ticket or shaken a door.

And to really top things off, Allen and I wound up divorced after all and he'd gone off somewhere else, leaving me stuck here with this Mickey Mouse job and no way at all to go home and no use anyway, since they'd filled my slot by now.

And Steve—well, if he hadn't been married, it would have been very nice to know Steve was here, because let's face it, he's an interesting guy, but he was most thoroughly married and the FBI frowns on its agents playing around.

So I went on sorting parking tickets, and never mind the tears in my eyes. Policemen can cry in uniform if they want to. Policewomen can't.

"Lorene?"

"Sir?" I answered mechanically, before looking up at Sergeant Collins. Detective sergeant, not uniform sergeant.

"Do you know Stephen Hallett?"

"Yes, sir, why?" Was there some reason why I shouldn't?

"What do you know about him?" Collins sat down companionably on the corner of the table, but his posture was anything but relaxed.

"What do you mean, what do I know? I know a lot of stuff."

"Tell me some of it."

"Well, he's a super-good investigator, one of the best I ever met from the FBI. I mean—oh, you know, most of them don't really—"

"Investigate. I know. Go on."

"He's a nice guy. By that I mean when he's tired and cross he makes sure whoever's around knows he's cross because he's tired, not because somebody did something. But he doesn't get cross much."

"What about his personal life?"

I shrugged. "He's married. So was I, then."

"What kind of marriage?"

"Why on earth do you want to know that?"

"Because two hours ago he called 911 and said, 'You better send somebody out here. I think I just killed my wife.' And we did, and he had. Now, what kind of marriage?"

Numbly, I bent over to pick up the ticket book I seemed unaccountably to have dropped on the floor. "Okay," I said, with, I suppose, some vague hope that telling the truth would help him, "okay, okay—kind of marriage. They—I don't know, Steve isn't the sort of person to go around crying on people's shoulders, but I had the feeling it—just wasn't working, not as a marriage anyway. The only time he said anything to me, we were talking one day and he'd just lost one in court that he should have won, and I said he must have had a lousy jury. And he said he wished Evelyn would say that, but she'd probably just say he was stupid, so he wouldn't tell her about it at all. And one day—the guys were talking. We had a series-type rapist, and you know how guys talk, and they'd forgotten I was there. Steve said the rapist was getting more than he was. So I said since he was married he ought to be able to solve that problem, and he sort of grinned, but his eyes looked—funny."

Sergeant Collins looked at the table, and then he got off it and quit trying to pretend we were buddies. "You like him?" he asked, standing straight beside me.

"I like him."

"Even if he did kill his wife?"

"I don't know that he killed his wife."

"He says he did."

"I still don't know that he did. Why did you come tell me this anyway? I'm no detective, not here, not now."

"Because," Sergeant Collins said, "he says he'll sign a rights waiver and tell what happened if he can tell you, and only if. Will you get a statement from him?"

"Yes."

"We'll tape-record it. Be sure you understand that. Just because he's your friend doesn't mean—"

"Look," I flared at him. "I'm not going to cover up for him and he knows it and he wouldn't ask me to. And if you feel that way, you'd better sit in on it."

"Not necessary," Collins said. "But what I'm afraid of is—he's smart. You know that. And I'm afraid he'll on purpose blurt out something as soon as you go in, because he knows you, and then turn around later and claim he wasn't advised of his rights. So I told him, and I'm telling you, that if either of you says one damn word to the other, even if it's just hello, before I get that tape recorder turned on, you go right back out the door. And I want the rights waiver signed before I leave the room."

"You should have already got it signed," I pointed out not very politely.

Collins sighed, deliberately audibly. "We got one at the scene. But I don't want him to be able to claim later he was too shocky to know what he was signing. So we get another one signed now."

"Right," I said, wondering why he was sounding so belligerent to me. *I* hadn't done anything, after all. . . . But then I stopped wondering and followed him into the little interrogation room that looked just exactly like the one at home. Steve was sitting in that straight chair that's always reserved for suspects, the chair that's not quite uncomfortable, but certainly not quite comfortable either.

He looked just the way he always looked, his coat neat and his tie straight, but his eyes when he turned toward me seemed almost as empty as his holster. Don't speak, I reminded myself, but impulsively I reached for his hand. He looked startled. Then, with a long shuddering sigh, he leaned forward, pulling me toward him, burying his face in the blue serge of my shirt. Unexpectedly, I found my hands on his shoulders.

Dragging my hands away, Sergeant Collins caught him by the left shoulder and shoved him back into the chair. "Take off your gunbelt," he ordered me curtly. "Put it in my office."

"Right," I said, seething inside. What did he expect, that Steve was going to grab my pistol and use it to escape? But then I glanced at Steve and realized that was *exactly* what Sergeant Collins expected, and Steve realized that even if I didn't. So I walked out the door and into the small office next to it, took off my black basketweave belt, wrapped it around my still-holstered revolver, laid it on Sergeant Collins's desk, and returned, to smile at Steve with one corner of my mouth. He lifted an eyebrow at me and tried to smile back, but he kept both hands on the table, quite still.

The tape recorder was running now. Sergeant Collins gave the date. "Offense, homicide," he said. "Victim, Evelyn Hallett. Suspect, Stephen Hallett. Interviewer, Policewoman Lorene Taylor. Now, go ahead." He shoved the rights waiver over to me. Apparently I was in charge of getting it signed. He hadn't mentioned that before.

I looked over at Steve, wondering how I was supposed to handle this if I was also not supposed to say one word until after the rights waiver was signed, and then I slid it on over to Steve. He looked at it, looked at the tape recorder, and looked back at me.

This was assuming the proportions of surrealism. It was some kind of bloody awful, rotten joke. Steve and I *together* had read people their rights; we'd worked together on a lot of cases. In a town just big enough to have two or three federal agents, but not big enough for a regular field office, the federal agents rely on local police support. *I hate this*, I thought bitterly, and then reminded myself that Steve undoubtedly was hating it a lot more. So I made the little speech, winding up with the usual "Do you understand these rights as I have explained them to you?"

Stupid question. This guy had a law degree. "Yes, I do." Very formal. Steve's voice, the first time I'd heard it in seven months, oddly husky, but with his usual strength.

"Do you wish to give up the right to remain silent?"

"Yes, I do."

"Then sign right there, please."

Sergeant Collins signed under Steve and then departed, closing the door very quietly. I wondered who he thought he was kidding. I'd already noticed that the "mirror" in this holding room was a window from Sergeant Collins's office, and Steve certainly knew it, too. Anybody who didn't realize Sergeant Collins was putting that window into use—well, that person hadn't been in police work as long as I had.

But of course I had to pretend I didn't know it, and so did Steve. "What happened?" I asked.

He closed his eyes, swallowed, reopened his eyes. "I killed Evelyn."

"Why?"

"Why?" He paused, as if to think about it, and his voice sounded rambling as he began to reply. "I'm six foot three. She's—she was—five foot two and ninety-five pounds. . . . I don't know why, Lorene. I shouldn't have—I shouldn't have needed to."

"Did you need to?"

"I guess I must have." The voice wondering as well as wandering. "I did, didn't I? So I guess I must have needed to, or at least I thought then I did."

I know how to question prisoners. You don't show any impatience, you take as long as it takes, you ask questions right—but this wasn't just any prisoner hauled in off the street, this was Steve. "Look, darn it," I said, "I don't know anything at all about this except they told me to come in here and take a statement from you, and, Steve, you ought to have sense enough to know I'm confused enough as it is. Now, will you for cryin' out loud tell me what happened?"

He jumped as if I'd awakened him from a half-sleep, and tears began to form in his eyes as if only his daze had kept them at bay. "I'm sorry," he said. "I—look, I'm sorry, Lorene, I just—they're out there at my house, the crime-scene people, and—Evelyn's just lying there and they say they won't move her for hours, and I never worked for a killing for cryin' out loud, but how they can just leave her—and they brought me up here and and—they won't even put a sheet over her, and I—I quit loving her a long time ago but I did love her once—It's Evelyn, and she's dead—like that—and they won't even cover her up."

"You're not there to see it."

"But I know."

"All right," I said. "I have worked killings, and I wouldn't move her yet either. And I never covered up a corpse in my life, unless it was outside. You've worked crime scenes. To them this is just another crime scene. Now will you *please* tell me—"

"All right. All right." Oddly, reminding him it was just another crime scene seemed to calm him a little. "I was working on a—You don't need to know that."

Bureau security, even now, I thought irrelevantly.

"Anyhow, I was working and I called my office to check in and they said Evelyn wanted me to call her, and I did. She asked me to come home for lunch. I didn't know why. We hadn't been getting along very well, and we'd agreed, oh, a year or so ago, that when I got transferred she'd just stay there. The only reason she changed her mind and came with me after all, when I did get transferred last month, was she'd lost her job about then and thought maybe she could find one here. Did you know I was here?" he asked irrelevantly.

"Yes. I saw you three weeks ago."

"How come you didn't yell at me or something, when I didn't see you?"

"Why should I?"

He looked hurt. "I thought we were friends."

"Then how come you didn't know where I went?"

"I was out of town for a trial," he said. "And when I got back, I—when I got back I went in the detective bureau and was talking to people and you weren't there and I figured you were on leave or something. But you kept on not being there. And then I asked Ransom where you were and he said, 'Gone.' I said, 'Gone where?' and he said, 'She's not with us anymore.' He acted like he didn't know where you went. Or didn't want to tell me. And so I shut up. I'd have found out if I needed to, but I didn't, and I figured if you didn't tell me you must not want me to know. So—"

He shut up suddenly, tightening his lips together, as if by doing that he could stop the slow drip of tears from his eyes.

"I wanted you to know," I said, afraid even that was saying too much. "But right now—" I nodded to the tape recorder.

"Oh, yeah," he said. "Today. Right. She, uh, she thought she could find a job here but she didn't. At least not yet."

"Go on."

"So I didn't know why she wanted me home for lunch." He shook his head. "That doesn't connect, does it, Lorene? What I mean is, she didn't love me, she didn't even *like* me anymore, so why the hell did she want to have lunch with me? But I had time, and so I said okay. When I got there she was lying on the couch; that was nothing new, she'd been doing that a lot lately. She said, 'Hi, Steve,' and I said, 'Hi, Evie,' and I turned around to lay my pistol on top of the bookcase just like I always do first thing when I get home, and then when I turned back toward her she had a pistol in her hand."

"Yours?"

"No, I don't have but the one. I don't know where she got it from. I'd never seen it before. I asked her what she was doing and she said—real conversational, like she was telling me what the weather was—she said, 'I'm going to kill you.' So I thought she'd been drinking again—she'd been drinking a lot the last few months, claiming it was because she had a headache, like there was anybody in the world could drink that much and *not* have a headache—and I said, 'I'll come back later when you're sober,' and I started to head for the door."

"Without your gun."

"Yeah. Like that would really make any big difference. How often do I need a gun? So I started to head for the door, and she shot at me." It was evident the memory was still more startling to him than frightening. "That's the only time I've ever been shot at. She missed, of course. She's—she was—a very bad shot. I'd tried to teach her, back before we got married."

"Where'd the slug hit?"

"I didn't notice. Somewhere high to my right, I think."

"Too scared to notice?"

"Too startled. I didn't have the time to get scared till later. *You* know."

Of course he was right. I did know. "Then what?"

"Then of course I asked her why she did that, and she said, 'You aren't leaving this room.' I asked why again, and she told me. In—in somewhat thorough detail, only none of it made sense."

"In what way?" He shook his head instead of answering, and I said, "Steve, you're going to have to tell me."

"She said—" He shook his head again. "Look, I told you we weren't getting along. And so we weren't sleeping together. And I'm not saying it was all her fault but it damn sure wasn't all mine either. Things like that just happen. That's why divorce courts stay full." He paused; I wondered if he'd decided that was all he was going to say.

The pause continued, and I said, "I know. I've been in one myself lately. Go on."

"Have you?" He looked briefly interested at that, and then continued. "She was saying it was all my fault—all my fault she always had to work even she didn't want to, and that wasn't true. I make a decent living and she didn't have to work, but she always said she wanted to, and for the last couple of weeks she'd been mad all the time because she couldn't find a job she wanted. And she said it was my fault we don't have any children. Okay, when we first got married we were both still in school and we didn't want a family until that was behind us. And for the last couple of years, well, you don't acquire kids by spontaneous combustion. Look, I'd have been ready to have children, but not the way she was drinking, and we weren't sleeping together and she didn't want to anyway. But there were about three years between, and I don't know why she didn't get pregnant. Maybe one of us was sterile, I don't know. It certainly wasn't anybody's *fault*. It could be my problem, it could be hers, but guessing at it is stupid. I really always thought it was because she was so thin; she never would eat right, and she ran all the time, it was like she was living on Scotch and air, but that's beside the point."

"You're saying she was anorexic?" I asked.

Steve shrugged. "Anorexia, bulimia, how should I know? I never saw her vomiting on purpose, but I didn't see her eat very much, either. I mean, we could go out to dinner at the nicest restaurant in town and she'd order thirty dollars' worth of steak and lobster and eat three bites. Five, if I twisted her arm. I mean verbally. I wouldn't really—Oh, you know. That kind of thing. And the drinking—I knew she was depressed. I got her to go to a doctor and he put her on some kind of antidepressant—"

"Prozac?"

"No, just some sort of—I don't remember, it ended with 'ine.' He said it would take about three weeks for it to work. She took it three days and flushed the rest down the toilet. Said she hated to take stuff."

"So she was depressed and she wouldn't do anything about the depression. And she was drinking heavily."

"Yeah," Steve said. "And she—she'd been acting like she hated me, like it was all my fault she felt like hell. Well, it wasn't. It wasn't my fault she didn't know what she wanted. It wasn't my fault she fought with all her friends until she didn't have any left. It wasn't my fault she didn't get along with her parents and didn't have any brothers or sisters. I couldn't make her take antidepressants. I couldn't make her stop drinking. I couldn't create a job for her when there wasn't one. If I tried to take her out—dancing, or movies, or something—she wouldn't go."

"And that's the background," I said.

"That's the background," he agreed.

"So getting back to today—she started spewing out all this stuff, and you said you were going to leave and come back when she was sober, and she shot at you, and then?"

"And then—she was pointing the gun at me, and I could see that she was cocking it again—she didn't need to, it was double-action, but I guess she wasn't strong enough to fire it double-action, and I tried to take it away from her and I got hold of her hand and the gun went off and she went limp and there was blood everywhere—"

He was trained to deal with emergencies. But this was his own personal emergency, of a kind no one ever expects to have to deal with, and he was shaking all over.

Making my voice as impersonal as possible, I asked, "Was the gun still in her hand?"

"Yes, and she was still breathing, so I tried to call an ambulance and the phone was dead, so I ran next door to get the neighbors to call an ambulance, but they weren't home, so I had to run around to the resident manager's office and I guess I should have told her to call the police, but I didn't even think of it, I did it myself—"

"Reporting Evelyn already dead."

"Lorene, with that much blood—"

"All right, go on," I said, this time wishing I'd kept my mouth shut.

"So then I ran back to the apartment to see if I could do anything about the bleeding before the ambulance got there, and she was dead."

"What kind of gun was it?"

"A twenty-two. A crummy little R.G., I think. I saw it when we were fighting over it. I never looked at it afterwards—I didn't want to—but I'm pretty sure it was an R.G."

"Steve," I pointed out, "that's not murder. If it happened the way you said—"

"I never said it was murder. I said I killed her."

"I'm not even sure of that, from what you've said. Anyway, let me get a typewriter in here and let's get it down on paper. Do you mind if the sergeant sits in?"

"Not now."

"Then why didn't you want him to start with?"

"Because I knew he wouldn't believe me. You might. And the reason—it doesn't make sense to me, so why should it to him? And if I started crying—Lorene, I knew he was going to watch and listen anyway." He looked bitterly at the one-way window. "But if I started crying at least I wouldn't have to look at him watch me." Not totally unpredictably, he did start crying then. "I just wish I'd known she hated me that much—she talked about it, but I thought at least half of it was talk—there should have been something I could do, even if it was only to get the hell out of there—"

"Steve," I said, "she could have left if she'd wanted to. Couldn't she?"

"Yeah. She had money. She had charge cards. She could have found a job in a bigger town, easy. And—I wouldn't have gone chasing after her to bring her back. And she sure as hell knew that."

"Now can he go home?" I asked thirty minutes later, as Sergeant Collins looked with some visible satisfaction at the written and signed statement.

"Go home? Hell, no, he can't go home."

"Why not?"

"This is a very pretty fairy tale." Collins laid the paper down on his desk. "But the woman was shot once with a thirty-eight. There wasn't even a twenty-two in the room.

And no bullet holes in there either, except the one in her."

"Maybe the other bullets went out the window. And there are R.G. thirty-eights. Maybe he was mistaken."

"You're telling me an FBI agent can't tell the difference between a twenty-two and a thirty-eight?"

"You ever look at a gun from the front end?" I asked softly. "I mean, a gun in business, not one that you're cleaning? A twenty-two looks like a cannon."

He looked at me. "You know?"

"I know."

"Okay," he said, "I'll have to take your word for it. But there wasn't an R.G. thirty-eight in there either. There was no gun of any description whatsoever except his service revolver. And it's an apartment. There aren't any windows in the living room that open, which means a bullet would have to break glass to go out, which means it didn't happen because there's no broken glass. And that service revolver, which he says hasn't been fired since he cleaned it after going to the range two weeks ago, was lying on the couch with a fouled barrel. Oh yes, that phone. You can bet it was out of order. The wire was cut where it came into the house and taped back together. . . . Now would you like to go break the news to your buddy that I'm taking out a warrant for him for capital murder?"

I let myself in with Steve's key, which he had slipped into my hand while the sergeant was gone to get the warrant signed and nobody was watching from the other side of the fake mirror. Then he'd laughed at himself, because he didn't have to give me the key so stealthily and because there were other things he had to give me too, things that couldn't be hidden.

The stench of blood, of death, hung over the room. I told myself it was a crime scene, no more than a crime scene. I knew crime scenes; I'd coped with plenty of them. I'd read the reports, and I knew nothing had been carried away except the body and the revolver.

I also knew I was breaking the rules, and I didn't care. It was only department rules, not the ones that matter.

No fingerprint powder, of course. Steve lived here, and there had been no reason to look for anybody else's. A yellow chalk outline where the body had lain on its back on the beige carpet. Blood—it was a lot of blood; I'd seen shotgun killings bleed less than that. It appeared to me she'd fallen back on the couch bleeding and then rolled onto the floor still bleeding. If the bullet had cut an artery, and then her heart had gone on pumping even after her brain was dead—that happens, of course, I'd once seen a heart go on beating for half an hour after the brain had been literally blown out of the skull from a shotgun blast.

But I didn't remember even that one having so much blood.

I forced my attention away, to the investigation I'd come here to do. What was that on the wall? If it was a bullet hole, to corroborate Steve's story—no. Damn. Something waxy, like a kid's crayon, except that it was pretty high for a kid to reach, and white besides.

"If I have to," I'd told Steve, "I'll work it all over there from the beginning on my own. But if I go over there, I'm going to search. Really."

He'd answered, "Search," and he'd known what I meant when I said it. He'd even insisted on signing a consent to search form, to make sure everything was legal—well, semi-legal; nobody had witnessed the document—even if it didn't follow departmental rules.

I had to give him one more warning. "If you're lying, Steve, I'll find it out."

"I know," he said. "That's why I want you to go."

So I was here, in a two-bedroom apartment. There was nothing in the living room of great interest. A beige couch, unimaginative decorator style, the kind rental places supply, with no cushions except those that came with it. No plants, no china ornaments, no pictures on the walls. End tables, chairs—Steve, unlike most men with whom I'd come in contact, didn't have a recliner, not that that meant anything. Stereo, TV, a few books.

Most of what little that was in the room looked as if it was Evelyn's. Some college textbooks, her diploma and transcripts lying on an end table, dust on top of them as if they'd been lying there for several weeks. Well, of course she was job hunting, but what a funny double major, drama and political science. I couldn't imagine what kind of work she'd down—or expected to do—with that combination.

I made myself dig down in the sides and back of the chair despite the lack of plastic gloves and my own squeamishness, which has, for I hope obvious reasons, become more pronounced of late. I might as well not have bothered; all I found was a balloon and a fingernail file, both very bloody. Laying them down, I went to wash my hands. The bathroom off the hall was just a bathroom. A toothbrush, an electric razor, pre-shave and aftershave lotion, towels and washcloths and soap. This must be Steve's bathroom. Evelyn must have used the one off the master bedroom.

Bedrooms. Master bedroom first. King-sized bed, unmade. Dresser—I wasn't used to crime scenes involving my friends, and this felt more like prying than investigating. But I found no gun hidden in Steve's underwear, or in Evelyn's, or in the bathroom, which contained talcum powder, Lady Shave, bubble bath, and a lot of makeup, most of it dusty, as if it hadn't been used in weeks.

The smaller bedroom, Steve's, I suppose, was mostly filled with boxes, still unpacked, many of them taped shut. A single bed, sheet thrown back, with a man's undershirt and a towel lying on it, and an alarm clock and a shoeshine kit (not dusty) on the table beside it. A few of Steve's clothes had been in the second closet in the larger room, but most of them were in here. No dresser, which explained why his underwear was in Evelyn's dresser. The boxes of .38 wadcutters on a closet shelf, right beside the box of .38 copper jackets was totally expected; Steve was conscientious about going to the firing range two or three times a month.

The boxes were all neatly labeled—books, dishes, theatrical props—for all that meant, and some of them appeared, from the condition of the tape, never to have been unpacked even the last time they had moved.

I went back into the living room. A stereo cabinet full of records—I wonder, I thought, and knelt in front of it.

"Looking for something, Lorene?"

It was at that moment—until I realized it was Sergeant Collins behind me, speaking to me, and my heart slowed its gallop just a bit—that I realized what people meant when they said they nearly jumped out of their skin.

"I expected to find you over here, as soon as we booked him in and found out his door key was gone. Still convinced he didn't do it?"

"I can see why you think he did do it," I said, "but he didn't. Though I'll agree his version isn't accurate either."

"He did shoot her, Lorene, there's no getting around that."

"I'm even beginning to doubt that."

"Look, I'd be willing to agree maybe there was some kind of struggle, only not quite the way he tells it. Or I'd be willing to agree she somehow goaded him into shooting her, and he's scared to admit it. Or I'd be willing to agree he's so shook up he doesn't even really know what happened. But if the first is true, then where the hell is the twenty-two? And if the second is true, then why is he telling such a silly story? And if the third is true—and it's really the most likely—then why does he go on insisting he's telling the exact truth?"

"The way I see it," I replied, "is that if what he thinks happened didn't, and if what you think happened didn't, then there should be something here to say what did happen. And for starts, I'm looking for that twenty-two."

"You really believe him, don't you?" Collins said.

"Yes. I do."

"And you know him. I don't, not really. But you're telling

me somebody like you and me, somebody that carries a pistol all the time, isn't capable of killing?"

"I didn't say that." My head was aching abominably. "I'm sure he's capable of killing—just like you and me. If it had been the way he told it, yes, that could happen. Or even, if he'd shot back reactively when she shot at him, that could happen, but he wouldn't lie about it. But—what you say happened—that's not killing. That's murder. And no. He's not capable of that. And what are you doing here?"

"Search warrant," Collins said, waving it at me. "Because I got to thinking. You believe him. And you're a good cop."

"Somebody noticed?"

"Somebody noticed. And I'll admit I don't know the man and you do, and sometimes I do jump to conclusions. He's got to be smart to have the job he has, and a smart man isn't going to think we'd mistake a thirty-eight slug for a twenty-two. Even if he panicked, he'd tell a better lie than that. And if he was too shocky to remember what happened, he'd admit it. So—I want to know what really happened."

"He's shocky," I said. "But he knows what he did and what he saw. So . . ." I broke off, turned back to my search.

Sergeant Collins leaned forward. "Back up, that record you just tipped out, what's—"

I was way ahead of him, and I intercepted his hand, automatically taking command of the scene because I'd done it so many times before. "Don't touch it until I've photographed it."

It was an R.G. twenty-two. It contained two rounds, both empty. Sergeant Collins, holding it gingerly, so as not to disturb fingerprints, sniffed at it. "Umm-humm," he said.

"I told you—"

"All right, you told me, but the fact remains she was killed with a thirty-eight and it's about a hundred percent sure it was his. Anyhow, if that gun was fired in here, where'd the bullets go? For that matter, where'd they come from? I didn't find any twenty-two ammo here, and if you had, you'd have told me already."

I looked slowly around the room, up at the ceiling, across the walls, down at the bloody mess on the couch and the floor, and quite suddenly I knew what happened, knew exactly what happened just as well as if I'd been here watching. Now all I had to do was prove it, but that depended on a lot of things. "Did they do a gunpowder residue on her hands?" I asked.

"No, just his. Do you want one on her? You don't usually get anything from a twenty-two, don't you know that?"

"An R.G. you will," I answered. "And you're lucky if it's not shaving lead." I had a long scar across my thumb from test-firing a misaligned R.G. .22. I would not soon forget the gunpowder that accompanied the sliver of lead thrown backwards toward my hand.

"So you want me to have somebody—"

"Not now," I said, standing again. "I'll do it myself. Come on, I know what happened here. Have you got—" And I went on giving orders, as I had done for years up until seven months ago, and neither the sergeant nor I quite noticed. "I don't know what kind of equipment you have here, do you have a trace-metal kit, because if you don't we're going to have to—"

"We have one," Sergeant Collins said slowly, "but I don't think I ever saw it used. What do you mean, you know what happened?"

"I'll tell you later. Let's get a gunpowder-residue kit and a trace-metal kit and go to the morgue."

"What are you trying to prove?"

"You'd never believe me, so I'm just going to have to show you."

"You want me to turn off all the lights in the morgue?" the attendant asked incredulously, thirty minutes later. "What are you, some kind of—" He shut up then, catching the sergeant's eye fixed on him.

"After I spray this stuff on her hands and turn on the black light," I said, "I sure do. Okay, now—look."

In the darkness, the dead woman's hand glowed eerily. On her right palm, outlined with the glow, were the initials "R.G." from the metal insert on the plastic grips of an R.G. .22. And on her left palm, also glowing, was the horse insignia of a Colt .38. Her right index finger and left thumb both glowed with the outlines of triggers.

"She shot herself," I said.

"But how?" Steve demanded an hour later, sitting at the sergeant's desk in blue jail coveralls.

"Once we knew what we were looking for, it was easy to find," I told him. "She knew theater. She knew props. You load a bullet with soft wax and a primer, and it makes a satisfactory pop and does little or no damage. In a box that had been opened and resealed, we found an entire case of prop bullets—and she'd used at least two. The wax was spattered on the wall about three feet from the front door, and on the ceiling above the couch. You can fill a balloon with animal blood and puncture it—we got the lab people out of bed, and they said the blood on the couch was beef blood."

"But how—"

I went on to tell him how I'd pulled the balloon and the nail file she'd used to puncture it out from under the cushions. "She'd disabled the phone on purpose, after she called you. Her fingernails were on the roll the tape came from; we found them as soon as we thought to look. She knew where you always put your gun when you came in. She knew how you'd react, thinking she was hurt. When you ran for the phone, she stuffed the balloon behind the sofa cushions and threw the twenty-two behind the records—it's got her prints on it and nobody else's. Then she grabbed your gun—her prints are on it too, overlaying yours—and sat on the couch facing in towards the back of it, held the pistol at arm's length so there wouldn't be muzzle burns and so that the gun would be on the couch when she landed on the floor, and pulled the trigger."

"But why?" Steve demanded. "I mean—All right. I knew she was suicidal. That was why I wouldn't have a pistol in the house other than mine, why I never left it where she could get it. And before she filled that prescription I called the doctor to be sure there wasn't enough in it to be fatal. I wouldn't have been surprised if—but—why in the hell would she want to set me up? That doesn't make any sense at all."

I looked at Sergeant Collins, who stood abruptly and turned to look out the high barred window at the side of his desk. We'd argued about who was going to tell Steve the rest of it; neither of us wanted to.

"She hated you," Collins said abruptly. "She hated you a lot more than you knew. As you said, she blamed you for her depression. And she wanted you to be as miserable as she'd been the last few years."

"Wait a minute," Steve said. "How do you know all this?"

"She kept a diary," I said. "We found it. She blamed you—said she'd have been perfectly happy if—"

"If I'd been willing to live the way she wanted to live, yeah," Steve said. "I heard that from her quite a few times—that, and I was boring and unimaginative—Oh hell. Thing is—I *couldn't* live the way she wanted to. And the combination—she wanted to party every night *and* she wanted children and a decent job—all those don't combine very well. Nobody has that much time. I wouldn't do the partying, and she couldn't find the job, and the children didn't come. What was I supposed to do about all that?"

It made sense. It also sounded as if I had heard more than enough on this topic. "Steve," I asked, "why did you say you killed her?"

"Because I thought it was the twenty-two. And big as I am, I ought to be able to take a gun away from a woman without hurting her. So—if I couldn't—if I didn't—then I thought I must've somehow subconsciously wanted to kill her."

"Baloney," I said. "I'd like to see either one of you take a gun away from me—Hey, I didn't say both at once, dammit, give me back my gun!"

Sergeant Collins laid the pistol, which I continue to maintain he would never have gotten one on one, down on his desk. "Why did you tell me not to have them do a gunpowder residue on her, and then you went and did one?"

"Because you can do a trace metal first and then a gunpowder residue, but if you do it the other way around the acid in the gunpowder-residue kit destroys the trace metal and then you get a negative trace metal. Everybody knows that." I wasn't even ashamed of the smugness I could hear in my voice.

Both men were staring at me. "Everyone?" Stephen Hallett asked.

SIDESHOW

==

by B. K. Stevens

Standing on tiptoe, her pert, rounded chin tilted bravely upwards, Cherry Benson would barely clear five foot one. She was about forty years old and softly plump, dressed in a simple black dress that looked, on her, demurely feminine, not at all severe. She had baby blue eyes and long lashes and rosy cheeks and a sweet, open face, and she wore a tiny cluster of bright red artificial cherries nestled coyly among her golden curls. She was, I knew, exactly the sort of woman that Iphigenia Woodhouse instinctively despised.

When I showed Cherry Benson into the office, Miss Woodhouse gave her an appraising look, then scowled and stood up, positively looming over her desk, as if to emphasize the difference between Cherry Benson's daintiness and her own sturdy bulk. Miss Woodhouse is about ten years older than Cherry Benson and almost a foot taller, with a build most linebackers only dream of—not an ounce of flab, but solid layers of muscles everywhere that they might conceivably come in handy. As always, she wore a tailored skirt and blouse and no makeup, and had pulled her graying, slightly frizzy black hair straight back from her face. She gave Cherry Benson a stare that's been known to send police captains and minor drug lords scurrying for cover.

"Mrs. Benson," she said coldly. "How nice. Sit down. Unless you came about the Cronin kidnapping, in which case you might as well leave now. I don't interfere with ongoing police investigations. That *is* why you came, isn't it?"

Miss Woodhouse never goes out of her way to cater to new clients—I've often wished that she *would* cater, just a little, so that we might get just a few more clients, and my paycheck might be just a little larger—but I'd never seen her so positively eager to push business out the door. Cherry Benson's palpable sweetness must really have been irritating her.

Mrs. Benson seemed oblivious to the problem. "Well, I *did* come about poor little Billy Cronin," she said, settling easily into one of the straight-backed wooden chairs facing Miss Woodhouse's desk. "I'm not asking you to *interfere*— I'd *never* ask anyone to interfere with the police—but I *do* have some special concerns, concerns that the police can't necessarily keep *foremost* in their minds, and I was thinking perhaps they could use a little *help*. If you give me five minutes to explain, perhaps you'll agree." She glanced toward the bay window at the east side of the office, where a woman in her late seventies sat in a red-cushioned rocking chair, tugging at a mass of knots just barely recognizable as macrame, paying no attention to any of us. Cherry Benson smiled at her warmly, then looked back at Miss Woodhouse. "Some of the details might be a little *upsetting*. Perhaps that lady might be more comfortable if we—"

"That lady," Miss Woodhouse cut in, "is my mother, Professor Woodhouse. Upsetting details do not make her uncomfortable. She customarily sits in on my consultations with clients. She finds them diverting. Does that make *you* uncomfortable, Mrs. Benson?"

Some prospective clients walk out when Miss Woodhouse announces that her mother is staying, some put up a fuss, some stammer and swallow hard and accept it but clearly don't like it. Cherry Benson looked like she honestly didn't mind. She aimed another bright, sweet smile in Professor Woodhouse's direction.

"I'm happy to meet you, Professor Woodhouse," she said. "I'll be grateful for any advice you might have for me."

Smarter and tougher than she looks, I thought, and gave her credit. Miss Woodhouse scowled again, evidently not pleased about failing to scare Cherry Benson off. "You asked for five minutes," she said. "You've got it. Harriet, take notes."

Hardly a necessary order, since I already had my pad and pencil ready, but I guess it was Miss Woodhouse's way of showing she was in control, at least of me. Cherry Benson set a stack of photographs and newspaper clippings on the desk.

"Well," she said, "you obviously already know something about our tragedy, but let me start at the beginning, just to make sure I don't leave anything out. I run Cherry's Children's Center. Dear Billy Cronin has been one of our students almost since he was born. He started out as a Little Lamb, of course, and then moved on to the Kuddly Kittens, and just last month he graduated to our toddler class, the Playful Pups."

"Fascinating," Miss Woodhouse said, from behind clenched teeth.

Cherry Benson winked at her kindly. "Now, Billy's teacher in Kuddly Kittens was poor dear Susan O'Reilly. Billy adored her so much that his parents often hired her to babysit for him on evenings or weekends. Susan was babysitting for him last Sunday afternoon, as you probably know."

"As everyone in the state of Maryland knows by now," Miss Woodhouse said impatiently. "And someone came along, snatched Billy Cronin, cracked open Susan O'Reilly's skull, and dumped her in the Cronin's swimming pool. So far, no ransom demand or other word from the kidnappers, no trace of Billy Cronin, thousands of cops combing the entire East Coast with no results. You have my sympathy, Mrs. Benson. It must be very hard, having a student kidnapped and a staff member killed. But I don't see how I can help. The police are already doing everything possible."

"Oh, but the police are making some *dreadful* mistakes," Cherry Benson protested. "You may scarcely believe this, Miss Woodhouse, but they seem to think that Susan was involved in the kidnapping somehow, that she was part of some terrible *conspiracy* to sell Billy on some sort of black market. They've been saying that perhaps her accomplice turned on her and killed her, to avoid sharing the profits. Can you imagine! Saying such a thing about poor Susan, after she died fighting to save poor Billy!"

Miss Woodhouse pursed her lips, looking interested for the first time. "What are their reasons for suspecting her?"

Cherry Benson lifted her hands to signal bewilderment. "No *real* reason. Oh, they say she ran up some big credit card bills in the last few months, and that shows she was desperate for money—but *all* young people are careless with money from time to time. And they say there were no signs of forced entry at the Cronin house, so Susan apparently opened the door for the kidnapper. But she was so trusting; it wouldn't be hard for a kidnapper to think up a story that would make her open the door. Isn't that a much *likelier* explanation? Especially when you consider how sweet Susan was. Here. Just *look* at her."

Cherry Benson pushed the stack of photographs and clippings across the desk, and Miss Woodhouse started flipping through them, slowly and thoughtfully. "So, you want an investigation to clear Susan O'Reilly's memory—is that it?"

"That's *partly* it." Cherry Benson dabbed at her forehead with a lace-edged handkerchief embroidered with a tiny portrait of Snoopy. "The police seem to think someone else at our center helped Susan plan the kidnapping. You know how much bad publicity there's been about day-care centers, how willing people are to think that we abuse children and do all *sorts* of naughty things. It's *such* a burden to bear. Anyway, the police have been at the center constantly, questioning all of us, making us very nervous, very unhappy. And the reporters—they're worse than the police. An absolute *gang* of them show up at the center every day, pointing their cameras at us and shouting the cruelest questions. We've lost half our students already, and I don't know how long the other parents will hold up. Even the ones who believe in us all very *deeply* can't stand to have their children exposed to all this, and I can hardly blame them."

It did sound awful. Miss Woodhouse passed me the pictures, and I found myself gazing down at Susan O'Reilly's high-school graduation portrait. She sure didn't look like a kidnapper. She looked nice—not pretty, really, but nice, the sort of ordinary, quiet, almost mousy girl you might not notice for years but could really get to like. I turned to a newspaper photograph and felt a sharp pang of loss, almost as if I *had* known her and liked her. Some ambitious photographer had dangled out of a helicopter to get this shot of Susan O'Reilly floating facedown in the swimming pool, her lacy summer dress spread out on the water. By the side of the pool was an overturned child-sized chair, with a battered-looking stuffed bear lying next to it. It was about as poignant as a picture can get. The photographer will probably get a Pulitzer, I thought, and felt like punching him.

Miss Woodhouse was getting interested in the case—I could tell from the way she was tapping her pencil against her chin to a slow, regular beat. "It's not just Susan O'Reilly's memory you want to clear, then. It's your own reputation. Your business is being hurt by all the bad publicity."

"Yes, and the entire staff is *so* demoralized. Why, just this morning, my secretary quit. She couldn't take the pressure any more, she said, not a single day more of it. And my poor teachers! The police have been bearing down especially hard on two of them. There's Anita Cox—she's the Playful Pups teacher, and she shared an apartment with poor Susan. I suppose the police suspect her just because of that. And then there's our Busy Beavers teacher, Doug Haley."

The pencil-tapping came to an abrupt halt. "*Doug* Haley?" A *man?* You have a *male* day-care teacher?"

Cherry Benson wagged a finger in gentle remonstrance. "Now, that's *just* the sort of attitude that's making them suspect poor Doug. People think it's *odd* and *suspicious* that a man would make a career of taking care of children, but why *should* it be? Dear Doug *loves* children, and he's *wonderful* with them. But the police are treating him like some *freak*. And it doesn't help that he dated Susan, even though it ended *months* ago."

I heard a sudden, sharp series of snaps behind me and glanced toward the bay window. Professor Woodhouse was glaring silently, holding out her hand. Of course. She wanted to see the pictures. I scurried across the room, ashamed that she'd had to snap her fingers to get my attention. She took the pictures from me with her left hand—her right, by now, was hopelessly entangled in her macramé—and smiled graciously, to show she wasn't holding a grudge. She never does, against me.

Miss Woodhouse had progressed from tapping her pencil to chewing on it, a sure sign that she was thinking over the case, and that she wanted a cigarette. But, of course, she'd never light up in front of her mother. "Exactly what do you want me to do, Mrs. Benson?"

"Why, I want you to investigate," Cherry Benson said promptly. "I want you to prove that no one at my center had anything to do with this terrible kidnapping. I want you to prove that we're all completely innocent." She paused. "And, of course, if you could also find poor little Billy and bring him home safely, that would be nice, too."

Miss Woodhouse shook her head. "I could look into the

case. But you might not like what I'd find. Frankly, I wouldn't be surprised if the police are right. Someone on your staff might very well be involved. And if I discovered that, I'd have to—"

A loud hiss from the east side of the room cut her off. We all jumped, and looked toward the bay window, and saw Professor Woodhouse holding up the newspaper photograph.

"I want to know more," she said sharply, "about the teddy."

Cherry Benson was the first to find her composure. "About what, dear?" she asked.

"Don't you 'dear' me, young woman," Professor Woodhouse snapped. "You haven't known me long enough—and if you *do* get to know me, you might change your mind. Now. The teddy bear in this picture looks like it's been dragged about a fair amount. Was it the little boy's favorite?"

"Well, yes," Cherry Benson said, obviously confused. "He took it with him everywhere, and always slept with it at naptime. If another child so much as touched it, he'd bellow so loudly that he'd throw the entire center into an uproar."

Professor Woodhouse nodded with satisfaction. "Iphigenia, you may take the case. You need not fear discovering anything that would distress Mrs. Benson—who, by the way, might just as well face facts, grow up, and find herself a real first name."

Miss Woodhouse's entire manner had changed, as it always does when her mother speaks to her. Her shoulders slumped meekly, her head drooped, and her eyes took on a look of mingled devotion and terror. "Of course, I'll take the case, if you advise it, Mother," she said, her voice maybe one-tenth as loud as it had been a minute ago. "But doesn't it seem a little early to be sure of what we'll discover? The police must—"

"The police are blind, opinionated fools," Professor Woodhouse shot back, "which is probably why you got along so well with them when you played at being a policewoman. The kidnapper must have wanted to keep the little boy quiet. Anyone who worked at the day-care center must have known that the little boy would fuss and cry constantly if he didn't have his teddy. The kidnapper left the teddy behind. Ergo, the kidnapper did not work at the day-care center. You may take the case."

Miss Woodhouse didn't look entirely convinced, but naturally she didn't argue. "Thank you for your observation, Mother," she said. "I had missed that point completely."

"Of course you did," Professor Woodhouse said, not at all appeased. "My observation required some insight into children. You have no such insight, never having taken the trouble to give me a grandchild."

"I'm very sorry," Miss Woodhouse said, slouching down still further in her chair. "But you didn't want me to get married."

Professor Woodhouse snatched up her macrame again. "Don't you dare try to blame your failures on me, you nasty girl," she said, tugging violently at the knots. "Had you ever presented me with a suitable candidate, I might perhaps have changed my mind."

So that was how I ended up at Cherry's Children's Center at six o'clock the next morning, posing as the new secretary. It felt a little ironic: I had spent most of my adult life working as a secretary, had trained to be a private detective because I was itching for a complete change of pace—and still, it seemed, I always ended up answering phones and typing letters and taking notes at meetings. Still, this *was* my very first full-fledged undercover assignment, so I was mostly thrilled.

Cherry Benson was mostly thrilled by the arrangement, too, partly because she needed a substitute secretary and partly because she didn't want her teachers to know she'd hired a detective—that, she thought, would make them jumpier than ever. Much better to slip me quietly into the scene, to help her handle unpleasant phone calls and to forage discreetly for scraps of information about Billy Cronin. Privately, Miss Woodhouse told me that I should also learn all I could about the staff. Even if the teddy bear evidence *did* seem to indicate that none of them had actually carried out the kidnapping, we still had to worry about conspiracy possibilities. So I was to keep an eye on everyone.

My first hour of undercover work passed quietly, following Cherry Benson around as she showed me through the center and briefed me on its routines. Starting tomorrow, I'd be the first staff person to arrive in the morning, to finish up leftover paperwork and make sure everything was ready for the children.

"Now, this is the Busy Beavers' Den," Cherry Benson said, leading me into a large, sparkling room with red and white gingham curtains hanging in the oversized windows. She pointed up to the exposed ceiling beams. "Lisa Kramer has her birthday tomorrow, and her parents are bringing in a piñata for the party—we'll have to haul a ladder out of the storeroom and hang the piñata from one of those beams. Can you handle that?"

"No problem," I said. "Is tomorrow morning soon enough?"

"Fine," she said, and we finished our tour of the building. All the classrooms were tidy and cheerful, with brightly colored chairs and tables, stacks of toys lining the walls, books displayed invitingly on shelves. Not a bad place for kids to spend their days, I thought, and tried to imagine dark conspiracies being plotted in these sunny rooms. It was a ludicrous image.

The press didn't seem to share my opinion. By six thirty minivans clogged the street outside the day-care center, and reporters began scrambling out, getting their cameras into firing position. When the teachers started to arrive, they had to pass through a gauntlet of shouted questions and accusing lenses. Then a rusting green Ford pulled into the driveway, and the reporters surged around it, louder and more insistent than ever. I felt sorry for the tall, sandy-haired young man who climbed out of the car and had to edge sideways through the reporters, shrugging and head-shaking his way to the center's door as they shoved microphones into his face. Nobody should have to fight that hard to get to work.

He was flushed and shaky by the time he got to the office. "Golly!" he said, wiping his forehead with his hand. "I need a drink." He staggered toward the miniature refrigerator, grabbed a can of apple juice, popped it open, then looked me over apprehensively. "You're not a reporter, are you? Or a cop?"

"No," I said. "I'm Harriet Russo, the new secretary."

"The new—oh, that's right. I heard Alice got scared off yesterday." He put down his apple juice and walked over to shake my hand. He was generally skinny but had a round, almost chubby face, with a blunt nose and very large, very nervous brown eyes. "I'm Doug Haley, the Busy Beavers' teacher. You must have guts, signing on here at a time like this. It's a great place, really, but awful crazy right now. I hope it quiets down soon."

It showed no signs of quieting down immediately. There was another roar from the press outside, and we both looked out the window to see a short, wiry young woman with a mass of curly red hair emerging from her car and plunging resolutely toward the door, swatting at reporters with her purse. "That's Anita Cox," Doug said, smiling affectionately. "She's the Playful Pups' teacher. Now, *there's* the definition of guts."

She stalked into the office, Doug introduced us, and she gave my hand a single, decisive shake. "Welcome to hell, Harriet," she said. "I hope those damn bloodsuckers didn't give you a hard time when you got here."

"No, I arrived before they did," I said, a little awed by the deep, clear intelligence burning in her eyes. She was barely five feet tall, but somehow she reminded me of Miss Woodhouse.

"Smart move." She glanced at Doug's can of apple juice. "Hitting the stuff already? It's not even seven o'clock."

"Well, I had a rough night." Doug said, cringing in apology. "These two cops showed up at my apartment and questioned me for three hours. They kept asking the same thing over and over, wanting to know why Susan and I broke up. What could I tell them? I never understood it myself. I liked her, I thought she liked me, we went out, everything seemed to be going great, I was thinking about a ring, and then—boom! She gives me this speech two months ago, says she can't ever date me again and can't explain why. I guess she just decided she didn't like me that much after all. What could I do? I accepted it, that's all. But those cops acted like there had to be more to it, like I was hiding some big guilty secret."

Anita patted him on the shoulder. "That's the way cops are. They're going after you because you're the obvious suspect. They always go after the obvious suspect. But don't worry. It'll work out all right in the end—it always does. We'd better get to our classrooms." She shot me a wry smile. "If the cops show up here and ask *you* any questions, Harriet, just stonewall. Don't even give them your Social Security number or they'll try to pin the murder on you. Maybe that sounds ridiculous, but cops do things like that all the time. Trust me."

The cops never showed up that day—a major relief, since by now a fair number of Annapolis cops knew me from my work on Miss Woodhouse's other cases, and I was nervous about having my cover blown. At three o'clock Cherry Benson bustled into the office.

"Could you do me a big favor, dear?" she asked. "Could you go to poor dear Susan's funeral? I'd planned to go myself, but Anita says she absolutely has to go, so I'll have to cover her class—I can't ask you to do *that*, because you're not certified. And I need someone to represent the center at the funeral, to convey our condolences to dear little Billy's parents. Anita volunteered, but she—well, she's a dear, but she's not always quite as *tactful* as one might wish, you know?"

I didn't really know, but after just one short conversation with Anita, I could guess. I reached for my purse. "I'm happy to help," I said with complete sincerity. I'd been dying to go to the funeral. In practically every mystery novel I'd ever read, the detective learned a lot from going to funerals.

The cemetery was on the other side of town. Anita led the way in her car, and I followed in mine. It was a sad, noisy scene. Scores of reporters, dozens of cops trying to blend into the crowd of mourners; but there weren't many mourners. Billy Cronin's father was there—I recognized him as the fresh-faced yuppie type I'd seen dodging the cameras in quick clips on the local news. He was maybe a few pounds over the target but undeniably gorgeous, with blond hair and big blue eyes and the cutest little chipmunk cheeks. Standing next to him was a taller, darker, slightly older, much craggier man, with "lawyer" written all over him. The only other genuine mourners were a middle-aged woman in a shabby overcoat, Anita, and me.

"This is awful," I whispered to Anita as a harassed-looking priest mumbled his way through the service. "Why didn't more people come? Where are her parents?"

"Dead," Anita said curtly. "Killed in a car accident, both of them, six months ago. And she was an only child. The woman in the crummy coat is her father's sister—she must be the one paying for this. She was the only living relative Susan had, as far as she knew." She looked around the cemetery, obviously dissatisfied. "I thought maybe we'd at least have some music. I thought maybe some of her father's friends would come. But I guess they're on the road, like he always was."

"Poor Susan," I said, and meant it. Everything I had learned about her life made it sound bleaker and lonelier.

At least the service was brief. The priest said some fairly

standard things about tender young shoots nipped in the bud, prayed a bit, and that was all. He closed his Bible, and the pitiful excuse for a crowd started to break up.

Time for me to express Cherry's Children's Center's personal condolences. I made my way over to Mr. Cronin, with Anita Cox following right behind me.

Jeff Cronin was making furtive swipes at his nose with a rapidly decomposing Kleenex. "We never should have moved here," he was saying to the lawyer. "We *knew* that the East Coast was dangerous, that it's the wrong place to raise a child. And now look what's happened. Billy gone, and poor Susan dead."

The lawyer murmured something consoling, but it didn't seem to amount to much—the usual "there, there" type of thing—so I felt justified in interrupting. "Mr. Cronin," I said, stepping forward, "I'm the new secretary at Cherry's Children's Center. Cherry asked me to say how terribly sorry we all are, how much we hope that Billy will be safe at home very soon."

He seemed about to say something, but the lawyer held up a hand to stop him. He was in his mid-forties, obviously worked out, might have been handsome if it weren't for the chronic sneer. "Mr. Cronin acknowledges your expression of sympathy," he said, "but he has no comment to make at this time. If Mrs. Benson has anything further to communicate, tell her to contact my office, P. Philip Barnard, Attorney-at-Law. The Cronins are weighing their litigative options and do not wish to have any direct contact with any representatives of the center."

"No, Phil," Jeff Cronin objected, "that sounds too cold. Kathy and I don't blame Cherry for—"

The lawyer shook his head. "Don't close off any avenues, Jeff, not until you've had a chance to assess the situation. Here, I'll drive you home. Margaret will fix you something soothing, and maybe later, if you and Kathy feel well enough, we can all drop by the club together."

I saw Jeff Cronin cringe at that. Well, of course. Who'd

want to go out to dinner at a time like this, to put up with a lot of nosy sympathy and prying questions? No, he and his wife would naturally want to stay home tonight, to perch by the phone and hope for good news from the police or, at least, for a ransom demand from the kidnappers. But he had the look of a weak-willed, compliant sort of guy who might end up at the club whether he wanted to or not. He gave us a nod—a sympathetic one, I thought—and let the lawyer lead him to his car. Anita, watching them, seemed positively hunched up with hostility. "God!" she said. "I need a drink. And I *don't* mean apple juice."

Another perfect opening. "I could use one, too," I said. "Do you want to go to a bar? You don't think the reporters would follow us there, do you?"

Anita snorted kindly, pitying my ignorance. "Are you kidding? Of course they would. Perfect front-page photo—two of Cherry's employees get sauced in public, demonstrating our decadence and lack of family values. Let's go to my place."

This was almost too easy. Once again, I followed in my car as she drove through the narrow, brick-paved streets of Annapolis's historic district. We stopped at a quaintly substandard, white-clapboard house. Downstairs, two apathetic local artists silkscreened T-shirts for tourists. Upstairs was the one bedroom apartment Anita had shared with Susan O'Reilly.

"This is it," Anita said, pushing the door open. She cast a bitterly sorrowful look around the living room. "Susan slept on the couch, let me have the bedroom. That was just like her—too nice for her own good. Well. I'm getting changed. Wine's in the fridge, real stuff's in the cupboard next to the sink." She went into the bedroom and closed the door behind her.

I looked around the living room, desperate to investigate but not sure where I should start. There was a coat closet just inside the front door, and that seemed as good a place as any. I opened the door cautiously, afraid of squeaking, and saw that the closet hadn't been used for coats after all. It was Susan's personal closet. Well, that made sense, if she'd let Anita have the bedroom. The closet was about as full as it could get—crammed at the back, half a dozen pairs of Levis at various stages of the fading process, some well-worn sweaters and blouses and a few sensible skirts, raggedy sneakers and two pairs of scuffed loafers on the floor. And, in front, carefully spaced and encased in plastic covers, eight gorgeous dresses of the knock-you-dead-and-destroy-your-paycheck variety, three pairs of designer jeans, a cashmere sweater, two silk blouses, several pairs of fantastic shoes with perilously high heels. One of the dresses still had the price tag on it, and a glimpse at the digits sent me into hyperventilation. So, I thought. That's how Susan O'Reilly ran up those big credit card charges.

I eased the closet door shut and walked over to a double bookcase set against the wall. Scanning the left-hand side, I spotted a lot of my old friends—all the Lord Peter novels, all the Miss Marples, a bunch of Rabbi Smalls and Peter Shandys and Annie Laurances and Jacqueline Kirbys. Good taste, I thought—but one really shouldn't neglect Inspector Wexford and Alan Grant, not to mention dear Hercule. The right-hand side of the bookcase had a distinctly different character. *Forbidden Love, Secret Lust, Hidden Passion, Love Forbidden, Lust in Hiding, Passionate Secret*. All the covers featured longhaired maidens swooning in the arms of men with brooding eyes, massive chests, and excessive biceps. Wondering which of the roommates was addicted to this stuff, I picked up *Hide the Lustful Secret* and saw a bookplate on the title page—"From the Library of Susan Penhurst O'Reilly." Well, that settled it.

There's nothing wrong with picking up a book while you're waiting for your hostess to join you. When I heard the bedroom door open behind me, though, I was feeling so sneaky and self-conscious that I jumped involuntarily, stuffed the book into my purse, and spun around quickly, facing Anita with my most innocent smile. "Just looking at your shelves," I said. It sounded about as stupid as you'd guess it would sound.

I had expected her to exchange the dark sweater and shirt she'd worn to the funeral for something more comfortable, like jeans. Instead, she'd put on a tweed suit. She looked at me curiously. "Didn't you get yourself a drink?"

"No, I—I thought I'd wait for you," I said, still working too hard at sounding innocent.

She shrugged and walked into the kitchen. "Well, okay. I'm afraid I'll have to kick you out in just a little while, though. I've got an appointment to keep."

That was a disappointment. I'd hoped we'd get down to some serious drinking and commiserating, that she'd loosen up and talk about Susan. As it was, I had time for just one glass of wine, and she downed two quick Scotches but didn't loosen up at all—just stared off into space, emitting absentminded monosyllables in response to my clever conversational maneuvers. After half an hour, she stood up abruptly.

"Thanks for the drink," I said, taking my cue. "I'll see you at work tomorrow. I sure hope the reporters don't surround the place and turn it into a circus again."

"It's not a circus—just a sideshow," she said, still sounding absentminded. She was digging around in her suitcase-sized purse, as if checking to make sure she had her keys. "And we can't count on any big change by tomorrow. Soon, though."

By five o'clock, I was back at Woodhouse Investigations. Miss Woodhouse was downstairs in the converted parlor that serves as her office, sitting at her computer, the telephone receiver cradled under her chin. That's how she does most of her investigating, since Professor Woodhouse gets cranky whenever her daughter leaves the house. As for the professor herself, she sat in her rocker, popcorn fragments of various hues set out before her on a folding table, cementing together a mosaic portrait of Mick Jagger. She gave me a happy little wave, and her daughter finished her call and swung around in her swivel chair.

"So, Harriet." She didn't even try to keep the sarcasm out of her voice. "Back from your day at Babysitting, Incorporated. Learn anything useful?"

"Not really," I admitted. "I met everyone on the staff and got some scattered impressions—"

"I'm not interested in scattered impressions," Miss Woodhouse cut in. "Any solid suspicions?"

"No," I said, blushing. "Everyone seemed really nice. I *did* go to Susan O'Reilly's funeral, and I met Mr. Cronin, but his lawyer wouldn't let him speak to me. He seems to think the Cronins should sue the center."

"Ah, yes. The lawyer." She flipped through a yellow pad filled with pencil notes. "P. Philip Barnard. Haven't you heard of him, Harriet? He's a real hotshot, lots of society clients. Just the sort of pompous bastard who'd argue that the center was negligent for hiring Susan O'Reilly and misleading the Cronins into thinking she was reliable. He and his wife—she's a physician—are also close personal friends of the Cronins. Just about their closest, judging from what I heard today. Barnard used his connections to get the Cronins their membership in the Bay Club—four months ago, I think."

"He must have a lot of connections," I said, impressed. I'd had some contact with the Bay Club on the very first case I'd worked on with Miss Woodhouse, and I knew that most of its members had lived in Annapolis for generations. "The Cronins are pretty new to the area, aren't they? He said something about wishing they'd never moved to the East Coast."

Miss Woodhouse nodded. "They moved here from Minneapolis just over a year ago. Jeff Cronin's an engineering prodigy, got a gold-plated job with Westinghouse. And Kathy Cronin's a commercial real estate whiz, found herself a nook at Central Properties. So they're loaded. Pretty good prospects for underpaid, ransom-hungry day-care workers."

"I guess," I said reluctantly, hating to think it. "But there *hasn't* been any ransom demand. And if you could've just *seen* the place, Miss Woodhouse. It's so *cheerful*, so *wholesome*, and all the people there really seem to love children."

"Of course they do," she said curtly. "They're paid to seem to love children, and I'm sure they perform their act well. But when you get right down to it, they're babysitters, nothing more, people too stupid and unambitious to attempt—"

"Not another word, you nasty girl," Professor Woodhouse said sharply. She was plastering down the pink popcorn fragments so energetically that Mick Jagger's mouth had assumed truly monstrous proportions. "And just where would *you* be, I'd like to know, if it hadn't been for the babysitters who kept you from destroying yourself while I was teaching? After Mr. Woodhouse went on his journey, after I was left with an oversized, egotistical toddler to support, what would have become of us if I hadn't been able to entrust you to those wonderful, warmhearted women? They weren't just acting a part—they really *did* love children, even a messy, ungrateful, nasty child like you. They wiped your nose and taught you to wash your hands and helped to make you into the barely tolerable young person you are today."

"I'm very sorry, Mother," Miss Woodhouse said, looking thoroughly ashamed. "You're right, of course—you're always right. I shouldn't speak so thoughtlessly. Here, let me fix your dinner. The grocery delivered a lovely, plump chicken today. I thought I might cut it up and fry it and—"

"*Fry* it?" Professor Woodhouse said, scandalized. "If that isn't just like you. We shan't fry it, of course. How disgustingly greasy. We shall soak it in vermouth, stuff it with onions and olives, and roast it. Harriet, I shall require your help. And later, I shall want to hear about everything you saw and heard and thought today. My daughter may not be interested in your scattered impressions, but *I* am."

Unfortunately, Professor Woodhouse dozed off between the onion and olive stuffed chicken and the chocolate chip pie. I helped Miss Woodhouse put her to bed, then went home to my own apartment. Our dinner conversation had been dominated by anecdotes proving just how alarming and unsatisfactory a child Miss Woodhouse had been, so we didn't have a chance to say anything more about the case that night.

The next morning I arrived at Cherry's Children's Center promptly at six. A place like that feels slightly spooky at such an early hour—it's so obviously designed to be filled by little bodies charging about that it doesn't feel quite right when it's empty. I walked resolutely to the office and double-checked yesterday's attendance figures, class plans, audio-visual signout sheets. Everything seemed to be in order, except that Anita Cox had signed out a tape recorder and a camera and had apparently forgotten to return them before she left for the day. Well, I'd ask her about them as soon as she arrived.

I noticed a pansy-bordered Post-it note Cherry Benson had stuck on the calendar. That's right—Lisa Kramer's birthday party. I glanced around the office and saw the huge bunny-shaped piñata her parents had dropped off, stuck in a corner. Now to haul out a ladder and string the piñata up from one of the exposed beams in the Busy Beavers' Den. No problem.

But as I was lugging the ladder out of the storeroom, I heard a sound I shouldn't have heard—a thin, high wail. Dear God, I thought. That's a child crying—a very small child. How could parents forget to pick up their child? How could Cherry be careless enough to leave when there was still a child trapped inside the center?

I let the ladder thud to the floor and ran. There was the child, all right—and not just any child. It was Billy Cronin, filthy and groggily frantic but easily recognizable from the newspaper photographs, sitting in the hall outside the Busy Beavers' Den and sucking his thumb like it was a caviar

lollipop. I raced over and picked him up. I didn't think about
disturbing evidence, didn't think about anything except that
here was a child no one had ever expected to see alive again,
twitching and wailing softly and obviously in need of
comfort.

"There, there, Billy," I crooned. "It's all over. You'll be
back with Mommy and Daddy soon. Everything's fine."

He didn't agree. He sobbed and hiccuped and took his
thumb from his mouth long enough to jab it toward the
doorway. Confused, I stepped into the Den and saw that
everything was far from fine. In the middle of the room, a
red wooden chair was lying on its side; directly above it,
something was already hanging from one of the exposed
beams. It wasn't a piñata. It was Anita Cox.

That was the end of my first undercover assignment. In
a panicky blur, I dragged the ladder over, scrambled
up, pressed my fingers against Anita's throat and wrists,
searched for a pulse, knew I wouldn't find one. No living
person's neck had ever drooped at that impossible angle. I
scooped Billy up and ran back to the office, then dialed 911,
Miss Woodhouse, and the Cronins, in that order. I was still
listening to Kathy Cronin's joyful, unbelieving sobs when
the first police cars roared into the driveway. I can't describe
Billy's reunion with his parents because I didn't see it. I
didn't see much of anything that happened at the center that
morning—a glimpse of Jeff Cronin and his lawyer being
led into the Playful Pups' Palace by a detective, and that was
about it. I spent the next few hours closeted in the Kuddly
Kittens' Korner with a succession of cops—first cops in
uniforms, then cops in suits—repeating my statement
maybe a hundred times. Around ten, Miss Woodhouse
showed up. She stood by and listened to my recital—after
all those repetitions, I had it pretty smooth—then put her
hand on my shoulder and gave the latest cop a withering
stare.

"Can't you let her go now, Harry?" she asked. "She's got

nothing more to say. She's my assistant, she was here on assignment, she happened to be the one to find the baby and the body. And she's had one hell of a morning. Give her a break."

The cop stood up and sighed. "Yeah, I guess we're done with her. Okay, miss. You can go. But stay available."

Miss Woodhouse walked me out to my car. "What's going on?" I asked. "How are they interpreting all this?"

She shrugged. "Well, the captain—never particularly renowned either for his powers of observation or for his deductive capacities—says this proves that Susan O'Reilly and Anita Cox planned the kidnapping together. Something went wrong Sunday—a quarrel about splitting the money, probably—and Cox killed O'Reilly. Then Cox took the kid, drugged him, and stashed him somewhere, thinking she'd carry out the scheme herself. Ransom, most likely, or some blackmarket baby sale. But she didn't have the guts to go it alone, and her conscience was bothering her because she'd killed her friend. She stewed a few days, then left the baby in a safe place, stood on that red chair, wrapped a jumprope round her neck, took the leap."

"I just can't believe that," I said, shaking my head. "Anita had something on her mind yesterday, but I'll swear she wasn't feeling guilty. Angry, yes. Cocky. Not guilty. Isn't anyone even considering any other explanations?"

"One person is." From the look in her eyes, I could tell she meant the homicide lieutenant she'd been engaged to years ago. "He doesn't think it's suicide—her neck was broken, and he says the drop from a chair wouldn't be enough to do that. Plus her face doesn't look nearly as awful as you'd expect with a homemade hanging. So he thinks a third person might be involved in the conspiracy, and maybe this third person killed both O'Reilly and Cox. He's taken Doug Haley in for questioning. Either way, it's fatal publicity for our client. I'd say Cherry's Children's Center has served its last peanut butter and jelly sandwich."

With that gloomy prediction in mind, I drove back to

Woodhouse Investigations. Professor Woodhouse was waiting for me. She'd finished her Mick Jagger mosaic and was hard at work on Keith Richards. She had a matched set planned, to hang above the living room mantel, and had already purchased the antique frames. "My poor little Harriet," she said, rapping her cane on the floor to signify sympathy. "Iphigenia told me about the nasty thing you found. How terribly upsetting! How shocking for a sweet, innocent girl like you to witness something so gory and violent! You must make us a nice pot of tea and sit down in Iphigenia's nice, comfy chair and give me all the details."

It took a long time. She wasn't satisfied with my initial description of the suicide scene, pressed me for more concrete adjectives, eventually had me draw her a detailed sketch of the room and the body. Then we moved on to everything I had heard and seen yesterday—all my conversations with Anita and the other people at the center, the funeral, the apartment Anita had shared with Susan O'Reilly. Professor Woodhouse seemed especially interested in my description of the bookshelves.

"An interesting selection of detective novels," she observed. "Did they belong to Miss O'Reilly or Miss Cox?"

"To Anita Cox, probably," I said, smiling a little. How typical for a former professor to fixate on books. "At least, I know the romance novels were Susan O'Reilly's. I saw her nameplate in one of them—and then Anita came into the room suddenly, and I ended up stuffing the book into my purse. Geez, that's right. I must still have it." I pulled it out and handed her *Hide the Lustful Secret*. "Here. You can see for yourself."

Professor Woodhouse adjusted her spectacles and peered at the nameplate. "This Susan Penhurst O'Reilly was unmarried?"

"That's right," I said, nodding.

"O'Reilly," she said, squinting thoughtfully. "An Irishman. That would fit. Do you know what her father did for a living?"

"No," I said patiently. After several months at Woodhouse Investigations, I'd gotten used to the way the professor's mind wandered off in trivial, irrelevant directions. "Anita said he used to be on the road a lot. Maybe he was a salesman."

Professor Woodhouse shook her head. "Not a salesman. Well. It all seems quite plain, doesn't it?"

"Miss Woodhouse thinks so," I agreed sadly. "She says Susan and Anita must've planned the kidnapping together, and then they got into a fight when Anita came to take little Billy, and—"

"Little Billy! Little Billy!" Professor Woodhouse said, disgusted. "How weary I am of hearing about that tiresome little Billy and that melodramatic kidnapping. Kidnapping! You must push yourself to think more logically, Harriet. Consider Susan Penhurst O'Reilly. Here you have a quiet young girl wearing sweatshirts and sneakers, working at a day-care center, reading romance novels and dating a fellow day-care worker in her spare time. Then, quite suddenly, she tells the young man she can see him no more, and she exhausts her credit buying expensive dresses. How would you explain such a metamorphosis?"

I thought hard. "Well, I guess she was getting sick of her way of life, and she wanted more money, maybe so she could attract more exciting men. That's why she and Anita planned the kidnapping and—"

"Not another word," she said severely, "about this so-called kidnapping. Has it never occurred to you that she might have *already* attracted a more exciting man?"

I stared at her. This "so-called" kidnapping? A more exciting man? Then it came to me. "Jeff Cronin," I gasped. "He's incredibly cute—blue eyes and blond hair and chipmunk cheeks—he could pass for Robert Redford's pudgy younger brother. And all those books about hidden, secret, forbidden loves—oh my God! Susan was having an affair with Jeff Cronin! And maybe he sneaked back to the house to see her, and she threatened to tell his wife, and they fought, and he accidentally killed her, and he panicked, and he took Billy, but of course it wasn't a *real* kidnapping since it was his own son, and he—"

Professor Woodhouse held up her hand. "You are making progress. You lack a well-disciplined intellect, my dear Harriet, but all things considered, you are doing quite well. Now. Tell me what you make of Anita Cox. A camera and a tape recorder checked out from the center, probably concealed in that voluminous purse you observed yesterday evening. Changing into a suit after the funeral. Miss Marple on her shelves, but no Hercule Poirot. Lord Peter, but no Inspector Wexford. Rabbi Small, but no Alan Grant. What do you infer from all this?"

Not much, at first. "I guess she liked reading about amateur detectives, not policemen," I said tentatively. "That would fit—she made a crack about how the police always go after the obvious suspect. As for the camera and the tape recorder—oh, professor! Now I see. Anita knew about the affair with Jeff Cronin. She was Susan's roommate and best friend, after all. So Anita figured Jeff Cronin had killed Susan, and she thought she could be some kind of amateur detective herself, and she went off to confront him or collect evidence—she *did* say something about a big change, like she expected the case to crack open soon. But it didn't work. Jeff Cronin realized what she was up to, and he killed her and made it look like a suicide. Oh, that *has* to be it! I *knew* Anita was too nice to be mixed up in a kidnapping."

Professor Woodhouse slapped my hand. "I *told* you I didn't want to hear another word about kidnapping. Nevertheless, on the whole, you are doing quite well. Your theory is consistent and fairly plausible. It is not yet accurate, but that is perhaps too much to expect. You still lack one vital fact. And that is the fact I must verify now." She plastered a bright red popcorn lump on the end of Keith Richard's cigarette and pushed the mosaic aside. "Harriet, get the car. We are going for a drive."

"For a drive?" I said, amazed. Professor Woodhouse almost never leaves the house. "Where would you like to go, professor?"

"To the house of Cora Elizabeth Penhurst." She stood up, leaning heavily on her cane. "It is a large house, very white, columns essentially Doric though too fussy about the top, mildly ostentatious but on the whole quite dignified. I cannot at the moment recall the address, but I am sure I shall recognize the house, and the street. I gave a most stimulating lecture there some thirty years ago, for the Daughters of the American Revolution, titled 'Medea and Jason: The Dysfunctional Family in Classical Literature.'" She frowned, as if not sure that she'd gotten it exactly right. "Or words to that effect. At any rate, there was a lively exchange over sherry afterwards, Cora Elizabeth Penhurst was a gracious hostess, and for a time we struck up a sort of friendship. Not a particularly close friendship, mind you, nor a permanent one, for eventually she became a nasty old woman. But I shall never forget her." She picked up her shawl. "And now I wish to see her again."

I didn't want to go. Miss Woodhouse was bound to come home any time, and I wanted to know what was happening with the case, but Miss Woodhouse had made it clear when she hired me that I was always to do anything her mother asked, so I got my purse. I scrawled a quick note for Miss Woodhouse—"Visiting C. E. Penhurst"—and helped the professor to the car.

We drove around Annapolis for half an hour before she spotted a street that looked right, and then it took us a long time to find the house. It was off by itself, smack on the banks of the Severn, and it fit her description exactly—big, white, many-columned, ostentatious in a dignified way. She hadn't mentioned the immense grounds or the private dock, but they didn't surprise me. This was how the richest, oldest families in Annapolis lived. The middle-aged woman who answered the door also fit right into the picture. Straight-spined, unsmiling, tweed and starched linen, thoroughly respectable—just the sort a wealthy old woman like Cora Elizabeth Penhurst would hire as her housekeeper and companion.

"Mrs. Penhurst is out on the east lawn, taking the afternoon air," she said, speaking only to Professor Wood-house. I was obviously beneath her notice. "I shall give her your card, and see if she is at liberty to receive you."

Wow. Now the whole visit felt worthwhile. I'd never thought I'd actually hear somebody outside of a movie say something that snooty. The housekeeper left us standing in a plant-and-doily-filled parlor, then came back in a few minutes.

"Mrs. Penhurst will see you now," she said impassively and led us through the house to the east lawn.

Cora Elizabeth Penhurst sat in a wheelchair, her body tiny and brittle, her sparse white hair barely covering her scalp, her bright little eyes nearly enveloped in wrinkles. A copy of today's *Capital* lay on her lap. "Professor Minerva Wood-house," she said, and I was amazed by the clarity and strength of her voice. "I remember you. You delivered a lecture on Medea. At the time, I thought her approach rather too extreme, your analysis rather too sympathetic. I have since reconsidered."

"Yes, they *can* be trying," Professor Woodhouse said, settling her bulk into one of the white wrought-iron chairs set out on the lawn and motioning me toward another. "My own daughter, for example. She could have had a brilliant academic career, but she chose to become a policewoman. And then, for a time, she thought of marrying a Jew."

"A Jew!" Mrs. Penhurst said, scandalized. "That is even worse." She curled her thin upper lip and scowled at me. "This is the imprudent young woman?"

"No," Professor Woodhouse said. The housekeeper came out again, carrying a silver tray with a cut glass decanter and glasses. She poured us each some sherry and then stood back, ready to serve again. Professor Woodhouse emptied her glass at one gulp. "This is Harriet Russo," she said. "A Papist of Italian origin, but decent. Not like most of them."

I swallowed my sherry and held out my glass for a refill, too stunned to speak. How could Professor Woodhouse say a thing like that? I'd known she was conservative, of course, but I'd never thought she was so prejudiced. And although Miss Woodhouse had never told me just why she broke off her engagement, I hadn't gotten the impression that religion was the real obstacle. Well, I was certainly learning a lot this afternoon. And I wasn't so sure that I liked Professor Woodhouse very much any more.

"That is rare," Mrs. Penhurst was saying. She took a healthy sip of her sherry. "Mind you, I try not to be too narrow in my views. A flute—I think I could have tolerated a flute. Perhaps even a clarinet. But a saxophone? What civilized person ever played a saxophone? And no trace of propriety, of true harmony. All cacophony and madness and disorder. And the rampant ethnicity of it! She made a choice I could not possibly accept. What rational person could blame me?"

"Not I," Professor Woodhouse said stoutly. I was finding the conversation very difficult to follow. Well, what could you expect? They were both nearly eighty. Naturally they were talking nonsense. I concentrated on enjoying my sherry, which was very mellow, very smooth, very soothing. Smoothing and soothing, I thought, and half-giggled at the sound of it.

Professor Woodhouse shot me a warning glance and drained her own glass. "I certainly do not blame you, Cora," she said, and leaned forward, lowering her voice. "But you blamed yourself, did you not?"

It could have been a shrug, or a shudder—I wasn't sure. Mrs. Penhurst's shoulders definitely quivered for a moment. "Well, well. Unforeseen events sometimes force reconsiderations, elicit regrets, even when one's actions have been absolutely above reproach. Finality, you know. It makes one think of one's own end and weakens one's resolutions. For a time, I doubted myself. I thought of making amends. Not with the original offenders—that would have been distasteful, and it was by that time at any rate impossible. But with the result." She picked up the *Capital*, stared at it, sighed, let it drop back into her lap. "I was wrong to doubt. Subsequent incidents have confirmed that. Unsound at the root, unsound at the bud. Only those who have proved themselves to be reliable deserve to be rewarded. I know that now, and I shall make everything once again as it was. I shall never doubt myself again."

"That," said Professor Woodhouse, "is exactly what I came here to learn." Then abruptly, her chin sank down on her chest, and her eyes closed.

The housekeeper stepped over to Mrs. Penhurst. "I'll see your guests out. You mustn't tire yourself, Cora."

Cora. I would have expected the housekeeper to call her Mrs. Penhurst. They must have been together a long time for Mrs. Penhurst to accept such informality. But I was suddenly too tired to try to figure it out. My head was aching something awful, and my eyes seemed to be getting blurry. Not terribly surprising, really—nothing but tea and toast all day, and then two glasses of sherry. Or was it three? Listening to these four old ladies ramble on had really gotten me confused.

No—only two old ladies. The housekeeper wasn't old, and there was no fourth person. Or was there? With an effort, I lifted my head up and tried to count. Mrs. Penhurst in her wheelchair, Professor Woodhouse sitting next to her, the housekeeper standing nearby—and yes, there was another person. Not an old lady, though. Not a lady at all. I tried to focus on his face. I'd seen it before.

The housekeeper was standing over me now, pushing my forehead back with one hand, pulling on my cheeks with the other, staring into my eyes. How rude. I started to push her away but lost interest in the attempt before my hand made it halfway to her arm. "She's nearly out," I heard her saying, in a voice that sounded miles away. "She won't give you any trouble. And the professor's asleep already. Now what? Car or boat?"

"Better use the car," the man's voice said. He came closer to me, but I still couldn't figure out who he was. For some reason, I got a flash of the covers of Susan O'Reilly's romance novels, of the dark, craggy men with their brooding eyes and sneering lips. Not Robert Redford, I thought groggily. He'd never make one of those covers. They go for the Heathcliff type. "We'll have to get rid of their car eventually anyway," Heathcliff was saying. "And I don't think anybody would believe they'd take a boat out. The old lady's too senile to pilot, and I heard the girl's from Ohio—she may never have been on a boat in her life. We'll have to think of a quiet road, with a stiff drop. Maybe we should wait until after dark."

"No," the housekeeper said sharply. "Get them out of here right away. That detective's probably home by now. When she sees that her mother's missing, she'll start looking for her."

"She'd never in a million years think to look *here*," Heathcliff said. He had grabbed me under the arms and was starting to pull me out of the chair. I tried to resist, but my body felt too heavy. It took all my energy just to listen to his words. "We've managed everything just fine," he said. "Thank God you came over today. Nobody's got any reason to connect Aunt Cora to any of this."

Aunt Cora. It was very confusing, because Heathcliff was an orphan—how could he have an aunt? I forced my eyes all the way open, looked him straight in the face, and saw that it wasn't Heathcliff at all. "P. Philip Barnard, Attorney-at-Law," I said out loud, and suddenly I knew what the *P* stood for.

"Damn!" He let me drop back into the chair. "I thought you said she was nearly out, Margaret. She recognized me."

"It won't do her any good," the housekeeper said—but

by now I'd realized she wasn't a housekeeper. P. Philip Barnard had called her Margaret. He had a wife named Margaret. "Just dump them far away from here, and make sure the gas tank explodes. We don't want a coroner finding traces. Tomorrow I'll convince Aunt Cora that she heard about the accident on the radio and dreamed the whole visit. It won't be hard. I gave her a pretty good dose, too. Just get the girl in the car. I'll take Aunt Cora inside and then give you a hand with the professor. She looks heavy."

He was already obeying her. He grabbed me again, heaved me over his shoulder, and started carrying me across the lawn. Strong guy, I thought. My head and arms were dangling upside down over his back, the only thing I could see was a whizzing mass of green, my mind was spinning in and out of focus wildly, but I could still give credit where credit was due. P. Philip Barnard must have a massive chest and excessive biceps, just like the heroes in Susan's novels. And he was married, so that made him a hidden, secret, forbidden object for her loves and lusts and passions. He probably wouldn't have much trouble getting a dreamy, romantic girl like Susan to fall for him. And he certainly wouldn't have any trouble hitting her over the head and tossing her in a swimming pool, or strangling Anita Cox and stringing her up from a ceiling beam. Or pushing a car off an overpass to cover up his latest two murders.

That last image was potent enough to make its way through the swirling thoughts in my brain. Gotta do something, I thought, straining for coherence. I'm a black belt—oughtta be able to do something. I made myself stop gazing at the grass, pleasant as it was, and took a good gaze at P. Philip Barnard's back. Hanging upside down over your opponent's back isn't a particularly good position for an attack, but I thought I could reach his kidney. Could I muster up a punch? Somehow, I'd have to—and I'd better do it now, before I passed out completely. I took the deepest breath I could manage, concentrated as hard as I could, succeeded in reducing the fog in my brain to a mere mist, made a fist, lifted my arm up over my head, aimed for P. Philip Barnard's kidney, swung my arm down, and connected.

All things considered, it must have been a pretty good punch. P. Philip Barnard gasped in pain, arched his body backwards, and dropped me. So now I was lying on my back on the grass, much to weak to think about getting up—also not an ideal position for an attack, but at least I could reach his ankles. I called up a mental image of a car exploding with Professor Woodhouse and me inside, felt suitably motivated, and made myself roll toward the stunned, panting lawyer. I put every bit of concentration I had left into getting my arms around his ankles, then tightened my grip. He swore, tottered, fell flat on his face. I heard a scream and hoped it was his, but I couldn't be sure—for all I knew, it could be mine. Another scream, and this one definitely wasn't coming from either one of us. It was too far away. A horrible image flashed into what was left of my mind—that bitch Margaret, hurting poor, helpless Professor Woodhouse. I had to finish this guy off and get back to her.

With a fresh spurt of strength, I squeezed his ankles more tightly, pushed my face against his pants leg, found some skin, sank in my teeth. He yelped in agony and tried to roll onto his back, but I wouldn't let him. Then he had curled around on the ground and was trying to pry my arms away from his ankles, my teeth out of his leg. I squeezed my eyes shut, gripped him more fiercely, bit down harder. I don't know just what I was hoping to accomplish—to puncture a vein, maybe, and make him bleed to death. I certainly hope I wasn't planning to eat him.

I don't know how long we struggled like that, or how long it would have taken him to realize that he'd make more of an impression by punching me in the face than by tugging at my arms. The next things I remembered were the muffled sounds of a car pulling up, a door slamming, feet running. And then, miraculously, Miss Woodhouse's voice.

"On your feet, Barnard," she said sharply. "Let her go."

But he wasn't the one who had to let go, and getting on his feet wasn't something he could manage just then. I heard him swear and felt him stop struggling, but at the moment these didn't seem like adequate reasons for removing my teeth from his leg. I clamped down again, and he bellowed with pain.

"Damn it!" he cried. "Get her off me!"

"It's all right, Harriet," Miss Woodhouse said. "I have a gun. You can let him up."

Perfectly reasonable advice, of course, but I was pretty far gone, and my mind had room for just one idea—bite the lawyer. I didn't even open my eyes. Miss Woodhouse was losing patience.

"For heaven's sake, Harriet," she said. "What's wrong with you? And where's Mother? When I saw your note, I—oh, there you are, Mother. Are you all right?"

"Of course I'm all right," Professor Woodhouse said, and her voice sounded just as crisp as it always does. "But *what* is the matter with Harriet? Harriet! Get up this instant! Is this any way for a lady to behave?"

Drunk, drugged, or sober, I could never disobey Professor Woodhouse. Her words made it through the haze, and I let go. By the time I'd worked my eyelids to a halfway up position, P. Philip Barnard was struggling to his feet, starting to reach for something inside his coat. Miss Woodhouse flattened him with one swift kick that left his nose as bloody as his ankle, then looked at her mother and me with open astonishment.

"I called the police," she said. "I thought they'd beat me here, but I see they're taking their time. What on earth happened, Mother?"

"I hardly know," Professor Woodhouse said, looking uncharacteristically baffled. "I was having a chat with Cora Elizabeth Penhurst, and Harriet was giggling and behaving badly. Then I must have dozed off. Terribly rude—I do hope Cora will forgive me. And then I was dreaming that I was with the Spartans at Thermopylae, being attacked by a Persian with exceptionally bad breath. I defended myself quite ably, as I recall, and awoke feeling refreshed and invigorated." She shrugged. "But I can*not* explain the scene that greeted me when I opened my eyes. Cora was no longer there, and that housekeeper of hers was lying on the ground with a bloody nose, quite unconscious. I trust you summoned an ambulance as well as the police, Iphigenia. She may require medical attention."

She required, in fact, hospitalization. Professor Woodhouse had left her with a broken nose and two cracked ribs and a mild concussion. If the professor really *had* been at Thermopylae, the Spartans might have had a chance. I stayed at the hospital for a few hours, too, until the doctors were sure that the drug Margaret Barnard had put in my sherry had worn off completely. It was the same kind of drug, I learned later, that she'd used to keep little Billy Cronin quiet when she and her husband had him hidden in their summer home in Ocean City. It always helps to have a physician in the family if you're planning a kidnapping. As for Professor Woodhouse, she refused to go to the hospital at all, and the paramedic who tried to get close enough to examine her had to admit that there was probably no need. She was fine. All she'd needed was a ten minute nap, and she'd recovered from the drug completely. I try to tell myself it was because she hadn't had as much sherry as I did. But I don't think that's the real reason.

Anyway, we were both lucky. P. Philip Barnard had seen Miss Woodhouse at the day-care center that morning, had asked a cop about her, had found out who I really was. Then, when his wife called him at his office to say that Professor Minerva Woodhouse and Miss Harriet Russo had come by to see his aunt, he'd panicked. He figured that we were starting to make the connections he hadn't wanted anyone to make. He'd told his wife to drug us, that he'd come right over to get rid of us. Luckily, by that time Miss Woodhouse had talked her ex-fiancé into letting her see the apartment Susan O'Reilly and Anita Cox had shared. She'd spotted one of those bookplates in another romance novel and seen that Susan's middle name was Penhurst—and since she'd already known that P. Philip Barnard's first name was Penhurst, too, she started making some connections of her own. She came home, and—well, you know the rest.

Or most of it. The three of us finally got a chance to put all the pieces together over supper that night. Miss Woodhouse made cold chicken sandwiches and opened up a bottle of Professor Woodhouse's olive and onion marinade, and we settled down in front of the television to enjoy a cosy meal.

"You should have told me about the bookplate, Harriet," Miss Woodhouse said reprovingly. "Penhurst and O'Reilly don't exactly sound like names that naturally go together."

I nodded in apology, not daring to point out that Miss Woodhouse hadn't shown much interest in hearing anything I had to say yesterday. "So Susan O'Reilly was Cora Elizabeth Penhurst's granddaughter?"

"That is correct," Professor Woodhouse said. "Wheel of Fortune" had just ended, so she picked up the remote and found "Green Acres." "As I told you, Cora could be an extremely nasty old woman. When her only daughter defied her by marrying an Irish jazz musician, Cora disowned her and refused to have anything further to do with the couple—or with the daughter they eventually produced. I doubt that young Susan ever met her grandmother, or understood the true origin of her middle name. Cora's daughter was probably just as proud, in her own way, as her mother. And I hope, dear Harriet, that you will understand why I felt constrained this afternoon to refer to your religion and your national origin in such a disrespectful way. I was pretending sympathy with Cora's outdated and thoroughly unjustified views, in hopes of drawing her out."

"I understand," I said warmly, and meant it. "And then Susan's parents were killed in that car accident six months ago, and Cora Penhurst felt guilty. So she decided to make amends by naming Susan as her heir after all."

Miss Woodhouse passed me the marinade and I nodded. "And that meant substantially disinheriting her nephew and lawyer, Penhurst Philip Barnard. An awkward decision, since he'd already lost a good bit of Susan's inheritance through gambling and bad investments. He had to get rid of her, in a way that would raise no suspicions and leave the old lady more than ever convinced that she'd been right to despise her daughter and granddaughter. He must have done a fair amount of research on Susan, to find out about her connection with the Cronins and her penchant for forbidden romances. After that, it was all fairly easy—play up to the Cronins, meet Susan through them, seduce her, make her promise to keep the affair secret to protect his marriage, arrange a rendezvous while she was babysitting at the Cronin house." She sighed. "And then kill her, and take little Billy to make it look like kidnapping and disguise the real motive for the murder. No one ever asked who would have a reason to kill Susan—it never occurred to the police to wonder if she might be an heiress. Everyone assumed that she was simply an incidental victim in a kidnapping, possibly a conspirator."

"Especially," Professor Woodhouse put in severely, "since people are so eager to regard day-care centers with suspicion, to see the people who work there as sinister figures prone to abuse and neglect and all manner of evil. You yourself, Iphigenia, display this same reprehensible tendency. Like so many young women of your generation, you pretend to liberality and sisterly feeling, but you are utterly intolerant of women whose lives differ in any respect from your own. Consequently, you were blinded by contempt and failed to see that this entire kidnapping was a mere sideshow, a means to mask a murder."

"I know," Miss Woodhouse said, spearing an olive with

her fork dejectedly. "I was wrong. Thank you for pointing it out."

"Well, at least Cherry's Children's Center has been completely vindicated," I said, eager to ease her misery. "I'm sure Cherry will get all her old students back. And little Billy Cronin is safe and sound, back home with his parents." A horrible thought came to me. "What were the Barnards planning to do with Billy? What would have happened to him if Anita hadn't forced the issue by confronting Barnard and giving him a reason to return Billy to the center? Would they have killed him?"

"Possibly," Miss Woodhouse said, shrugging. "Neither of the Barnards is talking much, so we may never know for sure. My guess is that they were waiting to see how things developed. They wanted the suspicion for the kidnapping to fall on someone else, and the people at the day-care center were the most obvious targets. If the Barnards could build that suspicion by having Billy show up alive somewhere, fine. If they decided it would be better to have his body found on Cherry Benson's doorstep, they would have done that. I don't think they were eager to commit a second murder. But as Anita Cox found out, they wouldn't hesitate to do it if they thought it was necessary." She looked over at her mother, and her eyes were suddenly misty. "They didn't hesitate about deciding to commit a third murder, either, or a fourth. I just thank God they didn't get the chance."

Professor Woodhouse snarled at her and set to work on her nearly completed Keith Richards mosaic. "I, too, thank God," she said, "since it is customary to do so on such occasions. You needn't think, however, that I thank *you*, you nasty girl. Had you thought just a bit more clearly and had been just a bit more open to the insights Harriet was ready to offer you, you might have spared us a most tiresome ordeal. As it was, you arrived just after the nick of time. Harriet and I were handling matters quite competently

on our own. Your help was tardy and ultimately super-
fluous."

"That's not fair," I began to protest, but Miss Woodhouse
passed me another sandwich and waved me off.

"Mother is quite right," she said, smiling. "As always."

BODY ENGLISH

::

by S. J. Rozan

It was the first case I took that I didn't want. My instincts
were right, too, because it also turned out to be the first case
that made me wonder whether I wanted to be a private
investigator for the rest of my life.

"And she doesn't really even want me, either," I fumed.
I was ranting to my sometime partner, Bill Smith, at the
Peacock Rice Shop on Mott Street. "Because I don't know
Mandarin. She almost stomped out when she found that out.
Stuck-up Taiwan lady! And she absolutely refused to speak
Cantonese. She insisted we speak English. Can you believe
that?"

"I always insist you speak English," Bill pointed out. He
lifted sautéed squid from the serving dish into his rice bowl.

"Don't start!" I speared my chopsticks into a mass of
deep green watercress in glistening sauce. "You big coarse
clumsy foreign characters are exactly what the problem is,
anyway."

Bill stopped a piece of squid just short of his mouth.
"Foreign?"

I was feeling argumentative and crabby. "I grew up in this

118

country. *Some* people spent their childhoods trotting around the world."

"That was my adolescence, and you grew up in Chinatown, which you've always said is another *planet*. Listen, Lydia, how about we talk about the case before you stab me with a chopstick?"

"Let me eat first," I said sulkily. I tried the squid; it was pungent and tender. It cheered me up a little, and the smoky, jasmine-scented tea cheered me more. Maybe my blood sugar was just low. "Actually," I said aloud, "maybe I was just nervous."

"Mrs. Lee made you nervous?"

I hated to admit it, but it was true. "She's a very powerful woman in Chinatown. She owns four big factories here." "Factory" was Chinatown for "sweatshop," but Bill knew that. "My mother was terrified I'd offend her. It would have humiliated my mother if Mrs. Lee hadn't approved of me."

"But you say you didn't."

"No, but she hired me. She won't criticize me publicly while I'm working for her. That would make her look foolish, you see. Hiring someone as obviously inadequate as I am."

"I think you're adequate. I think you're way beyond adequate. Don't glare at me, tell me about the case. You're hiring me. What are we doing?"

"Following a woman. I figured you'd be good at that."

"Only if she's gorgeous and small and Chinese and furious like you."

He drank some beer, and I glared at him.

"I know why you're mad." He put the bottle down. "You hate this woman for making you nervous. You wanted to turn her down, but you had to take her case so your mother wouldn't lose face, and now you're stuck. Boy, you really hate being told what to do, don't you?"

"You should know." I finished the squid. The stainless steel teapot wasn't empty yet, so I poured another cup.

Bill waited until I'd finished before he took out his cigarettes. "Is it all right?"

I didn't know if he was asking me if he could smoke now, or if I felt better. "Go ahead." Then I sighed, ran my hand through my hair. "I guess you're right."

"Well, that's rare enough." He dropped a match in the white ashtray with the red peacock on it. "Then the case is okay, it's the client who bothers you?"

I shook my head. "I don't like this case."

"Why? What's it about?"

"Mrs. Lee wants us to follow her son's financée. A woman named Jill Moore."

"She doesn't sound Chinese."

"That's sort of the point. She's tall and blond and according to Mrs. Lee completely untrustworthy. Mrs. Lee thinks she's cheating on her son."

"Does her son think so?"

"No, and Mrs. Lee doesn't want him to know what we're doing until we have proof."

"Do you know him? The son?"

"I nodded. "Lee Kuan Cheng. Kuan Cheng Lee to you. He's a few years younger than me, but when you grow up around here, you sort of know everybody."

"What's he like?"

"When he was twelve he took on my twin cousins in the schoolyard because they beat him out on a math test. He's very competitive. They fought like weasels in a sack; I had to separate them. I think I still have a scar."

"Can I see it?"

"Not a chance."

"Sounds like your cousins were sort of competitive, too."

"In my family? Don't be ridiculous."

Bill tipped the ash off his cigarette. "So what don't you like about it?"

"She wants it to be true."

"Mrs. Lee does?"

"Yes. She was sitting there with an I-told-you-so smile, as

though she'd already proved it. 'Jill Moore like rice,' she said. She looked like—what is it you people say? The cat that ate the canary?"

"That's what we people say. What does that mean, to like rice?"

"Yellow fever. Whites who are attracted to Asians just because we're exotic, or whatever it is your people think we are."

"Paranoid."

"Is that attractive?"

"On you it is. Go on."

I sighed, but I went on. "Jill Moore and Kuan Cheng are both NYU students. Kuan Cheng is getting an MBA, so he can go into his mother's business. Jill Moore's in Asian Studies."

"That's suspicious."

"Mrs. Lee thinks so. Kuan Cheng took Jill over to Mrs. Lee's apartment about six weeks ago, trying to make a good impression on the future mother-in-law. It was the first and only time they've ever met. She got Jill alone for twenty minutes, and based on that conversation, she's sure Jill Moore is only interested in Kuan Cheng for some perverse white-creature sexual reason."

"Don't knock white-creature sexual perversions until you've tried them."

"Oh, drop it, will you?" Sometimes I'm in the mood for that sort of stuff from Bill, but not always. "Anyhow, when I asked Mrs. Lee what made her suspect that, she gave me this superior look and said, 'Just, mother know. You follow, you see.' I wanted to sock her."

"Sounds to me like she wants to break up what she considers an unsuitable match for her baby. That's not admirable, but it's not unusual."

"Yeah, but I like happy endings. If Jill Moore and Kuan Cheng Lee love each other, what business is it of his mother's? I mean, who *asked* her? But if I can't get proof that he's being cheated on, she won't believe it's because she was wrong. She'll go around telling all of Chinatown what an incompetent detective I am. That would be terrible for my mother."

"So," Bill said, "you can't win either way. If she's right, you'll be disillusioned. If she's wrong, you'll be in trouble."

"That's it," I sighed. "Exactly."

The waiter appeared, smiling shyly. He brought us the check, and two glass bowls of quivering maroon gelatin, each crowned with an almond cookie.

"What's that?" Bill eyed his bowl suspiciously.

I looked over to the door where Mr. Han, the proprietor, smiled broadly at me. I called to him in Chinese; he answered.

"It's a bean paste jelly his new chef makes," I told Bill. "He says even white people like it."

"At least he admits I'm a person."

"Well, he didn't exactly say that." He put his cigarette out, and we tried the jelly. It was sweet, tasting delicately of lychee and orange.

"Tell him I like it," Bill said.

I called to Mr. Han again. From his post by the door he smiled and bowed.

"What you're speaking with him," Bill said, "that's Cantonese?"

"Uh-huh. Only spoken by peasants like Uncle Hun-jo and me. I'm sure Mrs. Lee understands it, since she's lived in Chinatown twenty years, and she wouldn't stoop to speak such a harsh, nasty-sounding language."

"Is it nasty-sounding?"

"Of course not."

"I didn't think so."

Out on the crowded sidewalk the November air was cold. High thin clouds diluted the sunlight, and a breeze herded papers this way and that in the gutter, practicing for winter.

Walking north, we maneuvered around old Chinese ladies with short gray hair and padded jackets, picking over vegetables shoulder to shoulder with uptown shoppers who didn't know the names of the greens they were buying. A group of camera-hung tourists peered into guidebooks at the streets I grew up in. Vendors hawked cotton socks and radio-controlled toy cars, calling in broken English, "Three, five dollar!" and, "See it goes!" The street vendors are often the newest immigrants; sometimes those are the only English words they yet know.

"I think Mrs. Lee speaks better English than she lets on, too," I said to Bill as we crossed Canal. "Or at least understands more."

"Her English wasn't good?"

"It was snooty and condescending, but her grammar was terrible. I think she refuses to learn it better, or to speak it as well as she already knows how. It would be giving in."

We single-filed past the sidewalk tables at a cafe in what used to be Little Italy and is still called that, though every other storefront sign now is in Chinese. "So," Bill said, "what now?"

"Now we go lurk outside Jill Moore's afternoon class and see how far we can tail her without getting spotted."

"Together? About a foot and a half."

Bill's thirteen inches taller, eighty pounds heavier, and twelve years older than I am, with big hands and a face that sort of shows he's been a P.I. for twenty years. I'm small, though I'm always saying I'm quicker and he's always saying I'm in better shape than he is. And we both know I'm a better shot, though it was he who taught me to shoot. I practice a lot.

And besides all that, of course, I'm Chinese. And he's not. We do make a weird-looking pair.

"No," I said. "Not together. We lurk in different places."

It's a technique he taught me, and we use it often. It's good to have two people on a tail because subjects can be surprisingly sneaky about losing you, even when they don't know you're there. The only reason not to do it is if the client can't afford it. When I'd quoted rates to Mrs. Lee,

she'd balked—"Too much. Inexperience child. I pay half."—
and we'd had to haggle, but I'd expected that, so I'd started
high. Now, for what she thought she was paying for me, she
was getting both me and Bill.

I considered that a bargain.

Jill Moore's afternoon class met in an old white big-
windowed NYU building on the east side of Washington
Square. Tracking her down had taken me most of the hour
between the time Mrs. Lee had sniffed her disdainful way
out of my office and the time I'd met Bill for lunch. I'd had
to use two different voices on the phone. For the Student
Life Office I was a confused clerk from the Bursar's Office
who'd gotten Jill Moore hopelessly mixed up with Joe
Moore, or Joan Moore, or God knows who. The other voice,
when I'd gotten Jill Moore's address and schedule, was for
Asian Studies.

"Herro," I'd said, blurring the distinction between L's and
R's the way we're all supposed to. "I am Chin Ling
Wan-ju—" that was the true part "—ah, guest lecturer in
Flowering of Ming Dynasty Art, today. Supposed to speak
on 'Spirit Scrolls of Ming Emperors.' So foolish, lose all
direction. Tell me, please, where to meet?"

They were glad to.

Bill pointed out, when I told him about it, that they might
have been glad to if I'd just called up like a regular person
and asked. But I always like to try out my moves when I get
a chance.

Armed with the photograph Mrs. Lee had given me from
the afternoon with her daughter-in-law-elect, Bill settled
on a bench at the edge of the park with the other bums. I felt
his eyes on me as I crossed the street to the classroom
building.

I entered the building along with a group of four NYU
women, one in jeans, one in sixties daisy-patterned leg-
gings, two in short skirts. I made three in short skirts. The
guard at the security desk, who would have stopped Bill in

a second, hardly even looked at me, except to evaluate my legs relative to the other legs sticking out of the skirts.

We all got on the elevator, but I got off first, on the third floor. I went around the corner to the room where someone was lecturing to a hall full of students on The Flowering of Ming Dynasty Art. Not on Spirit Scrolls, presumably, even if there really were such things, which I doubted.

I settled myself on the floor at the other end of the hall where I'd have a good view of the classroom door and took *The Catcher in the Rye* out of my leather knapsack. I'd read it when I was fourteen and it hadn't done a thing for me, but I thought maybe, in this setting, I'd give it another chance.

After fifteen minutes of giving it another chance a bell clanged and all hell broke loose. Doors burst open everywhere. The advance guard—students whose next class was all the way across campus—charged out of the classrooms and were in the elevator or bouncing down the stairs before the profs had finished giving the reading assignments. Then came the slower ones, juggling books, notebooks, backpacks, and handbags the size of carry-ons. Textbooks thumped closed and zippers zipped and kids called to each other down the hall in exuberant voices and lots of different accents.

I stood, slipped my knapsack on, searched the faces pouring out of the lecture hall for the one in Mrs. Lee's photograph.

Jill Moore was not hard to spot. She wore a white shirt and blue jeans, dangling brass earrings, and, I noticed, a small diamond ring on her left hand. That encouraged me. A woman who was cheating wouldn't wear her engagement ring while she did it, would she?

Of course, rings are easy to take off.

As Jill Moore made room in her canvas carryall for her notebook, a handsome Asian man worked his way through the throng. He called her name. She turned, spotted him, smiled playfully. He reached her, seemed to be asking a question, but they were speaking low; I couldn't hear them. Still smiling, she shook her head, then looked around quickly. She leaned close and whispered something. He nodded. Then she squeezed his arm, twinkled her eyes, and was gone down the stairs.

I clumped down after her, thinking damn, damn, damn. I didn't know who that guy was, but he wasn't Kuan Cheng Lee.

I followed Jill Moore for the rest of the afternoon, through Washington Square Park where the fallen leaves were restless on the asphalt paths, to the NYU library where she studied for two hours and I decided to give away my copy of *The Catcher in the Rye.* After that we shopped a little along Sixth Avenue, had cappuccino at the Caffe Lucca—she indoors, I out—and then, around seven, we wandered back to an old brick building on MacDougal Street. The whole time I could feel Bill nearby, always down the block or across the street from us, a figure at the corner of my eye who wasn't there when I looked.

The MacDougal Street building was what I'd been given as Jill Moore's address by the helpful secretary at the Student Life Office. I watched her go in, and I watched the lights come on in a fourth floor front apartment a minute later.

Across the street and down a little was another cafe. That's what I love about New York. I don't know how P.I.'s do this in the suburbs.

I settled at a table by the window in time to see Bill stroll around the corner and disappear. If the apartment building had a rear exit into an alley, I wouldn't see him again for a while. He'd plant himself there, waiting until Jill Moore came out that way, or until I found him to say we were knocking off for the evening. This case was mine, so that decision was mine to make.

There must have been no alley because he was back in a few minutes, lighting a cigarette on the street corner. I stuck my head out the cafe door, waved for him to come in.

He joined me at my round wooden table, ordered espresso and a Napoleon. I got peppermint tea.

"Thanks, chief," Bill grinned when the waiter was gone. "It was getting cold out there."

"Well, she may be in for the evening," I said. "If she's not, we can leave here separately."

But it turned out she was. As we sipped our drinks I told Bill about the man Jill Moore had huddled with outside of class. He said that seemed innocent enough to him, and I said the same thing, but I wasn't so sure, and neither was he, although he didn't say that. After about an hour we ordered an antipasto and shared it, dividing up chewy pepperoni, vinegared hot peppers, creamy rounds of provolone.

"How can you eat this after pastry?" I demanded.

"It's the white trash way of life."

"See," I said glumly. "The fact is we will never understand each other."

"And if we don't," Bill said, unearthing an anchovy and depositing it on my plate, because they're my favorite, "is that necessarily because I'm white and you're Chinese?"

"Yes," I said. "It necessarily is."

When we'd come in, there had been opera in the air, dramatic voices crashing together or lamenting separately in ways I was sure would break my heart if I understood them. After that there had been silence softened by murmured conversations. Now the elegant mahogany-skinned waiter clicked a new tape into the tape deck, and the swift notes of a piano tinkled around us. Bill's face grew distracted, just for a moment; maybe someone else wouldn't have noticed.

"Do you play this?" I asked him.

"Yes."

"What is it?"

"Beethoven. The Waldstein Sonata. I don't play it this well."

"Do you—" I began. Bill put a sudden hand on my arm.

"Look," he said, nodding toward the window. "Is that the guy you saw this afternoon?"

The outer door to Jill Moore's building stood open. As we watched a young Asian man took the stoop steps two at a time, then unlocked the inner door and let himself in. He was carrying a knapsack and a bag of groceries.

"No," I said. "That's Kuan Cheng Lee."

Nothing else happened that evening. Kuan Cheng, according to his mother, had an apartment on East 9th Street. "Good for son," she'd informed me. "Live by own self, learn manage household. Later will able treat mother proper way." I didn't know what sort of household Kuan Cheng would learn to manage in a 9th Street walkup, nor had I been sure that this wasn't just Mrs. Lee saving face by pretending to approve of her son's moving out. What was clear was that she intended, eventually, to establish herself in whatever household he set up. Well, as a Chinese mother, that was her right.

Kuan Cheng didn't come out, and no one else we cared about—meaning no Asian men—went in, and around ten I called it off. I paid the check, took the receipt for Mrs. Lee, and left a big tip. Bill and I walked south on Sixth to Canal in the chilly blue New York night. Traffic rushed up Sixth in a hurry to get someplace, it wasn't clear where.

At Canal we arranged to meet the next morning and start all over again. We kissed goodnight lightly, the way we always do, and I felt a little guilty and confused, the way I always do. Bill wants more than that from me, but he understands how I feel, and though he comes on a lot in a kidding sort of way, he never pushes it. Somehow that makes me feel guilty and confused.

Then we parted. Bill turned right to his Laight Street apartment and I turned left, to Chinatown.

The morning was overcast and chillier than the day before had been. Jill Moore had a nine o'clock class; at a quarter to nine Bill and I watched from separate corners as she and

Kuan Cheng Lee came out of her building and walked up MacDougal Street. They were smiling and talking, Jill Moore's eyes twinkling as they had the day before, with the other Asian man.

The day was pretty boring, and I began to feel bad for Bill, who spent most of it on park benches. He doesn't like to be cold. I was fine, sitting in the hallway of the white building, in the student cafeteria (which was noisier than I ever remember my college cafeteria being), in the library, and then back in the white building. I had ditched *The Catcher in the Rye* and wrapped *Surveillance and Undercover Operations: A Manual* in brown paper so I had something to read in the long stretches between clanging bells.

Jill Moore's afternoon class let out at three thirty. I was sitting on the windowsill at the end of the corridor when her lecture hall door opened. She was among the first out, hefting her bag, hurrying to the stairs. She galloped down them, and I followed her in a crowd of rushing people. I didn't get a chance to shove *Surveillance and Undercover Operations* back in my knapsack until we were striding across Washington Square Park. Jill Moore had much longer legs than I do—well, who doesn't?—and I began to wish for my Rollerblades, except that I had no idea where we were going. I also had Bill, who was keeping up with her pretty well, strolling along in a bum sort of way.

My idea about where we were going was right, and as Jill Moore unlocked the door to her building, Bill and I converged on the cafe across the street. The window tables were taken, but it was a small cafe; we could see the old brick building from the table we chose.

"Jesus Christ," Bill said, breathing on his hands to warm them. "I ought to charge you double for freezing."

"You ought to wear silk underwear."

"Will you buy it for me? I'll model it."

The thought of Bill striking model's poses in silk underwear almost made me spray my peppermint tea all over the table.

"Go ahead," he said. "Laugh at me. I—" He stopped. I followed his gaze out the window, and we saw what I'd been hoping we wouldn't.

The handsome young Asian man Jill Moore had twinkled her eyes at yesterday came quickly down MacDougal from the direction of NYU. He looked around, entered her vestibule, rang an apartment bell. He was buzzed in.

"Oh, damn," I said, in a little voice.

We watched; nothing else happened; we drank a little. With a lift of his eyebrows Bill offered me some apricot tart. I turned it down.

The guy didn't come out.

"Kuan Cheng has an afternoon class," I told Bill. "A seminar. His mother told me. Tuesdays and Thursdays until six."

"Otherwise his schedule coincides pretty much with hers?"

I nodded.

"So this is the only time she can be sure of being alone."

"I guess."

Bill sipped his cocoa. "Listen," he said. "This isn't your problem. You were hired to find out what's going on. Now your job is to take the client proof. How people behave isn't your problem."

"I know," I said. "But I like happy endings."

We discussed the fact that it might not be what it looked like, and of course that was true. We also discussed more practical things, like how to get photographs of whatever it was. This is where investigating in the suburbs has its advantages. You can't slink through the shrubbery and shinny up the drainpipe when the subject's in a fourth floor walkup on MacDougal Street.

You can, however, climb to the opposite roof.

Bill zipped his jacket and left. I watched Jill Moore's window. The shade, which she had pulled last night after she'd switched on the lights, was still lifted, and the lights were off. We had reached that time of year when it begins to get dark by four thirty. I was hoping we'd have time to find a place to look into the window before Jill Moore felt she needed lights and drawn shades.

Or, maybe, for what she was doing, she wouldn't need lights at all.

Bill was back in ten minutes. "Okay," he said, sitting down. "The building directly across from her, where the Laundromat is. I talked to the super."

"And he just said go ahead?"

"I gave him fifty dollars."

"Fifty?" I was aghast.

"The guy could get in trouble. The guy could lose his job. The guy could smell a quick buck when it came his way."

"Well, I guess it's okay. I guess Mrs. Lee won't mind paying that to get the goods." I knew she wouldn't. I paid the check, went out the door Bill held open for me.

At the Laundromat building we rang the super's bell. An unshaven man emerged from a rear apartment, led us wordlessly up slanted stairs to the roof. He unlocked the bulkhead door for us.

"You be sure to close the damn thing tight, you come in," he growled at Bill.

"Sure," Bill said. "Thanks."

The super grunted, looked once at me, turned and shuffled downstairs.

The building was lower than Jill Moore's building across the street; the roof was about half a story higher than her window. The asphalt roofing slanted up to the top of the cornice at the front.

I lay on my belly on the asphalt and took the binoculars out of my knapsack. Peering through them over the cornice I had a perfect view into Jill Moore's window.

"What's happening?" Bill was low beside me.

"It's a living room. They're drinking tea and talking." I crawled back down a little and passed him the binoculars.

He peered over the top of the cornice.

"The light's fading. If you're going to take pictures, you'd better do it soon."

"This isn't very juicy stuff to take pictures of," I grumbled, but I got out the camera, attached the telephoto lens, and clicked away. I took half a roll, then waited in case Jill Moore and the unknown Asian did something more dramatic. Instead, Jill Moore got up, turned on a lamp in the living room, and drew the shades.

"Fooey," I said.

"We can come back Thursday, if you want," Bill said.

"Personally I don't want. But Mrs. Lee might want."

We went back in the bulkhead door—closing it tight— and down the street. We trudged south on Sixth Avenue; the air was cold and the car horns blared at each other illtemperedly.

"I don't understand white people," I said. "I really don't. You saw her this morning with Kuan Cheng. She was *happy*. She's enjoying this. She's having a great time. You white people."

"Hey," Bill said. "I didn't do it."

"Yeah, but I'll bet you understand it. Romantic love isn't even a Chinese concept. Your people invented it. How come you mess around with it like this?"

I knew I was being unfair to him, and he knew not to answer.

I called Mrs. Lee as soon as I got back to my office. "I have something I think you'll want to see," I said. "I left some film to be developed. They say I can pick it up at six." I didn't ask her to meet me. That would be too forward, not respectful. If what I said was of interest, she would tell me what she wanted me to do.

"I come your office," Mrs. Lee told me. "Six thirty. You there. On time."

"Yes," I said, controlling my temper. "I'll be there. On time. Thank you, Mrs. Lee." I hung up the phone furious with myself. Thank you? *Thank you?*

I went home, kissed my mother, and told her Mrs. Lee and I were getting along fine. I grabbed my Rollerblades before she could ask me any questions and speedskated through the spookily empty downtown streets to Battery Park. I worked out hard, until it was time to skate back to Chinatown and give Mrs. Lee proof that there are no happy endings.

I called Bill early the next morning. "I gave her the pictures," I said.

"How did she like them?"

"She loved them. She gave me this horrible smile—all hard around the edges, you know?—and said, 'Mother know. Mother always know best for son.' I said they weren't doing anything interesting in the picture, just talking, and that usually in this sort of situation I'd recommend keeping the surveillance going another few days."

"What'd she say?"

"She sort of smirked. 'Oh-ho, greedy girl. Not need, not pay. Plenty here. How much bill?' I worked it out and she paid, right there, in cash."

"So that's it."

"Well," I said, "well, no."

"Oh-ho," Bill said. "Masochist girl. You want follow Jill Moore more."

"That's right." I ignored his phony Chinese accent, which was really pretty good. "I know it's none of my business—"

"I'll meet you in half an hour outside her building."

I hesitated. "I'm not sure I can pay you," I said. "I mean, the case is over."

"There are other ways you could pay me."

"Yes, but I won't."

"I know. But just think of the debt you're racking up."

"Junk bonds," I said.

We followed Jill Moore for the next two days. She was taking her classes: Ming Dynasty Art; Admiral Perry and the Opening of Japan; Topics in South Asian Political History; and Women in Chinese Culture. You'd better study harder in that one, I thought. I hung around all her classrooms, and even sat in on the Ming Dynasty Art lecture. It was pretty interesting, nice slides of glazed bowls and sumptuous silk robes. I tailed her to lunch, to the bookstore, and to the library, where she hauled a thick green book and a spiral notebook out of her bag and was so deep in concentration when I walked by her that she didn't even look up. I walked by the other way, too. I just wanted to see what she was doing.

"That was a little risky," Bill said later that afternoon, in the cafe I'd come to think of as ours. It was Thursday by now, the day Kuan Cheng Lee had a seminar until seven.

"I know," I said. "I shouldn't have. I was bad."

"So what was she doing?"

"Nothing interesting. Translating very, very elementary Mandarin. Filling a notebook full of clumsy characters."

"Like me? Big coarse clumsy foreign characters?"

"Is that still bothering you? I'm sorry I said that. I didn't mean it."

"It doesn't bother me. I just wanted to make you feel guilty."

"It's a cheap shot, making a Chinese daughter feel guilty. Anybody can do it. Oh, Bill. Oh, damn. Look."

Bill turned where I was pointing. Hurrying up MacDougal Street was the handsome Asian fellow. He had three textbooks under his arm and he was in such a rush to get to Jill Moore's doorbell that he dropped one of them on his toe as he leapt up the stoop.

"Serves him right," I announced, as we watched him hop around for a minute, then scoop up the thick green book and hit the bell. He was buzzed, limping, in.

"That's unworthy," Bill reprimanded me. I didn't listen, because I'd just had a thought.

I wanted to tell Bill about it—god, I hoped I was right!—but I didn't get the chance. As I opened my mouth, Kuan Cheng Lee raced down the sidewalk and up the same stoop. He let himself in the vestibule door, but not before his jacket blew open in a gust of wind.

He had a gun.

Bill must have seen it, too, because he jumped from the table at the same time I did. We charged out the cafe door, leaving the elegant waiter open-mouthed.

By the time we got to the vestibule the door was closed, and we lost seconds trying to be buzzed in. You always can in New York and eventually we did, but not before my heart was pounding crazily and I'd caught such an adrenaline rush that I wanted to kick the door in myself.

Bill went first because he can take stairs two at a time. I dashed up straight flights and around landings after him. A baby howled behind a door. Bill's footsteps thumped over my lighter, faster ones: then the sound of his changed as he hit the fourth floor and ran down the hall. He was almost at the front apartment's door when we heard a shot.

If you hadn't known, it could have been carpentry, hammer hitting wood. But he knew. Bill pounded on the door. "Police! Open up!" Crude, but effective. All sound stopped within.

I reached the door. "Lee Kuan Cheng!" I called. "It's Lydia Chin. Let me in. Don't shoot again."

Bill and I flattened ourselves on either side of the door, guns drawn, backs against the wall. Down the hall a door cracked, a face peered out, "Police!" Bill barked. "Get back inside!"

The face retreated hastily.

"Someday you'll get in trouble for that," I whispered.

"I always do."

"Can you break it in?"

He looked at the door, nodded.

"Kuan Cheng!" I called again. "Let me in! Let me talk to you. Don't hurt anyone, Kuan Cheng."

Nothing happened. Bill's eyes met mine. He backed a little, then threw himself against the unsuspecting door. It shuddered; he did it again, harder, and the door flew open, hinges shrieking. Bill went in low with it. I dived in even lower, so that any bullets Kuan Cheng fired would have a chance to miss us in the empty doorway.

But he didn't fire any. He stood in the kitchen, maybe eight feet from us, face twisted in anger and fear. His skin was shiny with sweat. He held his elbows locked, his gun gripped in both shaking hands. Bill and I held guns on him, too, which meant if we were lucky one of us would survive this.

Great.

"Kuan Cheng, don't," I said. "Put it down." I wasn't sure he could hear me over the beating of my heart.

He spoke. "She took a lover!" His voice was loud and hoarse. "Not even married yet, and she took a lover. Humiliated me everywhere! My *mother* knows! I'll kill her. I'll kill them both!"

"No," I said.

"No," a woman's cracked voice came from the shadowed room behind Kuan Cheng. "No!"

I peered down the hallway to the living room. In the fading light from the windows I saw Jill Moore kneeling, her arms wrapped protectively around the other man, the handsome Asian, whose white shirt showed a dark stain at the shoulder. His eyes were wide open with fear.

"Please!" Jill Moore's high, quavering voice was close to hysterical. "Kuan Cheng! It's not what you think!"

"Oh, no?" He whipped the gun in their direction, and his skin flushed darker.

"No," I said, grabbing for his attention. He was close to hysterical, too, and the sight of the other man in Jill Moore's arms wouldn't do him any good. "Kuan Cheng, he's not her lover."

He spun back to me. "Not her lover?" he sneered. "What, her younger brother?"

"No," I said. "He's her Mandarin teacher."

Disbelief, confusion, and anger chased each other across his face.

"Jill!" I yelled. "Am I right?"

"Yes!" she called. Her voice cracked again. "Kuan Cheng, I was going to surprise you. I didn't want you to know until I could speak it well." She made a small sobbing sound.

Kuan Cheng, his gun still trained on me, his body rigid and tense, glanced quickly into the living room, then back to me. He said nothing.

I stood slowly, lowered my gun, and put it in my belt clip. I looked at Bill. Sweat beaded his forehead and the back of his hands as he answered my look. Then he holstered his gun, too, and stood up.

God, I thought, if you shoot now, Kuan Cheng, shoot me, because I couldn't live with the guilt. Kuan Cheng didn't shoot anybody. He didn't put his gun down, either. He didn't move, just stood, paralyzed by indecision and disbelief.

"Kuan Cheng?" Jill's voice was clearer, though soft. "It was for your mother. I wanted her to like me."

Kuan Cheng laughed a short wild laugh. "My mother? That's ridiculous. What makes you think my mother will like you if you speak Mandarin?"

Jill said, "Because she said so."

My blood froze. No one spoke. There was silence everywhere.

Jill hurried on, trying to reach him. "That day at her apartment? She said if I learned to speak her language I'd be showing the proper respect. Then she'd accept me as a daughter-in-law. I mean, she never said she'd like me, but I thought it was a beginning. I wanted it to be as right as I could make it." In the dusk a tear glistened on her cheek.

"My mother said that?" Kuan Cheng whispered.

"Yes. She even found Chyi-Jou to teach me. We started that week."

"My god," I said low, unbelieving. I looked at Bill. Anger

shone in his eyes; his jaw was tight. He knew, too. I said it anyway. "We were set up."

He nodded.

In the darkness of Jill Moore's apartment, Kuan Cheng lowered his gun.

We stopped the bleeding from Chyi-Jou Kwong's shoulder, called an ambulance, and concocted a story: Kuan Cheng had bought the gun for Jill, for protection. Neither of them knew how to use it, and it went off. Bill and I were on our way there, just for a visit, because I'm an old friend of Kuan Cheng's. We heard the shot and assumed there was trouble, thus the scene in the hallway.

We pulled it off, though it was sort of a pain, Bill and me at the 6th Precinct for an hour answering the same questions separately until the cops gave up. Kuan Cheng was arrested for gun possession, but Chyi-Jou Kwong wasn't badly hurt and Kuan Cheng was a model of upwardly mobile Asian youth. A good lawyer would be able to wiggle him out of anything serious. I was mad enough to let him figure his own way out of spending the night in jail, but Bill pointed out that it was our licenses on the line if Kuan Cheng, in his perilous emotional state, blew the story.

So I called Mrs. Lee and told her where he was and what had happened, and suggested she send him a lawyer fast.

"How'd she take it?" Bill asked as we left the police station. Tenth Street was carpeted with fallen leaves; streetlights shone gently on brick rowhouses. It all seemed lovely and peaceful, but I was cold. And I knew that behind those cosy facades lurked legions of mothers gleefully plotting to doublecross their sons.

"She wailed. She yelled. She called him a stupid boy. She said it was all the white witch's fault. Then she said it was all *my* fault. Then I hung up on her."

"Without telling her where to get off?"

"Well," I admitted, "I told her a little bit where to get off. Because it won't get around and embarrass my mother.

From now on, I guarantee Mrs. Lee will pretend she never heard of me."

We stopped at a corner to let a car drift past.

"How did you know?" Bill asked. "That he was teaching her Mandarin."

"The book he dropped on his toe. It was the same one she was translating Mandarin from at the library. She's not taking any Mandarin courses, so I guessed he was her tutor. But I never guessed Mrs. Lee had set us all up."

Bill said nothing, just lit a cigarette and let me go on, thinking sad thoughts out loud.

"The thing is," I said, "I can't believe a mother would do that. Do you know what she said, when I called her on it?"

"Tell me."

"'Mother know best for son. White witch bad wife, undutiful daughter-in-law.' That was all she cared about—that Jill Moore wasn't the daughter-in-law of her dreams. What kind of mother is that?"

"Human," Bill said. "Flawed. Too desperate to see past herself."

"Desperate?" I snorted. "Selfish. Diabolical. Manipulative. A classic Chinese mother."

"Is your mother like that?"

"Of course not! Just because she doesn't like *you*—"

"Will it help if I learn Cantonese?"

I stopped, looked at him, and laughed. Then I hugged him.

When we started forward again the night wasn't as cold and the houses weren't as hostile.

"Maybe it's not that I don't understand white people," I said. "Maybe I don't understand anybody."

"Who does?"

"You do. Here's this woman who sets up her own son, and he almost kills a whole bunch of people including us, and you just say, 'She's human.'"

"That doesn't mean I understand her. Just that I know not to expect too much."

"Maybe nobody understands anybody." That thought made me cold again.

Bill took my hand. "Come on." We turned up a quiet street. "There's a cafe with a fireplace, where they play Vivaldi. I'll buy you a hot apple cider."

I didn't have to say anything because he was reading my mind.

THE GENERAL'S TASK FORCE

==

by Pearl G. Aldrich

"I have something for the Task Force." Colonel Jackson's voice was always cloak-and-daggerish when she reported a case. "It's a bad one, Top. The woman's afraid even to walk from the Annex to the barracks."

The Navy Annex, which housed Marine Corps Headquarters, is across the street from Henderson Hall where the barracks are located. Both are a couple of blocks up the hill from the Pentagon, all tucked into urban northern Virginia.

"Has she been assaulted, ma'am?" The Task Force handled sexual harassment (physical) differently from sexual harassment (administrative).

"Not yet," the colonel assured me, "but it could happen any time."

"Enlisted woman, male officer?" I reached for a case entry form. "Enlisted man, woman officer? Two enlisted people? Two officers?"

"Enlisted woman, one male officer, one noncom. A major and a sergeant. She's a PFC."

It was a bad one, all right. Two career men had ganged up

141

on a woman just two years into her first enlistment. She had joined the Corps right out of high school. Miracle she hadn't turned to drugs or gone on unauthorized absence. But she'd endured the harassment with strength and courage. The men, reaching across her for papers, had rubbed an arm against her breasts, cupped a hand on her buttock whenever they stood beside her, and whispered sexual innuendos nonstop all day.

While I was recording the details, the sergeant's name, George Castleman, echoed in my head. Castle? Cas? I couldn't make the connection.

The report was printing out when the general marched in. As usual when she went by, I heard a band playing, saw colors flying and troops passing in review. A tall, stately blonde, she looked grand in dress blues. My husband says I think any woman in military uniform looks good. "And don't we?" I always challenge him, but it's an amicable argument. After all, we met, married, and remained in the Corps.

Anyhow, I first saw the general on parade, and the impression never faded. She hadn't made general yet, and I wasn't a top sergeant. Officially, my rank is sergeant major, but "Top" is Marine-speak for the highest enlisted rank. I'm told I'm one of the youngest women ever to make it.

"Top," the general called from her office where she was reading the forms I had handed her. As I entered, she said, "Real pieces of work, these two. I wonder how many women they've already worked over, driven out, et cetera. Perfect candidates for the cure."

Our program, Operation Cure and Prevent (CAP), is based on the old adage, what's sauce for the goose is sauce for the gander. The general pitched it to the Joint Chiefs of Staff when they were getting heat from the Senate Armed Services Committee and the media about sexual harassment.

The chiefs wanted a quick fix to get the media off their backs, so they bought the general's Task Force, announcing it as an experimental program. If successful, it would be exported to other duty stations, they told the television cameras, then forgot about it. Aides commandeered a couple of offices from the Manpower and Personnel Directorate and squeezed out a budget—all small—then they forgot it, too.

But the women didn't. I was one of a long line requesting assignment on the Task Force staff and was lucky enough to be selected. Then I discovered I was it, a staff of one. But the general overcame that. She put the word out for volunteers, and the poured in.

The general had opened the safe and taken out CAP's secret roster of a hundred carefully screened military and civil service women, plus a paid auxiliary that I'd named "Downtown Girls" from Washington's Fourteenth Street red light district. I never knew how she recruited them.

I sat down beside her desk, and in a few minutes we selected the thirty women for this alert. The general is easy to work for once you get used to her impersonal approach. Never a personal word either to you or about herself. As the Brits say, she kept herself to herself.

Back at my desk, calling for women for a night drill didn't take long because, after the problems of reaching them for training, I made sure everyone had a telephone answering machine. When I finished saying, "CAP Alert. Night drill," and giving date, time, and place, I called my husband.

He was at home, on leave, getting ready to take our daughter to visit his parents in Iowa. "Do you know a George Castleman?" I asked. "The name seems familiar to me."

Len laughed. "Don't you remember?" he asked. "When we were in Germany? That over-age-in-grade sergeant who hit on you every time we saw him at Koenigshof?" That was our favorite beer garden in Stuttgart.

"Oh, of course," and I had a flashback of a squat,

belligerent man who looked like a frog, bulging eyes and all.

"Old Cassy must be about due for retirement," Len said—and old enough to be that PFC's father, I added silently. "He used to be a hard charger, drank hard, fought hard, chased women even harder. You know the type, think they're the only *real* Marines left and hang together to drink and grouse."

"His wife must put up with a lot," I commented.

Len didn't answer for a few seconds. "You know, hon, I'm not sure he had one." He carefully didn't ask why I wanted to know but, like the great guy he is, generously gave additional information.

I never told Len what the Task Force did, but the way things got around the Corps—a worldwide gossip factory—he knew and was wondering where Cassy figured. But we'd agreed long ago not to interfere in each other's careers. Over time, we'd developed an attitude of "I'll be blind, but don't expect me to be stupid."

While the general was on the phone, collecting background on the men, I hopped the shuttle to the Annex to check out the woman and the situation. Not all women reporting sexual harassment were on the side of the angels, and we might have to abort the Alert. It had happened before, and to prevent it, I'd gotten pretty good at evaluating the woman and the situation.

From the Annex bus stop, I climbed the flight of broken steps, passed the guard, and headed for the Marine Corps Headquarters entrance, then up the ladder to the inspector general's wing on the second deck. When I reached the right office, I saw PFC Smithson sitting at her computer at the back of the usual closetlike space. Sergeant Castleman, unmistakably the same, was at a desk near the door, and the major had his own small office off to the side.

"Cassy," I said, entering the office. "Private Smithson is being reassigned. Her relief will report tomorrow."

"Well, of all people!" he exclaimed, standing up. "How

the hell are you! What's old Len doing? Both of you stationed here now?"

He rattled on as though we were buddies while I looked Smithson over. She was spruce and trim in her uniform—what my father called bright-eyed and bushy-tailed and what I judged to be well brought up, respectful, and diligent. She glanced at me curiously. Colonel Jackson had told her someone would contact her, but she didn't know who or when.

When Castleman had made all he could of our very brief acquaintance, I told Smithson, "Get your personal gear, Private, and come with me. Now!" The command in that last word was for Castleman, not Smithson.

As she began stuffing things into her purse, a voice called from the major's office. "Private, get your ass in . . ." he started, but Castleman cut him off.

"Major, Smithson's ordered out," his voice full of syrupy regret. When the major appeared in his doorway, Castleman introduced us. By the time we completed protocol, Smithson was ready and eager to leave.

Rather than wait twenty minutes for the next shuttle, I flagged a taxi. "Pentagon, River Entrance," I told the driver. During the short drive, I asked Smithson, "How did you hear about the Task Force?"

Her answer was one I had grown to expect: "One of the noncoms in the barracks told me."

"What did she tell you?"

"Just that it was a way to exit a bad situation without a major flap." Her eyes filled with tears and she dug out a Kleenex, apologizing as she did so. "I'm sorry, Top. I know I'm not living up to standards, but they wore me down."

"That's all right, Smithson," I said sympathetically. "They don't prepare you for this kind of stress in boot camp."

"I sure didn't expect it. I thought if I did a good job, worked as hard as I could, I'd be okay," she went on.

"Not in this man's world, but this really has nothing to do

with you as a person. It's a power play. Why didn't you request mast?" I asked, knowing from Colonel Jackson that she didn't request permission to see her commanding officer.

"I was afraid I'd get in trouble." Another familiar answer.

The taxi dropped as close to the entrance as it could get, and we headed into the Pentagon. She stopped at the head to pull herself together before meeting the general, and I continued to the office, reporting the Alert was a go. Smithson wasn't out for revenge or on an ego trip.

When Smithson reported to the general, her shoulders were squared, back rigid, apprehension in every line. The general said, "At ease, Private. As of now, you're reassigned to Personnel at 'A' Company. Report to Captain Livingston at 0800 hours tomorrow, but before you're dismissed today, I need your story. Sit down and start at the beginning. What happened?" Then she closed the door. Smithson was going to be fine. It was now Castleman's and the major's turn.

That evening, after taking Len and Carolyn to National Airport, I returned to the Pentagon for the briefing. We mustered in the conference room of Strategic Plans and Policies Directorate on the second deck of E Ring. One of those accidentally appropriate assignments, I thought.

Implementing CAP was a complex administrative operation, but the general had honed to the max her major talent for manipulating military paperwork. Accessing the volunteers' time when needed and putting a contract in place to fund the Downtown Girls were part of her administrative magic.

When everyone was present, the general began the briefing from the forms I'd initiated, then said, "We'll administer the cure to the major exclusively during duty hours. Castleman is the primary target. He's a hard case."

Castleman had a long history of fighting and causing various types of disruptions. The shrink's diagnosis, antisocial personality disorder, included aggressive sexual behavior with an inability to form a lasting intimate relationship with a woman. As I remembered, dodging him was a daily supplement to the morning run.

"He was a drill instructor at Parris Island, but was relieved of duties for thumping. Translated into civilian, that means hitting recruits or using other harsh physical treatment in the name of training," the general explained.

Mention of PI brought back the scuttlebutt that went around the post when Castleman arrived in Germany. Word was that one of his recruits had been permanently injured, although Cassy hadn't been court-martialed or even charged with an offense.

After a short Q&A, the general read the roster of women to replace Smithson and spread large helpings of sauce over those two ganders. We needed a group. Although the men enjoyed the sexual fun at first, they soon tired of it and requested the woman be replaced. She was—with another Task Force member who continued ladling out the sauce. I provided Castleman's address to the Downtown Girls so they could link up with him off duty.

But Cassy's case went off the rails from the beginning. For starters, he reacted with anger. The corporal who replaced Smithson reported that Cassy shoved her into a filing cabinet and hissed in her ear, "Keep your hands off me, girl, or I'll put you on report."

"Back off," the general told her. "Concentrate on the major," and increased the number of women on duty in the halls.

We didn't limit the laying on of hands to women working in the target's office but placed others all over the building and in all the lines—cafeteria, credit union, dry cleaners. The only place a man could get away was in the head, and how many times a day could you go there?

I usually spent some time in the halls also, keeping track of what was going on. This time, I also kept an eye on Cassy. As the pressure built, he looked angrier and angrier, and I instructed the women to act quickly and move out fast. I didn't want anyone punched out.

Cassy's reaction to the Downtown Girls conformed to the pattern only for the first night. The Girls reported that he welcomed them, laughed, and said, "Ah, my boys. What'll they think of next?" when they said a friend had sent them as a gift—the reason they always gave.

Most men kept going three to five nights before trying to cry off, but on the second night, Cassy told the Girls to take the night off. He'd tell the boys they'd been, but of course they stayed. The third night, he wouldn't let them in, yelling through the door, "Go away and don't come back." It created a little rumpus, but they forced their way inside. When they reported, they told me they didn't know if they'd be able to get in the next night. If they couldn't, they didn't want to lose their money. I assured them they wouldn't.

Meanwhile, back at headquarters, the major crumbled on the fourth day—the fastest on record—begging the corporal to leave him alone. Please just leave me alone. What kind of woman are you? Why are you doing this to me? I never did anything to you.

When the general got that report, she paid her official visit, SOP when the pressure took effect. She would sit beside the man's desk and ask, "Does the saying, 'What's sauce for the goose is sauce for the gander,' mean anything to you?"

When they got it, they agreed they now knew what sexual harassment felt like. God, did they know! To a man, they promised on the Bible, on their mother's grave, on their firstborn child, they would never, ever do it again. They were cured for life. "Honest to God, ma'am, *never* again!" This time, as the major escorted her to the door, he said, "Don't worry about me, ma'am. I never acted that way before. I don't know what got into me."

I was watching them nearby, waiting for Cassy to report for duty—he was showing up later every day—or I'd have seen him come stamping down the hall. As the major turned back to his office, the general turned toward the hall and met Cassy face to face.

In her unflappable way, she asked, "Does 'What's sauce for the goose is sauce for the gander' mean anything to you?"

Saying, "Excuse me, ma'am," in a voice that only his years in the Corps kept polite, he carefully stepped around her into the office and stood behind his desk. She turned and stood looking at him. I moved into the doorway and looked at him, too. He looked dreadful: deep, black circles under his eyes with fatigue in every wrinkle. I almost felt sorry for him.

"I asked you a question, Sergeant," the general said quietly.

With effort and without expression, he answered, "I know what it means, ma'am . . ." his eyes flashed anger ". . . and where it's coming from. Every man at headquarters knows."

"This treatment will continue until you put in for retirement," the general told him. "Do it or I'll initiate charges that will result in a dishonorable discharge and loss of pension." She turned smartly, I stepped aside, and she marched down the hall. The band was still echoing in my head as I turned back to Cassy.

He was glaring through the door. "Damn bitch," he snarled. "Every base she's been on she's hassled guys just having a little fun." He turned the glare on me. "And you, what the hell you doing, working for *her?* How the hell Len let you . . ."

"Shut up, Cassy," I ordered, "and sit down," but he'd already flung himself into his chair, full of fury and frustration, still snarling. "Goddamn bull dyke. A real man oughtta bust her ass . . ."

"Cassy!" I broke in, slamming my hands on his desk, leaning over, and putting menace in my low-pitched voice. "Clean your mouth! Or I'll have it cleaned for you officially!" My mother, a Marine in World War II, had warned me when I enlisted that the men would call you a lesbian if you had women friends and a whore if you dated men. She was right, and the gossip never stopped. Because she was such a loner, the general's sexual preference caused more speculation than usual.

Cassy was breathing hard but shut up, and I moved into the chair beside his desk. "The commandant supports this project," I said. "Do as the general said or I guarantee you'll lose your benefits."

"Don't worry, I'll get my benefits . . ." the sneer was loud and clear ". . . and a lot more. My boys are taking care o' that. Nothin' that bi . . ." he looked at me and shifted ground ". . . nothin' she can do to queer that." He propped his head on his hands. "Benefits. What a crock. Hash marks up to my elbow and still a sergeant. And a *woman* made general!" The contempt in his voice was corrosive.

Then he turned on me. "Even you got promoted over me. While you were walking around the base in a maternity uniform. *Maternity* uniform, for Chri'sake. A *Marine* in a maternity uniform! God-almighty!" He stopped and looked down at his hands, clenched on his desk. Then he looked me straight in the eye with the sincere look guys like that put on when they want to con you. "What did Smithson tell you about me?"

"You mean how you harassed her?"

"Harassed, hell!" he snorted. "Just fun and games, and she couldn't take it. Some Marine she is. No, I mean about my personal business."

"What she said is confidential." Smithson hadn't said anything, but I wasn't going to tell him until I knew what he was after. Unfortunately, he didn't pursue it.

"Get the hell out of here," he ordered. "Go home where you belong. I got work to do."

I didn't move. "Why'd you re-up every time?" I asked. "You didn't have to."

"That was the deal," he said.

"Deal?" I echoed.

"C'mon, you're no recruit. You know what happened at PI. Everybody in the world knows," meaning the Corps.

That's our world. "No court martial, no promotion, no nothing; just thirty lousy years of nothing. They wouldn't even send me to Nam." He heaved a sigh. "I thought they'd forget after a couple years, but at the end of every hitch, someone showed up to remind me."

"What happened to the recruit?"

He bent his head over the desk. "Paraplegic," he muttered.

"And you thought they'd *forget*?" I exclaimed.

"He was a pantywaist, a sissy, prob'ly a fag . . ."

"And you were going to make a man out of him," I broke in.

"Naw, I was going to make a Marine outa him. Something you and her . . ." nodding toward the door ". . . don't know nothing about. It was an accident for Chri'sake. Afterwards I wanted out, court martial, admin discharge, one way or the other. I coulda started over, maybe been a cop, made chief by now, but the kid was a relative of Chesty Puller's, for Chri'sake, and the family didn't want no publicity." General Puller was a Marine's Marine. Of course no one would forget.

I stood up. "Put your papers in, Cassy. I'll make sure they're processed on the double."

I was so downhearted when I left, I was almost home when I mentally kicked myself for not asking who his boys were. The Downtown Girls said he thought his boys arranged for their visit, and he said they were making sure he had more than his pension to retire on. Who could they be? He had no sons; at least, none he claimed. He hadn't been assigned to a company since Parris Island, and I didn't think he was into Scouts or Big Brothers. Not the type.

When the phone rang, it was after midnight. I was just dozing off and jumped for it, scared something had happened to Len or Carolyn, but all I heard at first was a jumble of sounds, then a woman yelling, "Get Top, get Top."

"Yes?" I asked. "Who's this? What's wrong?"

A calm voice said in the background, "I'll talk to her," then in my ear, "Top, can you come to our place? Something happened, and Yvonne's freaked."

I recognized the calm voice as one of the Downtown Girls but not on this alert; Yvonne was on Cassy's team.

"I'll be right there," I said, reaching for my clothes. "Try to calm her."

The Downtown Girls lived in a garden apartment on Alexandria's west side. When Rachel let me in, I could see Yvonne flaked out on the couch. She looked as though she'd been in a fight. Her hair was straggling, and her makeup smeared. One satin sequined shoe lay on the floor, its three inch heel broken off, the other shoe lay on the floor. Her black lace pantyhose and slinky, skintight hot pants were ripped.

I took her hand, her fingers with their clawlike false nails and their glittering designs clutching tight. "What happened, Yvonne? Did he assault you?" I asked.

"He didn't do nothin'. He's dead. Blood all over 'im. Flat out dead . . ."

"Dead? What do you mean, dead?" I asked, my voice rising with shock and surprise.

"Whaddya mean what do I mean? Dead is dead. Whaddya think I mean?"

"You fought with him and killed him? Is that what you're telling me? Did you call the police?"

"Po-leese? You crazy or what?" Yvonne shrieked, sitting up, hair sticking out, long earrings flapping. "Me call po-leese? No way, no how, no ma'am. I jus' got my butt outa there."

"Chill out, Vonne," Rachel said. "Just chill out. Top'll handle this." Her soothing voice worked on me, too.

"Where's Sherry?" I asked quietly. "Wasn't she with you?"

"She talkin' to the man," said Yvonne. "We wife-in-laws. Rach, I'm dry." One shoe off and one shoe on, she limped into the kitchen while I looked questioningly at Rachel.

"We have the same husband," she said.

Bigamy? I thought, totally bewildered.

"Our man," Rachel said impatiently. It still took me a minute to realize she meant "pimp." This was as close to their real life as I'd come. They came to briefings dressed like everyone else and on the phone, we talked about their assignments as though they were doing office work.

When Yvonne returned, glass in hand, I asked, "What happened? How did your clothes get all ripped up? Did he do it?" I was assuming they had a brawl, she and Sherry knocked Cassy out, then panicked, thinking he was dead. "You got to Sergeant Castleman's apartment as usual?" I prompted, and she nodded. "Then what happened?"

"We knocked, he didn't answer, and Sherry goes, 'We gonna break in?' an' I go, 'On'y if we hafta,' so we knock some more. Call his name. Bang on the door, an' it just open'." She paused to take a swallow from her glass. "He was in the living room, deader'n a mackerel, so we hightailed outa there."

"If you didn't fight with him, how'd you get so messed up?" I didn't really believe her story.

"Sherry an' me, we got our feet all mixed up and fell down the stairs. Honest to Gawd, Top, that's what happened."

"What are you going to do?" Rachel asked as I stood up and slung my purse on my shoulder.

"I don't know yet," I said. "The first thing is to check Cassy out. See what condition he's in."

"I tole you!" Yvonne yelled. "He's dead!"

"I'll be in touch later," I said as I went to the door.

Back home, I paced the living room, trying to develop a plan. I knew Marine regs inside out, but no regulation I ever heard of covered this situation. When the general told me the day I reported that CAP was breaking new ground, I didn't know how truly she spoke.

I drank two pots of coffee, waiting for morning. The general was on duty promptly at 0700 hours every day. Two minutes past the hour, I dialed the office and reported the situation and my suspicions, recommending that we turn the problem over to the civilian authorities.

The line was silent for a few seconds, then she said, "No, CAP can't be involved, and the connection between the Downtown Girls and CAP must be kept out of sight. However, top priority is to determine Castleman's condition. Start at his quarters," and she hung up.

Oh, hell, that's the last place I want to go, I muttered, even as I got the map of Northern Virginia. As I drove, I saw Cassy lived in an older section of Alexandria, mostly boxlike, red brick, two story, one-family houses and boxlike, red brick, four story apartment houses.

When I turned off Mt. Vernon Avenue onto Cassy's street, I could see a lot of cars and people bunched near the end of the next block. As I got closer, the cars turned out to be police, some people moving purposefully about, some just rubbernecking. I parked and joined the rubberneckers, comparing Cassy's address with the one where all the activity was taking place. As I feared, they were the same, one of the four story apartment houses. I got as far as the front door when a uniformed police office stopped me.

"You can't go in right now," she said. "Do you live here?" She was taking in my uniform.

"I've come to see another Marine who lives here," I said. "Someone have an accident or a fight?"

"Are you a relative?" she asked.

I shook my head. "We're stationed together." That covered it without lying.

"Wait here a minute," and she walked back into the building. She returned with a man in a business suit who started from square one. "Do you live here, miss?"

"Sergeant," I corrected automatically. "No, as I told the officer, I came to see a Marine who lives here. Why are you asking?"

"Are you a close friend of his?" he asked, ignoring my question.

"His?" I countered. I had to find out if they were here because of Cassy. "What makes you think it's a man?"

"Just answer my question," he said.

"No, I won't answer your question until I know why you're asking and what your authority is. The Marine I came to see may have nothing to do with who you came to see."

He tried to stare me down, but it didn't work. Finally he said, "Come on inside." He led the way to a small alcove that held mailboxes and two beat-up wing chairs. "There's a man upstairs with Marine uniforms in his closet and his I.D. says he's one George Donald Castleman, sergeant. Is that who you came to see?"

"Yes," I said. "Why are you going through his apartment? What's the problem?"

"Don't worry. We leave things as neat as we find 'em. You his girlfriend, his . . . uhm . . . significant other?"

"No. I told you. We're stationed together."

"Why are you here?"

"Why are you?"

"Stop wasting time," he said irritably. "I wouldn't be here if it wasn't serious."

"Serious?" I echoed. "Is he injured? Who are you?"

"Detective Alexander Rojas, Alexandria Police Department," he said, automatically reaching into a pocket for his I.D. "Yes, he's been injured."

"How bad?" I didn't dare ask if George was dead.

"Tell me your name first."

I told him my name, then added, "Cassy'd been looking pretty bad the last few days, reporting for duty later and later, so before the major put him on report, I came over to see if he was SIQ—that is, sick in quarters," hoping that would move things on.

"And that's it?" he asked.

"Yes, sir. That's it. Is he badly injured?" but the detective just asked, "Where's he stationed?"

"Quit playing cat and mouse with me, Detective Rojas.

We have procedures to follow when a noncommissioned officer is injured."

"I know," he said. "There's lots of military living around here. Sergeant Castleman was fatally assaulted last night, but I couldn't tell you until I knew if you were close . . ." As his voice went on about an autopsy and notifying next of kin, I reached out for one of the chairs and sat down. My God, those women *did* kill him, I thought. How can we keep CAP out of it now? The whole program will go down the drain. My thoughts were skittering about when I picked up a note of urgency in the detective's voice. "Miss? Are you all right? Miss?"

"Sergeant," I repeated. "Who killed him? How did he die?"

"We don't know yet. The neighbor who found him heard loud voices and banging around several nights recently. Women coming and going, just generally lots of commotion."

"How did he die?" I repeated. "Shot? Stabbed? What?"

"He was hit on the head repeatedly," Rojas said. Blood all over him, Yvonne had said.

"I must get back," I said, standing up. "He was assigned to the Inspector General's Section, Headquarters, Marine Corps. Report the death to headquarters and liaise with the MPs. I'll notify our people," meaning the general. "I'd like to visit his quarters for a minute," maybe I'd see something, although I had no idea what, "and talk to the neighbor who found him."

"Sorry, no can do. It's a crime scene, and we're not finished yet. The I.D. people are there, and the neighbor is down at headquarters making a statement. That is, if she's calmed down, she's making a statement. Thanks for saving me some time, Sergeant," he went on. "I don't have to go through the whole routine with the military personnel locator."

I just nodded and moved out to my car. The rubberneckers had mostly left, and the street was back to its residential mid-morning quiet. Now that I know, what do I do first? I thought as I drove back to Mt. Vernon Avenue. Report to the general or question Yvonne and Sherry? I don't recall making a conscious decision, but like a homing pigeon, the car just headed for the Pentagon.

The general was waiting for my report. "We're up to our ears in alligators, ma'am," I started, walking into her office and closing the door.

"No way can we keep CAP out of this," I concluded. "The neighbor who found him talked about the women. The police will find them, and the publicity will kill CAP." I started pacing agitatedly. "It was working so well, really ready to export to other stations." In fact, I was doing a final scrub on a report recommending just that. "Now it's all going down the drain . . ."

"There are ways to handle this without endangering CAP, Top," the general said. "I'll talk to the two women. Tell them I'm on my way," and she marched out.

I called Yvonne, getting her out of bed and grumpy, then I caught the Metro to Pentagon City, one stop from the Pentagon itself, and went to a restaurant in the mall where I could sit quietly with a glass of wine and think.

Totally unlikeable as Cassy was, I'd rather he had left the Corps a retiree. On the other hand, I couldn't forget the recruit he might just as well have murdered.

But that wasn't the current problem, and I switched from the moral to the practical. Yvonne and Sherry had probably killed Cassy accidentally. They'd made no effort to hide their presence, yelling back and forth with Cassy through the door. They'd clattered up and down the stairs. They'd been noticed, and they'd be found. My problem was damage control.

For that, I needed to know what the police were doing. Would that detective tell me anything? Probably not, but I'd try anyhow, I decided as I paid for lunch and went back to my office. When I reached the detective, he was very cordial but only because he wanted information.

"I'm glad you called, Sergeant," he said. "You can fill in some of the blanks about Castleman. The neighbors say he was frequently seen in the company of teenage boys and one at least, must have been his son. You can save me valuable time if you tell me where the boy lives. It'll take two weeks going through your procedures."

They must have been the ones Cassy called "my boys," but I wasn't ready to share that with the detective yet.

"I can check it out," I told him. "Can you give me a few more details? Did they live with him or visit at regular times, like weekends? You know, the way kids do after a divorce."

"Apparently nothing regular."

"The neighbor who found him?" I suggested.

"Mrs. Gonzales? Naw, she works nights in a restaurant. That's how she came to find him, coming home late. Going upstairs, she saw his door open and . . ." He stopped as he remembered who he was talking to. "Call me when you get the address."

"Right," I said. Yes, sir, I'll execute your order immediately, but for CAP. I called Cassy's office and asked the corporal if he kept a personal file there.

"You know he's dead?" she asked. "I can't find one. The major was looking, too. He wasn't a nice man, Sergeant Castleman, but it's a shame anyway." After a moment's silence, she asked in a low voice, "Will people blame his death on the Task Force?"

"I hope not. Is the major in?"

When he came on the line, I said the appropriate things, then asked, "Can you tell me where his son and wife, or ex-wife, live? The police need the address." I hoped he was too shocked to ask me why the police didn't go through channels. Or why I was even in contact with the police.

"He never mentioned dependents."

"Did he ever say 'my boys' or anything to give the impression he had children? Or he was working with a boys' club?"

The major came up negative, so I called several of Len's friends. They all knew Cassy and told me old gossip. One of them had served with him in Hawaii and confirmed what Len had suspected: Cassy never married. He also confirmed my evaluation that Cassy wasn't into community service.

Before I could do anything else, the phone started to ring nonstop. News of Cassy's death was getting around headquarters, and Task Force members were concerned. Several women said they'd served with Cassy at various stations, but nothing new surfaced.

When the general got back, she looked very worried. "I'm satisfied the Girls are in the clear," she announced, going into her office and closing the door. I wasn't, but I didn't have time to develop a strategy to find out what her decision was based on. Visiting Mrs. Gonzales, the neighbor who found Cassy, was next on my agenda, so I put the Downtown Girls on the back burner.

At home, I changed my uniform for civilian slacks and a sweater, called Len at his folks' and talked to everybody. It was so comforting to hear their voices, warm and loving. It really set me up.

All was quiet when I reached Cassy's apartment house. No police, but no parking, either. Everyone was home from work. I parked in a restaurant lot on the corner of Mt. Vernon Avenue.

Cassy's apartment was on the top deck, and I assumed Mrs. Gonzales lived nearby if she had to pass his door on her way home. I planned to knock loudly on his door, and when no one answered, I'd knock on hers. But I didn't have to. After I called, "Cassy!" in my command voice, which could carry clearly across a drill field during a fly by, a harried looking woman, with eyes red from crying, stuck her head out of the door across the hall.

"You a relative?" she asked.

If I hadn't known Cassy was dead, that question would have seemed peculiar, but I answered, "No. A friend."

"You come before in the nigh'?" I shook my head, moving toward her.

"Something wrong?" I asked sympathetically, a sympathy I really meant even if the rest was playacting.

She nodded, wiped her eyes, and opened her door with a gesture inviting me in. Her apartment looked as though it had just been cleaned for a white glove inspection.

"Sit down, sit down." She hustled a bucket of cleaning stuff to the kitchen. "Is terrreeble." She rolled the *r*'s with extra emphasis and sat down, too. "I send my 'usband with children to my sister. I don't go to work tonigh' but I must do something." She was twisting her hands in her lap. "The sergeant, he's dead." I gasped and looked suitably shocked, and she nodded understandingly. "I fin' him last nigh' when I come home from work. Terrrreeble! Terrrreeble!"

She was a waitress in the restaurant at the corner where I'd parked and had noticed Cassy's door open when she got home after work. That was unusual, so she called his name several times and stuck her head in. She thought his apartment had been robbed while he was out, but she found him. She didn't add much to what I'd pieced together from Yvonne and the detective, but told it with graphic detail, crying and twisting her hands. It had been awful for her.

"Why did you ask if I'd come other nights?" I asked when she'd calmed down.

"Women come," she said with a shrug. "Men, too. I don't see. I just hear something before I go to work. My 'usband say sometime men come later, too. Make much noise."

"Were you friends? You and your husband and the sergeant? Talk together?" I was floundering, out of my element. I couldn't say anything like, "Corporal, I want a straight answer and I want it now!"

"No, not friends. We say 'hello,' 'how are you.' No more. At restaurant, he order food, talk more, but not friends."

I leaped at her mention of the restaurant. "He ate there a lot?"

"Oh yes, many times," she said with the first smile I'd

seen. "He love food of my country, but no *salsa*. Too hot, he say," and she rubbed her stomach as he probably had done.

"Did the women and the young men eat with him?" I asked, wondering if the police knew that.

"Women, no," she replied. "Young men, sometime."

Cassy's boys? The teenagers the detective mentioned? "The same young men all the time?" I asked, feeling my way.

"Two, yes. Others sometime. One old, like sergeant. They know each other long time, he say."

"The two boys, what did they look like?"

She started to answer, but before she could, we heard voices in the hall. Mrs. Gonzales and I looked at each other in surprise, then went to the door to see what was going on.

A natty little man stood with the general before Cassy's door, trying one key after another in the lock. She was in civilian slacks and a blue Jordache shirt and looked straight through me.

"Not to worry," he told Mrs. Gonzales. "I'm just showing this lady the sergeant's apartment. It won't be ready for occupancy until the end of the month, but I didn't think looking would hurt. Ahhh . . ." He turned the knob. "It wasn't locked after all. Very careless."

He opened it, and two guys tried to run through us, but four people clustered in the narrow doorway formed a solid barrier. They backed off, struggling to look cool, as though their actions had been perfectly normal.

"What are you boys doing here?" the natty little man asked fussily and stupidly broke the barrier to walk in and confront two muscular young men caught where they had no business to be. Fortunately for him, they retreated the few steps of the short hall to fidget in the opening to the living room. I closed ranks so the general and I filled the doorway, but Mrs. Gonzales pushed between us and the little man, walking toward the two boys.

"You," she said. "I know you. You eat with sergeant in my restaurant. He killed last night, and police want to ask about him. Come, I give you detective number." She was almost face to face with them when she gasped. "What you do? Police leave room nice."

The two flashed signals at each other with their eyes, and the one with stringy blond hair said, "Cassy dead? We didn't know," but I didn't believe him. I'd dealt with too many Marines who sounded just like that when they were lying.

"Are you related to Cassy?" I asked. Unexpectedly, they both laughed, punching each other's arms.

"Well, no, lady, not exactly," the other one said. "More like brothers in arms, we might say," proud of being so clever.

"What kind of arms are you talking about?" asked the general.

"Huh? Whaddaya mean?" Smartass stalled for time.

"What're your names?" I asked, wondering how I could get them to stay put until I got the police here.

"Oh, just call us Tom and Jerry," said Smartass, back to speed.

"What are you doing here?" the general asked.

"We come over alla time," the blonde said. "Cassy gave us a key. See?" He held it up by a metal ring.

"Why did you try to run when we opened the door?" she asked.

"Just surprised, that's all," Smartass said, shrugging. "No big deal."

"Mrs. Gonzales," I said, "please call the detective. We'll all wait here until he arrives."

"Sure, sure," she said and went out between the general and me. That's when the boys made their move, pushing through us and running down the stairs. Both the general and I started after them, but the fussy little man and Mrs. Gonzales got in our way and the street was empty when we got outside. They could be behind any bush or down any driveway, I thought, looking up and down the street.

I turned to the general, who was doing the same thing. "Ma'am, I'm going to call the police and describe those boys. You don't need to be involved." She nodded and, without a word, marched briskly toward Mt. Vernon Avenue.

God, I thought, walking back upstairs, if the media found out a woman general was involved in the murder of a male sergeant, all hell would break loose. Her reputation, her career—mine, too, probably—and CAP would die a very public death, and all the women's services would suffer. I hoped she gave the real estate agent a phony name.

On the landing, I saw the doors to both apartments were open. Mrs. Gonzales and the little man were talking in hers, so I went into Cassy's to look around. What did those boys want? They didn't find it, unless it was so small they could stick it in their tight jeans without a noticeable bulge.

Mrs. Gonzales was right. The living room was a mess, thoroughly ransacked. The bedroom was the same: mattress thrown off the bed, drawers dumped out on the floor, shoes and suitcases thrown out of the closet. The suitcases had been broken open and all Cassy's mementos—a photo album, plaques and mugs from his service stations—strewn about. In the closet, his dress blues hung in a plastic cleaners' bag alongside his other uniforms and a couple of civilian jackets. I looked around until I heard people coming up the stairs. It was Detective Rojas and another man.

"I'm not surprised to find you here," he said to me. "Not pleased, but not surprised. Mrs. Gonzales said something about boys in the sergeant's apartment who attacked you and a woman who was eager to see his apartment. Is it *really* so desirable that she had to see it this very night?"

I only said, "Mrs. Gonzales was right. I got a good look at the two boys. I can give you their description."

"Where's the woman?" he asked.

"She left," I said. "Didn't want to be involved."

He gave me a sharp look but didn't say anything else. When I'd finished describing the boys, I agreed to go to his office and look at photos. He said he'd call when they were available.

By this time, Mr. Gonzales had come home and Mrs. Gonzales was crying again. That poor lady was having a very bad day. I told him goodbye, expressing my sympathy and hoping she'd get some rest, and went home.

The next morning, when I reported for duty, the general was reading the case file. I kept detailed reports on every Alert, and she had spotted Cassy's reference to "my boys" providing money to supplement his pension.

"They're the two last night," she announced with authority.

"Yes, ma'am. There might be more than two involved in this money-making operation."

"Drugs?" she asked. "Those two looked pretty clean."

"Yes, ma'am," I agreed. They didn't twitch, their noses didn't run, their reactions were good, their eyes and skin clear. "It's not usual, but they could sell it without taking it."

"It's a possibility."

"Those boys and the Downtown Girls might have met and tied up together."

"Absolutely not," the general said emphatically. "The Girls are out of it. Castleman was overseas often enough to develop contacts for drugs. Get a track on his assignments in the Middle and Far East."

"Yes, ma'am," I said and went to my desk to call Personnel. She really bought the Girls' story, I thought, but they were still my best bet. I couldn't think how, but what the boys were looking for had to figure somewhere in this mess. That was the first priority. I would focus on the Girls later.

The Personnel duty sergeant answered the phone, and I asked for Captain Wilson. She and I had served in Guam together and had been pretty close before she reported for Officer Candidate School. After we caught up with each other, I asked for a printout of Cassy's eastern assignments, then took off for headquarters.

When I reached Cassy's office, the corporal was going through his desk. "The major asked me to clear it," she told me. "I'm going to put the files back into the cabinet and just toss the rest."

"I need to take a look," I said. "Pick up a printout from Captain Wilson in Personnel for me. And corporal . . ." she paused in the doorway ". . . Take your time."

She smiled, understanding that I had no official status here, but I knew she'd figure it had something to do with CAP.

"Right, Top," and she took off.

If the civilian police came up with a reason to search Cassy's desk, they had to ask the MPs. That would take a while, so I had first crack at it.

I went through every file in the desk but found only official documents. I piled them on the corporal's workstation so she could refile them as she planned. Then I emptied all the drawers. At the back of one, I found several packets of pornographic pictures, really explicit. Hoping no one would walk in, I thumbed through them for notations or hidden notes. Nothing, so I ripped them up and buried them at the bottom of a trashcan.

Next, I pulled the drawers off their runners, stacked them to one side, and crawled underneath the desk to see if anything was taped to the inner sides. Nothing there but dust, which I got all over my uniform shirt and slacks. Backing out, I knocked over the stack of drawers. The third one I picked up was upside down, and as I swung it over, the dividers fell out. One came apart, and an envelope dropped out. Inside the envelope was—wow!—a key. Am I Nancy Drew or what? Was there anything that explained it? No, the desk produced nothing more.

Sitting in Cassy's chair, I looked at my find. It could have been the key to everything. I couldn't tell what it fit by looking at it, but a locksmith probably could.

When the corporal returned, printout in hand, I asked her, "Do you know if the sergeant had a private business?"

"Sorry, Top, I really haven't been here long enough to

know much about what goes on. How about the PFC I replaced? The woman they harassed?"

"Good idea," I told her and walked across Southgate Road to "A" Company in Henderson Hall. Captain Livingston, Smithson's new boss, and I had served together at Camp Pendleton. She was more than casually interested in CAP.

"Smithson is good," she told me. "I'm glad to have her aboard, but tell me about Sergeant Castleman. Do the police know who killed him?"

I shook my head. "I need to talk to Smithson, Skipper."

"Sure thing, Top."

When Smithson reported, I asked, "Did you ever hear Sergeant Castleman refer to 'my boys'?"

"On the phone, he called a guy named Johnny 'my boy.' Just a joke, you know. I thought Johnny was one of the lifers he served with. They drank together a lot, and he rented a truck from him several times."

"Was the sergeant running a private business?"

"I don't know," Smithson said. "I didn't hang around him any more than I had to. I just couldn't help overhearing some things."

"Of course," I said. "I don't want to rake up painful memories, but I need one last item. Do you recognize this?" I handed the key to her, but she'd never seen it before.

"Top," she said hesitantly as she returned the key, "did I cause his death? You know, going to the Task Force?"

"Of course not," Captain Livingston and I said simultaneously. I continued, "You weren't the only one he harassed, just the one who had somewhere to go."

"And the courage to do it," the captain put in.

"Yes," I agreed. "His death is an external issue," hoping I was right.

After Smithson left, Captain Livingston asked, "What are you up to, Top?"

"Damage control. I need to find out what this key fits so I can point the police in that direction and away from CAP.

Maybe one of Cassy's old buddies might know," thinking of Len's friends who'd served with Cassy. They'd know who his people were.

The captain reached for a copy of *Henderson Hall News* and flipped through it until she found the page she wanted. Folding the paper back, she handed it to me, pointing to the classified ads for trucking companies. Being owned by former Marines was the big pitch in every one. "Way to go. I was thinking only of active duty men."

"And look at this," she said, digging her key ring from her purse and laying one of the keys beside mine on her desk. "Very similar, aren't they?" I agreed. "It's for a heavy duty padlock. When I was assigned here and Joe went to Norfolk, we rented our house to the Pastors. You remember them?" I nodded. "We put our stuff in one of those public storage places and we bought the best lock we could get."

"Hey, maybe we'll keep CAP alive, after all."

"Keep me posted," she said. "Anything I can do, let me know."

Crossing Southgate Road, I saw the shuttle waiting and ran for it. Back in the office, I put the printout of Cassy's eastern assignments on the general's desk, sat down at mine, and planned what to say to the trucking companies. In the next couple of hours, I collected a lot of information about rates, times, and renting trucks before I found Cassy's old friend, Gunny Moore. From the day he made gunnery sergeant, only his mother, and maybe his wife, used his real first name.

I had started each call by saying, "Sergeant Castleman told me about your company . . ." and this man was the first to respond to the name.

"Good old Cassy," he boomed genially in my ear. "We go way back, y'know. Started together at PI. How is the old . . ." he coughed to give himself time to change the B word he was going to use to a polite one. "How's the old boy? Seen him recently?"

"Not for a couple of days," I replied truthfully. "I hear you did a lot of trucking for him."

"Hauled a few loads for him. Down the Carolinas."

"You hauled the loads?" I asked. "I must have misunderstood. I thought he rented trucks from you, and your rates were lower than U-Haul."

"Oh, well, yes and no. Actually, I don't rent trucks. I was just doing an old buddy a favor," and he swiveled away from the subject. "What can I do for you, sergeant?"

"Take some furniture out of storage and move it to my parents' house in Norfolk," I lied. Mom and Dad sold that house when they retired to Arizona.

"I reckon I can handle that," he said. "Where's your gear?"

"Same storage as Cassy's," I said, taking a shot in the dark.

"Well, he's got stuff in more than one of them places over on Pickett. Which one's yours?"

I couldn't answer that, so I bought some time. "You better give me some prices first, Gunny. Then I'll talk it over with my husband and we'll get back to you."

"Call any time," he said. "I'm usually here till twenty, twenty-one hundred. Most folks call after they get off duty," and I added his prices to all the others I'd collected. If anyone ever needs them, here they are, I thought, making a file for them.

Those places over on Pickett, he had said, and that evening I followed Pickett's meandering path through Alexandria. On the west side, it became commercial. I saw four public storage places and decided to try Cassy's key in as many padlocks as I could. I couldn't get into one place without a coded gate card, but the next one was open. I drove in between two buildings—one, round, in the middle; the other, curved like a C, with solid walls facing the outside. I parked and, expecting a challenge from security any minute, tried the key in every padlock. Nothing on both counts.

The next one, up a small, steep hill, was built on the same principle but in a rectangle, the drive a straight line between the two buildings with the doors facing in. Here security was at least visible, but I showed the key to the guy who came to see what I was doing, and he went back to his television set.

At the tenth door, the key slid into the lock as though it had reached home. As I heaved the up-and-over door, I hoped I'd find the answer to Cassy's murder. If it was in what I found, I needed an interpreter. The area was a neatly arranged warehouse, each row of boxes clearly labeled— TVs, VCRs, computers, printers, CD players, electronic typewriters.

Nothing sinister here, I thought as I closed the door and secured the padlock. Cassy had obviously started a business to supplement his pension and "my boys" worked for him. Damn and blast, I had thought I'd really found something; I drove home really pissed. It took a long conversation with Carolyn and Len to put me back in a good humor.

The next morning Detective Rojas called to tell me the pictures had come in. When could I go through them? "The sooner the better," I told him. "How about this afternoon?"

The general looked tired and worried, almost haggard when I went into her office. I wanted to say something sympathetic, but you couldn't with her—so business as usual. I laid on her desk a hard copy of what I fervently hoped would be the final version of the CAP report. Five drafts was more than enough. She handed me some routine paperwork and looked up with a touch of impatience when I didn't leave immediately.

"Ma'am, I have more information about Sergeant Castleman's activities . . ."

"Well?" she asked, giving me permission to continue by motioning to the chair near her desk. I told her about finding the key, Gunny Moore, and the storage space. "The police detective has some kind of photo lineup for me to look at this afternoon. Maybe I'll identify the boys, and the police can solve the murder without involving CAP."

"I know Sergeant John Moore," she said. "We served together on Okinawa. He's running a trucking company here?" I told her its name and address and left for my appointment.

The police department was in Alexandria's new Detention Center, a big red brick complex at the end of a maze of streets south of historic Olde Towne (established in 1749 the signs say), almost under the Capital Beltway.

When Rojas laid before me five yearbooks from T. C. Williams High School, I laughed. "All your criminals in high school?"

He looked uncomfortable but just said, "Don't bother with all the pictures. Just the seniors. Want some coffee?"

Even just the seniors was a big job—several hundred each year. At first, I enjoyed looking at the fresh, young faces—like recruits—but by book three, they all looked alike. Then I actually found one of the boys—the Smartass. His face was just as cocky two years ago as it had been the other night. The stringy blonde turned up in the same book.

I sat back, feeling I'd really accomplished something this time, and looked around for Rojas. He'd gone about his business after he brought me the coffee. With partitions bracketing off each desk, I couldn't tell where everyone was, so I went looking.

He was sitting at a large table with a group of men and women, both uniformed and plainclothes. Everyone stopped talking when I appeared. "I found them," I announced. A babble broke out, while Rojas grinned with satisfaction. "The blonde is Hurley Anderson and the other, Lazar White."

"Yah, yah," he crowed at his colleagues. "Thought I was off my head, didn't you?" Then he turned to me. "Thank you, Sergeant. You've proved a point I've been trying to make for a couple of months. George," he looked at a uniformed patrolman, "get the sergeant some real coffee, not that slop we give visitors." George brought me not only a cup of great coffee, but a piece of pie, too. After three hours of heavy concentration, it hit the spot.

Those two boys worked for a company that cleaned stores and offices, many of which had been robbed. The detectives working the robberies had noted that the company cleaned every one of the places and thought they had the thieves. Most of the crews were illegals, Hispanics with little English, but they all checked out. Always with large numbers of people the nights of the robberies. If they stole anything, the detectives figured it was one or two TVs or VCRs for their own use. Not the truckloads that had disappeared.

The few Anglos who took jobs with the cleaning service did so only until they could find something better. Except for these two. They had stayed with the company for a year and, according to the manager, become strong right arms.

"I keep my fingers crossed," she had told the police. "I expect them to vanish any minute because they can do better than this. In fact, they belong in college. They're reliable and conscientious; hard workers, too. Always ready to fill in for no-shows, and I have more of those than I care to count."

"You think they're the robbers?" I asked, my mind running immediately to Cassy's warehouse. That would point them away from CAP, even though the boys would probably tell them where Cassy's invoices were.

"Their alibis the nights of the robberies are ironclad," a woman in plainclothes said. "Would you believe, with their families every damn time?"

"That in itself is suspicious," a man said. "It's unreal for those two to spend so much time at home. Their counselors at T. C. Williams just laughed when I brought it up."

"So they have to be involved, but indirectly," Detective Rojas said. "They probably set up the robberies."

"They haven't the know-how," the plainclothes woman objected. "There's someone else; someone experienced in running large-scale robberies."

"But their being at the sergeant's in suspicious circumstances is the first time we've been able to tie them to a crime, and now we can put some teeth into questioning them."

"Right on!" "Yeah, man." "Good stuff," came from the group, but I felt let down. "How does this connect with Sergeant Castleman's murder? That's why I'm here, you know," I reminded Rojas.

"In good time," he said. "In good time. This is the way police work is done." He was annoyed. Well, so was I.

"Before I leave you to your police work, then, here's some new information. I found this key in the sergeant's desk," laying it on the table. "I wondered what those boys were looking for and conducted my own search . . ." and briefed them on what I had found. When I finished, Rojas sent two detectives with the key to check out the storage space.

The plainclothes woman escorted me to the door, saying, "I've a feeling you won't leave this alone. That sergeant's death is too important to you. If you need help, my name's Lydia Malone. Here's my card with office and home numbers."

As I drove home, I reviewed the situation. CAP was okay so far. The police knew nothing about it or the Downtown Girls, and Detective Rojas was really more interested in the robberies than Cassy's murder. If Yvonne and Sherry killed Cassy by accident, I needed to know for sure. I didn't want anything to blindside CAP later, so, no, I couldn't leave it alone. I'd sort out right and wrong when I knew.

By then I was unlocking my front door and decided to think out what to do next during supper. All I came up with was a visit to Gunny Moore. He probably couldn't help, but I wanted to meet him anyway, I like old salts like him. My father is one.

It was dark when I finally found his office in a cruddy warehouse in a back alley at the northern edge of Alexandria, between old U.S. 1 and the railroad tracks. I'd expected better, but I guessed a trucking company didn't need a trendy office. The only light was a dim one coming through the dirty glass of the warehouse door, so I headed for it. I was fairly close when someone—Hurley Anderson—opened it.

"You do a number on us, Gunny, it'll be your balls in a sling. What's between you and Cassy don't cut any ice with us. We just want our money."

Gunny laughed, a hearty, rolling guffaw. "Shove off, boy. You're outranked. All you need to remember is which side your bread's buttered on. Just keep doing what we tell you. What I tell you, I mean, now Cassy's gone."

"We want our money this Saturday. We're taking off," came Lazar White's voice.

"Now you listen to me, boy, and listen good." Gunny's voice became angry and menacing. "Cassy put that money and that key somewheres. He was going off his rocker, what with all his disappointments eating away at him. He had to be nuts to doublecross me. Me! The only guy in the Corps he could count on. And I trusted *him*. I cut him in every place I was assigned—Nam, Guam, Okinawa—me where all the goods was and him at home port to sell it. I cut him in here, too, and he screwed me. When I found he never deposited the money like he was s'posed to, and no trace of the last three loads . . . well, 'nuff said." His anger had run out; his voice was quiet now. "Don't worry. I'll find it all. You two still got a job to do, so don't hang around here."

They laughed. "We got that job taped. Those dummies think we're doing 'em a favor, letting 'em do all the work." They slammed the door and horsed their way around the warehouse. I was still standing in the dark, listening to them revving an engine, when the boys' headlights, swinging around the building, picked up a figure running for cover. The driver slammed on the brakes, and both boys jumped out and took off after it. At the same time Gunny opened his door and stood framed in the light.

"Who's there?" he called.

"It's me, a friend of Cassy's," I answered. I didn't want to be caught hiding in the dark. "I just came to talk to you," trying to make my voice sorrowful.

"Well, come on in," he said, the genial old sergeant again. "Any friend of Cassy's is a friend of mine."

"What's with the people in that pickup?"

"Just some crazy kids," he said, peering to see beyond the light. "Come on in," he said again and ushered me into the dirtiest place I'd ever seen. Engine parts, tools, dirty clothes, greasy rags, and junk were scattered all over. Seeing the expression on my face, he said, "I spent most of my time in the Corps policing up or making sure others did. I don't hafta now, so I just relax. I thought I knew all Cassy's people, but I don't recall you. What's your connection?"

"I'm civil service at headquarters."

"Must have been a terrible shock. His death, I mean. Here, siddown." He shoved ratty magazines, empty food cartons, a couple of wrenches, and some other stuff off the ripped plastic upholstery of a rickety dinette chair.

I was trying to think how to start, when the door was yanked open and a hand propelled the general inside. I thought for a horrible moment she was going to fall flat on her face on the dirty floor. She stumbled, but by some miracle of balance and willpower, stayed upright.

"It's that ditzy woman from the apartment," Anderson was saying as he followed her in, but stopped abruptly when he saw me. White crashed into him, almost knocking him down.

"That's the other one!" Anderson exclaimed. "What're they hanging 'round for?"

"I got 'er," White said with satisfaction, clenching and

unclenching his fists, jittering on his toes. The general's face and hands were bruised, and she looked as though she'd rolled in oily dirt. "She slipped and kept rolling around so's I couldn't get a good hold, otherwise I'd've gotten some blood." White teetered on braced legs, flexing his shoulders. "You stupid old bitch," he told the general. "Think a couple feeble karate moves could deck me?"

I got up to give her my chair, but she straightened her back and didn't move. "Maybe you better sit down, ma' . . . miss." Old habits die hard. Gunny had to shift from "ma'am" to "miss" in midword.

"What we gonna do with 'em?" Anderson asked, dancing around, shadowboxing. Both were all pumped up. "I'm ready for some fun. Laze and me'll take the young one; she's kinda cute. You can have the beat-up oldie, Gunny. More your style." He and White laughed.

"Never mind that right now," Gunny said. "I'll figure something out. You two still have those jobs to close out tonight. We don't want anyone getting suspicious, so don't break up the routine."

"Oh right."

"Yeah, man, that's right."

With a couple of leers in my direction, they charged out, slamming the door. I could hear them laughing and chattering until they revved the engine of their truck and took off in a splatter of gravel.

While Gunny was getting rid of the boys, the general sat down. She looked pretty battered. In spite of what White said, I could see blood oozing from cuts on her hands and trickling from her hair. "Where's your first-aid kit, Gunny?" I asked.

"The colonel's pretty tough, as I recall," Gunny answered. "She'll be okay while you two explain yourselves."

"General," I snapped. "Those cuts could get infected if they're not cleaned."

"Uhmmm," he said to her, raising his bushy, salt and

pepper eyebrows. "So you made it? Everyone on Okinawa knew how damned ambitious you were. Too ambitious to act like a normal woman. If you are a normal woman."

"You're a disgrace, Moore," the general rapped out. "You and Castleman. If I could have proved you were behind the thefts, you'd both still be in the brig."

He smiled complacently. "Nothing you could do about it then; nothing you can do about it now, and being a general ain't nothin' to me."

It now all fit together. "You killed Cassy, didn't you?" I asked. "And Anderson and White were searching his apartment for a key—the key to a storage space where he'd hidden electronics equipment you had stolen, right?"

He picked up a wrench and sat rubbing it. "So I say right, so what?"

"So nothing," I lied. "I just wanted to know for sure who killed him."

"Like hell," he laughed. "Think I believe that crap?" Then with a quick change of mood, "Where's the key? That merchandise belongs to me."

"I gave it to the police. Told them what it fit—and where."

"The hell you say!" He leaped up and came at me with the wrench upraised, yelling, "Damn you, interfering bitch!" as he aimed at my head. I sidestepped, but not far enough. The wrench caught me a glancing blow on the shoulder, numbing my whole arm. I pivoted to face him and knocked his arm aside as he was raising it again. He dropped the wrench, grabbed me by the shoulders, ran me back into the wall, banging my head against it until something made him drop me. I slid to the floor, dizzy and disoriented, seeing through a haze. He and the general were just shapes, moving together.

I heard him laugh and say, "Want to mix it up, Colonel m'love? Com'on, baby, I wanted to grapple with you for a long time, only you're gonna get a little extra punishment for shipping me out of Okinawa. I could've made lots more money before normal rotation."

While he was talking, they tangled somehow. I heard grunts and thuds, but I couldn't tell much. My head was fuzzy, but when I could see better, I looked around for a weapon. All I saw was the wrench he'd dropped. I was crawling toward it when the general warned "Top!" in time for me to roll out of the way of a kick from his heavy boots. I managed to get to my knees before he could get close. When he kicked again, I grabbed his foot and twisted it. He landed with a satisfying thump. The general knelt on his back, pinning him down, twisting his arm up behind him, pushing his face against the floor.

"Hey!" His voice was muffled. "Get the hell off!"

"What was that about mixing it up with the colonel, you maggot? Pull, you bastard, pull hard so I can break your arm. After all the trouble you gave me in Okinawa, I'd love it."

While she was letting off steam, she yanked the belt from her slacks, grabbed his other arm, and lashed them together above the elbow. I pulled my belt off, sat on his kicking legs, and looped it around his ankles. The general got off his back, and I tied the ends of the two belts together, arching his back enough to be uncomfortable.

If I could have found some duct tape, I'd have taped his mouth. He swore up a storm, threatening horrible revenge. "Shut up," I told him, "or I'll use this wrench on you like you did on Cassy."

"You'll never prove it," he snarled. While he continued to curse and threaten, I dug out Lydia Malone's card and dialed her number. When I finished briefing her about why and where I was holding Moore, she told me to stay until she and Rojas got there.

"Ma'am," I said to the general, who was dabbing at her bruises and looking like the cat that swallowed the canary. "The police ETA is about fifteen minutes."

"Right," she said, looking at Moore, who was trying to roll around. "So the Girls really didn't do it."

"Hey, let's make a deal," Moore called. "We're all Marines here. No point in letting civilians in on this."

"Semper Fi," the general said and marched out. The military band in my head was back on duty, but some of the musicians were playing sour notes. Damn and blast! Shared intelligence and planning could have produced a coordinated operation—with the same result. She got her satisfaction taking Moore down, but we both could have been badly hurt, if not killed.

I brooded on the problem of working in the dark while Moore alternately begged to be untied and threatened to "blow that bitch out of the water." By the time a squad of police arrived, sirens blaring, lights flashing, guns in hand, I was feeling pretty good about what Detective Rojas called my "collar."

"This the turkey you want roasted?" Rojas asked when he saw Moore. "Trussed him up all by your hundred and twenty pound self, did you?"

"Combat readiness," I told him. "Part of every Marine's equipment."

"Which includes wearing two belts in case you need to tie someone up?"

Before I could think of an answer to that, one of the uniformed cops said, "We better untie him. We don't want him yelling police brutality."

While they cuffed Moore and read him his rights, Lydia and I left for the police station where I spent the next several hours filling out forms, answering questions, and signing statements. No one asked me again about the two belts. Patrol officers picked up the two boys, leaving two sets of parents in shock. It was dawn when, after a shower to wash off the crud from Moore's dirty floor, I fell into bed.

The general called in sick and didn't report for duty for almost a week. I wondered how badly she was hurt. I ached some, but X rays showed no bone damage where Moore had hit me with the wrench. The media reported the murder as a falling out among thieves and moved on to juicier things.

When the general returned to duty, all I saw was a bruise on her right cheekbone. She kept her hands out of sight, but of course, business as usual. I had put entry forms for two new Alerts in her in box. One checked out; the other was revenge for being dumped. Not easy to take, but it wasn't sexual harassment. She put the fifth version of the CAP report in her out box, mercifully marked for distribution.

"Top," she said as I started to leave. "A debriefing is in order."

"Yes, ma'am," I said, turning back to find her with a braced-for-action set to her shoulders.

"How are you feeling?"

"Fine, ma'am," I answered, hiding my astonishment at this first-ever inquiry. "Nothing serious. How about you?" I ventured.

She displayed her bandaged hands, then pointed to her head with a slight smile. "Several stitches up there, some aches and pains." She took a deep breath and looked at me with such intense determination that the color of her eyes seemed brighter. "I showed weakness."

"No, ma'am, not that I saw," I said emphatically.

"It was about the Downtown Girls. They blackmailed me, said they'd reveal their connection to CAP, and I caved in. You didn't believe me when I told you they were innocent."

"Yes, ma'am—er, no, ma'am. I wondered what proof you had."

"Just my fear. I had too much to lose. Top, we're going to have to figure out some way to keep the pressure on the men off duty without using the Girls."

"The Alert that's a go . . ." pointing to her in box ". . . is in the barracks. A man harassing a woman who lives down the hall. Plenty of volunteers to continue the cure after duty hours without using the Girls' —er—specialty."

"Right," she said. "In the meantime, we'll put together an ad hoc committee of experienced volunteers and do some brainstorming. Meanwhile, let's get this cure under way."

"Yes, ma'am," I said. Asking about my health? Saying *we* and *let's*? Will wonders never cease? As I marched out, the band struck up.

THE MAGGODY FILES: D.W.I.

======================================

by Joan Hess

Thursdays aren't the busiest day for outbursts of criminal activity in Maggody, Arkansas (pop. 755). Neither are Sundays, Mondays, Tuesdays, and Wednesdays. Long about Friday, things pick up in anticipation of the weekend, although when we're talking grand theft auto, it means some teenager took off in his pa's pickup. A hit-and-run has to do with a baseball and a broken window at the Pot o' Gold trailer park. The perpetrator of larceny tends to be a harried mother who forgot to pay for gas at the convenience store, most likely because one of the toddlers in the back seat of the station wagon chose that moment to vomit copiously into the front seat.

I say all this with authority, because I, Ariel Hanks, am the chief of police, and it's my sworn duty to drag the errant driver home by his ear, and send the batter over to mumble a confession and offer to make reparation. Why, I've been known to go all the way out to Joyce Lambertino's house to have a diet soda and a slice of pound cake, admire her counted cross-stitch, and take her money to the Kwik-Stoppe-Shoppe. And bring her back the change.

Other than that, I occasionally run a speed trap out by the skeletal remains of Purtle's Esso Station, where there's a nice patch of shade and some incurious cows. I swap dirty jokes with the sheriff's deputies when they drop by for coffee. Every now and then I wander around Cotter's Ridge, on the very obscure chance I might stumble across Raz Buchanon's moonshine still. It's up there somewhere, along with ticks, chiggers, mosquitoes, brambles, and nasty-tempered copperheads.

The rest of the time I devote to napping, reading, wondering why I'm back in Maggody, and doing whatever's necessary to eat three meals a day at Ruby Bee's Bar & Grill. The proprietor (a.k.a. my mother) is a worthy opponent, despite her chubby body and twinkly eyes. She's adjusted to having her daughter do what she considers a man's job, and she's resigned to my divorce and my avowed devotion to the single life. This is not to say I don't hear about my failings on a regular basis, both from her and her spindly, redhaired cohort, Estelle Oppers, who runs a beauty shop in her living room—and is as eager as Ruby Bee is to run my life. But I don't believe in running; there's nothing wrong with a nice, easy walk (except on Cotter's Ridge, and that's already been mentioned).

But the particular Thursday under discussion turned ugly. I was at the PD, yanking open desk drawers to watch the roaches scurry for cover. When the telephone rang, I reluctantly shut the drawer and picked up the receiver.

"Sheriff Dorfer says to meet him by the creek out on County 103," the dispatcher said with her customary charm. "Right now."

"Shall I bring a bucket of bait and a six-pack?"

"Just git yourself over there, Arly. Sheriff Dorfer's at the scene, and he ain't gonna be all that tickled if you show up acting like you thought it was a picnic."

It was not a picnic. I parked behind several official

vehicles, settled my sunglasses, and slithered and slipped down a fresh path of destruction to the edge of Boone Creek. Harve Dorfer was talking to a man in a torn army jacket who was wiping blood from his face with a wadded handkerchief. A pair of grim deputies watched. Beyond them lay a lumpish form covered by a blanket. The rear half of a truck stuck out of the water as if poised in a dive.

"You're a real work of art," Harve growled, then stalked over to me, an unlit cigar butt wedged in the corner of his mouth. He aimed a finger at me, but turned and looked at his deputies. "Les, you and John Earl take this stinkin' drunk up to the road and have the medics check him. If nothing's broke, take him to the office and book him. If something is, go along with him and wait at the emergency room until he's patched up. Then take him to the office and throw the whole dadgum book at him."

I studied the object of Harve's displeasure. Red Gromwell was local, a young guy, maybe thirty, with a sly face already turning soft and greasy hair the color of a rotting orange. At the moment, he had a swollen lip, the beginnings of a black eye, and a ragged streak of blood down the side of his face. His knuckles were raw. His jacket was stained with blood, as were the baggy jeans that rode low on his hips out of deference to his beer gut. He gave me a foolish grin, dropped the handkerchief, and crumpled to the ground. The deputies hauled him to his feet, and the three began to climb toward the road.

"Drunker than a boiled owl," Harve said, firing up the cigar butt. "Says he and a guy named Buell Fumitory was out riding around, sharing a bottle and yucking it up. All of a sudden the truck's bouncing down the hill like one of those bumper cars at the county fair. Says he was thrown out the window and landed way yonder in that clump of brush. Buell over there wasn't as lucky."

I folded my arms and tried to be a cool, detached cop. My eyes kept sneaking to the shrouded body on the ground, however, and I doubt Harve was fooled one whit. I tried to swallow, but my mouth was as dry as the dusty road behind us. "Did Buell drown?" I asked.

"I can't say right offhand. He was banged up pretty bad from hitting his face against the steering wheel who knows how many times. It doesn't much matter—in particular to him. Red said by the time he could git himself up and stagger to the edge of the water, it was clear there wasn't anything to do for Buell. He did manage to climb back to the road and flag down a truck driver who called us."

"Red's not the heroic sort," I said, shaking my head. "He'd just as soon run down a dog as bother to brake."

"You know him?"

"Yes indeed. He works at the body shop and brawls at the pool hall. I had some unpleasant encounters with him after his wife finally got fed up with him and filed for divorce. Twice I drove her to the women's shelter in Farberville and urged her to stay for a few days, but she scooted right back and refused to file charges, so there wasn't much I could do."

"One of those, huh?" Harve said through a cloud of noxious cigar smoke.

"One of those." I again found myself staring at the blanket. "Buell Fumitory kept to himself, so I don't know much about him. He moved here . . . oh, a year ago, and worked at the supermarket. He came into Ruby Bee's every now and then for a beer. He seemed okay to me."

"According to this Red fellow, Buell was driving at the time of the accident. I reckon it's too late to give him a ticket." Harve snuffed out the cigar butt and looked over my shoulder. "Here come the boys with the body bag. Tell ya what, Arly," he said, putting his arm around me and escorting me up the hill, "I'm gonna let you have this one for your very own. I need Les and John Earl to finish up the paperwork on those burglaries over in Hasty, and I myself am gonna be busier than a stump-tailed cow in fly time with office chores."

I shrugged off his arm. "Like posing for the media with

the latest haul of marijuana? This sudden activity doesn't have anything to do with the upcoming election, does it?"

"You just hunt up the next of kin and write me a couple of pages of official blather," he said. Trying not to smirk, he left me at the road and went down to supervise the medics.

As I stood there berating myself for getting stuck so easily with nothing but tedious paperwork, a tow truck came down the road. Once the body and the truck were removed, the squirrels would venture back, as would the birds, the bugs, and the fish that lurked in the muddy creek. The splintered saplings would be replaced by a new crop. Three months from then, I told myself with a grimace, there would be nothing left to remind folks about the dangers of D.W.I. In some states, it's called other things. In Arkansas, we opt for the simple and descriptive Driving While Intoxicated. Might as well call it Dying While Intoxicated.

"It doesn't make a plugged nickel's worth of sense," Ruby Bee proclaimed from behind the bar. She rinsed off the glasses in the sink, wiped her hands on her apron, and gazed beadily at Estelle, who was drinking a beer and gobbling up pretzels like she was a paying customer.

"That sort of thing happens all the time," Estelle countered. "They were drunk, and anybody with a smidgen of the sense God gave a goose knows it's asking for trouble to go drinking and driving, particularly on those twisty back roads. Remember that time I was coming back from a baby shower in Emmet, and this big ol' deer came scampering into the road, and I nearly—"

"Nobody said there was a deer involved. Lottie said that Elsie happened to hear Red talking to some fellow at the launderette earlier this morning, and he said Buell was singing and howling like a tomcat and was a sight too far gone to keep his eyes on anything else on the road." She began to dry the glasses on a dishrag, all the while frowning and trying to figure out what was nagging at her. "The thing is," she added slowly, "I didn't think Buell was like that. He was always real nice when he worked in produce. One time I bought a watermelon, and when I cut—"

"I don't see why he couldn't have been real nice and also been willing to drink cheap whisky and take a drive."

"I ain't saying he wasn't," Ruby Bee said, still speaking slowly and getting more bum-fuzzled by the minute. "But I'll tell you one thing, Estelle—he never came in here and guzzled down a couple of pitchers like Red did. Like Red did before I threw him out on his skinny behind, that is. It like to cost me three hundred dollars to get the jukebox fixed. And to think he busted it just because his ex-wife was drinking a glass of beer with that tire salesman!"

"He was hotter than a fire in a pepper mill, wasn't he?" Estelle said as she picked up a pretzel. "I wish somebody'd find the gumption to mention to him that what his ex-wife does is none of his business. It ain't like he bought a wife; he was only renting one. It's a crying shame he wasn't the one to end up in the creek so Gayle can get on with her life and stop having to peek over her shoulder every time she steps out of the house."

"How'd she take the news?"

Estelle lowered her voice, although anybody could see there wasn't another soul in the barroom, much less hanging over her shoulder like a lapel. "Well, Lottie said Mrs. Jim Bob happened to run by Gayle's with some ironing, and Gayle wouldn't even come to the door. Mrs. Jim Bob saw the curtain twitch, so she knew perfectly well that Gayle was home at the time."

"I don't see that she has any reason to . . ."

Estelle gave her a pitying look. "To avoid Mrs. Jim Bob? I'd say we all had darn good reasons to do that. I could make you a list as long as your arm."

"Unless, of course . . ."

"Unless what?"

"Well, if Gayle was . . ."

"I do believe you could finish a sentence, Mrs. Dribble Mouth, and do it before the sun sets in Bogart County."

Not bothering to respond, Ruby Bee stared at the jukebox with a deepening frown. "You know," she said about the time Estelle was preparing to make another remark, "the last time I saw Gayle at the Emporium, she was looking right frumpy. What she needs is a perm, Estelle, and you're the one to give it to her. I suspect it'll have to be for free; she barely makes minimum wage at the poultry plant in Starley City. Why doncha call her right now and make an appointment?"

"For free?" Estelle gasped. "Why in tarnation would I do a thing like that?"

Ruby Bee curled her finger, and this time she was the one to speak in a low, conspiratorial voice. Estelle managed not to butt in, and ten minutes later she was dialing Gayle Gromwell's telephone number.

The next morning I got the address of Buell Fumitory's rent house from the manager at the supermarket. He told me that Buell had worked there for most of a year, caused no trouble, took no unauthorized days off, and got along with the other employees.

Armed with the above piercing insights, I drove out past Raz Buchanon's shack to an ordinary frame house in a scruffy yard. A rusty subcompact was parked beside the house, but no one answered my repeated knocks. I considered doing something clever with a skeleton key or a credit card to gain entry. However, having neither, I opened the front door and went inside.

The interior was as ordinary as the exterior. It was clearly a bachelor's domain. There were a few dirty ashtrays and a beer can on the coffee table, odds and ends of food in the refrigerator, chipped dishes and a cracked cup in the cabinets. The only anomaly was a vase with a handful of wilted daisies, but even tomato stackers can have a romantic streak.

I continued on my merry way. The bedroom was small and cluttered, but no more so than my apartment usually was. The closet contained basic clothing and fishing equipment. The drawer in the bedside table had gum wrappers, nail clippers, a long overdue electric bill, and an impressive selection of condom packets. Perhaps somebody in the morgue would encourage Buell to continue practicing safe sex in the netherworld.

In the distance, most likely at Raz's place, a dog began to bark dispiritedly. As if in response, the house creaked and sighed. It wasn't a mausoleum, and I wasn't about to lapse into a gothic thing involving involuntary shivers and a compulsion to clutch my bosom and flutter my eyelashes. On the other hand, I recalled the blanketed body alongside the creek, and I wasted no time, pawing through dresser drawers until I found a stack of letters and an address book.

I sat down on the bed and flipped through the latter until I found the listing for Aunt Pearl in Boise. If she was not the official next of kin, she would know who was. The letters turned out to be commercial greeting cards, all signed with a smiley face. I made a frowny face, stuffed them back in the drawer, and returned to the PD to see if Aunt Pearl might be sitting by her telephone in Boise.

She was, but she was also hard of hearing and very old. Once I'd conveyed the news, she admitted she was the only living relative. Her financial situation precluded funeral arrangements. I assured her that we would deal with it, hung up, and leaned back in my chair to ponder how best to share this with Harve. There was very little of value at Buell's house. A small television, furniture that would go to the Salvation Army (if they'd take it), and a couple of boxes of personal effects. The pitiful car would bring no more than a hundred dollars.

The pitiful car. I propped my feet on the corner of the desk and tried to figure out why there was a car, pitiful or not, parked at Buell's house. He did not seem like a two-car family. Glumly noting that the water stain on the ceiling had expanded since last I'd studied it, I called the manager at the supermarket and asked him what Buell had driven. He grumbled but agreed to ask the employees, and came back with a description of the subcompact.

Red Gromwell drove an ancient Mustang; I'd pulled him over so many times that I knew the license plate by heart. The pickup truck in the creek had been gray, or white and dirty. I thought this over for a while (bear in mind it was Friday morning, so I wasn't preparing to foil bank robberies or negotiate with kidnappers).

I called the sheriff's department and got Harve on the line.

"You're not backing out on the D.W.I. report, are you?" he asked before I could get out a word. "I hate to stick you with it, Arly, but I'm up to my neck in some tricky figures for the upcoming quorum meeting, and one of the county judges says—"

"What'd you do with Red Gromwell?"

There was a lengthy silence. At last Harve exhaled and said, "Nothing much, damn it. We kept him in the drunk tank for twelve hours. This morning he called his cousin for bail money and strolled out like a preacher on his way to count the offering. I checked with the county prosecutor, but it ain't worth bothering with. If he'd been driving, we could cause him some grief. Not that much, though. Get his driver's license suspended, slap him with a fat fine. The judge'd lecture him for twenty minutes, and maybe give him some probation. The prisons are stuffed to the gills right now, and I sure don't need to offer the likes of Red Gromwell room and board, courtesy of Stump County."

I waited until he stopped sighing, then asked him to ascertain the ownership of the truck that had been pulled out of Boone Creek. He huffed and puffed some more while I wondered how badly the PD roof was leaking and finally agreed to have Les call the tow shop (sigh), get the truck's plate number (siigh), and call the state office (siiigh) to see who all was named on the registration.

On that breezy note, we parted. I did some noisy exhaling of my own, but all it accomplished was to make me woozy.

It occurred to me that I was in need of both local gossip and a blue plate special, so I abandoned any pretense of diligent detection and walked down the road to Ruby Bee's Bar & Grill, the hot spot for food and fiction.

It was closed. Irritated, I went back to my car, drove to the Dairee Dee-Lishus where the food was less palatable but decidedly better than nothing, and promised myself a quiet picnic out by the rubble of the gas station. Twenty minutes later, I was turning down County 103.

"It'd be cute all curly around your face," Ruby Bee said brightly. "Brush those bangs out of your eyes and wear a little makeup, and you'd look just like a homecoming queen."

"I don't know," Gayle Gromwell said. She didn't sound like she did, either. She sounded more like she was real sorry about coming to Estelle's Hair Fantasies, even if the perm was free. Nobody'd said the event was open to the public.

Estelle nudged Ruby Bee out of the way. "I happen to be professionally trained in these matters," she said with a pinched frown. "Now, Gayle honey, I have to agree that those bangs make you look like a dog that came out of the rain a day late. I'm just going to snip a bit here and there, give you some nice, soft curls, and then we'll see if maybe you don't want an auburn rinse."

Gayle looked a little pouty, but this wasn't surprising, since she wasn't much older than twenty and still had a few blemishes and the faint vestiges of baby fat. She slouched in the chair and gazed blankly at the image in the mirror, refusing to meet Estelle's inquisitive eyes or even Ruby Bee's penetrating stare. "Oh, go ahead and do whatever you want. I know my hair looks awful, but I don't care. Why don't you shave it off?"

"It's going to be real pretty," Estelle said nervously. This wasn't what she and Ruby Bee had hoped for, although Gayle had come and that was the first hurdle. She wiggled her eyebrows at Ruby Bee. "Don't you think Gayle here will have every boy in town chasing after her?"

Ruby Bee knew a cue when she heard one. "I just hope Red's simmered down. Remember when he put his fist through the jukebox because of that tire salesman? They charged me three hundred dollars."

They both looked at Gayle wondering what she'd say. Her eyes were closed, but as they watched, a tear squeezed out and slunk down her cheek alongside her nose. Within the hour, they had the whole teary, hiccuppy, disjointed story.

"Two weeks ago?" I echoed, admittedly less than brilliantly. "The truck was purchased two weeks ago?"

"A private sale," Les continued. "I tracked down the previous owner, who said he'd advertised the damn thing for three weeks running and was about to sell it for scrap when some guy showed up with a hundred bucks."

"Some guy? What did he look like?"

"Nothing special. Dark hair, wearing jeans and a work shirt, sunglasses, cap. Average height and weight, no initials carved in his forehead or neon antlers or anything."

"And he didn't catch the guy's name, I suppose?"

"You suppose right. This was strictly cash-and-carry."

I tried once more. "What about the registration papers?"

"Never transferred."

I hung up and went to the back room of the PD to glower at my evidence. It didn't take long. The bloodstained handkerchief was in one plastic bag and an empty liter whisky bottle in another. I hadn't been in the mood to take scrapings of mud from the bank or water from the creek. Harve, the deputies, the medics, and the tow truck operator had all tromped around; if there had been a telltale footprint, it had been obliterated (and I couldn't imagine a footprint telling much of a tale, anyway).

There was no point in dusting the bottle for fingerprints. If I bothered, and then found Red and took his to compare,

I'd have a lovely match. It was a policeish activity, but also a futile one. As for the handkerchief, I knew where the blood came from and I didn't care where the handkerchief did.

And I knew where the truck came from, but I didn't know who had bought it or why. I realized I again was making a frowny face. This was of no significance, but it led my thoughts back to the smiley faces on the cards, and that led me to the contents of the bedside drawer, the daisies, the white pickup truck, and before too long I was staring at the whisky bottle and wondering how I could prove Red Gromwell had murdered Buell Fumitory—soberly and in cold blood.

Then I realized I had the evidence in front of me. I went back to the telephone, called Les, and said, "Do you have a date tonight?"

"I don't think my wife will approve, but what do you have in mind?"

"What happened to Gayle's hair?" I said to Ruby Bee as I watched Gayle and Les settle in a back booth. "Didn't her mother warn her about sticking a fork in a socket?"

Ruby Bee leaned across the bar and whispered, "This ain't the time for smart remarks. I don't seem to recollect anyone complimenting you on that schoolmarm hair of yours. I happen to have something that you might find interestin', if you can shut your mouth long enough to hear it."

I meekly shut my mouth, mostly because I might have time to eat a piece of pie before the fireworks started. Before I could hear the big news, Estelle perched on the barstool next to me, craned her head around until she spotted Gayle, and then turned back with a self-righteous smile. "I just knew that auburn rinse would be perfect. If Arly here would let me restyle her hair, she'd look just as nice as Gayle."

"So that's why I had to eat at the Dee-Lishus today," I said accusingly. I resisted the urge to run my fingers through my hair, which would have undone my bun and left me vulnerable to further cosmetological attacks. "Just once I wish you two would stay off my case. Believe it or not, I am more than capable of—"

"Gayle was having an affair with Buell," Ruby Bee said.

I did not relent. "I figured as much, and I did it all by myself. I did not require the assistance of two overgrown Nancy Drews to—"

"And Red found out," Estelle said. "Last week he busted in on 'em and made all kinds of nasty threats. I find that a mite suspicious, considering what happened last evening." She blinked at Ruby Bee, not blankly but frostily. "If Arly already knew about Gayle and Buell, why did I end up doing her perm for free?"

Ruby Bee retreated until she bumped into the beer tap. "Arly doesn't know everything. Just ask her if she knows that Buell didn't like to go carousing like some, and hardly ever got drunk on account of the medication he took for a recurring bladder problem. And wouldn't have gone riding around with Red if his life depended on it."

"Don't ask me anything," I rumbled. I was about to elaborate on my irritation when I spotted Red coming across the dance floor. He still looked a bit battered, the black eye having blossomed and the swollen lip giving him a petulant sneer. He was not wearing blood-stained clothing, however, and he moved easily for someone reputedly thrown fifty feet from a careening vehicle.

He froze in the middle of the floor, ignoring the couples cruising around him. His fingers curled into fists, and a muscle in his neck bulged like a piece of rope. Clearly, the first of the bottle rockets was lit. I slid off the stool and caught up with him as he reached the booth where Gayle and Les were sitting.

"What the hell did you do to your hair?" he asked Gayle. When she shrugged, he jabbed his thumb at Les.

"Who's this?"

She looked up defiantly. "None of your business, Red.

We've been divorced for two years now, and you ain't got any right to act like a crybaby if I go out with someone."

"I didn't act like a crybaby when I caught you in bed with that wimp from the supermarket, did I?" he said, looming over her. "Guess you won't be romping with him any more, unless you aim to crawl in the casket with him."

Les put down his beer. "Now, wait just a minute, buddy. This woman doesn't have to take that kind of talk from—"

"Shut up or I'll shove that glass down your throat," Red snarled. "Now, listen up, Gayle Gromwell. You git yourself out of that booth and on your way home afore I drag this mama's boy outside to rearrange his pretty little face."

"You can't tell me what to do," she said sulkily.

Red pulled back his hand to slap her, but I grabbed his arm and hung on until he relaxed. "Gayle's right, Red—you can't tell her what to do," I said. "She's a single woman, and she's allowed to date whomever she chooses. In this case, she's chosen to date a deputy sheriff, which means you're threatening an officer of the law. In front of an entire roomful of witnesses, too."

He realized all the customers were watching and, from their expressions, enjoying the scene. Ruby Bee thoughtfully had unplugged the jukebox so nobody would miss a word.

"Okay," he muttered to me, then stared at Gayle. "You keep in mind what I said to you the other night, you hear?"

I tapped him on the shoulder. "Was this when you invited your old pal Buell to share a bottle of whisky and enjoy the moonlight?"

"Naw, that was yesterday after work. I went by his house to tell him I was wrong to bust down the door like I did. I told him that sometimes I go kind of crazy when I think about Gayle with another man. He was right understanding, and pretty soon we decided to run into Farberville and get ourselves a bottle. We was talking about deer season when he lost control of the truck. You know what happened then."

"Yes, I do," I said, nodding. "Why was Buell driving the

truck you bought in Little Rock two weeks ago? You paid good money for it, and I'm surprised you weren't driving."

The bruises under his eye stayed dark, but the rest of his face paled. "I dunno. I thought he was soberer than me."

"It's a good thing you weren't in the Mustang, isn't it?" I continued, still pretending we were having a polite conversation. "I know you're awfully fond of it."

"Helluva car," he said.

"Which is why you bought the truck. You weren't about to total your Mustang that way. I checked around town today, and nobody saw you and Buell driving down the road in the white pickup." I crossed my fingers. "But Raz saw you drive by his place in the Mustang late afternoon, and come back by. He didn't see Buell then, but I guess he'd need X-ray vision to see a body in the trunk, wouldn't he?"

"What are you saying?" Gayle said, gulping. "Did he kill Buell?"

"I already told the sheriff all about it," Red muttered.

I shook my head. "You told the sheriff a stale old fairy tale, Red. You went to Buell's and beat him up, put him in the trunk, and drove to your place to switch vehicles. Then you collected the whisky, went out to the hill on County 103, and sent Buell down the hill and into the creek. He was unconscious, so he didn't have much of a chance to get out of the truck."

He gave me a frightened look. "You got any proof, cop lady?"

"You drained the bottle after the wreck, so we'd figure you were drunk. I found it in the woods. If you had it with you in the truck, then you and it went flying out the window together. Why didn't it break?"

"That doesn't prove anything."

"You'd better hope Buell's fingerprints are on it," I said, "and that the alcohol level in his blood indicates he was drunk." I waited politely, but he didn't seem to have much to say. "Oh, yes, and there's one more thing, Red. You'd better start praying the blood on that handkerchief matches your type and doesn't have any traces of the medication Buell was taking."

"Medication?" Red said, sounding as if he were in need of some at the moment. He didn't improve when Les stood up, recited the Miranda warning, and cuffed him.

Once they had gone, I glowered at Ruby Bee until she headed for the jukebox, then sat down across from Gayle. "Red'll be out on bail by Monday. I suggest you spend the weekend thinking about why you're willing to play the role of victim. Get some counseling at the women's shelter if it'll help, and change the lock on your front door."

Her smile was dreamy. "Who'd have thought Red would actually kill somebody over me?"

"One of these days he'll kill you," I said, then left her to her pathetic fantasies and went back to the PD to brood.

During the course of the weekend, I'd be obliged to run in some drunks, bust a couple of minors in possession, and intervene in domestic disputes. With luck, we'd all survive, and on Monday morning, bright and early, I'd grab my radar gun and a good book, and head for that patch of shade . . . unless I decided to take a hike on Cotter's Ridge. You just never know where crime will erupt in Maggody, Arkansas (pop. 755).

ARRIE AND JASPER

=======================================

by Amanda Cross

My aunt Kate Fansler doesn't care for children. I'm her niece, but I never really got to know her till we ran into each other when I was a student at Harvard. It's true my cousin Leo spent a summer with her, and lived with her a year or so when he was in high school, but he wasn't really a child in high school, and during that summer she had a hired companion for him and sent him to day camp besides. Kate always refused to become defensive about this. "I know it's an eccentric attitude," she admitted, "but not a dangerous one. The worst fate I've ever inflicted on any child is to avoid it. As it happens, however," she added, "I did once more or less solve a case for a child. Do you think that will serve to redeem me in the eyes of those with maternal instincts?"

Kate was in her office at the university, about to conclude that her office hour was over and the thought of a martini with Reed could be realistically contemplated, when she heard a timid knock. She looked through the glass in the top half of her door and saw a silhouette reaching only a few inches above where the glass began. She opened the door to find herself confronting a girl child wearing a school uniform, glasses, braces, and a frown. Kate stared at the child so long she asked if she might come in. Kate apologized and ushered her in, closing the door.

"Forgive me," Kate said. "I was just a bit startled. You look rather young for graduate school. Or even for college, if it comes to that. Are you lost?"

"I've come to hire you as a detective," the child said. "I have money. My father says you probably couldn't find a herd of buffalo in a field covered with snow, but I figure if he doesn't like you you must be good."

"My dear young woman," Kate said, dropping back into the chair behind her desk, "I don't know which misapprehension to confront first. But, in the order in which you offered them, I'm not a detective, either private or police—they work at that job a lot harder than I do. I have detected from time to time, but I never take money, it might cloud the fine, careless rapture of the adventure. I don't know who your father is, and I'm somewhat concerned that you hold his opinion in such low regard."

You might think all this verbiage would have frightened the kid, but she held her ground admirably. "I hope I didn't offend you about the money," she said, returning her wallet to her pocket. "I would be very glad of your help."

"It doesn't sound to me as though your father would approve of your seeking my help, nor of my offering it. Who is your father? Someone I know?"

"His name is Professor Witherspoon," the child said, assured that his name was sufficient to establish his identity and credentials in Kate's eyes. She was quite right. Witherspoon was a member of Kate's department, and to say that he and Kate never saw eye to eye on anything was to put their relationship in its least emotional terms. Kate was frank to admit that she could never decide if he was a monster or a lunatic. The best that could be said on her side was that most of the department agreed with her. Kate eyed his progeny with some dismay.

"It sounds to me as though I'm the last person you should come to. Am I to gather that your dislike of your father is sufficient to recommend to you someone he despises?"

The girl had no trouble with this one, either, merely nodding. "I think he's the most awful man I know," she added. "I didn't come to you just for that reason, though. My sister took a class with you, and she considered you worthy of recommendation."

"Well," Kate said with some relief, "I'm glad to hear there is one member of your family that you like. But I can't say I ever remember having a Witherspoon in my class. I don't remember all my students' names, but I have a feeling I would have noticed hers."

"Roxanna has taken our mother's name—Albright. I'm going to do the same as soon as I can. I'll have to wait at least until I leave high school. My sister is a lot older than me. She's very smart and very beautiful; not like me."

"You look fine to me," Kate said. She meant it. Kate is the best disregarder of beauty in any conventional sense I've ever met, and if a person is glamorous or studiously well dressed, they have to go a long way to gain her trust.

"I don't look like my mother," the child said with evident regret. "Also, I'm strabismic and have an overbite. Put differently," she added, "my eyes have difficulty focusing on the same object, and my upper and lower jaws fail to meet properly. I think it's because I was such a disappointment. I was unexpected, you see, but they hoped—that is, my father hoped—that at least I would be a boy. I wasn't," she added sadly, in case Kate had any doubt.

Had the kid but known it, she had picked the quickest way to Kate's sympathics. I think Kate asked her what she wanted in order to get her off the topic of her drawbacks.

"I want you to find my dog," she said.

About this time, I'm sure, Kate was beginning to think of that martini with something close to passion. "I wouldn't know how to begin to look for a lost dog in this city," she said. "I'm afraid it may have been snatched by someone, or else wandered off. Have you tried the ASPCA?"

"He wasn't lost, he was stolen. And not on the streets, out of the apartment. The doorman saw someone leaving with Jasper under his arm. And the apartment wasn't broken into. Which means it was an inside job."

Kate took the bull by the horns (the same bull, according to Witherspoon, which she would be capable of overlooking in a china shop). "Do you suspect your father?" she asked.

"I don't know what to suspect." The kid sighed. "But Jasper meant, means, an awful lot to me." And she began to cry. She raised her glasses and wiped her eyes on her sleeve.

"What kind of dog was he?" Kate asked for something to say. "I gather not a mastiff if someone could carry him out."

"He's a Jack Russell terrier. The breed isn't yet accepted by the American Kennel Club, though it is by the English. Jack Russell terriers are small, very low to the ground, white with brown faces and ears, and tough as anything. Don't you see, it had to be someone Jasper knew, someone he thought was taking him out. He loves to go out," she added, sniffing, "but he's a fierce watchdog with anyone he doesn't know."

"You haven't told me your name," Kate said.

"Arabella. It was my father's mother's name. She was a suffragette who chained herself to fences. My father hated her. People like my sister call me Arrie."

Of course it occurred to Kate that the kid needed a therapist, not a detective, and she also probably needed a new father and a new dog. "What about your mother?" she asked. "You haven't mentioned her."

"She's away trying to stop drinking. She's much younger than my father. She was a graduate student. She's his second wife. We have two much older stepsisters from his first marriage. My father has never been able to produce a son, to his sorrow. I hope my mother gets better. The man where she is says the whole family ought to help, but my father hasn't the time. My sister and I went down there once." She trailed off.

Poor Kate didn't really know what to do. She wanted to help the kid, but there didn't seem to be any evident practical course of assistance. Arrie seemed to understand her dilemma. "You could think about it," she said. "My sister says you're very good at thinking about things. Only try not to think too long because I'm very worried about poor Jasper. He can be very trying to people who don't understand him."

"And with that," Kate said, relating the scene to Reed over her second martini, her first having been required simply to calm her down and stop her babbling, "she left with a lot more dignity than I was exhibiting. What the hell am I to do? Could you call some old pal from the DA's office to undertake a dog search on the side?"

Kate's husband answered her real question. "The doorman saw someone leave with the dog under his arm, as I understand it. The dog wasn't struggling, indicating that it wasn't being nabbed by a stranger but by someone it knew. You better find out more about the family."

"It doesn't sound like a family I want to know much more about. Perhaps we should offer to adopt Arrie and get her another Jasper."

"You have got to begin drinking less," Reed said with asperity. "We are a happy, adult couple, let me remind you—you have no trouble remembering it when you're sober. You aren't going to turn maternal on me after all these years?"

"Fear not. Just wait till *you* meet Arrie. Not to mention her father, the esteemed Professor Witherspoon."

"What is he a professor of, exactly?"

"Exactly is the word. He deals in manuscripts, the older the better, and in a foreign tongue. There is nothing about them he doesn't know, to do him justice. The trouble is, he doesn't know anything else. Confront him with an idea and he turns into a dangerous, oversized porcupine with a very loud voice. He detests every new discipline or theory or concept of teaching, and if he had his way the first woman faculty member would never have been hired. He's done his best to keep our numbers down. Women students, needless to say, are a different matter. He carries on with them in a manner designed to give sexual harassment a new name. Women students should be grateful to sit at his feet and submit themselves in other suitable poses; he doesn't want them as colleagues. He is also pompous and leering, but we might as well keep this discussion on an impersonal basis, as is my wont."

"That fills out the picture without getting us anywhere, wouldn't you say?"

"I've *been* saying, ever since I got home. What, dear man, is my next move?"

"Something will occur to you," Reed said with confidence.

The next day, Arrie's sister Roxanna Albright phoned Kate's office for an appointment. With enormous relief, Kate agreed to see her. Roxanna, being beautiful and older, could be counted on not to get to Kate in the same way Arrie had. No doubt they could arrive at a practical conclusion to the whole problem, insofar as it allowed of one. Perhaps it would be best to begin by advertising for Jasper, hanging plaintive signs on lampposts, that kind of thing.

Roxanna, whom Kate had unsuccessfully attempted to call to mind from some years back, exceeded all expectations. She was gorgeous—there was no other word. She must, Kate thought, have undergone some sort of transformation in the intervening years; not to have noticed her would have been like overlooking Garbo.

"I don't know whether to apologize or implore," Roxanna said when they had both sat down. "Arrie didn't consult me before coming. We'd talked about you once at dinner and I'd expressed my admiration. The fact that you had successfully undertaken some detective commissions was mentioned."

"As well as the opinion that I couldn't find a herd of buffalo in a white field; I know. But does the fact that your father despises me really qualify me to help Arrie? If so, I hope you'll tell me how."

"Oh, dear. Tact is something Arrie doesn't so much scorn as ignore."

"I quite agree with her," Kate said. "Tact should never interfere with one's getting at the facts. Your father, for example, lacks not tact but any concept of what the facts are."

"How well you put it," Roxanna paused as though considering how to go on. "I think the world of Arrie," she said. "Arrie's convinced she's an ugly duckling; I talk of a swan, which in time she will become. Arrie's going to do just fine. But, except for me, she doesn't get much undemanding affection, or really any affection at all. Except from Jasper, of course, which is what made this so awful. Jasper's a very responsive dog—he and Arrie have a relationship I can only call passionate.

"That's why I wanted to come in person to tell you that he's back, and apparently no worse for his strange adventure. We got a note, printed capitals on plain paper, saying he could be found at five P.M. tied to the gate of the playground at Seventy-second Street and Fifth Avenue. Of course Arrie was there on the dot, and so was Jasper. I've really only come to thank you for your kindness, not throwing her out, listening to her. It was a horrible three days. Even my father's glad the dog's back, and that's saying a good deal. You've been very kind."

"There was no ransom asked? No demand at all?"

"None. My father pointed out to Arrie that if she went ahead of time, as she wanted to do, the kidnapper might see her and not return Jasper. It's the only helpful thing he's said in living memory, so I suppose this whole affair is remarkable for that alone." Roxanna rose.

"I know," she said, "that Arrie will write to you and thank you for your sympathy and kindness. I thank you, too . . ."

The next day, however, brought not a letter from Arrie, but Arrie herself. She had waited patiently during Kate's office hour until the last of the students had gone. She had Jasper with her, hidden in a very large sack. She let him out in Kate's office, explaining that she had brought him because she hardly dared leave him alone if she didn't absolutely have to, and because she thought Kate might like to meet him, having been so kind about his disappearance.

Jasper was a bundle of energy, perhaps ten inches high and eighteen inches long. He looked as though he could take on with ease anything five times his size. Having dashed about with relief at being out of the sack, necessitated by the university's No Dogs signs, Jasper sat down at Arrie's feet and looked up at her adoringly. Kate began to feel she was being forced to watch a Disney movie that threatened never to end. Arrie, perhaps sensing this, became very business-like.

"Jasper and I are not here only to thank you," she said. "We wish to engage your services to find out who took him. Unless I know, you see," she added, "I'll never be able to feel safe in leaving him again. I'm sure you can understand that."

Kate was silent, which wasn't—as she was the first to admit—her usual part in a conversation. She had to recognize a clear reluctance to abandon this child to an additional unknown. Her father was clearly as reliable as a lottery and her sister affectionate but hardly able, and certainly not obliged, to provide parent attentions. The dog seemed to be the only steady factor, and Kate understood that Arrie's desire for assurance was certainly justified. How, on the other hand, to provide it?

"I've come with a suggestion," Arrie said, reaching over to stroke Jasper, who sat expectantly—Kate doubted if the dog ever sat any other way—at her side. "My father is relieved that I have Jasper back. So is my sister. I think they'd be willing to agree if I invited you to dinner."

"To case the joint?" Kate asked. Dinner with Professor

Witherspoon, Roxanna, and Arrie, to name only the minimum cast of characters, struck Kate as likely to be bizarre.
Apart from everything else, Witherspoon was the sort of
man who, alone with three females, becomes either auto-
cratic or flirtatious, neither of them modes dear to Kate's
heart. On the other hand—

Arrie had smiled at Kate's question. "Tomorrow night?"
she suggested. "Seven o'clock? I've written down the
address and phone number. Jasper and I will be grateful."

Kate nodded. What else was there to do? Not for the first
time, she thanked the gods—Kate, when not agnostic, was
firmly polytheistic—that she had very little to do with
children in this life.

At least one of Kate's trepidations about the dinner chez
Witherspoon was allayed immediately upon her entrance:
there were two men in addition to the professor. At least that
cause of Witherspoon's pontification or sprightliness had
been removed. Roxanna introduced a young man almost
as gorgeous in his way as she was in hers—Desmond
Elliott, an actor. What possibly else, Kate thought, shaking
hands. Arrie she greeted with warmth and a wink. Jasper
had been, it appeared, exiled for the duration. The other
guest was an older man, who, it became immediately clear,
was allied with Witherspoon and against the others. Why,
Kate wondered, was that so clear? Equally clear, somewhat
less inexplicably, was the fact that Mr. Johnson was a
lawyer, who had joined them for dinner when Arrie's
invitation to Kate superseded his planned dinner a deux with
Witherspoon.

The professor had decided upon graciousness. He was the
host, and while in his house Kate would be treated like a
woman guest, neither more nor less. With relief, Kate sank
into a chair, accepted a drink, and embarked upon a sea of
meaningless chitchat. This torture was somewhat amelio-
rated by Desmond Elliott's amusing account for the actor's
life—made up, it appeared, in equal parts of being a waiter

and performing in small, unprofitable companies of great artistic integrity so far off Broadway as to be in another state.

Roxanna was a pleasant hostess, keeping an eye on everyone's comfort but not buzzing about or insisting upon anything. When they moved in to dinner, she brought things gracefully to the table. She and Desmond were the mainstays of the conversation, although Witherspoon made some acidic comments to Kate about their department which Kate did her best to ignore. It is difficult, while eating your host's meat, to convey to him that you disagree with everything he is saying and everything he is likely to say. They finally reached the blessed subject of the university's administration, in disdain for which even sworn enemies could agree.

As the company returned to the living room for coffee, Arrie asked Kate if she would like to say hello to Jasper. Kate eagerly agreed, and followed Arrie down the hall to a closed door, behind which sharp barks of anticipation could be heard. "Quiet, Jasper," Arrie said, revealing a history of complaints, from whom it was not hard to guess. "Up." The dog danced on his short hind legs and Arrie took from her pocket a chunk of chicken breast. She tossed it into the air and Jasper caught and swallowed it in one grateful gulp, then sat, hoping for more.

"You have a nice room," Kate said.

"Yes, I used to have a tiny room off the kitchen, but Roxanna took that since she doesn't really live here most of the time. There's really just me and my father now."

"And Jasper," Kate said, it being the only cheerful fact that occurred to her. "Did you father buy him for you?" she added hopefully.

"No. Roxanna did. Dad said I couldn't keep him. But then he changed his mind. Roxanna made him."

"Desmond's nice," Kate observed. It *was* odd how conversation deserted her in the presence of the very young.

"Very nice. I'm glad he was here. I don't care for Mr. Johnson."

"Does he come often?"

"No, he's never really been here before. I've just talked to him on the phone when he calls my father. Roxanna says he's simultaneously illiterate and imperious." Kate tried not to grin, and failed. They laughed together, and Jasper rose to his hind legs, joining in.

"I still need to know who took him," Arrie said before they rejoined the others.

Reed had promised that something would occur to Kate, but all that occurred to her was gossip. And for departmental gossip, the ultimate source was Richard Frankel. Dean Rosovsky, when he retired from his high post at Harvard, reported in *Harvard Magazine* that the first duty of a dean was to listen to gossip. Kate, not to be outdone by any dean, took the advice to heart. Richard, reached by telephone, was graciously pleased to make an appointment the following day for lunch.

Kate contemplated his face across the luncheon table with pleasure. Richard combined the best features of an imp and a youthfully aging and gay (in all senses of the word) uncle. He was, in fact, quite heterosexual and a convinced bachelor, having convinced everyone of this except himself. He still hoped to meet the right woman in the next day or so and launch himself on a satisfactory career of marriage and fatherhood. Like a number of people Kate had observed over the years, Richard, marvelously suited to his life and vigorously happy, was unaware that his deep satisfaction arose in part from the delusion that he was abjectly in need of passionate love, babies, and a deep and lasting relationship. Kate liked him enormously.

She did not immediately ask about Witherspoon. To have evinced that much interest would have started Richard's investigative motors and Kate did not wish to reveal her relationship with Arrie. But it was easy to work the conversation around to Witherspoon, whom Richard, together with the greater part of the department, despised with a vigor only mitigated by the pleasure they got in talking about how awful he was. Witherspoon, Kate was forced to realize, had provided a good deal of pleasure in his curmudgeonly life, none of it intended.

Richard knew all about the wife tucked away in a nearer version of Betty Ford's detoxification facility. "Before my time, of course, but the usual story. He pursued her with tales of his unsympathetic wife—now she's the unsympathetic wife. They never learn, poor dears. One hopes the graduate students these days are too smart to marry him, if not quite smart enough to dodge entirely. I met the wife once. He had me to dinner in the early days, before I turned out to be modern altogether. Obviously a lady, and punishing him and herself for her stupid mistake. They have two daughters, an absolutely mouthwatering creature called Roxanna and an afterthought called Arabella. The names are enough to give you an idea of the marriage. It's widely assumed that Arabella isn't his child."

Kate stared at him. "On what grounds?" she finally asked.

"I think it was the poor thing's final attempt to bolt, before she drowned herself in alcohol, reinforced by prescription drugs. Considering his record of fornication and adultery, you'd think he'd have turned a blind eye, but not our Witherspoon."

"Why not?"

"Kate, my sweet, you don't seem your usual quick-witted self, if you'll forgive my observing it. Must you go on grunting monosyllabic questions?"

"I'm sorry, Richard. I'm always astonished at how much life is like prime-time soap operas."

"Which I'm certain you never watch. They are unreal only in the way outrageous situations follow hard upon each other and in the luxury of the surroundings. Actually, they are otherwise just like life, if you're a shit like Witherspoon—which of course most of them are. Have you some special interest in him? A renewed fascination with manuscripts?"

Kate laughed. "If I could take the smallest interest in manuscripts, it wouldn't be renewed. It would be a new and sudden aberration. Actually, I had dinner there the other evening and was overwhelmed with curiosity. Roxanna used to be a student of mine, and she asked me." Richard would wonder why she hadn't mentioned this in the first place. The reason was clear to Kate: it had entailed lying.

"Ah—I wondered why your interest was so suddenly awakened. The rumor is that he now wants a divorce and most of what there is of her worldly goods. In exchange, he'll pretend to relinquish with infinite sorrow custody of Arabella."

"Do you mean he'll get her to pay him alimony?"

"Don't ask me the details, but that's often how it works out these days. The woman gets the children and the man gets the property."

"Surely the woman gets to keep what she brought into the marriage."

"No doubt," Richard dryly said, "but since all this wife brought in was her misguided affection for Witherspoon that's unlikely to serve her very well. Of course, she may have some family bonds stashed away, in which case he'll do his best to get them. The man can always afford the better lawyers, alas."

"No doubt the men look at it differently," Kate said, her mind elsewhere.

"We certainly can guess how Witherspoon looks at it. And he's got two daughters from the former marriage, both unlikely to have great sympathy with the poor alcoholic. Maybe Roxanna and Arabella will come to her defense. I had the most awful row with him, you know, not too long ago. That's why it's an additional pleasure to contemplate his absolute awfulness. He worked every angle to get tenure of one of his acolytes, a twerp with his nose in manuscripts and his brain in a sling. Witherspoon got his way, of course, and I was marked down as an enemy—a mark not of distinction, since there are so many of us, but of honor. The only good part of the story is that the twerp left to devote himself wholly to some manuscript collection. Did Witherspoon behave himself at dinner?"

"Oh, yes. The older daughter is very gracious and I like the younger one. I'm surprised the wife had the gumption to have a love affair."

"Its end was no doubt the inevitable last straw. Witherspoon made no bones about the fact that if the child had been a boy he would have forgiven everything. He's that kind of monster."

"Do you think he's really the father?"

"God knows. Roxanna is pretty, definitely his, and she's gorgeous, so who has an opinion about genes? Of course, the wife was pretty luscious in those days—he'd never have bothered otherwise, that being all women are good for."

"Do you know anything about the lover? He sounds mysterious, like the tutor who might have been Edith Wharton's father."

"I know the scuttlebutt. He was thin with glasses and buck teeth, and very sweet. He was an adjunct teacher in art history, which she dabbled in. I don't know what became of him. Gossip has it they used to walk around the campus holding hands. I feel sorry for her."

Kate was amazed, not for the first time, at the extent of her colleagues' interest in one another's lives. Richard was, of course, unofficial keeper of the gossip and since his heart was in the right place she was willing to decide that this was a valuable function. What Witherspoon would have thought of it was another question. Did she care what Witherspoon thought about anything, or only what he did?

What had he done, apart from being a failure as a human being and a father? Kate decided to walk for a while after bidding Richard a grateful farewell.

She wandered around the city streets, noticing dogs (no Jack Russell terriers) and the general air of menace which by now everyone in New York, and probably elsewhere, took for granted: it seemed the mark of an age. Compared to which, Kate told herself, the momentary absence of a dog was hardly to be counted. And yet that had been, somewhere along the family chain, a failure of trust which was how menace began. Was it Kant who said that trust was the basis of civilization?

Letting her attention wander unbidden over the cast of characters at that dinner, and in Richard's account of the Witherspoons, Kate found herself eventually at Central Park and East Seventy-second Street. She sat on a bench to observe the spot where Jasper had been tied when Arrie retrieved him. It was a well chosen location, easily approached and abandoned from four directions, sufficiently crowded with people and dogs entering and leaving the park to make one more man and dog unnoticed.

Man? A man had removed Jasper from the building, according to the doorman's report. Dogs were not allowed in the playground, so a number of them were tied to the entrance, waiting with accustomed patience or anxiety for their people on the other side of the fence. By the time Kate had to leave to meet her class, she had made up her mind.

"It is, of course, none of my business," Kate said to Roxanna as they had a drink before ordering their dinner. "That phrase is always a sign that someone thinks it is her business, or has determined to make it so. Do you mind?"

"Hardly," Roxanna said. "I used to wonder what it would be like to have dinner with Professor Fansler. Thank you for the privilege: my business is your business."

"Very graciously put. Perhaps you'd better order another drink."

"Oh, dear," Roxanna said.

"I intend nothing more sinister than blackmail," Kate said reassuringly.

"I know—on behalf of Arrie. Blackmail won't be necessary. From you, that is—I've already employed it on her behalf. Is that what you guessed?"

"It would hardly be fair to get you to tell me what happened and then claim to have guessed it all."

"Okay," Roxanna said. "You tell me. And I'll take that second drink. May I correct you as you go along?"

"Please do," Kate said. "My hope is that you'll end up assuring me about poor Jasper's safety."

Roxanna nodded.

"Your father, the revered Professor Witherspoon, has been after what money he can get out of your mother. Doubtless he has another young lady in tow. I say 'lady,' because I don't really think a *woman* would have anything to do with him. Did he try to retrieve from your mother something he had given her and now wanted to give to another? A ring? A brooch? It can't have been too big or Jasper wouldn't have swallowed it, however imbedded in a piece of meat. Although the way he gulps while dancing around on his hind legs, anything is possible."

"Not a ring," Roxanna said. "An emerald. He'd had it taken out of the ring and he was going to get it reset. It's the most valuable thing my mother had—it was in her family for years. They may have pawned it, but they never sold it."

"He pretended to her it needed to be reset?"

"Nothing so civilized. She would have been suspicious at any kindly offer, I'm afraid. He talked her out of taking it to the detoxification place, said it might be stolen. She didn't believe him, but when he put his mind on something she didn't have a chance. I heard them arguing about it one night. So did Desmond, the guy you met—he was there with me. He held me back from interfering and he was right."

"He's very handsome, even for an actor," Kate said.

"He's especially handsome for a lawyer, which is what he is," Roxanna responded. "We were trying to allay my father's suspicions. He knew we'd overheard him. So when he emerged that evening, we pretended innocence, on Desmond's advice, and I introduced him to Dad as an actor. His looks, as you observed, made that easy."

"I've lost count," Kate said, "but I don't think I'm doing too well. Shall we order dinner?"

"The details need cleaning up, but you certainly seem to be onto the main story line. Go on."

"There isn't much more. Somehow, later, needing to hide the stolen emerald, the professor fed it to Jasper. Anyone who observed Jasper's routine with Arrie would have thought of it, whether the motive was greed or detection. Was he going to kill the dog?"

"Of course. Or pay someone else to. Fortunately, I guessed what he was up to. I had caught him examining the stone. I demanded it and he wouldn't give it to me. Sometime later, he came in to promise me he wouldn't take it out of the house. There was something about the exact way he said it that made me suspicious. I pretended to calm down and then went to look for the stone. It wasn't where it was supposed to be. My father went into calm assurances that he didn't have it and hadn't hidden it, urging me to search him. He was smug about it! That, and the sight of Jasper dancing around, gave me the idea. He had fed it to the dog in a hunk of meat, intending to have the dog 'get lost.' When I figured this out, we really had a knockdown fight. I couldn't believe he'd really do that to Arrie."

"Where was Arrie?"

"Locked in the bathroom, crying. She hated the fights. She used to stuff her ears with toilet paper. He and I fought about a lot of things, though never as violently as this. In the end, I threatened him. You see, my mother had mentioned her ring when Arrie and I went to see her—she wanted Arrie to have it but Arrie said I should have it because I was beautiful. Mother hugged Arrie and said, 'You take care of Roxanna—it's far, far better not to be beautiful, believe me, my darling.'"

"And you got Desmond to leave with the dog under his arm. I gather Jasper had got to know him by now."

"Jasper takes a long time to get to know people well

enough to let people pick him up. He may be small, but he's tough. That was me."

"In drag?"

She nodded. "Great fun. I got the idea from Sherlock Holmes. 'My walking clothes,' Irene Adler called them. Desmond borrowed the suit for me from someone my size. The doorman didn't raise an eyebrow."

"So you took Jasper—where?"

"To Desmond's, where I stay most of the time. I walked him, and never have I used a pooper-scooper more diligently. At first we thought we'd keep him in, but poor Jasper is well trained. I tell you, retrieving that emerald from Jasper made me feel like someone in Dickens's *Our Mutual Friend*. I well remember you talking about that novel."

"You said you'd get the emerald back if he behaved?"

"More than behaved. I had Desmond as a witness and advisor. I said Arrie and Jasper were to live with me, that he was to give my mother a divorce under fair terms: he could keep the apartment, he had to continue to support Arrie till she finished her education, my mother was to get half his pension, and if he didn't agree I was going to drag him into court accused of theft and abusive conduct."

"And he bought it?"

"Not entirely. I had to give him the emerald and a few other things besides. But I figured I didn't need it and Arrie didn't need it. It hadn't done my mother much good—and it was worth her freedom and ours. I also told him I had a student lined up ready to bring charges of sexual harassment. I scared him. He even cooperated about Arrie's retrieving Jasper. I was going to make him leave the dog at the playground, but I didn't want him to take out his frustrations on the poor beast so I did that, too. Desmond came with me between two closings. Desmond's been great."

"He sounds rather unusual for a lawyer."

"He is. He's quitting. He says there's no point spending

your life suing about water damage and helping one firm take over another. I don't know what he's going to do."

"You might suggest acting," Kate said. "And being a waiter on the side."

"He's thinking of becoming a detective," Roxanna said. "A private eye. Perhaps he could get in touch with you for pointers."

Kate decided not to look for irony in this. "What next?" she asked.

"It's Arrie's vacation next week. We're going down with Desmond to visit my mom. I think with some real encouragement, and the knowledge that the professor is out of her life, she may actually make it. She never took up drinking or prescription drugs until she met him. But she's going to need a lot of help."

"Speaking of 'none of my business,'" Kate said, "may I ask an outrageous question? Just tell me to go to hell if you don't want to answer it. Is the professor Arrie's father or was there someone else?"

"I'll answer that question on one condition," Roxanna said. "That you agree to do me an enormous favor, no questions asked. Is it a bargain?"

"I'll have to think about it," Kate said. "I don't believe in blind promises."

"And I don't believe in gossip—not all of it. My mother did moon around with another guy. His main attraction was that he wasn't lustful. My father is very lustful. He insisted on his rights. That's how he thought of them—as rights. And he still wanted a son."

"You've been angry at him a long time, haven't you?" Kate said.

"I'm getting over it, with help. I don't want Arrie to go through the same thing. Of course, I couldn't have done it without Desmond—especially since the professor had that sleazy lawyer on his side. Mr. Johnson. You met him, too."

Kate looked into her coffee cup. "All right," she said. "It's a bargain."

Roxanna looked up questioningly.

"I'll keep Jasper for Arrie while she's gone. Reed will be overjoyed.—That is, I'll pretend we have him forever, and when he finds out it's only a week or so he'll be overjoyed."

"I think women are reprehensible," Roxanna said, "don't you?" And they laughed together. Kate even found herself wishing Arrie and Jasper had been there.

DEADLY FANTASIES

=======================================

by Marcia Muller

"Ms. McCone, I know what you're thinking. But I'm not paranoid. One of them—my brother or my sister—*is* trying to kill me!"

"Please, call me Sharon." I said it to give myself time to think. The young woman seated across my desk at All Souls Legal Cooperative certainly sounded paranoid. My boss, Hank Zahn, had warned me about that when he'd referred her for private investigative services.

"Let me go over what you've told me, to make sure I've got it straight," I said. "Six months ago you were living here in the Mission district and working as a counselor for emotionally disturbed teenagers. Then your father died and left you his entire estate, something in the neighborhood of thirty million dollars."

Laurie Newingham nodded and blew her nose. As soon as she'd come into my office she'd started sneezing. Allergies, she'd told me. To ease her watering eyes she'd popped out her contact lenses and stored them in their plastic case; in doing that she had spilled some of the liquid that the lenses soaked in over her fingers, then nonchalantly wiped them on her faded jeans. The gesture endeared her to me because I'm

217

sloppy, too. Frankly, I couldn't imagine this freshly scrubbed young woman—she was about ten years younger than I, perhaps twenty-five—possessing a fortune. With her trim, athletic body, tanned, snub-nosed face, and carelessly styled blonde hair, she looked like a high school cheerleader. But Winfield Newingham had owned much of San Francisco's choice real estate, and Laurie had been the developer's youngest—and apparently favorite—child.

I went on, "Under the terms of the will, you were required to move back into the family home in St. Francis Wood. You've done so. The will also stipulated that your brother Dan and sister Janet can remain there as long as they wish. So you've been living with them, and they've both been acting hostile because you inherited everything."

"Hostile? One of them wants to *kill* me! I keep having stomach cramps, throwing up—you know."

"Have you seen a doctor?"

"I *hate* doctors! They're always telling me there's nothing wrong with me, when I know there *is*."

"The police, then?"

"I like them a whole lot less than doctors. Besides, they wouldn't believe me." Now she took out an inhaler and breathed deeply from it.

Asthma, as well as allergies, I thought. Wasn't asthma sometimes psychosomatic? Could the vomiting and other symptoms be similarly rooted?

"Either Dan or Janet is trying to poison me," Laurie said, "because if I die, the estate reverts to them."

"Laurie," I said, "why did your father leave everything to you?"

"The will said it was because I'd gone out on my own and done something I believed in. Dan and Janet have always lived off him; the only jobs they've ever been able to hold down have been ones Dad gave them."

"One more question: Why did you come to All Souls?" My employer is a legal services plan for people who can't afford the going rates.

Laurie looked surprised. "I've *always* come here, since I moved to the Mission and started working as a counselor five years ago. I may be able to afford a downtown law firm, but I don't trust them any more now than I did when I inherited the money. Besides, I talked it over with Dolph, and he said it would be better to stick with a known quantity."

"Dolph?"

"Dolph Edwards. I'm going to marry him. He's director of the guidance center where I used to work—still work, as a volunteer."

"That's the Inner Mission Self-Help Center?"

She nodded. "Do you know them?"

"Yes." The center offered a wide range of social services to a mainly Hispanic clientele—including job placement, psychological counseling, and short term financial assistance. I'd heard that recently their programs had been drastically cut back due to lack of funding—as all too often happens in today's arid political climate.

"Then you know what my father meant about my having done something I believed in," Laurie said. "The center's a hopeless mess, of course; it's never been very well organized. But it's the kind of project I'd like to put my money to work for. After I marry Dolph I'll help him realize his dreams effectively—and in the right way."

I nodded and studied her for a moment. She stared back anxiously. Laurie was emotionally ragged, I thought, and needed someone to look out for her. Besides, I identified with her in a way. At her age I'd also been the cheerleader type, and I'd gone out on my own and done something I believed in, too.

"Okay," I said. "What I'll do is talk with your brother and sister, feel the situation out. I'll say you've applied for a volunteer position here, counseling clients with emotional problems, and that you gave their names as character references."

Her eyes brightened and some of the lines of strain

smoothed. She gave me Dan's office phone number and
Janet's private line at the St. Francis Wood house. Preparing
to leave, she clumsily dropped her purse on the floor. Then
she located her contact case and popped a lens into her
mouth to clean it; as she fitted it into her right eye, her foot
nudged the bag, and the inhaler and a bottle of time-release
vitamin capsules rolled across the floor. We went for them
at the same time, and our heads grazed each other's.

She looked at me apologetically. One of her eyes was
now gray, the other a brilliant blue from the tint of the
contact. It was like a physical manifestation of her somewhat schizoid personality: down-to-earth wholesomeness
warring with what I had begun to suspect was a dangerous
paranoia.

Dan Newingham said, "Why the hell does Laurie want to do
that? She doesn't have to work any more, even as a
volunteer. She controls all the family's assets."

We were seated in his office in the controller's department of Newingham Development, on the thirty-first floor
of one of the company's financial district buildings. Dan
was a big guy, with the same blond good looks as his sister,
but they were spoiled by a petulant mouth and a body whose
bloated appearance suggested an excess of good living.

"If she wants to work," he added, "there're plenty of
positions she could fill right here. It's her company now,
dammit, and she ought to take an interest in it."

"I gather her interests run more to the social services."

"More to the low life, you mean."

"In what respect?"

Dan got up and went to look out the window behind the
desk. The view of the bay was blocked by an upthrusting
jumble of steel and plate glass—the legacy that firms such
as Newingham Development had left a once old-fashioned
and beautiful town.

After a moment Dan turned. "I don't want to offend you,
Ms. . . . McCone, is it?"

I nodded.

"I'm not putting down your law firm, or what you're trying to do," he went on, "but when you work on your end of the spectrum, you naturally have to associate with people who aren't quite . . . well, of our class. I wasn't aware of the kind of people Laurie was associating with during those years she didn't live at home, but now . . . her boyfriend, that Dolph, for instance. He's always around; I can't stand him. Anyway, my point is, Laurie should settle down now, come back to the real world, learn the business. Is that too much to ask in exchange for thirty million?"

"She doesn't seem to care about the money."

Dan laughed harshly. "Doesn't she? Then why did she move back into the house? She could have chucked the whole thing."

"I think she feels she can use the money to benefit people who really need it."

"Yes, and she'll blow it all. In a few years there won't *be* any Newingham Development. Oh, I know what was going through my father's mind when he made that will: Laurie's always been the strong one, the dedicated one. He thought that if he forced her to move back home, she'd eventually become involved in the business and there'd be real leadership here. Laurie can be very single-minded when she wants things to go a certain way, and that's what it takes to run a firm like this. But the sad thing is, Dad just didn't realize how far gone she is in her bleeding heart sympathies."

"That aside, what do you think about her potential for counseling our disturbed clients?"

"If you really want to know, I think she'd be terrible. Laurie's a basket case. She has psychosomatic illnesses, paranoid fantasies. She needs counseling herself."

"Can you describe these fantasies?"

He hesitated, tapping his fingers on the window frame. "No, I don't think I care to. I shouldn't have brought them up."

"Actually, Mr. Newingham, I think I have an inkling of what they are. Laurie told her lawyer that someone's trying to poison her. She seemed obsessed with the idea, which is why we decided to check her references thoroughly."

"I suppose she also told her lawyer who the alleged poisoner is?"

"In a way. She said it was either you or your sister Janet."

"God, she's worse off than I realized. I suppose she claims one of us wants to kill her so he can inherit my father's estate. That's ridiculous—I don't need the damned money. I have a good job here, and I've invested profitably." Dan paused, then added, "I hope you can convince her to get into an intensive therapy program before she tries to counsel any of your clients. Her fantasies are starting to sound dangerous."

Janet Newingham was the exact opposite of her sister: a tall brunette with a highly stylized way of moving and speaking. Her clothes were designer, her jewelry expensive, and her hair and nails told of frequent attention at the finest salons. We met at the St. Francis Wood house—a great pile of stone reminiscent of an Italian villa that sat on a double lot near the fountain that crowned the area's main boulevard. I had informed Laurie that I would be interviewing her sister, and she had agreed to absent herself from the house; I didn't want my presence to trigger an unpleasant scene between the two of them.

I needn't have worried, however. Janet Newingham was one of those cool, reserved women who may smolder under the surface but seldom display anger. She seated me in a formal parlor overlooking the strip of park that runs down the center of St. Francis Boulevard and served me coffee from a sterling silver pot. From all appearances, I might have been there to discuss the Junior League fashion show.

When I had gotten to the point of my visit, Janet leaned forward and extracted a cigarette from an ivory box on the coffee table. She took her time lighting it, then said,

"*Another* volunteer position? It's bad enough she kept on working at that guidance center for nothing after they lost their federal funding last spring, but this . . . I'm surprised; I thought nothing would ever pry her away from her precious Dolph."

"Perhaps she feels it's not a good idea to stay on there, since they plan to be married."

"Did she tell you that? Laurie's always threatening to marry Dolph, but I doubt she ever will. She just keeps him around because he's her one claim to the exotic. He's one of these social reformers, you know. Totally devoted to his cause."

"And what is that?"

"Helping people. Sounds very sixties, doesn't it? That center is his *raison d'etre*. He founded it, and he's going to keep it limping along no matter what. He plays the crusader role to the hilt, Dolph does: dresses in Salvation Army castoffs, drives a motorcycle. You know the type."

"That's very interesting," I said, "but it doesn't have much bearing on Laurie's ability to fill our volunteer position. What do you think of her potential as a counselor?"

"Not a great deal. Oh, I know that's what she's been doing these past five years, but recently Laurie's been . . . a very disturbed young woman. But you know that. My brother told me of your visit to his office, and that you had already heard of her fantasy that one of us is trying to kill her."

"Well, yes. It's odd—"

"It's not just odd, it's downright dangerous. Dangerous for her to walk around in such a paranoid state, and dangerous for Dan and me. It's our reputations she's smearing."

"Because on the surface you both appear to have every reason to want her out of the way."

Janet's lips compressed—a mild reaction, I thought, to what I'd implied. "On the surface, I suppose that is how it looks," she said. "But as far as I'm concerned Laurie is welcome to our father's money. I had a good job in the public relations department in Newingham Development; I saved and invested my salary well. After my father died, I quit working there, and I'm about to open my own public relations firm."

"Did the timing of your quitting have anything to do with Laurie's inheriting the company?"

Janet picked up a porcelain ashtray and carefully stubbed her cigarette out. "I'll be frank with you, Ms. McCone: it did. Newingham Development had suddenly become not a very good place to work; people were running scared—they always do when there's no clear managerial policy. Besides . . ."

"Besides?"

"Since I'm being frank, I may as well say it. I did not want to work for my spoiled little bitch of a sister who's always had things her own way. And if that makes me a potential murderer—"

She broke off as the front door opened. We both looked that way. A man wearing a shabby tweed coat and a shocking purple scarf and aviator sunglasses entered. His longish black hair was windblown, and his sharp features were ruddy from the cold. He pocketed a key and started for the stairway.

"Laurie's not here, Dolph," Janet said.

He turned. "Where is she?"

"Gone shopping."

"Laurie hates to shop."

"Well, that's where she is. You'd better come back in a couple of hours." Janet's tone did little to mask her dislike.

Nor did the twist of his mouth mask *his* dislike of his fiancée's sister. Without a word he turned and strode out the door.

I said, "Dolph Edwards?"

"Yes. You can see what I mean."

Actually, I hadn't seen enough of him, and I decided to take the opportunity to talk to him while it was presented. I thanked Janet Newingham for her time and hurried out.

• • •

Dolph's motorcycle was parked at the curb near the end of the front walk, and he was just revving it up when I reached him. At first his narrow lips pulled down in annoyance, but when I told him who I was, he smiled and shut the machine off. He remained astride it while we talked.

"Yes, I told Laurie it would be better to stick with All Souls," he said when I mentioned the context in which I'd first heard of him. "You've got good people there, and you're more likely to take Laurie's problem seriously than some downtown law firm."

"You think someone *is* trying to kill her, then?"

"I know what I see. The woman's sick a lot lately, and those two—" he motioned at the house "—hate her guts."

"You must see a great deal of what goes on here," I said. "I noticed you have a key."

"Laurie's my fiancée," he said with a puritanical stiffness that surprised me.

"So she said. When do you plan to be married?"

I couldn't make out his eyes behind the dark aviator glasses, but the lines around them deepened. Perhaps Dolph suspected what Janet claimed: that Laurie didn't really intend to marry him. "Soon," he said curtly.

We talked for a few minutes more, but Dolph could add little to what I'd already observed about the Newingham family. Before he started his bike he said apologetically, "I wish I could help, but I'm not around them very much. Laurie and I prefer to spend our time at my apartment."

I didn't like Dan or Janet Newingham, but I also didn't believe either was trying to poison Laurie. Still, I followed up by explaining the situation to my former lover and now good friend Greg Marcus, lieutenant with the SFPD homicide detail. Greg ran a background check on Dan for me, and came up with nothing more damning than a number of unpaid parking tickets. Janet didn't even have those to her discredit. Out of curiosity, I asked him to check on Dolph

Edwards, too. Dolph had a record of two arrests involving political protests in the late seventies—just what I would have expected.

At that point I reported my findings to Laurie and advised her to ask her brother and sister to move out of the house. If they wouldn't, I said, she should talk to Hank about invalidating that clause of her father's will. And in any case she should also get herself some psychological counseling. Her response was to storm out of my office. And that, I assumed, ended my involvement with Laurie Newingham's problems.

But it didn't. Two weeks later Greg called to tell me that Laurie had been taken ill during a family cocktail party and had died at the St. Francis Wood house, an apparent victim of poisoning.

I felt terrible, thinking of how lightly I had taken her fears, how easily I'd accepted her brother and sister's claims of innocence, how I'd let Laurie down when she'd needed and trusted me. So I waited until Greg had the autopsy results and then went to the office at the Hall of Justice.

"Arsenic," Greg said when I'd seated myself on his visitor's chair. "The murderer's perfect poison: widely available, no odor, little if any taste. It takes the body a long time to eliminate arsenic, and a person can be fed small amounts over a period of two or three weeks, even longer, before he or she succumbs. According to the medical examiner, that's what happened to Laurie."

"But why small amounts? Why not just one massive dose?"

"The murderer was probably stupid enough that he figured if she'd been sick for weeks we wouldn't check for poisons. But why he went on with it after she started talking about someone trying to kill her . . ."

"He? Dan's your primary suspect, then?"

"I was using 'he' generically. The sister looks good, too. They both had extremely strong motives, but we're not going to be able to charge either until we can find out how Laurie was getting the poison."

"You say extremely strong motives. Is there something besides the money?"

"Something connected to the money; each of them seems to need it more badly than they're willing to admit. The interim management of Newingham Development has given Dan his notice; there'll be a hefty severance payment, of course, but he's deeply in debt—gambling debts, to the kind of people who won't accept fifty-dollars-a-week installments. The sister had most of her savings tied up in one of those real estate investment partnerships; it went belly up, and Janet needs to raise additional cash to satisfy outstanding obligations to the other partners."

"I wish I'd known about that when I talked with them. I might have prevented Laurie's death."

Greg held up a cautioning hand. "Don't blame yourself for something you couldn't know or forsee. That should be one of the cardinal rules of your profession."

"It's one of the rules, all right, but I seem to keep breaking it. Greg, what about Dolph Edwards?"

"He didn't stand to benefit by her death. Laurie hadn't made a will, so everything reverts to the brother and sister."

"No will? I'm surprised Hank didn't insist she make one."

"According to your boss, she had an appointment with him for the day after she died. She mentioned something about a change in her circumstances, so I guess she was planning to make the will in favor of her future husband. Another reason we don't suspect Edwards."

I sighed. "So what you've got is a circumstantial case against one of two people."

"Right. And without uncovering the means by which the poison got to her, we don't stand a chance of getting an indictment against either."

"Well . . . the obvious means is in her food."

"There's a cook who prepares all the meals. She, a live-in

maid, and the family basically eat the same things. On the night she died, Laurie, her brother and sister, and Dolph Edwards all had the same hors d'oeuvres with cocktails. The leftovers tested negative."

"And you checked what she drank, of course."

"It also tested negative."

"What about medications? Laurie probably took pills for her asthma. She had an inhaler—"

"We checked everything. Fortunately, I caught the call and remembered what you'd told me. I was more than thorough. Had the contents of the bedroom and bathroom inventoried, anything that could have contained poison was taken away for testing."

"What about this cocktail party? I know for a fact that neither Dan nor Janet liked Dolph. And according to Dolph, they both hated Laurie. He wasn't fond of them, either. It seems like an unlikely group for a convivial gathering."

"Apparently Laurie arranged the party. She said she had an announcement to make."

"What was it?"

"No one knows. She died before she could tell them."

Three days later Hank and I attended Laurie's funeral. It was in an old-fashioned churchyard in the little town of Tomales, near the bay of the same name northwest of San Francisco. The Newinghams had a summer home on the bay, and Laurie had wanted to be buried there.

It was one of those winter afternoons when the sky is clear and hard, and the sun is as pale as if it were filtered through water. Hank and I stood a little apart from the crowd of mourners on the knoll, near a windbreak of eucalyptus that bordered the cemetery. The people who had traveled from the city to lay Laurie to rest were an oddly assorted group: dark-suited men and women who represented San Francisco's business community; others who bore the unmistakable stamp of high society; shabbily dressed Hispanics who must have been clients of the Inner Mission

Self-Help Center. Dolph Edwards arrived on his motorcycle; his inappropriate attire—the shocking purple scarf
seemed several shades too festive—annoyed me.

Dan and Janet Newingham arrived in the limousine that
followed the hearse and walked behind the flower-covered
casket to the graveside. Their pious propriety annoyed me,
too. As the service went on, the wind rose. It rustled the
leaves of the eucalyptus trees and brought with it dampness
and the odor of the nearby sea. During the final prayer, a
strand of my hair escaped the knot I'd fastened it in and
blew across my face. It clung damply there, and when I
licked my lips to push it away, I tasted salt—whether from
the sea air or tears, I couldn't tell.

As soon as the service was concluded, Janet and Dan
went back to the limousine and were driven away. One of
the Chicana women stopped to speak to Hank; she was a
client; and he introduced us. When I looked around for
Dolph, I found he had disappeared. By the time Hank
finished chatting with his client, the only other person left at
the graveside besides us and the cemetery workers was an
old Hispanic lady who was placing a single rose on the
casket.

Hank said, "I could use a drink." We started down the
uneven stone walk, but I glanced back at the old woman,
who was following us unsteadily.

"Wait," I said to Hank and went to take her arm as she
stumbled.

The woman nodded her thanks and leaned on me,
breathing heavily.

"Are you all right?" I asked. "Can we give you a ride
back to the city?" My old MG was the only car left beyond
the iron fence.

"Thank you, but no," she said. "My son brought me. He's
waiting down the street, there's a bar. You were a friend of
Laurie?"

"Yes." But not as good a friend as I might have been, I
reminded myself. "Did you know her through the center?"

"Yes. She talked with my grandson many times and made him stay in school when he wanted to quit. He loved her, we all did."

"She was a good woman. Tell me, did you see her fiancé leave?" I had wanted to give Dolph my condolences.

The woman looked puzzled.

"The man she planned to marry—Dolph Edwards."

"I thought he was her husband."

"No, although they planned to marry soon."

The old woman sighed. "They were always together. I thought they were already married. But nowadays who can tell? My son—Laurie helped his own son, but is he grateful? No. Instead of coming to her funeral, he sits in a bar. . . ."

I was silent on the drive back to the city—so silent that Hank, who is usually oblivious to my moods, asked me twice what was wrong. I'm afraid I snapped at him, something to the effect of funerals not being my favorite form of entertainment, and when I dropped him at All Souls, I refused to have the drink he offered. Instead I went downtown to City Hall.

When I entered Greg Marcus's office at the Hall of Justice a couple of hours later, I said without preamble, "The Newingham case: you told me you inventoried the contents of Laurie's bedroom and bathroom and had anything that could have contained poison taken away for testing?"

". . . Right."

"Can I see the inventory sheet?"

He picked up his phone and asked for the file to be brought in. While he waited, he asked me about the funeral. Over the years, Greg has adopted a wait-and-see attitude toward my occasional interference in his cases. I've never been sure whether it's because he doesn't want to disturb what he considers to be my shaky thought processes, or that he simply prefers to leave the hard work to me.

When the file came, he passed it to me. I studied the

inventory sheet, uncertain exactly what I was looking for. But something was missing there. What? I flipped the pages, then wished I hadn't. A photo of Laurie looked up at me, brilliant blue eyes blank and lifeless. No more cheerleader out to save the world—

Quickly I flipped back to the inventory sheet. The last item was "1 handbag, black leather, & contents." I looked over the list of things from the bathroom again and focused on the word "unopened."

"Greg," I said, "what was in Laurie's purse?"

He took the file from me and studied the list. "It should say here, but it doesn't. Sloppy work—new man on the squad."

"Can you find out?"

Without a word he picked up the phone receiver, dialed, and made the inquiry. When he hung up he read off the notes he'd made. "Wallet. Checkbook. Inhaler, sent to lab. Vitamin capsules, also sent to lab. Contact lens case. That's all."

"That's enough. The contact lens case is a two-chambered plastic receptacle holding about half an ounce of fluid for the lenses to soak in. There was a brand-new, unopened bottle of fluid on the inventory of Laurie's bathroom."

"So?"

"I'm willing to bet the contents of that bottle will test negative for arsenic; the surface of it might or might not show someone's fingerprints, but not Laurie's. That's because the murderer put it there *after* she died, but *before* your people arrived on the scene."

Greg merely waited.

"Have the lab test the liquid in that lens case for arsenic. I'm certain the results will be positive. The killer added arsenic to Laurie's soaking solution weeks ago, and then he removed that bottle and substituted the unopened one. We wondered why slow poisoning, rather than a massive dose; it was because the contact case holds so little fluid."

"Sharon, arsenic can't be ingested through the eyes—"

"Of course it can't! But Laurie had the habit, as lots of contact wearers do—you're not supposed to, of course; it can cause eye infections—of taking her lenses out of the case and putting them into her mouth to clean them before putting them on. She probably did it a lot because she had allergies and took the lenses off to rest her eyes. That's how he poisoned her, a little at a time over an extended period."

"Dan Newingham?"

"No. Dolph Edwards."

Greg waited, his expression neither doubting nor accepting.

"Dolph is a social reformer," I said. "He funded that Inner Mission Self-Help Center; it's his whole life. But its funding has been cancelled and it can't go on much longer. In Janet Newingham's words, Dolph is intent on keeping it going 'no matter what.'"

"So? He was going to marry Laurie. She could have given him plenty of money—"

"Not for the center. She told me it was a 'hopeless mess.' When she married Dolph, she planned to help him, but in the 'right way.' Laurie has been described to me by both her brother and sister as quite single-minded and always getting what she wanted. Dolph must have realized that too, and knew her money would never go for his self-help center."

"All right, I'll take your word for that. But Edwards still didn't stand to benefit. They weren't married, she hadn't made a will—"

"They *were* married. I checked that out at City Hall a while ago. They were married last month, probably at Dolph's insistence when he realized the poisoning would soon have a fatal effect."

Greg was silent for a moment. I could tell by the calculating look in his eyes that he was taking my analysis seriously. "That's another thing we slipped up on—just like not listing the contents of her purse. What made you check?"

"I spoke with an old woman who was at the funeral. She

thought they were married and made the comment that nowadays you can't tell. It got me thinking. . . . Anyway, it doesn't matter about the will because under California's community property laws, Dolph inherits automatically in the absence of one."

"It seems stupid of him to marry her so soon before she died. The husband automatically comes under suspicion—"

"But the poisoning started long *before* they were married. That automatically threw suspicion on the brother and sister."

"And Dolph had the opportunity."

"Plenty. He even tried to minimize it by lying to me: he said he and Laurie didn't spend much time at the St. Francis Wood house, but Dan described Dolph as being around all the time. And even if he wasn't he could just as easily have poisoned her lens solution at his own apartment. He told another unnecessary lie to you when he said he didn't know what the announcement Laurie was going to make at the family gathering was. It could only have been the announcement of their secret marriage. He may even have increased the dosage of poison, in the hope she'd succumb before she could reveal it."

"Why do you suppose they kept it secret?"

"I think Dolph wanted it that way. It would minimize the suspicion directed at him if he just let the fact of the marriage come out after either Dan or Janet had been charged with the murder. He probably intended to claim ignorance of the community property laws, say he'd assumed since there was no will he couldn't inherit. Why don't we ask him if I'm right?"

Greg's hand moved toward his phone. "Yes—why don't we?"

When Dolph Edwards confessed to Laurie's murder, it turned out that I'd been absolutely right. He also added an item of further interest: he hadn't been in love with Laurie at all, had had a woman on the Peninsula whom he planned to marry as soon as he could without attracting suspicion.

It was too bad about Dolph; his kind of social crusader had so much ego tied up in their own individual projects that they lost sight of the larger objective. Had Laurie lived, she would have applied her money to any number of worthy causes, but now it would merely go to finance the lifestyles of her greedy brother and sister.

But it was Laurie I felt worst about. And it was a decidedly bittersweet satisfaction that I took in solving her murder, in fulfilling my final obligation to my client.

COP GROUPIE

===================================

by Joyce Harrington

"But what does it feel like?" she persisted. "What does it really feel like? To kill somebody?"

I looked up at her face then, at her bright, gleaming eyes, at her lips that shone in the gloom with something slick. Lip gloss, I think they call it. It's supposed to make them look sexy. Avid.

"It feels," I said, drawing the moment out, taking a mouthful of drink. It tasted like medicine, but I had no disease it could cure. "It feels like nothing at all, and that's the truth." And that was a lie. She didn't deserve better.

"You're kidding me," she said. "It's got to feel like something. Are you carrying a gun now?"

"Always. It's my wife, my mistress, my best friend. I guess that lets you out." I figured her for one who would rise to the bait.

"Show me," she whispered. "Let me hold it for a minute."

The bar was old and dark. We sat in a leatherette booth with the air conditioning making eddies of chill around our ankles and our glasses sweating clear puddles onto the red Formica tabletop. She'd come in when I was about two drinks along and eyed me from the bar until I waved her over.

"Have another drink?" I asked her, and finished mine off. She was drinking gin and orange juice, a combination only a mother could love. Mine had, until the day she died.

This one called herself Rusty. She had red hair. It might even have been her own, bright carrot under bright lights, veering toward purple in the shadows that clustered around the booth.

I got up and went to the bar. It was a carry-your-own kind of place. No waitress. Not many customers either. Just some of the neighborhood old faithful clustered at the end where the television muttered a baseball game. It wasn't my neighborhood or my baseball game. Just a hot night in August when prowling the streets felt better than lying in bed, staring at the dark and trying not to think.

The bartender sloshed the drinks down in front of me and waited, incurious, for my money. I paid him, and left a chintzy tip in the spilled orange juice. It's only a mood, I told myself, you'll get over it. You'll feel better very soon now.

"So, tell me about yourself," I said, sliding back into the booth. I could have told her her life story. She probably could have told me mine, if she thought about it at all. And the two wouldn't have been so different.

When she got to the failed marriage part, and the kid who was living with her mother, she was ready for another drink.

"I'm buying this time," she said, "and then you can tell me what made you decide to be a cop."

She made a detour to the ladies' room on her way to the bar and I tinkered with the idea of walking out. It was the right thing to do. But as my mother always said, "Mikey, knowing the right thing is easy. It's doing it that's hard."

She came back, teetering a little in her high-heeled sandals, carrying a little bag of Cheez Doodles along with the drinks. "I wouldn't trust the food in this place. I peeked in the kitchen. What a pigpen!"

"People don't come here to eat," I said. "You hungry?"

"A little," she said.

I willed her to take the thought further and invite me up to her place. She didn't. "We can go someplace," I prompted.

"Maybe," she said. "Later. First, tell me what makes a guy like you take a job that pays you peanuts for risking your neck every day of your life." She sipped daintily at her drink, every inch a lady, but her eyes were unfocused.

I laughed. It was my bitter, rueful laugh number three. Not too bitter, only slightly rueful, with just a hint of self-deprecation. "My old man," I muttered, staring down at my knuckles. One of them had an old scab on it, almost ready to fall off. From the last time I'd had to get tough with someone. "My old man, he was a cop. Not a very good cop, or a smart one. I guess it runs in the family."

"Following in his footsteps, huh?" She was nodding as if she understood. "Only doing it your way. Better. You'll show him."

What could she understand? Nothing. Nada. Zilch. None of them would. Correction. None of them had. So here we go again, Mikey, lad.

I raised my head and looked around the bar. It looked familiar, but I couldn't remember if I'd ever been here before. There are hundreds, thousands of these dingy, evil-smelling neighborhood saloons all over the city. They take their flavor from their location—Irish, Italian, black, Hispanic—but they all seemed to have grown out of the hard sidewalks and the hard thirsts of the clientele. I ought to know. My old man had a thirst like a pile driver after they booted him off the force. He died in a booth just like the one we were sitting in. Could have been the same one for all I know. I was away at the time, on the road, seeing the great U.S. of A. and trying to figure out if there was some place in it for me.

I guess there is. And I guess I'm sitting in it.

"You're not very talkative." She'd polished off the Cheez

Doodles and was licking the yellow off her fingers, one by one. Trying to be provocative.

"Nothing much to tell. Ah, Christ! Let's get out of here. This place gives me the creeps."

"Me too," she said, gathering up her shoulder bag. She was wearing one of those short, tight skirts that clung to her rump and thighs like a second skin as far as it went before the real skin took over. A cropped sleeveless blouse left a stretch of tanned midsection bare to the night breeze. If there'd been a breeze. I walked behind her to the door, watching her haunches sway from side to side. Her blouse was almost sheer, and there weren't any bra straps showing through. She might as well have been naked, the bitch.

Outside, on the sidewalk, she looked both ways up and down the deserted street. "Maybe we should have called for a cab," she murmured, nervously. "We'll never find one here."

"Don't worry," I told her. "I've got my car. It's parked right down that alley." I nodded toward a narrow stretch of deep night between two shuddered industrial buildings across the street.

She smiled up at me. "I don't know why I'm being such a chicken," she murmured coyly. "I guess it's all those women you read about in the newspapers. How many have there been now? Five?"

"Six," I told her. And it was only partly a lie. Soon there would be six. "You shouldn't be out by yourself at night. Talking to strangers."

She shrugged, and her cropped blouse lifted to show the roundness of heavy breasts. "What can happen to me? I'm with a cop. You should try staying home alone, night after night. You could go bonkers."

So. She lived alone and didn't like it. Time for the direct approach. "You got anything to eat at your place? Like you said, on a job that pays peanuts, there's not much left over for elegant restaurant dining."

She frowned, but I could tell it was a pretense. "I really

shouldn't," she said. "What if you're not a cop after all? What if you're the one who's been cutting up all those girls?"

I pulled out my badge. "Show you my gun, too," I offered. "I'll even let you hold it. But not right here."

She guffawed. "I bet you will. I just bet you will."

She took my arm and let me guide her across the street and into the alley. As the darkness enveloped us, she pressed closer to my side. She was small. The top of her head barely reached my shoulder. And she was trembling.

"Don't be frightened," I whispered, bending low to nibble at her ear.

She jumped as if I'd bitten a chunk out of it. "Don't do that!" she squealed. But she clung closer to my side and when we reached my car, she got in quickly and locked the door.

She felt safe with me. And why not? A cop is supposed to protect dumb little bimbos from their own stupidity. Not to mention, they think cops are sexy as hell. That's why so many of them are cop groupies. That's why it's so easy to go home with them.

Her refrigerator held leftover Chinese food, a package of Devil Dogs, and a few lonesome eggs. I started whipping up an omelet using the tired shrimp and broccoli as a filling. She put some water on to boil for instant coffee.

"I never would have thought of doing that," she said of the omelet. "I'm not much of a cook. Usually, I eat at the restaurant where I work, but today was my day off."

While I was cooking and she was in the bathroom repairing her makeup, I checked out the kitchen drawers. It's always better to use one of their own knives. No need to dump it afterwards. No possibility of tracing it.

Nothing but a dime-store utility knife, none too sharp. But it would do.

The omelet was done and she was still in the bathroom. I'd let her eat first, tell her cop stories. That always got them excited. Then, when she couldn't wait to get her clothes off . . .

I knocked on the bathroom door. "Food's ready," I called out.

"Be right there," she answered.

And right there she was. Wearing a whore's delight of a negligee, red satin and lace with little black ribbons all over it. Some kind of heavy perfume that almost made me choke. This one was just asking for it. Well, I sure don't like to disappoint a lady.

I goggled at her and gave a long, low whistle. The expected response. She simpered at me. "You like?"

"I like a lot," I told her. "Maybe we should just forget about the omelet."

"Not a chance," she said. "I really am starving. It'd be real unromantic if my stomach started growling. Besides, I want to hear more about your adventures."

She actually said that. Adventures. Oh, Rusty, you little slut, could I tell you adventures! Things you'd really get off on. How I cut up those other five. How they begged me to stop. The things they offered to do if I would only not hurt them. They didn't understand that it's not sex. It's more of a clean-up action. Getting the trash off the streets. The human trash.

We sat down opposite each other on folding chairs at her little card table. Genteel as all get out, with a white tablecloth and mismatched china. The knife handy to cut up a half loaf of not quite fresh Italian bread.

She had put a tape in the cassette player. Somebody moaning about the woman he had always dreamed of. Her idea of music to screw around by. So predictable. This one was going to be easy. No sweat. In fact, it was all getting to be too easy. Not satisfying. Maybe it was time to broaden the hunting ground. Go for a higher class clientele. Think about it.

She was saying something. "Sorry," I said. "I was thinking about the case I'm working on."

"I said the omelet is very good. Aren't you going to have some?"

I chuckled. That always disarms them. "Sometimes I forget to eat. When I'm working or when I'm having a good time."

"So what case are you working on? Or can you tell? I don't want to hear any secret stuff."

Not much you don't. "Don't worry. I won't tell you anything that hasn't been in the papers already. I'm working on the stabbing of all those girls." That was no lie. "I guess I should say women, but a couple of them were just teenagers. It's disgusting the way they were cut up."

"Now don't go getting gruesome on me. I get enough bad dreams about it already."

I picked up the knife and hacked off a chunk of bread. "The killer used ordinary kitchen knives, just like this one."

She stifled a little shriek and swallowed hard at the food in her mouth. "Let's talk about something else," she whispered.

"No," I said. "I can't. This is what I live with. Day and night. I thought maybe you could take my mind off it."

She stared at me for a long moment, then murmured, "Heavy. Very heavy." She took hold of my hand, right hand, knife hand, and stroked it. Drew faint white lines on it with her pointed red nails. "Lighten up, Mike," she whispered. "This is supposed to be fun."

Still holding my hand, she drew me out of my chair and curled herself into my body. I put one arm, left arm, around her and held her close. Kissed her long and deep. And all the while my right hand was finding the knife on the table behind me, getting just the right grip on it. The only question that remained was whether to do it here or in the bedroom. She answered it for me.

With her lips locked on mine, she started swaying and guiding me toward the open bedroom door. I let her move me, inching backward while her body pressed urgently against me. Ah, Rusty, soon, soon you'll be free of all this.

You'll be purified. And you'll thank me for returning you to innocence.

The light in the bedroom was dim, the bed a gaudy display of lavender satin with a huge white teddy bear propped against the pillows. She broke away from me to fling herself on it and bury her face in the bear's synthetic fur. "I hope you don't think I make a habit of this," she whispered. "I really like you, Mike." The bed had a headboard—brass rails. Perfect.

"And I like you, Rusty. More than you know." The knife was hidden behind my back. I sat down on the bed and slipped it beneath one of the pillows. I got out the handcuffs, both sets.

She sat up when she heard their metallic rattle. She held the teddy bear in front of her, as if it could protect her.

"Oh no you don't," she said. "No kinky stuff. I don't care if you are a cop."

"But, Rusty, I'm not a cop now. I'm off duty. And you'll enjoy this. I promise." I flatter myself that I can be very persuasive. Some of the others had been reluctant, but I'd been able to win them over with promises of things they had never experienced. I wasn't lying to them.

But she was stubborn. And she was becoming suspicious. "I think you'd better go now," she said. Her grip on the bear had tightened and she was trembling. "I think you aren't a cop at all. I think you really are the one who's been killing all those girls."

I had to laugh. She was so serious, so scared. "And what if I told you I am? What would you do then?"

"Are you?" Her voice was weak. Her eyes filmed over with fear.

"Of course I am, Rusty. And since you've been so clever, I'm going to make sure you have the experience of a lifetime. And there's not a thing you can do about it." I reached for her arm with one set of handcuffs ready to snap closed.

"Oh, isn't there?" The gun appeared out of nowhere, or

rather out of the back of the teddy bear. "For one thing, I'm a police officer. And for another, I'm placing you under arrest."

"A decoy! Rusty, you should be ashamed of yourself." I was well within my rights to scold her. She looked and behaved like a whore. No self-respecting police officer should do that. Besides, my father always said they should never have allowed women on the force.

They took women on, but they wouldn't take me. Some bullshit about an old drug bust. I had to pretend, with a fake badge and a real gun. And the real gun was in my hand, aimed at Rusty's head. "You can shoot me," I told her. "But not before I get one off. At this range it'll be quick but it won't be pretty. I'd much rather take it slow and easy. The way I did with the others. Who knows? I might even let you live. Now, be a good girl and put that gun down!" The last was a shout. That was a mistake. It's always a mistake to lose control.

"Do you really think I'm here alone, without a backup?" she asked. "Do you think we don't know who you are, Mikey? We've been following you for weeks, ever since the last one. She lived long enough to tell us about a cop whose father was a cop. The same story you told me. She gave us a pretty good description. Poor kid, she didn't know what a phony you are. A nut case."

"You lie! She was dead!" Calm down, I told myself. This is not the way. The correct way is to remain calm and in charge.

But I really didn't want to shoot Rusty. There's no satisfaction in that. And I didn't care if she shot me. That was my great strength. That, and knowing that she'd rather make the collar than bring in a corpse. I reached again for her arm. She backed away and got off the bed.

"It was one of your father's old buddies who told us about you," she said. "He told us you were always doing weird things when you were a kid. Killing stray cats. Setting fires. Broke your mother's heart and drove your father to drink.

That's what he said. Always hanging around the precinct, making a pest of yourself. I remember his exact words. 'It's a damn good thing they didn't let him join. The guy's a looney.' Did you do those things, Mikey?"

"So what if I did? What are you trying to do? Make me believe I'm nuts? Think I'm going to break down and start feeling sorry for myself? Not a hope! I know what I'm doing, and I've wasted enough time listening to you. It's your call, Rusty, or whatever your name is. Either I blow your head off now, or you give me your gun and let me get on with it. Don't you see there's no way out of it?"

"Okay, guys," she called out. "I think we've got enough now."

The closet door opened and suddenly the room was full of large men with grim faces and drawn revolvers. I raised my own gun to my head but Rusty was on me like a pit bull, leaping over the bed, snarling and spitting. The gun went flying. I tried to dive for the knife under the pillow, but she kneed me in the groan and I bent double. And all the while the smell of her cheap perfume was in my nostrils.

The most embarrassing thing was that they cuffed me with my own handcuffs. And thought it was a big joke. One of them called me a cop groupie. They all laughed at that. Even Rusty. Too bad. I was really getting to like her. She would have been the best of them.

MATCH POINT IN BERLIN

::

by Patricia McGerr

Selena sat in the restaurant at Templehof Airport and decided to treat herself to a fancy pastry as her last memento of Berlin. The delicately flaked dough with its rich topping of whipped cream seemed somehow to symbolize the life to which she was returning. In June she had graduated from Vassar—Class of '55. In October she was to be married. The summer's tour of Europe had been a final fling before settling down with the well-bred pleasant young man of whom her parents so thoroughly approved. They would slide into the social rounds of Washington's bright younger set whose major anxiety was the proper chilling of wines and the harmonious blending of dinner guests. Life with Raymond would be a good life, easy, comfortable, sheltered. And oh, so unexciting.

Stop it! She pulled herself back from the edge of melancholy. It's the letdown of being at journey's end. Plus perhaps a slight case of pre-bridal jitters. She checked her watch: 7:40. They had told her when she arrived at the airport for the New York flight that there would be about an hour's delay in takeoff. So there were twenty minutes left to drink her coffee, eat her pastry, and say goodbye to adventure.

Her eyes went to the entryway where a young man was just coming in. Tall, lean-faced, rangy, he wasn't exactly awkward, yet his arms and legs seemed to move on not quite the same wave length. So different from Raymond, she thought involuntarily, with his neat precise movements, all so coordinated and so easy to classify. The stranger's face was serious, even set; yet seeing the deep clefts in each cheek she felt she knew how he would look when he smiled.

I'd like to know him, she told herself, and then, as his eyes seemed about to meet hers, she turned sharply away, with a vague sense of disloyalty to Raymond. She fixed her gaze on the pastry tray, which was only a few tables away, studying it as if all her hope of heaven depended on a right choice between Schillerlocken and Buttercremetorte. So intense was her concentration that she didn't see the small shabby man until he was beside her.

"Excuse, fraulein." His English was accented but fluent. "You are American, no?" The question was rhetorical. He slid into the other chair as he spoke. It was only when he was seated that she became aware—from his short quick breaths, the whiteness of his knuckles as he gripped the table edge—that this was no ordinary encounter; not a pickup, not a beggar, not a peddler. This was a man under shattering tension, a man ripped apart by terror.

"Fraulein." He leaned close to her. "I must speak quickly. It is necessary they see me talk with American. I have a list. It is important. It belongs to the Party. And it is trusted to me to deliver to our leader. But they say I am not loyal. They say I will sell this list to the Americans. This is not true. I sell nothing. All I have—" his clenched fist beat against his heart "—all I am is for the Party. But one accused me and they do not let me explain. They come in the night to kill me before I can sell the list. It is the names of those who work for the Party, those who are true and those who betray us. You understand?"

"No." Selena shook her head.

"No matter. It is necessary only they see me talk to you and see me give you something. So long they know I have the list, they think only to kill me before I can sell it. They give me no time to talk, to explain. But when they think I have deliver it already, they will not be in so much hurry to kill me. They will wish to have me alive, to take me to the leader and tell what I have done. Then I can give to him the list and prove that I am always loyal. So please to put your hands on the table, fraulein."

Instinctively she obeyed and his hand moved with snake-like speed to place in hers a small oblong box.

"Now put it quickly away," he ordered.

"But I—this list—I don't—"

"Quick, fraulein, bitte!" His tone was so urgent that she transferred the box to her purse and snapped it shut.

"Now is all right." His tension went out in a long slow breath. "They have seen. They think it is too late to stop me selling. They bring me now to the leader."

"But what have you given me? I don't want—"

"Nothing, fraulein. I give you nothing. The box with the list is here." He slapped his palm on his vest pocket. "When I go to the leader I give it to him and he knows Stanovski is loyal. What I give you is a box of matches, a box of matches only. But they will think it is the box with the list for long enough to save my life."

"But if it's so important—to both sides—and they think I have it—" He was rising to leave. She clutched his sleeve. "I mean, if they'd kill you for it, they might—"

"To you, fraulein, they can do nothing. With me it is different. Something happens on a dark street to me, one of their own people. I disappear, who cares? But you are American. You are here in the light with many people. Very soon you walk on your plane and then you are back in your own country. No one can hurt you. Besides in fifteen minutes, maybe less, I give the list to the leader and everyone knows you have nothing. Only a box of matches, fraulein. When I am gone you will use them to light your cigarettes and when you strike them you will remember that you have saved a life." He stood, heels close together, and made a formal bow. "Wiedersehen, fraulein."

She watched him walk, almost jauntily, to the exit. Two men met him there and they exchanged greetings. To a casual observer it might have been a reunion of old friends. But there was something in the eyes of the other two, something in the way they arranged themselves on each side, so close that he might almost be lifted between them, that was like an icy finger on Selena's spine. The little man, she realized, was an enemy agent, carrying information valuable to the other side. Yet watching him, so small and helpless between his two allies, she felt glad that he still had his precious list, glad he would be able to prove himself "loyal."

The waitress approached and cut off her view of the door. She looked blankly at the tray that had seemed, only a few minutes ago, so enticing—the thick chocolate, the gooey pineapple, the vivid cherry-and-banana.

"No," she said vaguely. "No, thank you."

Somehow she had lost her taste for pastry.

Instead she poured her second cup of coffee, reached into her purse for the cigarette that would, she hoped, be a sedative for her quaking nerves. Ordinarily the waiter would have been quick to light it, but now he was deep in argument with the pastry girl, presumably trying to explain why he had summoned her to serve cake to a lady who wanted none.

So Selena fumbled for and found her newest acquisition. It was, the little man said, a matchbox, just like the other boxes she had been buying for ten pfennigs all through Germany. She pushed it open and reached for a match.

But there were none. The box was empty. No, not empty. Only empty of matches. The panel slid a little way and stuck. And what made it stick was a thin strip of microfilm.

The list! Stanovski's list! In his fear and agitation he had reached into the wrong pocket, passed over the wrong box. Now he had nothing to give his leader, no way to prove his loyalty. He had delivered the list to an American. Who would ever believe he had done it by mistake? Or believing, make any differentiation between error and betrayal? The grim faces of his companions rose freezingly before her. And the leader, she thought, would be grimmer still. Unhappy little man.

But now—she pressed the box shut, thrust it back into her purse, and suddenly had sympathy only for herself. Now I have the list. I'm marked with having it. It was delivered to me with almost a blare of trumpets. And if those men were sent to take their colleague, dead or alive, to the leader, are there not others charged with—at any cost—recovering this filmstrip?

She glanced around the restaurant. It was full of people and none of them was looking at her. Yet it seemed—was it only her imagination?—that many eyes had dropped, turned aside, just before she looked their way. She stared through the distant glass wall into the dark. Out there was the runway down which her plane would come. She strained toward it, toward the safety of that cabin rising into the sky.

The American Embassy, she thought. No, that's in Bonn. In Berlin it's the United States Mission. They would want this list. I must take it to them. But to get up from the table, find a telephone, try to locate someone at the Mission and explain what she had—it was too much for her. You're safe here, Stanovski had said. Here there was light, there were people, and she couldn't bring herself to leave it for the unknown that might be just outside the door. I can't be a heroine, she decided. My best hope is to stay in this public place until my plane is announced. I'll turn the film over to the authorities when I'm safely in New York.

So Selena sat and sipped her coffee and planned to thrust herself into the very center of the group that would move through the exit to the field and onto the plane.

At last it came—the announcement for which she was waiting. "Achtung," and the loudspeaker and went on in German of which she caught the names of Hamburg, London, and New York, so she knew it was her flight being reported. But as the announcement continued, a dismayed murmuring rose from the people who understood it. More delay, Selena realized, and wondered how she could get through another half hour or more with the matchbox hotter in her purse than if all its original contents had been ablaze.

"Attention," said the loudspeaker and she learned forward to concentrate on the English translation. With each word her heart sank nearer to despair. Unfavorable weather conditions. Flight canceled. No more planes would take off from Berlin that night.

Around her the murmurs were tinged with irritation, anger, disgust. But Selena felt only numbness, as if a nightmare had taken hold and none of this could be real. There was no safe cabin to walk to, no plane to lift her high above danger. There was only darkness and fog and evil.

Around her people gathered up their wraps and bags, preparatory to returning to their homes and hotels for the night. These were people who would be inconvenienced, missing business appointments or social engagements, because of the canceled flight.

But I—Selena pressed her purse tightly against her stomach—I have no urgent appointments. An overnight delay will make no great difference. I have nothing to lose—nothing but my life.

A few people lingered to finish their coffee or dessert. Soon they would leave. The restaurant would close. The airport would be deserted. Then what would she do? Find a cab, go to a hotel, spend the night in Berlin. How far, she wondered almost with detachment, will I get? Will they wait till I'm well away from the airport or will it happen as soon as I step into the cab? When? And how?

If she could get to the airport authorities, tell them her story, perhaps they could protect her. But the reservation desk seemed an impossible distance away. Beyond the restaurant entry was a smaller room with tables and chairs in it and a place to check coats and hats. There might be people in this smaller room and there might not. Beyond the room was a broad expanse of corridor with doors opening from it that led—she didn't know where. To pass alone through all that empty space—no, it wasn't possible.

But there must be some way. Some help. All these people. I can't let them get away. If only I could speak a little of the language. Yet even if I did, how would I choose between a German who might befriend me and one of those who are waiting for me? How can I know whom to trust?

Once more she surveyed the restaurant. How, she asked herself, do you recognize an American? It's unfair, when everyone can tell I'm one, that I can't work it in reverse. In spy novels we give ourselves away by switching the fork from left hand to right after cutting our meat. But no one here is eating meat. And I've never heard of a distinctively American way of stirring coffee.

Behind her, a table nearby but out of range of her vision, a voice was raised to ask the waiter for the check. A clipped British voice with an imperious accent that assumed everyone everywhere must speak his language. An Englishman! She twisted in her chair till she could see him. A comfortable, middle-aged, Colonel Blimp-type Englishman. So it's all right. I'll tell him what's happened, he'll take me to the American consul and—but no.

Before she moved she tried to compose her thoughts. Better not run to him with a wild tale of spies. He'll think I'm mad and it will give me completely away to whoever's watching. Instead I'll go calmly to his table and say that I'm alone in Berlin and need an escort back to my hotel. Then, once we're safely away from the airport, I'll tell him the story.

She rose and held tightly to the chair to steady herself till the weakness was gone from her knees. Then she turned. Colonel Blimp was counting Deutchesmarks into the waiter's palm. But she hardly noticed the Englishman. For at the table behind and on the other side of hers was the young man she had seen earlier. And he was reading the European edition of the *New York Herald Tribune*. Reading the comics! So he was certainly an American. She wanted to shout the word aloud like a hymn. An American!

She almost ran to his table and the speech she had prepared for the Englishman tumbled from her lips.

"I'm an American and my flight home's been canceled. I'm all alone in Berlin and I—"

"Not any more you're not alone," he broke in cheerfully.

"You're with Simon Mead now and there's not a better handler of damsels-in-distress on the whole continent than Simon Mead—especially when they're cuddly green-eyed damsels with raven distresses. Sit down, we'll have a little drink and then fly out under our own power."

She took the chair he pushed out, but she felt a stabbing disappointment. When he came in, she thought, he looked so sturdy, so competent, so able to cope with any emergency. Why must he turn out to be so hearty and clownish?

"I don't want a drink," she said. "I don't want to stay here."

"Sure you don't," he agreed. "Nothing deader than an airport when the fog closes in. The fun and games all went thataway. So we'll go after them. I'll tell you where we're going to start." His voice dropped to a confidential whisper as if they were already alone in a candlelit room. "The Zigeuner Keller of the Haus Wien. Know what that means? The gypsy cellar of the Vienna café. And it lives up to its name. Music that will break your heart and goulash that will ruin your stomach. Then from there—"

"I don't want to go to a night club," she protested. "I thought maybe you could take me someplace quiet and—"

"Ah!" His breath came out on a long rollicking note and ended in a whistle. "Know something, kiddo, I had you pegged all wrong. I was sitting here thinking you were my kind of dish, but I said to myself, uh-hunh, that's an icicle, go up and you'll get the refrigerator door smack in your face. So I sit tight and you come to me. That's the kind of mistake I like to make."

"But I—"

"Don't worry, kiddo, if it's a quiet time you want, Mrs. Mead's boy Simon is for you. I've a nice cozy room, they'll send up some champagne, and we'll have ourselves a ball. Maybe you know my hotel?" Again his voice was caressingly low. "The Am Zoo. Funny name, huh? Means it's by the zoo. So you can listen to the lions roar outside and the wolf purr inside. How about that?" A grin creased his face, just the way she'd expected it would, but the sight gave her no satisfaction.

He rose and with a hand under her arm helped her from her seat and started toward the door. Unhappily, she let herself be drawn along, though only the memory of the perilous matchbox in her bag kept her from pulling away from him. His conversation, as they threaded their way through the other tables, continued to be loud, jovial, suggestive. But as they passed the entry there was a sudden change. His grin faded, his voice dropped, and there was left no trace of heartiness.

"I'll take them off your hands now," he said briskly. "Our friend's matches."

"You—" She pulled her arm free. So he was one of Them. Or one of Us. In that instant she didn't care which. All that mattered was that he wanted the list and she wanted to get rid of it. The film had been forced on her. She had no responsibility for it, no ability to keep it safe. Let this man have it. And, more important, let everyone know he had it.

She half turned back into the restaurant. Look at me, she wanted to shout. Whoever you are, wherever you are, look at me. She fumbled in her purse, held the little box conspicuously aloft, and jabbed it toward her companion. See that. It was half a prayer. You must have seen that. I've given it away. I don't have it any more.

Her palm met his briefly as she pressed the box into it. He

looked a little startled at the suddenness of her move but accepted the box and reached again for her arm.

"No," she said inanely. "I haven't finished my coffee. You go on. I'll stay here."

"Yeah?" He frowned, shrugged, was again the falsely jolly pickup. "Okay, this party was your idea, so you can call it off."

He swaggered away from her and disappeared into the room beyond. She walked back to her table, past Colonel Blimp who was stuffing his wallet into his pocket while he moved toward the exit. No need to speak to him now, she thought. I'm free of the list, free of danger. Yet the relief she should have felt was somehow missing.

The waiter hurried forward with her forgotten check. As she paid it and waited for her change, there was a commotion in the corridor, the sound of running feet and rising voices. No, she denied her fears. No, it's nothing to do with me. I can't go out there. Whatever's happening, I must stay here. But she ran, stumbling in her haste, to the door, past the checkroom, into the lobby where a chattering crowd had collected.

"What is it?" She seized the arm of the nearest man. "What's happened?"

He answered with a flow of German and she moved frantically on. Finally, near the outside exit, she found a woman who could speak English.

"The young man—the American—he has attack—a fainting fit. He falls and hits his head on the hard floor. But he has good luck that his friend is doctor. He takes him now to hospital."

"No!" Selena's agonized cry brought her only the curious glances of the nearest spectators. She pushed through them till she was at the door and could look out the glass into an open cab where Simon Mead's long form, limp now, his head dangling, was supported by a black-coated stranger.

"Stop!" She hurled herself past the obstructing bodies,

out onto the sidewalk. "That's not a doctor. He has no friend."

But the cab was already moving and gaining speed. The crowd was breaking up, its moment of drama ended, returning to its own concerns.

"Stop them," she said again without much hope and no one paid any attention. The cab reached the first bend in the drive, and would soon be out of sight.

I did this, she told herself, and the thought was a jagged wound. With my flaunting of the matchbox, my shoving it into his hand, I marked him for Them. Because I was afraid, I delivered him into their hands, sent him to—She couldn't finish the thought. She had to act.

Another car was at the curb, with an elderly couple inside giving instructions to a uniformed chauffeur. Selena pulled open the door, scrambled in, and almost onto the astonished owner's lap.

"Follow them!" The words took most of her remaining strength. "Follow that cab."

The man, his wife, and their driver stared at her in bewilderment. They say all Europe is corrupted with our American gangster movies, she thought bitterly, so that's a phrase they ought to understand. But they looked at her blankly, waiting courteously for some explanation of this wild American intrusion. And now the cab had vanished into the night. Only its license number, memorized without conscious volition, remained imprinted on her brain. Simon Mead was gone, he was helpless, and there was nothing more she could do.

But there must be. Her mind went back to those few minutes at his table. He had acted so well the part of brainless masher. He had talked a lot of nonsense. But he was there with a purpose, so his talk must have had a purpose too. He had told her his name, repeated it several times so she was sure to remember. And he had told her—what else? The name of his hotel.

Again his voice came back and the lowering of its tone

took on new significance. He was giving her information
that no one else should hear, telling her where help might be
found. But she, filled with her own fears, had not listened
carefully. Now she tried vainly to remember. It was her only
hope. His only hope. She had to recall the hotel name.
Something—yes, something about wolves and lions.

"Take me," she said to the driver, "to the zoo."

He looked past her at his employer. She turned to the old
man.

"A hotel," she begged, "near the zoo." She tried various
combinations. "Zoo Hotel? Hotel Zoo?"

"Hotel Am Zoo?" The woman supplied the name and
Selena nodded gratefully.

"Hotel Am Zoo," she repeated. "Oh, hurry, please!"

The man and woman looked at her, spoke gently to each
other. They could see she was in trouble, perhaps ill,
certainly hysterical. Short of physical ejection, there was no
way to get rid of her. That must have been their conclusion,
for the man turned at last to the driver and spoke a command
that contained the words "Hotel Am Zoo" and Selena
relaxed a little as the car got under way.

But only for a moment. Where was Simon now? What
were they doing to him? Would they take the list and let him
go? Or would they— Again her mind veered from inevitable conclusion. She sat on the edge of the seat and
clenched her hands till the nails bit into the palms and tried
to believe that it was not too late, that there was rescue for
Simon at the end of her journey.

They rode through dark streets, narrow streets, and finally
merged on the broad brightly lighted Kurfurstendamm. The
car slowed, came to a halt, and she saw with glimmering
hope the lettering of the Hotel Am Zoo marquee. She
pressed the woman's hand, murmured a breathless "Thank
you," and was out of the car before the chauffeur was
halfway round to open the door. In an instant she was in the
lobby, almost shouting Simon's name to the man behind the
desk.

"Mr. Mead is not in," the clerk told her. "You wish to leave a message?"

"No, I—" She tried to calm herself, to collect her thoughts. "Is there someone here—someone who knows him—that I could talk to?"

"There is Mr. Mead's friend, Mr. Hartman. You wish to see Mr. Hartman?"

"Yes, please. And hurry."

With what seemed to her maddening slowness he turned to the switchboard operator. After minutes that might have been hours a stocky young man with a crew cut came toward her.

"Bill Hartman," he announced himself. "You looking for Simon? He ought to be back in a few minutes. If you'll come with me—"

"No, they've taken him away. He's in danger. He—"

"This way." Firmly he took her arm and propelled her to the short flight of stairs that led to the hotel's lounge.

"There's no time to lose," she insisted. "You've got to get help, find him—"

"Of course," he said soberly. "But first I have to know what's happened."

The lounge was a railed balcony that looked down on the lobby, its only occupant a man glancing impatiently at his watch. Bill Hartman took her to the back into a small glass-enclosed room to which treelike plants in large pots gave the appearance of a conservatory. He put her into a chair and took one close beside her.

"Now," he said, "tell me what you know and then I'll know what to do."

The authority of his voice and eyes gave her reassurance. She took a deep breath and told him quickly but fully about events at the airport from Stanovski's appearance at her table to Simon's unconscious exit. She held back only one detail—the flourish with which she had passed over the matchbox. To admit her cowardice, to expose to his friend her betrayal of Simon, was beyond her strength.

"You're sure," he said when she finished, "of the license number?"

"Very sure. Will it help?"

"It's good," he said, "that they started with the letters KB. That means a West Berlin registration and makes it less likely that Simon's been taken to the Soviet Zone." He was on his feet, looking down at her thoughtfully. "Now about you. I ought to take you some place where you'll be guarded, out of—"

"No!" she said vehemently. "Don't waste time. They know I gave him the matchbox. No one's interested in me now."

"I suppose that's true." He frowned, came to a decision. "All right, stay here. It should be as safe a place as any. Don't move from this spot until either Simon or I come back for you."

She watched through the glass of her shelter as he hurried down the steps, through the lobby, out of the hotel. Then she sank deeper into her chair and tried to tell herself that it was going to be all right. But there was no solace in her thoughts. Berlin was a huge city filled with hiding places and hostile forces. What could Bill Hartman or a dozen Bill Hartmans do to find one cab or one man in all that dark expanse? Again she was pervaded with a sense of guilt, a yearning to go back beyond that moment when her only desire had been to shift her danger to someone else.

Simon wanted the list, she told herself. He had asked for it. He was at the airport to get it. Yet she could not escape the belief that if she had made a less public presentation, had stayed beside him, the end might have been different. How he must despise me! I can't bear to face him. Yet she knew that to face him was the one thing above all else that she wanted. Only let him come back, she prayed. What he thinks of me doesn't matter. Only let him be safe.

A page came up the steps and gave a message to the man in the lounge. The man scowled, looking again at his watch, and rose to leave. Selena reached into her purse for cigarettes and matches. She put a cigarette between her lips, but the page was behind her, lighter extended, before she could take out a match. Inhaling deeply, she watched the man go down the stairs and the boy follow him.

She tried to make her mind a blank, to fill it only with the action in the lobby below, the movement of clerks and porters, the comings and goings of the guests. The next man to enter was, though she could not see his face, a familiar figure. The airport's Colonel Blimp. How different things might have been if she had spoken to him instead of Simon.

The Englishman stopped for a few moments at the desk, took a quick look around, and then, nimbly for a fat man, climbed the steps. He crossed the empty lounge and entered Selena's enclosure.

"My dear." He stood beside her chair, smiling down at her. "It's good to see you. I hoped that I might find you here."

"You—" She looked up at him, puzzled. "I don't think—"

"I told the porter that I had come to meet my niece and described you. He sent me up here. Very convenient." He lowered himself into the next chair, pulled it closer to hers. "Now to business."

"I don't understand—"

"Please." He held up a plump well-manicured hand. "My time is too valuable to spend on games. You know why I am here. You have something that belongs to us. I have come for it. The matchbox, if you please."

"You're not an Englishman at all."

"It's a nationality," he said, "that I can counterfeit with great success. Very helpful in this business."

"Then you—you're a spy."

"We have the same trade, my dear. Only we work on opposite sides of the street. But I did not come to talk shop. Please return our property."

"I don't have it. I gave it away. You must have seen—"

"Yes, I saw. You made very certain that it was seen." He smiled at her and her cheeks flamed at the reminder. "You're a very clever girl. And you look so frivolous. Perhaps that is why you are valuable. Stanovski said that you were no one, that he had chosen you only because you were the first American he saw and he had given the list to you by mistake. At first we believed him. But no matter."

The shrug with which he dismissed Stanovski was casual, his smile still amiable. "He will bother us no longer with his lies. But you, my dear, I must admire your acting. You seemed so anxious to be rid of the matchbox, so uninterested in its contents. It was brilliant the way you used the young American as a decoy to throw us off your trail and onto his."

The young American. Of all the man had said, Selena's attention focused on that one phrase.

"The young American—where is he? What have you done with him?"

"So now you grow concerned for your dupe." He chuckled. "A little late, is it not? But then you are like me, ruthless when there is a job to do. The innocent must be used and cast aside. If they suffer—well, it teaches them the length of our arm."

"What did you do to him?"

"An oafish tourist. They should not be allowed to wander loose and get in the way of serious business."

"But he—is he—"

"When I found that he was nothing, only a fool, I could not waste more time on him. We searched and found that you had given him a box of matches. Real matches. That was brilliant, my dear. But fortunately, though I was deceived, I was not entirely sleeping. I left someone at the airport to see where you went and I was able to follow. Now I will take the box—Stanovski's box. The one with our list."

He extended his palm confidently and Selena's hand closed tightly over the box she still held, the box she had not needed to open because the page had lighted her cigarette. It's not possible, she told herself. It can't be that the little

man and I made the same mistake! He had intended to give
her the wrong box but had handed her the right one. She,
meaning to pass along the right one, had given Simon the
wrong one. So now she still had the film, the list that both
sides were so desperately seeking.

"You hesitate, my dear?" the fat man said cheerfully.
"Surely you don't think I would come to you without a
means of persuasion."

His hand dipped into his pocket and brought out a flat dark
piece of wood. His thumb pressed a lever and three inches
of narrow finely edged steel shot out. "If you have ideas about
calling for help, let me tell you that it would take less than
five seconds for this to slide between your ribs and into your
heart. Then I would need only to summon a porter to help
me carry my ailing niece to a taxi."

"You couldn't—you'd be stopped—you wouldn't—"

"Do you wish to put me to the test?" He switched the
blade back into its case, held it close to her side. She shrank
a little away, shaking her head without speaking. The
cigarette dropped from her fingers. He picked it up and
crushed it out neatly in the ashtray on the table in front of
them.

"You're very wise," he approved. "Perhaps I'm bluffing,
but in my trade you don't last long unless you're ready to
follow through on a bluff. Now you will give me the
matchbox."

"I—" Her throat was so dry she could hardly force the
words. She closed her eyes and tried hard to swallow. This
is what you wanted, she told herself. To be rid of the list, to
be free of involvement. All you have to do is hand it to this
man and it will be over. Otherwise—

"I don't have it," she said.

"Don't be foolish." For the first time there was a snarl in
his voice. "I know you have it. One way or another I'll get
it from you. It will be pleasanter if you cooperate."

Yes, don't be foolish, one part of her was saying. You
can't save the list, all you can do is get hurt. Give it to him

before he has to use force. But her will was saying an irrevocable no. Maybe she was a coward, maybe at the airport she had been ready to save herself at any cost, but she wouldn't act like that again.

Simon Mead had risked his life for this list. She couldn't now surrender it tamely. When he came back—if he came back—at least she wouldn't have to tell him that she had given it up without a fight. The knife case was hard against her side. All right, she wanted to shout wildly. You have me, but you still don't have your list.

"Here." She thrust her purse at him. "Look for it yourself."

He opened the bag and dumped its contents on the table. She took advantage of this distraction to put the hand that was farthest from him, the one that held the matchbox, over the side of her chair till her fingers touched the soft earth of a potted plant. Showing no haste that might betray her, she dug a hole buried the box, smoothed the surface of the soil.

"You see," she taunted as he probed the empty purse for hidden pockets. "I really don't have it."

"You don't have it in your bag," he amended. He swept the jumbled assortment back in and snapped the clasp. "It seems we must make a more thorough search than is proper for a hotel lounge. I must ask you to come with me."

He rose, fingering the knife with its unmistakable message. It's not too late, she thought. I could still give him the box and let him go away without me. Instead, she pressed hard against the chair, forcing herself to her feet. Only one thing seemed necessary—to get him away from the vicinity of the matchbox, away from this hotel before Simon came back to reveal his link with her.

They walked together down the steps. His hand was beneath her elbow, giving her chivalrous support. And the knife was in his hand.

"Your aunt will be pleased that I found you," he said as they passed the desk clerk. "She was afraid you might have left Berlin without seeing her again."

They walked out to the street. Kurfurstendamm was still as colorful, still as gay as the night before. Then she had been part of the gayety. Now she looked hopelessly at the milling throng on the sidewalk, the groups sipping drinks at the outdoor café, and wondered if she would ever be one of them again. A cab was waiting at the curb. Her companion helped her into it, seated himself at her side, then banged the door.

"The young lady is not being sensible, Josef," he told the driver. "She wishes to make us work to recover our property. You know where to take her."

Josef nodded, swung the car away from the curb, out into the traffic.

"I am sensible," Selena protested. "If I had it I'd give it to you. I know you'd find it anyway. So it would be plain silly to try to keep it hidden."

"Extremely silly," he agreed. "But I encounter many silly people. However, if you wish to change your mind and give me the list it will improve your situation. You must realize that you are now quite beyond help."

"I do realize it. And if I had the box I would give it to you. But I swear I don't have it. I—I gave it away."

"Really? To whom?"

"I can't tell you that."

"Ah, but you can. I think you'll find that there's nothing you can't tell me, after we've had our little time together. I told you my time is valuable, but I'll spend as much of it with you as is necessary. As for you, you have plenty of time—the rest of your life, in fact. Tell me, Josef." He leaned forward. "You've had experience with Americans. How long will it take to persuade our young friend to tell us everything we want to know."

"They're soft," the driver said contemptuously. "Ten minutes, if you're in a hurry."

"Ten minutes." He looked at her with lips thrust out, eyes narrowed speculatively. "Would you care to bet it takes longer?"

"No, I—" She pressed her hands together and strove for control. "I expect you can make me tell you everything I know. But I don't know anything. My orders were to go to the airport where a man would give me a matchbox. I was to take it to Hotel Am Zoo and someone would meet me in the lobby and take it from me. I did as I was told and that's all I know."

"And the person who took it from you. Who was that?"

"I don't know. I really don't." Draw them away from Bill Hartman, her mind warned, in case they learn that you spoke with him. "It was a woman. A woman I'd never seen before. She gave me the password and I gave her the matchbox. There was no need for me to know any more about her."

"Hmm." He rubbed his chin. "What do you think, Josef?"

"Could be," the driver answered. "They don't trust each other either."

"We'll see, " the fat man said. "If you stick to your story through the next few hours, we may begin to believe it."

He patted her hand as if he were in fact an affectionate uncle and she felt a deep inner squirming. Ten minutes, Josef had said. Would it take less time or more? She had no standards by which to measure her own endurance and Josef was evidently an authority. She might as well take his word for it that in ten minutes she'd blurt out everything about Simon and Bill and send them back to the Am Zoo to dig the list out of the dirt. She'd been given a second chance to be brave and she was going to fail more dismally than the first.

"Please—" She took a deep breath, gathering all her strength. "I know I can't hold out against you. So—I'm ready now to tell you the truth."

"Ah." The man beside her let out his breath in a slow murmur and in the front seat Josef's husky chuckle showed satisfaction at finding an American even softer than his estimate.

"I—" She spoke slowly, choosing her words with care. "It's true what I told you, about them not giving me any more information than I needed and my not knowing who any of the other people are. But when they didn't know I was still there, I overheard something."

"Yes?" he prompted. "You overheard?"

"The woman I gave the matchbox to was to go to a café. She was to stay there from ten o'clock until eleven and a man would come, say the password, and take the box."

"The name of the café?"

"If I tell you, if I point out the woman to you, will you let me go?"

"Your life in exchange for our list? It may be a good bargain. We'll discuss it when the list is in my hand. Quickly now, the name of the café."

Quickly, her mind echoed, quickly, quickly. But she could not speed up her memory. Twice Simon had lowered his voice. Once it was to mention his hotel and she had found Billy Hartman there. Surely the other time was also significant, a signpost to a place of refuge. She *must* remember what he said.

"It's a place I never heard of." She turned to her companion for help. "A strange name—I think it was Hungarian. Or maybe Viennese. There was something— yes, about a cellar. And gypsy music."

"Gypsy cellar," he suggested. "The Zigeuner Keller of the Haus Wien?"

"Yes, oh, yes." She almost hugged him in her relief. "That's the place."

"All right, Josef, get us there fast." The car swerved round a corner, gathered speed. "We must be there before ten, before our list changes hands again. You've taken us on a roundabout chase, my dear. The Zigeuner Keller is almost next door to the Am Zoo."

"I didn't know that. I told you I only heard of it by accident."

"For your sake," he said softly, "I hope you've told me the truth. If this is a trick to gain time or to get yourself back among people, I'm afraid you'll deeply regret it. A crowded restaurant is no safer for you than this car. Remember how easily I took you out of the hotel? And people who waste my time have a very bad effect on my temper."

"It's not a waste of time," she breathed.

The car, once again on Berlin's main street, drew up in front of a vividly decorated building of gray stone.

"Wait for us, Josef," the fat man said, and helped Selena out of the car.

He kept her arm as they approached the building and continued to hold it as they descended the steep stairs that led to the dimly lit cellar.

"Simon Mead," she muttered as the uniformed doorman bowed them in.

"Eh?" The fat man frowned at her. "What's that?"

"He told me his name," she answered. "The American at the airport." They were beside the cashier. The headwaiter rushed forward with elaborate welcome. "I think it was—" she raised her voice a little "—Simon Mead."

The headwaiter, with sure professional instinct, greeted them in English, offered them a choice of tables in the three-quarter-filled dining room.

"We're meeting friends," the man told him. "We'll just walk round the room and see if they're here yet."

They made a slow tour of the cellar, inspecting the animated couples, the family groups. Passing a cluster of waiters near the raised platform on which the orchestra was temporarily at rest, she spoke again.

"Yes," she said, "I'm sure he called himself Simon Mead."

"Still worrying about that tourist," her escort grumbled. "Get your mind on finding the woman for me or you'll have more personal worries than that."

They completed the circuit. He selected a booth near the far wall from which the entrance was visible and sat down close beside her.

"So," he said, "we are ahead of her. That is good. Unless she is not coming. That will be most unfortunate for you."

"I only told you what I heard. The arrangement was for her to be here. But that may have been changed. They may have made a different plan."

"Let us hope not, my dear," he said gently. "Let us both hope not."

The maroon-coated waiter was beside them with menus.

"Cognac," the fat man said. "And you, my dear? Do you wish to eat something?"

"Oh, no, nothing."

"Cognac," he repeated. "And mocha for the fraulein."

The waiter took the menus and scurried away.

"Now," he commanded, "keep close watch. We should not like to miss our friend."

Obediently she fixed her eyes on the entry. What now, she wondered desperately. How long will he wait before he knows that there is no woman, that I've lied to him? And when he knows it what will he do?

The waiter was back with their order. The fat man lifted the steaming pot, poured the thick strong coffee into her cup. Then he leaned back and took a connoisseur's sniff of his cognac. But he used only the hand farthest from her. The other remained on the bench, close to her side, so that she could always feel the curved wooden surface that masked the thin blade.

On the bandstand in front of her the orchestra finished their beers and went back to work. Violin, cello, piano, and marimba blended in a lilting tune with undertones of deep sadness. At the next table a boy reached for his girl's hand, gazed at her with misting eyes. Nearby, an exuberant diner waved his fork at the musicians in unison with the rhythm. From across the room came bursts of high-pitched laughter.

A short scream behind her brought her head around and she saw a spurt of flame. Fire! She felt a rising hope. If the restaurant's on fire there may be a chance for her to escape. But the blaze, she saw quickly, was only a row of skewered meat on which a waiter had poured brandy and touched a match. He waved it momentarily aloft before sliding it, still burning, onto a plate.

"Interesting," her companion murmured. "Have you ever seen a human torch, my dear?"

"No," she barely whispered.

"Much the same," he said. "Only of course we use gasoline. It's cheaper. Your woman should be getting here—if she's coming."

"Yes," she agreed. "She should be here soon."

She looked hopelessly round the room, from door to bandstand, past all the tables of happy people, to the back of the room where the white-capped heads of the chefs were visible above a screen. She looked at the screen, then looked away quickly, unable to believe her eyes. She glanced back and there was nothing there. Then a head bobbed up again—and it was Simon!

His eyes met hers, held them for an instant, and his hands, above the screen, moved apart in a sweeping gesture that told her to get away from the fat man, to free herself so that he could act.

There was no command she wanted to obey more. But there was no practical way to do it. Any movement on her part would only make her captor more alert. She wrenched her eyes from the kitchen, hoping that she had not given herself away. But her sudden tension could not miss being noticed.

"You have seen something?" the fat man said. "The woman—is she here?"

"I think so." Selena bit her lip, played for time. "Wait. Let me be sure."

Her eyes frenziedly roved the room, picked out a plump woman being seated by the waiter a few tables away. Her husband is probably checking his hat, Selena thought. But there may be time, just enough time, before he joins her.

"Yes, that's she." She pointed an unsteady finger. "In the red hat. She has the matchbox. But hurry. If she recognized me, sees us together, she may suspect—"

"Good." He slid his bulk from behind the table. "You've done well." He started away, turned back. "The password. What's the password?"

"Journey's end," she said.

He nodded soberly. In his trade, no doubt, he was used to odd phrases. He walked the few steps to the woman's table, looked down at her and spoke. She stared at him blankly and he spoke again, shouting to be heard above the music. The woman blinked, drew a little away in distaste, and he raised his voice just as the music came to a stop so that his repeated "Journey's end" boomed in the suddenly silent air.

"That's right." The answering voice was lower but audible to Selena's straining ears. "Your journey's ended, my friend."

Behind the fat man—close behind so that the weapon in the newcomer's pocket could press against the fat man's back—was Bill Hartman. And coming up to close the other flank was the cellist, incongruous in his yellow blouse and lavishly embroidered vest. The orchestra, a trio now, began a fresh tune, so Selena could hear no more of what was said. But she saw the fat man shrug his submission and move with the other two toward the door in a tableau reminiscent of her last view of Stanovski at the airport. This time, though, she felt no chill.

She didn't watch them all the way out. Suddenly Simon was at her side, his voice soft but imperative.

"You're all right?" She turned and his eyes seemed to be memorizing every detail of her face.

"Yes, I—I'm all right." She felt, now that it was finished, an overwhelming limpness. Then, as she looked at him, her strength came flooding back and she repeated with honesty and fervor, "I'm perfectly all right. But your friends— there's a man outside in a cab—"

"We've got him," Simon answered. "Everything's under control now."

"But you—" She looked at him more closely, saw with a

pang the red scar that ran from his hairline to an eyebrow. "You're hurt. What did they do to you?"

"It's nothing." He touched the mark lightly, laughed at her concern. "Don't worry about me. I'm indestructible. If you think this was a rough party, you should have been to the one in Hong Kong. Some day I'll tell you about it."

"Please do," she said eagerly, though her interest lay not in Hong Kong but in the promise contained in the words "some day."

"What happened tonight?" Selena went on. "How did you escape? At the airport you were unconscious. I saw them take you away." The memory came back with a vividness that made her shiver. "I thought they were going to kill you. And it was all my fault."

"Your fault?" His eyebrows lifted quizzically.

"I was so frightened." Fixing her eyes on her untouched coffee, she made her confession in a rush. "All I wanted was to save myself. That's why I made such a production of giving you the matchbox. I didn't think of the danger I was putting you into. The truth is, I didn't care. Not then, I didn't."

"As it turned out, that was the best job you could have done for me. Your big gesture made it easier for them to believe that you were using me, that I knew nothing about anything. By the time I came to, they'd finished their search and knew the list wasn't on me. All I had to do was go into my whiskey-brained playboy act till they were convinced they had the wrong man and you'd outsmarted them."

"And they let you go so easily?"

"An American tourist in the wrong hands can be a pretty hot potato. Let one disappear and it starts all kinds of big wheels in motion. Headlines, diplomatic notes, high-level conferences, low-level investigations. Soviet-American relations are too delicate to put all that strain on them for no reason. And the way I looked to them, I was no reason. Worth nothing to either side. So they dumped me on the nearest street corner and got back to business."

"And you're—" She had to resist an impulse to run her

fingers along the scar, to assure herself it was superficial. "You're all right?"

"Completely. The boy with the sandbag was careful to knock me out and nothing more. They wanted me in talking condition. But if you were worried about me, you can imagine how I've been kicking myself for throwing you to the wolves. Danger's my job. But you—"

He put his hand over hers, clasped it tightly as if to make sure she was really there. "Believe me, I thought you were well covered or I'd never have let them get the idea that you were the principal and I was your tool. The girl in the airport checkstand was working with us. Before they got to me, I had a chance to point you out and tell her to get you some guards. But you lit out too fast."

"I had to. When I saw them take you I had to try to find help."

"I know." He didn't release her hand. "I got a thousand-volt shock when I phoned the airport and found you'd gone out on the town alone. Then I got through to Hartman and he told me you'd showed up at the hotel. We raced back there and—" The pressure on her hand increased to the point of pain, but she didn't want it loosened. "The clerk said you'd left with your uncle. That's when I really panicked."

"But you found me," she soothed.

"Hartman kept his head," he continued. "He said since you got my message about the hotel, maybe the name of this place had stuck, too. We checked and found an American girl had been dropping my name and we knew we'd found you. Lord knows how you managed it, though. What witchcraft did you use to persuade our fat friend to go night-clubbing on the busiest night of his life?"

"I told him the list was—oh, I'd almost forgotten. The list is important, isn't it?"

"Worth everything you've been through for it," he said soberly. "The Reds have a cute trick of planting agents on our side and then expecting a double-cross. So they run periodic checks on their own team. This is the first time we've been able to run down one of their checkups. It will give us a valuable fix on who belongs to whom."

"Then we'd better get it." She started to rise. "It's in a pot at the Am Zoo."

"In a what? You'll have to decode that for me."

"I buried it," she said. "The list. In one of the hotel plants. We'd better hurry. If it's so important—"

"The list is all right." He held her down. "It's locked in a safe and photocopies are on their way to the proper places."

"How did you get it? Did you look in the pot?"

"You gave it to me." He studied her face as if he thought she might be feverish. "At the airport. Remember?"

"That was the wrong box. I made a mistake—"

"No, you didn't. The box you gave me had the microfilm in it. But I got rid of it fast. I hoped I'd get back to town whole. But that was something no one could guarantee. And the important thing was to save the list. So I passed it on to my friend at the checkstand before the other crowd closed in. I had another matchbox in my pocket. That's what made them think you'd done a sleight-of-hand. And I let them think it because I was sure that by then you were in a safe place. I didn't know I was getting myself off the hook by getting you on it."

"Then I didn't have the list? What I buried was just my own box of matches?"

"Let me get this straight." He spoke slowly, wonderingly. "Porky came to you and said you still had his film. And you believed him?"

"Yes, of course. I had another matchbox. I thought it must be the right one."

"But you refused to give it to him. Did he have a gun?"

"No, a—" Her voice shook a little at the recollection. "A knife."

"So you let him take you away. You thought you had what he wanted. You knew that all you had to do was hand him the matchbox and he'd leave you alone. Yet you deliberately hid the box and walked out with him. That took courage."

"No," she said. "I don't have any courage. I was scared to death. I've been scared from the beginning. I wasn't being brave. I just got mad."

"Maybe that's what makes heroes. Getting mad at the right time."

"But it was all for nothing," she said dolefully. "I could just as well have given him the box and saved all this fuss."

"Then you wouldn't have led Porky into our net. He and his friend Josef make a very good night's catch."

"They're important?"

"Not the biggest frogs in the puddle," he admitted. "But they make a fair splash. When they start talking—and a man like Porky, who's in it strictly for profit, doesn't need much encouragement to talk—I think we'll get some interesting revelations. You've been a valuable auxiliary, Selena."

"You—" She looked up, surprised. "You know my name?"

"Got it from the airline. You're the only passenger who didn't check in to change your reservation. It's the only concrete fact I have about you, but I intend to start a collection." His face lightened with the grin that would never lose its power to quicken her pulse. "For us, the journey's just beginning."

JEMIMA SHORE AT THE SUNNY GRAVE

==

by Antonia Fraser

"This is your graveyard in the sun—" The tall young man standing in her path was singing the words lightly but clearly. It took Jemima Shore a moment to realize exactly what message he was intoning to the tune of the famous calypso. Then she stepped back. It was a sinister and not particularly welcoming little parody.

"This is my island in the sun
Where my people have toiled since time begun—"

Ever since she had arrived in the Caribbean, she seemed to have had the tune echoing in her ears. How old was it? How many years was it since the inimitable Harry Belafonte had first implanted it in everybody's consciousness? No matter. Whatever its age, the calypso was still being sung today with charm, vigor, and a certain relentlessness on Bow Island, and on the other West Indian islands she had visited in the course of her journey.

It was not the only tune to be heard, of course. The loud noise of music, she had discovered, was an inseparable part of Caribbean life, starting with the airport. The heavy, irresistible beat of the steel band, the honeyed wail of the singers, all this was happening somewhere if not everywhere all over the islands late into the night: the joyous sound of freedom, of dancing, of drinking (rum punch), and, for the tourists at any rate, the sound of holiday.

It wasn't the sound of holiday for Jemima Shore, Investigator. Or not officially so. That was all to the good, Jemima being one of those people temperamentally whose best holidays combined some work with a good deal of pleasure. She could hardly believe it when Megalith Television, her employers, had agreed to a program which took her away from freezing Britain to the sunny Caribbean in late January. This was a reversal of normal practice, by which Cy Fredericks, Jemima's boss—and the effective boss of Megalith—was generally to be found relaxing in the Caribbean in February while Jemima herself, if she got there at all, was liable to be despatched there in the inconvenient humidity of August. And it was a fascinating project to boot. This was definitely her lucky year.

"This is my island in the sun—" But what the young man facing her had actually sung was "your *graveyard* in the sun." Hers? Or whose? Since the man standing between Jemima and the historic grave she had come to visit, it was possible that he was being proprietorial as well as aggressive. On second thought, surely not. It was a joke, a cheerful joke on a cheerful, very sunny day. But the young man's expression was, it seemed to her, more threatening than that.

Jemima gazed back with that special sweet smile so familiar to viewers of British television. (These same viewers were also aware from past experience that Jemima, sweet as her smile might be, stood no nonsense from anyone, at least not on her program.) On closer inspection, the man was not really as young as all that. She saw someone of perhaps roughly her own age—early thirties. He was white, although so deeply tanned that she guessed he wasn't a tourist but one of the small loyal European population of Bow Island, a place fiercely proud of its recent independence from a much larger neighbor.

The stranger's height, unlike his youth, was not an illusion. He towered over Jemima and she herself was not short. He was also handsome, or would have been except for an oddly formed, rather large nose with a high bridge to it and a pronounced aquiline curve. But if the nose marred the regularity of his features, the impression left was not unattractive. He was wearing whitish cotton shorts, like more or less every male on Bow Island, black or white. His orange T-shirt bore the familiar island logo or crest: the outline of a bow in black and a black hand drawing it back. Beneath the logo was printed one of the enormous variety of local slogans—cheerful again—designed to make a play upon the island's name. This one read: THIS IS THE END OF THE SUN-BOW!

No, in that friendly T-shirt, he was surely not intending to be aggressive.

In that case, the odd thing about the whole encounter was that the stranger still stood absolutely still in Jemima's path. She could glimpse the large stone Archer Tomb just behind him, which she recognized from the postcards. For a smallish place, Bow Island was remarkably rich in historic relics. Nelson in his time had visited it with his fleet, for like its neighbors Bow Island had found itself engulfed in the Napoleonic Wars. Two hundred or so years before that, first British, then French, then British again had invaded and settled the island which had once belonged to Caribs, and before that Arawaks. Finally, into this melting pot, Africans had been brought forcibly to work the sugar plantations on which its wealth depended. All these elements in various degrees had gone to make up the people now known casually among themselves as the Bo'landers.

The Archer Tomb, the existence of which had in a sense brought Jemima across the Atlantic, belonged to the period of the second—and final—British settlement. Here was buried the most celebrated governor in Bow Island's history,

Sir Valentine Archer. Even its name commemorated his long reign. Bow Island had originally been called by the name of a saint, and while it was true the island was vaguely formed in the shape of a bow it was Governor Archer who had made the change: to signify ritually that this particular archer was in command of this particular bow.

Jemima knew that the monument, splendidly carved, would show Sir Valentine Archer with Isabella, his wife, beside him. This double stone bier was capped with a white wood structure reminiscent of a small church, done either to give the whole monument additional importance—although it must always have dominated the small churchyard by its sheer size—or to protect it from the weather. Jemima had read that there were no Archer children inscribed on the tomb, contrary to the usual seventeenth-century practice. This was because, as a local historian delicately put it, Governor Archer had been as a parent to the entire island. Or in the words of another purely local calypso:

"Across the sea came old Sir Valentine—
He came to be your daddy, and he came to be mine."

In short, no one monument could compromise the progeny of a man popularly supposed to have sired over a hundred children, legitimate and illegitimate. The legitimate line was, however, now on the point of dying out. It was to see Miss Isabella Archer, officially at least the last of her race, that Jemima had come to the Caribbean. She hoped to make a program about the old lady and her home, Archer Plantation House, alleged to be untouched in its decoration these fifty years. She wanted also to interview her generally about the changes Miss Archer had seen in her lifetime in this part of the world.

"Greg Harrison," said the man standing in Jemima's path suddenly. "And this is my sister, Coralie." A girl who had been standing unnoticed by Jemima in the shade of the arched church porch stepped rather shyly forward. She, too, was extremely brown and her blonde hair, whitened almost to flax by the sun, was pulled back into a ponytail. His sister.

Was there a resemblance? Coralie Harrison was wearing a similar orange T-shirt, but otherwise she was not much like her brother. She was quite short, for one thing, and her features were appealing rather than beautiful—and, perhaps fortunately, she lacked her brother's commanding nose.

"Welcome to Bow Island, Miss Shore," she began. But her brother interrupted her. He put out a hand, large, muscular, and burnt to nut color by the sun.

"I know why you're here and I don't like it," said Greg Harrison. "Stirring up forgotten things. Why don't you leave Miss Izzy to die in peace?" The contrast between his apparently friendly handshake and the hostile, if calmly spoken words was disconcerting.

"I'm Jemima Shore," she said, though he obviously knew that. "Am I going to be allowed to inspect the Archer Tomb? Or is it to be across your dead body?" Jemima smiled again with sweetness.

"*My* dead body!" Greg Harrison smiled back in his turn. The effect, however, was not particularly warming. "Have you come armed to the teeth, then?" Before she could answer, he began to hum the famous calypso again. Jemima imagined the words: "This is your graveyard in the sun." Then he added: "Might not be such a bad idea, that, when you start to dig things up things that should be buried."

Jemima decided it was time for action. Neatly sidestepping Greg Harrison, she marched firmly toward the Archer Tomb. There lay the carved couple. She read: "Sacred to the memory of Sir Valentine Archer, first governor of this island, and his only wife, Isabella, daughter of Randal Oxford, gentleman." She was reminded briefly of her favorite Philip Larkin poem about the Arundel Monument, beginning, "The Earl and Countess lie in stone—" and ending, "All that remains of us is love."

But that couple lay a thousand miles away in the cloistered cool of Chichester Cathedral. Here the hot tropical sun burnt down on her naked head. She found she had taken off her large straw hat as a token of respect and

quickly clapped it back on again. Here, too, in contrast to
the very English-looking stone church with pointed Gothic
windows beyond, there were palm trees among the graves
instead of yews, their slender trunks bending like giraffes'
necks in the breeze. She had once romantically laid white
roses on the Arundel Monument. It was as the memory of
the gesture returned to her that she spied the heap of bright
pink and orange hibiscus blossoms lying on the stone before
her. A shadow fell across it.

"Tina puts them there." Greg Harrison had followed her.
"Every day she can manage it. Most days. Then she tells
Miss Izzy what she's done. Touching, isn't it?" But he did
not make it sound as if he found it especially touching. In
fact, there was so much bitterness, even malevolence, in his
voice that for a moment, standing as she was in the sunny
graveyard, Jemima felt quite chilled. "Or is it revolting?" he
added, the malevolence now quite naked.

"Greg," murmured Coralie Harrison faintly, as if in
protest.

"Tina?" Jemima said. "That's Miss Archer's—Miss Izzy's—
companion. We've corresponded. For the moment I can't
remember her other name."

"She's known as Tina Archer these days, I think you'll
find. When she wrote to you, she probably signed the letter
Tina Harrison." Harrison looked at Jemima sardonically
but she had genuinely forgotten the surname of the companion—it was, after all, not a particularly uncommon one.

They were interrupted by a loud hail from the road.
Jemima saw a young black man at the wheel of one of the
convenient roofless minis everyone seemed to drive around
Bow Island. He stood up and started to shout something.

"Greg! Cora! You coming on to—" She missed the rest
of it—something about a boat and a fish. Coralie Harrison
looked suddenly radiant, and for a moment even Greg
Harrison actually looked properly pleased.

He waved back. "Hey, Joseph. Come and say hello to
Miss Jemima Shore of BBC Television!"

"Megalith Television," Jemima interrupted, but in vain. Harrison continued:

"You heard, Joseph. She's making a program about Miss Izzy."

The man leapt gracefully out of the car and approached up the palm-lined path. Jemima saw that he, too, was extremely tall. And like the vast majority of the Bo'landers she had so far met, he had the air of being a natural athlete. Whatever the genetic mix in the past of Carib and African and other people that had produced them, the Bo'landers were certainly wonderful-looking. He kissed Coralie on both cheeks and patted her brother on the back.

"Miss Shore, meet Joseph—" but even before Greg Harrison had pronounced the surname, his mischievous expression had warned Jemima what it was likely to be "—Joseph Archer. Undoubtedly one of the ten thousand descendants of the philoprogenitive old gentleman at whose tomb you are so raptly gazing." All that remains of us is love indeed, thought Jemima irreverently as she shook Joseph Archer's hand—with all due respect to Philip Larkin, it seemed that a good deal more remained of Sir Valentine than that.

"Oh, you'll find we're all called Archer round here," murmured Joseph pleasantly. Unlike Greg Harrison, he appeared to be genuinely welcoming. "As for Sir Val-en-tine—" he pronounced it syllable by syllable like the calypso "—don't pay too much attention to the stories. Otherwise, how come we're not all living in that fine old Archer Plantation House?"

"Instead of merely my ex-wife. No, Coralie, don't protest. I could kill her for what she's doing." Again Jemima felt a chill at the extent of the violence in Greg Harrison's voice. "Come, Joseph, we'll see about that fish of yours. Come on, Coralie." He strode off, unsmiling, accompanied by Joseph, who did smile. Coralie, however, stopped to ask Jemima if there was anything she could do for her. Her manner was still shy but in her brother's absence a great deal more friendly. Jemima also had the strong impression that Coralie Harrison wanted to communicate something to her, something she did not necessarily want her brother to hear.

"I could perhaps interpret, explain—" Coralie stopped. Jemima said nothing. "Certain things," went on Coralie. "There are so many layers in a place like this. Just because it's small, an outsider doesn't always understand—"

"And I'm the outsider? Of course I am." Jemima had started to sketch the tomb for future reference, something for which she had a minor but useful talent. She forbore to observe truthfully, if platitudinously, that an outsider could also sometimes see local matters rather more clearly than those involved—she wanted to know what else Coralie had to say. Would she explain, for example, Greg's quite blatant dislike of his former wife?

But an impatient cry from her brother now in the car beside Joseph meant that Coralie for the time being had nothing more to add. She fled down the path and Jemima was left to ponder with renewed interest on her forthcoming visit to Isabella Archer of Archer Plantation House. It was a visit which would include, she took it, a meeting with Miss Archer's companion, who, like her employer, was currently dwelling in comfort there.

Comfort! Even from a distance, later that day, the square, low-built mansion had a comfortable air. More than that, it conveyed an impression of gracious and old-fashioned tranquility. As Jemima drove her own rented mini up the long avenue of palm trees—much taller than those in the churchyard—she could fancy she was driving back in time to the days of Governor Archer, his copious banquets, parties, and balls, all served by black slaves.

At that moment, a young woman with coffee-colored skin and short black curly hair appeared on the steps. Unlike the maids in Jemima's hotel who wore a pastiche of bygone servants' costume at dinner—brightly colored dresses to the ankle, white-muslin aprons, and turbans—this girl was wearing an up-to-the-minute scarlet halter-top and cutaway shorts revealing most of her smooth brown legs. Tina Archer: for so she introduced herself.

It did not surprise Jemima Shore one bit to discover that Tina Archer—formerly Harrison—was easy to get on with. Anyone who left the hostile and graceless Greg Harrison was already ahead in Jemima's book. But with Tina Archer chatting away at her side, so chic and even trendy in her appearance, the revelation of the interior of the house was far more of a shock to her than it would otherwise have been. There was nothing, nothing at all, of the slightest modernity about it. Dust and cobwebs were not literally there perhaps, but they were suggested in its gloom, its heavy wooden furniture—where were the light cane chairs so suitable to the climate?—and above all in its desolation. Archer Plantation House reminded her of poor Miss Havisham's time-warp home in *Great Expectations*. And still worse, there was an atmosphere of sadness hanging over the whole interior. Or perhaps it was mere loneliness, a kind of somber, sterile grandeur you felt must stretch back centuries.

All this was in violent contrast to the sunshine still brilliant in the late afternoon, the rioting bushes of brightly colored tropical flowers outside. None of it had Jemima expected. Information garnered in London had led her to form quite a different picture of Archer Plantation House, something far more like her original impression, as she drove down the avenue of palm trees, of antique mellow grace.

Just as Jemima was adapting to this surprise, she discovered the figure of Miss Archer herself to be equally astonishing. That is to say, having adjusted rapidly from free and easy Tina to the moldering, somber house, she now had to adjust with equal rapidity all over again. For the very first inspection of the old lady, known by Jemima to be at least eighty, quickly banished all thoughts of Miss Havisham.

Here was no aged, abandoned bride, forlorn in the decaying wedding-dress of fifty years before. Miss Izzy Archer was wearing a coolie straw hat, apparently tied under her chin with a duster, a loose white man's shirt, and faded blue jeans cut off at the knee. On her feet were a pair of what looked like child's brown sandals. From the look of her, she had either just taken a shower wearing all this or been swimming. She was dripping wet, making large pools on the rich carpet and dark, polished boards of the formal drawing room, all dark-red brocade and swagged, fringed curtains, where she had received Jemima. It was possible to see this even in the filtered light seeping through the heavy brown shutters which shut out the view of the sea.

"Oh, don't fuss so, Tina dear," exclaimed Miss Izzy impatiently—although Tina had, in fact, said nothing. "What do a few drops of water matter? Stains? What stains?" (Tina still had not spoken.) "Let the government put it right when the time comes."

Although Tina Archer continued to be silent, gazing amiably, even cheerfully, at her employer, nevertheless in some way she stiffened, froze in her polite listening attitude. Instinctively Jemima knew that she was in some way upset.

"Now don't be silly, Tina, don't take on, dear." The old lady was now shaking herself free of water like a small but stout dog. "You know what I mean. If you don't, who does—since half the time I don't know what I mean, let alone what I say. You can put it all right one day, is that better? After all, you'll have plenty of money to do it. You can afford a few new covers and carpets." So saying, Miss Izzy, taking Jemima by the hand and attended by the still-silent Tina, led the way to the farthest dark-red sofa. Looking remarkably wet from top to toe, she sat down firmly in the middle of it.

It was in this way that Jemima first realized that Archer Plantation House would not necessarily pass to the newly independent government of Bow Island on its owner's death. Miss Izzy, if she had her way, was intending to leave it all, house and fortune, to Tina. Among other things, this meant that Jemima was no longer making a program about a house destined shortly to be a national museum—which was very much part of the arrangement that had brought her to the island and had, incidentally, secured the friendly cooperation of that same new government. Was all this new? How new? Did the new government know? If the will had been signed, they must know.

"I've signed the will this morning, dear," Miss Archer pronounced triumphantly, with an uncanny ability to answer unspoken questions. "I went swimming to celebrate. I always celebrate things with a good swim—so much more healthy than rum or champagne. Although there's still plenty of *that* in the cellar."

She paused. "So there you are, aren't you, dear? Or there you will be. Here you will be. Thompson says there'll be trouble, of course. What can you expect these days? Everything is trouble since independence. Not that I'm against independence, far from it. But everything new brings new trouble here in addition to all the old troubles, so that the troubles get more and more. On Bow Island, no troubles ever go away. Why is that?"

But Miss Izzy did not stop for an answer. "No, I'm all for independence and I shall tell you all about that, my dear"—she turned to Jemima and put one damp hand on her sleeve—"on your program. I'm being a Bo'lander born and bred, you know." It was true that Miss Izzy, unlike Tina for example spoke with the peculiar, slightly sing-song intonation of the islanders—not unattractive to Jemima's ears.

"I was born in this very house eighty-two years ago in April," went on Miss Izzy. "You shall come to my birthday party. I was born during a hurricane. A good start! But my mother died in childbirth, they should never have got in that new-fangled doctor, just because he came from England. A total fool he was, I remember him well. They should have had a good Bo'lander midwife, then my mother wouldn't have died and my father would have had sons—"

Miss Izzy was drifting away into a host of reminiscences—and while these were supposed to be what Jemima had come to hear, her thoughts were actually racing off in quite a different direction. Trouble? What trouble? Where did Greg Harrison, for example, stand in all this—Greg Harrison who wanted Miss Izzy to be left to "die in peace?" Greg Harrison who had been married to Tina and was no longer? Tina Archer, now heiress to a fortune.

Above all, why was this forthright old lady intending to leave everything to her companion? For one thing, Jemima did not know how seriously to treat the matter of Tina's surname. Joseph Archer had laughed off the whole subject of Sir Valentine's innumerable descendants. But perhaps the beautiful Tina was in some special way connected to Miss Izzy. She might be the product of some rather more recent union between a rakish Archer and a Bo'lander maiden. More recent than the seventeenth century, that is.

Her attention was wrenched back to Miss Izzy's reminiscing monologue by the mention of the Archer Tomb.

"You've seen the grave? Tina has discovered it's all a fraud. A great big lie, lying under the sun—yes, Tina dear, you once said that. Sir Valentine Archer, my great great great—" An infinite number of greats followed before Miss Izzy finally pronounced the word "grandfather," but Jemima had to admit that she did seem to be counting. "He had a great big lie perpetuated on his tombstone."

"What Miss Izzy means—" This was the first time Tina had spoken since they entered the darkened drawing room. She was still standing, while Jemima and Miss Izzy sat.

"Don't tell me what I mean, child," rapped out the old lady; her tone was imperious rather than indulgent. Tina might for a moment have been a plantation worker two hundred years earlier rather than an independent-minded girl in the late twentieth century. "It's the inscription which is a lie. She wasn't his only wife. The very inscription should have warned us. Tina wants to see justice done to poor little Lucie Anne and so do I. Independence indeed!

I've been independent all my life and I'm certainly not stopping now. Tell me, Miss Shore, you're a clever young woman from television. Why do you bother to contradict something unless it's true all along? That's the way you work all the time in television, don't you?"

Jemima was wondering just how to answer this question diplomatically and without traducing her profession when Tina firmly, and this time successfully, took over from her employer.

"I read history at university in the U.K., Jemima. Genealogical research is my specialty. I was helping Miss Izzy put her papers in order for the museum—or what was to be the museum. Then the request came for your program and I began to dig a little deeper. That's how I found the marriage certificate. Old Sir Valentine *did* marry his young Carib mistress, known as Lucie Anne. Late in life—long after his first wife died. That's Lucie Anne who was the mother of his youngest two children. He was getting old, and for some reason he decided to marry her. The church, maybe. In its way, this has always been a God-fearing island. Perhaps Lucie Anne, who was very young and very beautiful, put pressure on the old man, using the church. At any rate, these last two children of all the hundreds he sired would have been legitimate!"

"And so?" questioned Jemima in her most encouraging manner.

"I'm descended from Lucie Anne—and Sir Valentine, of course," Tina returned sweet smile for sweet smile. "I've traced that, too, from the church records—not too difficult, given the strength of the church here. Not too difficult for an expert, at all events. Oh, I've got all sorts of blood, like most of us round here, including a Spanish grandmother and maybe some French blood, too. But the Archer descent is perfectly straightforward and clear."

Tina seemed aware that Jemima was gazing at her with respect. Did she, however, understand the actual tenor of Jemima's thoughts? This is a formidable person, Jemima was reflecting. Charming, yes, but formidable. And ruthless, maybe, on occasion. Jemima was also, to be frank, wondering just how she was going to present this sudden change of angle in her program on Megalith Television. On the one hand, it might now be seen as a romantic rags-to-riches story, the discovery of the lost heiress. On the other hand, just supposing Tina Archer was not so much an heiress as an adventuress? In that case, what would Megalith—what did Jemima Shore—make of a bright young woman putting across a load of false history on an innocent old lady? In those circumstances, Jemima could understand how the man by the sunny grave might display his contempt for Tina Archer.

"I met Greg Harrison by the Archer Tomb this morning," Jemima commented deliberately. "Your ex-husband, I take it."

"Of course he's her ex-husband." It was Miss Izzy who chose to answer. "That no-good. Gregory Harrison has been a no-good since the day he was born. And that sister of his. Drifters. Not a job between them. Sailing. Fishing. As if the world owes them a living."

"Half sister. Coralie is his half sister. And she works in a hotel boutique." Tina spoke perfectly equably, but once again Jemima guessed that she was in some way put out. "Greg is the no-good in that family." For all her calm, there was a hint of suppressed anger in her reference to her former husband. With what bitterness that marriage must have ended!

"No-good, the pair of them. You're well out of that marriage, Tina dear," exclaimed Miss Izzy. "And do sit down, child—you're standing there like some kind of housekeeper. And where is Hazel, anyway? It's nearly half past five. It'll begin to get dark soon. We might go down to the terrace to watch the sun sink. Where is Henry? He ought to be bringing us some punch. The Archer Plantation punch, Miss Shore—wait till you taste it. One secret ingredient, my father always said—"

Miss Izzy was happily returning to the past.

"I'll get the punch," said Tina, still on her feet. "Didn't you say Hazel could have the day off? Her sister is getting married over at Tamarind Creek. Henry has taken her."

"Then where's the boy? Where's what's-his-name? Little Joseph." The old lady was beginning to sound petulant.

"There isn't a boy any longer," explained Tina patiently. "Just Hazel and Henry. As for Joseph—well, little Joseph Archer is quite grown up now, isn't he?"

"Of course he is! I didn't mean that Joseph—he came to see me the other day. Wasn't there another boy called Joseph? Perhaps that was before the war. My father had a stable boy—"

"I'll get the rum punch." Tina vanished swiftly and gracefully.

"Pretty creature," murmured Miss Izzy after her. "Archer blood. It always shows. They do say the best-looking Bo'landers are still called Archer."

But when Tina returned, the old lady's mood had changed again.

"I'm cold and damp," she declared. "I might get a chill sitting here. And soon I'm going to be all alone in the house. I hate being left alone. Ever since I was a little girl I've hated being alone. Everyone knows that. Tina, you have to stay to dinner. Miss Shore, you must stay, too. It's so lonely here by the sea. What happens if someone breaks in?— Don't frown, there are plenty of bad people about. That's one thing that hasn't gotten better since independence."

"Of course I'm staying," replied Tina casually. "I've arranged it with Hazel." Jemima was wondering guiltily if she, too, ought to stay. But it was the night of her hotel's weekly party on the beach—barbecue followed by dancing to a steel band. Jemima, who loved to dance in the Northern Hemisphere, was longing to try it here. Dancing under the stars by the sea sounded idyllic. Did Miss Izzy really need extra company? Her eyes met those of Tina Archer across the lady's old strawhatted head. Tina shook her head slightly.

After a sip of the famous rum punch—whatever the secret ingredient, it was the strongest she had yet tasted on the island—Jemima was able to make her escape. In any case, the punch was having a manifestly relaxing effect on Miss Izzy herself. She became rapidly quite tipsy and Jemima wondered how long she would actually stay awake. The next time they met must be in the freshness of a morning.

Jemima drove away just as the enormous red sun was rushing down below the horizon. The beat of the waves from the shore pursued her. Archer Plantation House was set in a lonely position on its own spit of land at the end of its own long avenue. She could hardly blame Miss Izzy for not wanting to be abandoned there. Jemima listened to the sound of the waves until the very different noise of the steel band in the next village along the shore took over. That transferred her thoughts temporarily from recent events at Archer Plantation House to the prospect of her evening ahead. One way or another, for a brief space of time, she would stop thinking altogether about Miss Isabella Archer.

That was because the beach party was at first exactly what Jemima had expected—relaxed, good-natured, and noisy. She found her cares gradually floating away as she danced and danced again with a series of partners, English, American, and Bo'lander, to the beat of the steel band. That rum punch of Miss Izzy's, with its secret ingredient, must have been lethal because its effects seemed to stay with her for hours. She decided she didn't even need the generous profferings of the hotel mixture—a good deal weaker than Miss Izzy's beneath its lavish surface scattering of nutmeg. Others, however, decided that the hotel punch was exactly what they did need. All in all, it was already a very good party long before the sliver of the new moon became visible over the now-black waters of the Caribbean. Jemima, temporarily alone, tilted back her head as she stood by the lapping waves at the edge of the beach and fixed the moon in her sights.

"You going to wish on that new little moon?" She turned. A tall man—at least a head taller than she was—was standing beside her on the sand. She had not heard him, the gentle noise of the waves masking his approach. For a moment she didn't recognize Joseph Archer in his loose flowered shirt and long white trousers, so different did he look from the fisherman encountered that noon at the graveside.

In this way it came about that the second part of the beach party was quite unexpected, at least from Jemima's point of view.

"I ought to wish. I ought to wish to make a good program, I suppose. That would be a good, professional thing to do."

"Miss Izzy Archer and all that?"

"Miss Izzy, Archer Plantation House, Bow Island—to say nothing of the Archer Tomb, old Sir Valentine, and all that." She decided not to mention Tina Archer and all that for the time being.

"All that!" He sighed. "Listen, Jemima—it's good, this band. We're saying it's about the best on the island these days. Let's be dancing, shall we? Then you and me can talk about all that in the morning. In my office, you know."

It was the distinct authority with which Joseph Archer spoke quite as much as the mention of his office which intrigued Jemima. Before she lost herself still further in the rhythm of the dance—which she had a feeling that with Joseph Archer to help her she was about to do—she must find out what he meant. And, for that matter, just who he was.

The second question was easily answered. It also provided the answer to the first. Joseph Archer might or might not go fishing from time to time when he was off-duty, but he was also a member of the newly formed Bo'lander government. Quite an important one, in fact. Important in the eyes of the world in general, and particularly important in the eyes of Jemima Shore, Investigator. For Joseph Archer was the minister dealing with tourism, his brief extending to such matters as conservation, the Bo'lander historic heritage, and—as he described it to her—"the future National Archer Plantation House Museum."

Once again it didn't seem the appropriate moment to mention Tina Archer and her possible future ownership of the plantation house. As Joseph himself had said, the morning would do for all that. In his office in Bowtown.

They danced on for a while, and it was as Jemima had suspected it would be: something to lose herself in, perhaps dangerously so. The tune to "This is my island in the sun" was played and Jemima never once heard the graveyard words in her imagination. Then Joseph Archer, most politely and apparently regretfully, said he had to leave. He had an extremely early appointment—and not with a fish, either, he added with a smile. Jemima felt a pang which she hoped didn't show. But there was plenty of time, wasn't there? There would be other nights and other parties, other nights on the beach as the moon waxed to full in the two weeks she had before she must return to England.

Jemima's personal party stopped, but the rest of the celebration went on late into the night, spilling onto the sands, even into the sea, long after the silver of the moon had vanished. Jemima, sleeping fitfully and visited by dreams in which Joseph Archer, Tina, and Miss Izzy executed some kind of elaborate dance, not at all like the kind of island jump-up she had recently been enjoying, heard the noise in the distance.

Far away on Archer Plantation's lonely peninsula, the peace was broken not by a steel band but by the rough sound of the waves bashing against the rocks at its farthest point. A stranger might have been surprised to see that the lights were still on in the great drawing room, the shutters having been drawn back once the sun was gone, but nobody born

on Bow Island—a fisherman out to sea, for example—
would have found it at all odd. Everyone knew that Miss
Izzy Archer was frightened of the dark and liked to go to
bed with all her lights blazing. Especially when Hazel had
gone to her sister's wedding and Henry had taken her
there—another fact of island life which most Bo'landers
would have known.

In her room overlooking the sea, tossing in the big
four-poster bed in which she had been born over eighty
years ago, Miss Izzy, like Jemima Shore, slept fitfully. After
a while, she got out of bed and went to one of the long
windows. Jemima would have found her nightclothes, like
her swimming costume, bizarre, for Miss Izzy wasn't
wearing the kind of formal Victorian nightdress which
might have gone with the house. Rather, she was "using up,"
as she quaintly put it, her father's ancient burgundy-silk
pajamas, purchased many eons ago in Jermyn Street. And as
the last Sir John Archer, Baronet, had been several feet taller
than his plump little daughter, the long trouser legs trailed
on the floor behind her.

Miss Izzy continued to stare out of the window. Her gaze
followed the direction of the terrace, which led in a series of
parterres, once grandly planted, now overgrown, down to
the rocks and the sea. Although the waters themselves were
mostly blackness, the Caribbean night was not entirely dark.
Besides, the light from the drawing-room windows streamed
out onto the nearest terrace. Miss Izzy rubbed her eyes, then
she turned back into the bedroom, where the celebrated oil
painting of Sir Valentine hung over the mantelpiece dominated the room. Rather confusedly—she must have drunk
far too much of that punch—she decided that her ancestor
was trying to encourage her to be valiant in the face of
danger for the first time in her life. She, little Isabella
Archer, spoilt and petted Izzy, his last legitimate descendant—
no, not his last legitimate descendant, but the habits of a
lifetime were difficult to break—was being spurred on to

something courageous by the hawklike gaze of the fierce old autocrat.

But I'm so old, thought Miss Izzy. Then: But not *too* old. Once you let people know you're not, after all, a coward—

She looked out of the window once more. The effects of the punch were wearing off. Now she was quite certain of what she was seeing. Something dark, darkly clad, dark-skinned—What did it matter, someone dark had come out of the sea and was now proceeding silently in the direction of the house.

I must be brave, thought Miss Izzy. She said aloud: "Then he'll be proud of me. His brave girl." Whose brave girl? No, not Sir Valentine's—Daddy's brave girl. Her thoughts began to float away again into the past. I wonder if Daddy will take me on a swim with him to celebrate?

Miss Izzy started to go downstairs. She had just reached the door of the drawing room and was standing looking into the decaying red-velvet interior, still brightly illuminated, at the moment when the black-clad intruder stepped into the room through the open window.

Even before the intruder began to move softly toward her, dark-gloved hands outstretched, Miss Izzy Archer knew without doubt in her rapidly beating old heart that Archer Plantation, the house in which she had been born, was also the house in which she was about to die.

"Miss Izzy Archer is dead. Some person went and killed her last night. A robber, maybe." It was Joseph Archer who broke the news to Jemima the next morning.

He spoke across the broad desk of his formal office in Bowtown. His voice was hollow and distant, only the Bo'lander sing-song to connect him with Jemima's handsome dancing partner of the night before. In his short-sleeved but official-looking white shirt and dark trousers, he looked once again completely different from the cheerful ragged fisher-man Jemima had first encountered. This was indeed the rising young Bo'lander politician she was seeing: a member of the newly formed government of Bow Island. Even the tragic fact of the death—the murder, as it seemed—of an old lady seemed to strike no chord of emotion in him.

Then Jemima looked again and saw what looked suspiciously like tears in Joseph Archer's eyes.

"I just heard myself, you know. The Chief of Police, Sandy Marlow, is my cousin." He didn't attempt to brush away the tears. If that was what they were. But the words were presumably meant as an explanation. Of what? Of shock? Grief? Shock he must surely have experienced, but grief? Jemima decided at this point that she could at least inquire delicately about his precise relationship to Miss Izzy.

It came back to her that he had visited the old lady the week previously, if Miss Izzy's rather vague words concerning "Little Joseph" were to be trusted. She was thinking not so much of a possible blood relationship as some other kind of connection. After all, Joseph Archer himself had dismissed the former idea in the graveyard. His words about Sir Valentine and his numerous progeny came back to her: "Don't pay too much attention to the stories. Otherwise, how come we're not all living in that fine old Archer Plantation House?" At which Greg Harrison had commented with such fury: "Instead of merely my ex-wife." The exchange made more sense to her now, of course, that she knew of the position of Tina Harrison, now Tina Archer, in Miss Izzy's will.

The will! Tina would now inherit! And she would inherit in the light of a will signed the very morning of the day of Miss Izzy's death. Clearly, Joseph had been correct when he dismissed the claim of the many Bo'landers called Archer to be descended in any meaningful fashion from Sir Valentine. There was already a considerable difference between Tina, the allegedly sole legitimate descendant other than Miss Izzy, and the rest of the Bo'lander Archers. In the future, with Tina come into her inheritance, the gap would widen even more.

It was extremely hot in Joseph's office. It was not so much that Bow Island was an unsophisticated place as that the persistent breeze made air conditioning generally unnecessary. The North American tourists who were beginning to request air conditioning in the hotels, reflected Jemima, would only succeed in ruining the most perfect kind of natural ventilation. But a government office in Bowtown was rather different. A huge fan in the ceiling made the papers on Joseph's desk stir uneasily. Jemima felt a ribbon of sweat trickle down beneath her long loose white T-shirt, which she had belted as a dress to provide some kind of formal attire to call on a Bo'lander minister in working hours.

By this time, Jemima's disbelieving numbness on the subject of Miss Izzy's murder was wearing off. She was struck by the frightful poignancy of that last encounter in the decaying grandeur of Archer Plantation House. Worse still, the old lady's pathetic fear of loneliness was beginning to haunt her. Miss Izzy had been so passionate in her determination not to be abandoned. "Ever since I was a little girl I've hated being alone. Everyone knows that. It's so lonely here by the sea. What happens if someone breaks in?"

Well, someone had broken in. Or so it was presumed. Joseph Archer's words: "A robber, maybe." And this robber—maybe—had killed the old lady in the process.

Jemima began hesitantly: "I'm so sorry, Joseph. What a ghastly tragedy! You knew her? Well, I suppose everyone round here must have known her—"

"All the days of my life, since I was a little boy. My mama was one of her maids. Just a little thing herself, and then she died. She's in that churchyard, you know, in a corner. Miss Izzy was very good to me when my mama died, oh, yes. She was kind. Now you'd think that independence, *our* independence, would be hard for an old lady like her, but Miss Izzy she just liked it very much. 'England's no good to me any more, Joseph,' she said, 'I'm Bo'lander just like the rest of you.'"

"You saw her last week, I believe. Miss Izzy told me that herself."

Joseph gazed at Jemima steadily—the emotion had vanished. "I went to talk with her, yes. She had some foolish idea of changing her mind about things. Just a fancy, you know. But that's over. May she rest in peace, little old Miss Izzy. We'll have our National Museum now, that's for sure, and we'll remember her with it. It'll make a good museum for our history. Didn't they tell you in London, Jemima?" There was pride in his voice as he concluded: "Miss Izzy left everything in her will to the people of Bow Island."

Jemima swallowed hard. Was it true? Or rather, was it still true? Had Miss Izzy really signed a new will yesterday? She had been quite circumstantial on the subject, mentioning someone called Thompson—her lawyer, no doubt—who thought there would be "trouble" as a result. "Joseph," she said, "Tina Archer was up at Archer Plantation House yesterday afternoon, too."

"Oh, that girl, the trouble she made, tried to make. Tina and her stories and her fine education and her history. And she so pretty!" Joseph's tone was momentarily violent but he finished more calmly. "The police are waiting at the hospital. She's not speaking yet, she's not even conscious." Then even more calmly: "She's not so pretty now, I hear. That robber beat her, you see."

It was hotter than ever in the Bowtown office and even the papers on the desk were hardly stirring in the waft of the fan. Jemima saw Joseph's face swimming before her. She absolutely must not faint—she never fainted. She concentrated desperately on what Joseph Archer was telling her, the picture he was recreating of the night of the murder. The shock of learning that Tina Archer had also been present in the house when Miss Izzy was killed was irrational, she realized that. Hadn't Tina promised the old lady she would stay with her?

Joseph was telling her that Miss Izzy's body had been found in the drawing room by the cook, Hazel, returning from her sister's wedding at first light. It was a grisly touch that because Miss Izzy was wearing red-silk pajamas—her daddy's—and all the furnishings of the drawing room were dark-red as well, poor Hazel had not at first realized the extent of her mistress's injuries. Not only was there blood everywhere, there was water, too—pools of it. Whatever—whoever—had killed Miss Izzy had come out of the sea. Wearing rubber shoes—or flippers—and probably gloves as well.

A moment later, Hazel was in no doubt about what had hit Miss Izzy. The club, still stained with blood, had been left lying on the floor of the front hall. (She herself, deposited by Henry, had originally entered by the kitchen door.) The club, although not of Bo'lander manufacture, belonged to the house. It was a relic, African probably, of Sir John Archer's travels in other parts of the former British Empire, and hung heavy and short-handled on the drawing-room wall. Possibly Sir John had in mind to wield it against unlawful intruders but to Miss Izzy it had been simply one more family memento. She never touched it. Now it had killed her.

"No prints anywhere," Joseph said. "So far."

"And Tina?" asked Jemima with dry lips. The idea of the pools of water stagnant on the floor of the drawing room mingled with Miss Izzy's blood reminded her only too vividly of the old lady when last seen—soaking wet in her bizarre swimming costume, defiantly sitting down on her own sofa.

"The robber ransacked the house. Even the cellar. The champagne cases Miss Izzy boasted about must have been too heavy, though. He drank some rum. The police don't know yet what he took—silver snuff-boxes, maybe, there were plenty of those about." Joseph sighed. "Then he went upstairs."

"And found Tina?"

"In one of the bedrooms. He didn't hit her with the same weapon—lucky for her, as he'd have killed her just like he killed Miss Izzy. He left that downstairs and picked up something a good deal lighter. Probably didn't reckon on seeing her or anyone there at all. 'Cept for Miss Izzy, that is. Tina must have surprised him. Maybe she woke up. Robbers—well, all I can say is that robbers here don't generally go and kill people unless they're frightened."

Without warning, Joseph slumped down in front of her and put his head in his hands. He murmured something like: "When we find who did it to Miss Izzy—"

It wasn't until the next day that Tina Archer was able to speak even haltingly to the police. Like most of the rest of the Bow Island population, Jemima Shore was informed of the fact almost immediately. Claudette, manageress of her hotel, a sympathetic if loquacious character, just happened to have a niece who was a nurse. But that was the way information always spread about the island—no need for newspapers or radio, this private telegraph was far more efficient.

Jemima had spent the intervening twenty-four hours swimming rather aimlessly, sunbathing, and making little tours of the island in her mini. She was wondering at what point she should inform Megalith Television of the brutal way in which her projected program had been terminated and make arrangements to return to London. After a bit, the investigative instinct, that inveterate curiosity which would not be stilled, came to the fore. She found she was speculating all the time about Miss Izzy's death. A robber? A robber who had also tried to kill Tina Archer? Or a robber who had merely been surprised by her presence in the house? What connection, if any, had all this with Miss Izzy's will?

The will again. But that was one thing Jemima didn't have to speculate about for very long. For Claudette, the manageress, also just happened to be married to the brother of Hazel, Miss Izzy's cook. In this way, Jemima was apprised—along with the rest of Bow Island, no doubt— that Miss Izzy had indeed signed a new will down in Bowtown on the morning of her death, that Eddie Thompson, the solicitor, had begged her not to do it, that Miss Izzy *had* done it, that Miss Izzy had still looked after Hazel all right, as she had promised (and Henry who had worked for her even longer), and that some jewelry would go to a cousin in England, "seeing as Miss Izzy's mother's jewels were in an English bank anyway since long back." But for the rest, well, there would be no National Bo'lander Museum now, that was for sure. Everything else—that fine old Archer Plantation House, Miss Izzy's fortune, reputedly enormous but who knew for sure?—would go to Tina Archer.

If she recovered, of course. But the latest cautious bulletin from Claudette via the niece-who-was-a-nurse, confirmed by a few other loquacious people on the island, was that Tina Archer *was* recovering. The police had already been able to interview her. In a few days she would be able to leave the hospital. And she was determined to attend Miss Izzy's funeral, which would be held, naturally enough, in that little English-looking church with its incongruous tropical vegetation overlooking the sunny grave. For Miss Izzy had long ago made clear her own determination to be buried in the Archer Tomb, along with Governor Sir Valentine and "his only wife, Isabella."

"As the last of the Archers. But she still had to get permission since it's a national monument. And of course the government couldn't do enough for her. So they gave it. Then. Ironic, isn't it?" The speaker making absolutely no attempt to conceal her disgust was Coralie Harrison. "And now we learn that she wasn't the last of the Archers, not officially, and we shall have the so-called Miss Tina Archer as chief mourner. And while the Bo'lander government desperately looks for ways to get round the will and grab the house for their precious museum, nobody quite has the bad taste to go ahead and say so—no burial in the Archer Tomb for naughty old Miss Izzy. Since she hasn't, after all, left the people of Bow Island a penny."

"It should be an interesting occasion," Jemima murmured. She was sitting with Coralie Harrison under the conical thatched roof of the hotel's beach bar. This was where she first danced, then sat out with Joseph Archer on the night of the new moon—the night Miss Izzy had been killed. Now the sea sparkled under the sun as though there were crystals scattered on its surface. Today there were no waves at all and the happy water-skiers crossed and re-crossed the wide bay with its palm-fringed shore. Enormous brown pelicans perched on some stakes which indicated where rocks lay. Every now and then, one would take off like an unwieldy aeroplane and fly slowly and inquisitively over the heads of the swimmers. It was a tranquil, even an idyllic scene, but somewhere in the distant peninsula lay Archer Plantation House, not only shuttered but now, she imagined, also sealed by the police.

Coralie had sauntered up to the bar from the beach. She traversed the few yards with seeming casualness—all Bo'landers frequently exercised their right to promenade along the sands unchecked (as in most Caribbean islands, no one owned any portion of the beach in Bow Island, even outside the most stately mansion like Archer Plantation House, except the people). Jemima, however, was in no doubt that this was a planned visit. She had not forgotten that first meeting, and Coralie's tentative approach to her, interrupted by Greg's peremptory cry.

It was the day after the inquest on Miss Izzy's death. Her body had been released by the police and the funeral would soon follow. Jemima admitted to herself that she was interested enough in the whole Archer family, and its various branches, to want to attend it, quite apart from the tenderness she felt for the old lady herself, based on that brief meeting. To Megalith Television, in a telex from

Bowtown, she had spoken merely of tying up a few loose ends resulting from the cancellation of her program.

There had been an open verdict at the inquest. Tina Archer's evidence in a sworn statement had not really contributed much that wasn't known or suspected already. She had been asleep upstairs in one of the many fairly derelict bedrooms kept ostensibly ready for guests. The bedroom chosen for her by Miss Izzy had not faced onto the sea. The chintz curtains in this back room, bearing some dated rosy pattern from a remote era, weren't quite so bleached and tattered since they had been protected from the sun and salt.

Miss Izzy had gone to bed in good spirits, reassured by the fact that Tina Archer was going to spend the night. She had drunk several more rum punches and had offered to have Henry fetch some of her father's celebrated champagne from the cellar. As a matter of fact, Miss Izzy often made this offer after a few draughts of punch, but Tina reminded her that Henry was away and the subject was dropped.

In her statement, Tina said she had no clue as to what might have awakened the old lady and induced her to descend the stairs—it was right out of character in her own opinion. Isabella Archer was a lady of independent mind but notoriously frightened of the dark, hence Tina's presence at the house in the first place. As to her own recollection of the attack, Tina had so far managed to dredge very few of the details from her memory—the blow to the back of the head had temporarily or permanently expunged all the immediate circumstances from her consciousness. She had a vague idea that there had been a bright light, but even that was rather confused and might be part of the blow she had suffered. Basically, she could remember nothing between going to bed in the tattered, rose-patterned four-poster and waking up in hospital.

Coralie's lip trembled. She bowed her head and sipped at her long drink through a straw—she and Jemima were drinking some exotic mixture of fruit juice, alcohol free, invented by Matthew, the barman. There was a wonderful soft breeze coming in from the sea and Coralie was dressed in a loose flowered cotton dress, but she looked hot and angry. "Tina schemed for everything all her life and now she's got it. That's what I wanted to warn you about that morning in the churchyard—don't trust Tina Archer, I wanted to say. Now it's too late, she's got it all. When she was married to Greg, I tried to like her, Jemima, honestly I did. Little Tina, so cute and so clever, but always trouble—"

"Joseph Archer feels rather the same way about her, I gather," Jemima said. Was it her imagination or did Coralie's face soften slightly at the sound of Joseph's name?

"Does he? I'm glad. He fancied her, too, once upon a time. She is quite pretty." Their eyes met. "Well, not all that pretty, but if you like the type—" Jemima and Coralie both laughed. The fact was that Coralie Harrison was quite appealing, if you liked *her* type, but Tina Archer was ravishing by any standards.

"Greg absolutely loathes her now, of course," Coralie continued firmly, "especially since he heard the news about the will. When we met you that morning up at the church he'd just been told. Hence, well, I'm sorry, but he was very rude, wasn't he?"

"More hostile than rude." But Jemima had begun to work out the timing. "You mean your brother knew about the will *before* Miss Izzy was killed?" she exclaimed.

"Oh, yes. Someone from Eddie Thompson's office told Greg—Daisy Marlow, maybe, he takes her out. Of course, we all knew it was on the cards, except we hoped Joseph had argued Miss Izzy out of it. And he *would* have argued her out of it given time. That museum is everything to Joseph."

"Your brother and Miss Izzy—that wasn't an easy relationship, I gather."

Jemima thought she was using her gentlest and most

persuasive interviewer's voice, but Coralie countered with something like defiance: "You sound like the police!"

"Why, have they—?"

"Well, of course they have!" Coralie answered the question before Jemima had completed it. "Everyone knows that Greg absolutely hated Miss Izzy—blamed her for breaking up his marriage, for taking little Tina and giving her ideas!"

"Wasn't it the other way around—Tina delving into the family records for the museum and then my program? You *said* she was a schemer."

"Oh, I *know* she was a schemer! But did Greg? He did not. Not then. He was besotted with her at the time, so he had to blame the old lady. They had a frightful row—very publicly. He went round to the house one night, went in by the sea, shouted at her. Hazel and Henry heard, so then everyone knew. That was when Tina told him she was going to get a divorce and throw in her lot with Miss Izzy for the future. I'm afraid my brother is rather an extreme person— his temper is certainly extreme. He made threats—"

"But the police don't think—" Jemima stopped. It was clear what she meant.

Coralie swung her legs off the barstool. Jemima handed her the huge straw bag with the archer logo on it and she slung it over her shoulder in proper Bo'lander fashion.

"How pretty," Jemima commented politely.

"I sell them at the hotel on the North Point. For a living." The remark sounded pointed. "No," Coralie went on rapidly before Jemima could say anything more on that subject, "of course the police don't *think*, as you put it. Greg might have assaulted Tina—but Greg kill Miss Izzy when he knew perfectly well that by so doing he was handing his ex-wife a fortune? No way. Not even the Bo'lander police would believe that."

That night Jemima Shore found Joseph Archer again on the beach under the stars. But the moon had waxed since their first encounter. Now it was beginning to cast a silver pathway on the waters of the night. Nor was this meeting unplanned as that first one had been. Joseph had sent her a message that he would be free and they had agreed to meet down by the bar.

"What do you say I'll take you on a night drive round our island, Jemima?"

"No. Let's be proper Bo'landers and walk along the sands." Jemima wanted to be alone with him, not driving past the rows of lighted tourist hotels, listening to the eternal beat of the steel bands. She felt reckless enough not to care how Joseph himself would interpret this change of plan.

They walked for some time along the edge of the sea, in silence except for the gentle lap of the waves. After a while, Jemima took off her sandals and splashed through the warm receding waters, and a little while after that Joseph took her hand and led her back onto the sand. The waves grew conspicuously rougher as they rounded the point of the first wide bay. They stood for a moment together, Joseph and Jemima, he with his arm companionably round her waist.

"Jemima, even without that new moon, I'm going to wish——" Then Joseph stiffened. He dropped the encircling arm, grabbed her shoulder, and swung her around. "Jesus, oh sweet Jesus, do you see that?"

The force of his gesture made Jemima wince. For a moment she was distracted by the flickering moonlit swathe on the dark surface of the water. There were multitudinous white—silver —horses out beyond the land where high waves were breaking over an outcrop of rocks. She thought Joseph was point out to sea. Then she saw the lights.

"The Archer house!" she cried. "I thought it was shut up!" It seemed that all the lights of the house were streaming out across the promontory on which it lay. Such was the illumination that you might have supposed some great ball was in progress, a thousand candles lit as in the days of Governor Archer. More somberly, Jemima realized that was how the plantation house must have looked on the night of Miss Izzy's death. Tina Archer and others had borne

witness to the old lady's insistence on never leaving her
house in darkness. The night her murderer had come in from
the sea, this is how the house must have looked to him.

"Come on!" said Joseph. The moment of lightness—or
loving, perhaps?—had utterly vanished. He sounded both
grim and determined.

"To the police?"

"No, to the house. I need to know what's happening
there."

As they half ran along the sands, Joseph said, "This house
should have been *ours*."

Ours: The people of Bow Island.

His restlessness on the subject of the museum struck
Jemima anew since her conversation with Coralie Harrison.
What would a man—or a woman, for that matter—do for
an inheritance? And there was more than one kind of
inheritance. Wasn't a national heritage as important to some
people as a personal inheritance to others? Joseph Archer
was above all a patriotic Bo'lander. And he had not known
of the change of will on the morning after Miss Izzy's death.
She herself had evidence of that. Might a man like Joseph
Archer, a man who had already risen in his own world by
sheer determination, decide to take the law into his own
hands in order to secure the museum for his people while
there was still time?

But to kill the old lady who had befriended him as a boy?
Batter her to death? As he strode along, so tall in the
moonlight, Joseph was suddenly a complete and thus
menacing enigma to Jemima.

They had reached the promontory, had scrambled up the
rocks, and had got as far as the first terrace when all the
lights in the house went out. It was as though a switch had
been thrown. Only the cold eerie glow of the moon over the
sea behind them remained to illuminate the bushes, now
wildly overgrown, and the sagging balustrades.

But Joseph strode on, helping Jemima up the flights of

stone steps, some of them deeply cracked and uneven. In the darkness, Jemima could just see that the windows of the drawing room were still open. There had to be someone in there behind the ragged red-brocade curtains which had been stained with Miss Izzy's blood.

Joseph, holding Jemima's hand, pulled her through the center window.

There was a short cry like a suppressed scream and then a low sound, as if someone was laughing at them there in the dark. An instant later, all the lights were snapped on at once.

Tina was standing at the door, her hand at the switch. She wore a white bandage on her head like a turban—and she wasn't laughing, she was sobbing.

"Oh, it's you, Jo-seph and Je-mi-ma Shore." For the first time, Jemima was aware of the sing-song Bo'lander note in Tina's voice. "I was so fright-ened."

"Are you all right, Tina?" asked Jemima hastily, to cover the fact that she had been quite severely frightened herself. The atmosphere of angry tension between the two other people in the room, so different in looks yet both of them, as it happened, called Archer, was almost palpable. She felt she was honor bound to try to relieve it. "Are you all alone?"

"The police said I could come." Tina ignored the question. "They have finished with everything here. And besides—" her terrified sobs had vanished, there was something deliberately provocative about her as she moved toward them "—why ever not?" To neither of them did she need to elaborate. The words "since it's all mine" hung in the air.

Joseph spoke for the first time since they had entered the room. "I want to look at the house," he said harshly.

"Jo-seph Archer, you get out of here. Back where you came from, back to your off-ice and that's not a great fine house." Then she addressed Jemima placatingly, in something more like her usual sweet manner. "I'm sorry, but, you see, we've not been friends since way back. And, besides, you gave me such a shock."

Joseph swung on his heel. "I'll see you at the funeral, Miss Archer." He managed to make the words sound extraordinarily threatening.

That night it seemed to Jemima Shore that she hardly slept, although the threads of broken, half remembered dreams disturbed her and indicated that she must actually have fallen into some kind of doze in the hour before dawn. The light was still gray when she looked out of her shutters. The tops of the tall palms were bending—there was quite a wind.

Back on her bed, Jemima tried to recall just what she had been dreaming. There had been some pattern to it: she knew there had. She wished rather angrily that light would suddenly break through into her sleepy mind as the sun was shortly due to break through the eastern fringe of palms on the hotel estate. No gentle, slow-developing, rosy-fingered dawn for the Caribbean: one brilliant low ray was a herald of what was to come, and then, almost immediately, hot relentless sunshine for the rest of the day. She needed that kind of instant clarity herself.

Hostility. That was part of it all—the nature of hostility. The hostility, for example, between Joseph and Tina Archer the night before, so virulent and public—with herself as the public—that it might almost have been managed for effect.

Then the management of things: Tina Archer, always managing, always a schemer (as Coralie Harrison had said—and Joseph Archer, too). That brought her to the other couple in this odd, four-pointed drama: the Harrisons, brother and sister, or rather *half* brother and sister (a point made by Tina to correct Miss Izzy).

More hostility: Greg, who had once loved Tina and now loathed her. Joseph, who had once also perhaps loved Tina. Coralie, who had once perhaps—very much perhaps, this one—loved Joseph and certainly loathed Tina. Cute and clever little Tina, the Archer Tomb, the carved figures of Sir Valentine and his wife, the inscription. Jemima was beginning to float back into sleep, as the four figures, all

Bo'landers, all sharing some kind of common past, began to dance to a calypso whose wording, too, was confused:

"This is your graveyard in the sun
Where my people have toiled since time begun—"

An extraordinarily loud noise on the corrugated metal roof above her head recalled her, trembling, to her senses. The racket had been quite immense, almost as if there had been an explosion or at least a missile fired at the chalet. The thought of a missile made her realize that it had in fact been a missile: it must have been a coconut which had fallen in such a startling fashion on the corrugated roof. Guests were officially warned by the hotel against sitting too close under the palm trees, whose innocuous-looking fronds could suddenly dispense their heavily lethal nuts. COCONUTS CAN CAUSE INJURY ran the printed notice.

That kind of blow on my head would certainly have caused injury, thought Jemima, if not death.

Injury, if not death. And the Archer Tomb: my only wife.

At that moment, straight on cue, the sun struck low through the bending fronds to the east and onto her shutters. And Jemima realized not only why it had been done but how it had been done. Who of them all had been responsible for consigning Miss Izzy Archer to the graveyard in the sun.

The scene by the Archer Tomb a few hours later had that same strange mixture of English tradition and Bo'lander exoticism which had intrigued Jemima on her first visit. Only this time she had a deeper, sadder purpose than sheer tourism. Traditional English hymns were sung at the service, but outside a steel band was playing at Miss Izzy's request. As one who had been born on the island, she had asked for a proper Bo'lander funeral.

The Bo'landers, attending in large numbers, were by and large dressed with that extreme formality—dark suits, white shirts, ties, dark dresses, dark straw hats, even white gloves—which Jemima had observed in churchgoers of a Sunday and in the Bo'lander children, all of them neatly uniformed on their way to school. No Bow Island T-shirts were to be seen, although many of the highly colored intricate and lavish wreaths were in the bow shape of the island's logo. The size of the crowd was undoubtedly a genuine mark of respect. Whatever the disappointments of the will to their government, to the Bo'landers Miss Izzy Archer had been part of their heritage.

Tina Archer wore a black scarf wound round her head which almost totally concealed her bandage. Joseph Archer, standing far apart from her and not looking in her direction, looked both elegant and formal in his office clothes, a respectable member of the government. The Harrisons stood together, Coralie with her head bowed. Greg's defiant aspect, head lifted proudly, was clearly intended to give the lie to any suggestions that he had not been on the best of terms with the woman whose body was now being lowered into the family tomb.

As the coffin—so small and thus so touching—vanished from view, there was a sigh from the mourners. They began to sing again: a hymn, but with the steel band gently echoing the tune in the background.

Jemima moved discreetly in the crowd and stood by the side of the tall man.

"You'll never be able to trust her," she said in a low voice. "She's managed you before, she'll manage you again. It'll be someone else who will be doing the dirty work next time. On you. You'll never be able to trust her, will you? Once a murderess, always a murderess. You may wish one day you'd finished her off."

The tall man looked down at her. Then he looked across at Tina Archer with one quick savagely doubting look. Tina Archer Harrison, his only wife.

"Why, you—" For a moment, Jemima thought Greg Harrison would actually strike her down there at the graveside, as he had struck down old Miss Izzy and—if only on pretense—struck down Tina herself.

"Greg darling." It was Coralie Harrison's pathetic, protesting murmur. "What are you saying to him?" she demanded of Jemima in a voice as low as Jemima's own. But the explanations—for Coralie and the rest of Bow Island—of the conspiracy of Tina Archer and Greg Harrison were only just beginning.

The rest was up to the police, who with their patient work of investigation would first amplify, then press, finally concluding the case. And in the course of their investigations, the conspirators would fall apart, this time for real. To the police fell the unpleasant duty of disentangling the new lies of Tina Archer, who now swore that her memory had just returned, that it had been Greg who had half killed her that night, that she had had absolutely nothing to do with it. And Greg Harrison denounced Tina in return, this time with genuine ferocity. "It was her plan, her plan all along. She managed everything. I should never have listened to her!"

Before she left Bow Island, Jemima went to say goodbye to Joseph Archer in his Bowtown office. There were many casualties of the Archer tragedy beyond Miss Izzy herself. Poor Coralie was one: she had been convinced that her brother, for all his notorious temper, would never batter down Miss Izzy to benefit his ex-wife. Like the rest of Bow Island, she was unaware of the deep plot by which Greg and Tina would publicly display their hostility, advertise their divorce, and all along plan to kill Miss Izzy once the new will was signed. Greg, ostentatiously hating his ex-wife, would not be suspected, and Tina, suffering such obvious injuries, could only arouse sympathy.

Another small casualty, much less important, was the romance which just might have developed between Joseph Archer and Jemima Shore. Now, in his steamily hot office with its perpetually moving fan, they talked of quite other things than the new moon and new wishes.

"You must be happy you'll get your museum," said Jemima.

"But that's not at all the way I wanted it to happen," he replied. Then Joseph added: "But you know, Jemima, there has been justice done. And in her heart of hearts Miss Izzy did really want us to have this National Museum. I'd have talked her round to good sense again if she had lived."

"That's why they acted when they did. They didn't dare wait, given Miss Izzy's respect for you," suggested Jemima. She stopped, but her curiosity got the better of her. There was one thing she had to know before she left. "The Archer Tomb and all that. Tina being descended from Sir Valentine's lawful second marriage. Is that true?"

"Yes, it's true. Maybe. But it's not important to most of us here. You know something, Jemima? I, too, am descended from that well known second marriage. Maybe. And a few others maybe. Lucie Anne had two children, don't forget, and Bo'landers have large families. It was important to Tina Archer, not to me. That's not what I want. That's all past. Miss Izzy was the last of the Archers, so far as I'm concerned. Let her lie in her tomb."

"What *do* you want for yourself? Or for Bow Island, if you prefer."

Joseph smiled and there was a glimmer there of the handsome fisherman who had welcomed her to Bow Island, the cheerful dancing partner. "Come back to Bow Island one day, Jemima. Make another program about us, our history and all that, and I'll tell you then."

"I might just do that," said Jemima Shore.

MRS. HOWELL AND CRIMINAL JUSTICE 2.1

==

by Margaret Maron

Jeff Dixon watched with jaundiced eyes the dozen or so students drifting into his classroom. After three years, he could almost predict why each person had signed up for this summer course in criminal justice.

Take that clean-shaven young man in off-duty chinos and Izod shirt, for instance. He was probably capital police, bucking for plainclothes; an associate degree from Colleton County Technical College would almost cinch it.

Dixon was privately amused to note that he already had the textbook. Some of the guys never bothered; thought they could get through the course on sheer machismo. Like the blond kid strutting through the door now, his tie loosened, the top button of his blue uniform undone, and, even though he wore a wedding ring, already coming on strong to a couple of very pretty women ahead of him.

Dixon shuffled through the enrollment cards. They must

be the pair of SBI clerks from the ID lab outside the capital. Those two stocky black guys behind them he remembered from previous classes. CCBI. (Like the uniformed police departments, both the State and City-County Bureaus of Investigation gave their people time off from work for classes that would upgrade their ratings.)

"Excuse me, please?"

Hovering in the doorway was a well-dressed, slightly plump woman with smart gray hair and inquisitive green eyes. Probably looking for Needle-craft on the next floor, thought Dixon. Colleton Tech drew a lot of older women who took up new hobbies when their children left home.

"Criminalistics?" chirped the woman.

Nonplussed, Dixon nodded.

"Oh, good!" She clicked into the room on thin high heels and took a desk near the two SBI women.

Several nondescript males wandered in. Lower echelon patrolmen from some of the surrounding small towns, no doubt; encouraged to attend by their sergeants, but more motivated by VA stipends.

Last through the doorway was a thin, freckled woman in full summer uniform. A sleeve of her crisp blue shirt carried the identifying patch of the Lockton police department.

Lockton was a bedroom suburb, and he'd heard about officer Janet Jones from the captain there. The only woman in a twenty-man department, Jones was a divorcée, mid-thirties, who had talked her way onto the force after several years with the county rescue squad. She had a reputation for competence and hard work, and the captain was pushing her to advance.

The bell rang, and Dixon called the roll. The older woman's enrollment card carried a social security number and a name, Mrs. Marie Howell, but nothing to indicate why she was there.

As usual, Dixon began with a quick description of the course. "Welcome to Criminal Justice 2.1," he said. "Better known as Criminalistics I. We cover the fundamentals of investigation in this course—crime scene search, recording, collection and preservation of evidence, with investigation of specific offenses such as arson, narcotics, sex crimes, larceny, burglary, robbery, and homicide. The main thing I'll be stressing is the importance of common sense, thoroughness, and teamwork."

"If we're gonna form teams," said Blair, the blond hotshot, "I wanna be on her team." He leered at Sue Lee, the prettier of the two SBI women.

There was a snicker from some of the men in the rear, and the three professional women in the room exchanged here-we-go-again looks, but Mrs. Howell smiled at Blair as if she hadn't quite understood his remark.

Dixon brought them to order and continued his introductory lecture. Everyone began taking notes except Blair, who not only lacked notepaper, but had somehow lost his pen. Mrs. Howell lent him both.

By the end of the three-hour class session, Dixon had seen most of his first impressions confirmed. The discussion period brought intelligent comments from the SBI women, who were experienced in identifying partial fingerprints; thoughtful questions from the capital police officer and Janet Jones about why detectives took certain actions; and a running stream of smart-aleck remarks from Blair. Only Mrs. Howell had contributed nothing; and as class ended amid general conversation, Dixon said, "Mrs. Howell?"

She paused with a bright smile. "Yes?"

He held out her enrollment card. "There's a space here for noting if you're connected with a law agency. Yours is blank."

"Oh, I'm not anything official," she said. "Heavens, no! Do I have to be?"

"Not really, but I wondered . . ."

"Why I'm here?" Mrs. Howell looked self-conscious. "I thought it was a writing class."

"I beg your pardon?"

"I've always loved to write," she said shyly. "I write poems. Not very good ones, I'm afraid. And poetry's not very popular unless you're Robert Frost or Rod McKuen or somebody. Then I noticed that there are lots of mystery books on the newsstands and I thought they might be easy to write, only I don't know a thing about guns or poisons; so when I saw Criminalistics in the catalog, I hoped it meant the technical parts of crime-writing. Well, I see now that it didn't, but it sounds awfully fascinating and I hope you don't mind if I stay."

Dixon suppressed a smile. "Not at all," he said.

In the weeks that followed, Dixon was rather pleased with the way the class shaped. The women were more conscientious about assignments, and they plunged into experimental crime scene searches with so much enthusiasm that pride spurred the men into keeping up. Blair became the class kvetch, grumbling about tests and papers. He was the only one to pass out at the autopsy they attended. "Try to pretend he's just cutting up a chicken," Mrs. Howell advised.

Mrs. Howell brought a distinctly domestic touch to the course. Despite some elementary consciousness-raising from the younger women, she persisted in calling herself "just a housewife" and in seeing things in that light.

When they mixed plaster of Paris to cast shoe tracks, she likened it to making cream waffles. "Mr. Howell's terribly fussy about his waffles. Cook never gets them right so I always have to do it, and this is the exact consistency of my batter."

She was enchanted to learn of the chemicals available to crime labs: chemicals that could lift a gun's filed-off serial numbers, that would react with microscopic traces of blood, that could develop fingerprints several years old.

Janet Jones took her under her wing, explained police procedures and terminology, and let the older woman examine the handcuffs and gun she wore on her belt.

Mrs. Howell reciprocated with home-baked cookies; and during coffee breaks in the canteen, she tried out arcane plot devices on her classmates and pretended not to mind when they picked flaws in her motives and methods.

"Black widow spiders aren't all that deadly," one of the CCBI guys told her. "And even if they were, putting some in a man's bed wouldn't necessarily do the trick. He'd probably roll over and crush them before they bit."

"Then what about a rich woman who can't sleep because it's a scorching hot night and the air conditioner is broken," Mrs. Howell postulated. "She goes out to the car, cranks it up, switches on the air conditioner, and goes to sleep in the back seat. Her husband sneaks out, closes the garage door and stuffs rags in the exhaust pipe so that she dies of carbon monoxide poisoning."

"There would be smudges on the tailpipe," said the policeman from the capital.

"Maybe if he'd just replaced the exhaust system?" she asked hopefully.

"That'd make him the number one suspect. He'd be accused of premeditated tampering."

When Dixon discussed paraffin tests to determine whether someone had recently fired a gun, she was excited to hear that handling bologna would give an inconclusive reading.

"So a killer could conceal a gun in his lunchbox, shoot the victim, and then eat a bologna sandwich! Mr. Howell loves bologna," she confided. "He says people wouldn't be so snooty about it if it cost as much as roast beef. We have it for lunch all the time. It doesn't quite agree with me and Mr. Howell's really not supposed to have so much smoked meat, but you know husbands. They love to have their way."

She said it without the least trace of irony or resentment. Sue Lee sighed and once again began to explain some of the basic gains that women—even "just housewives"—had made in the last twenty years.

Dixon tried to be patient; but one day, after listening to

yet another zany murder plot in the canteen when he really wanted to talk to Janet Jones, he couldn't resist expounding the cold hard facts of life to his naive student.

"It's not 'Columbo' or 'Kojak' and half the time it isn't even 'Hill Street Blues,'" he said, ignoring Janet's frown. "Read the textbook, Mrs. Howell. There's only a seventy-three percent clearance rate on homicide, and it wouldn't be that high except that most murders are domestic and the killers don't even try to deny it. More murders go unsolved because of dumb, lazy detectives than because of smart killers."

Mrs. Howell's face fell, and Janet Jones glared at him. To take the sting from his words, he grinned at them both. "Look," he said, "go ahead with your plots. They'll make good reading; but just remember that in real life, there are more Blairs around a station house than Kojaks."

Mrs. Howell smiled back gamely. "The KISS system you tell us to follow—Keep It Simple, Stupid?"

"Oh now, I didn't mean—"

"No, you're probably right. I suppose it *is* stupid for a fifty-year-old housewife to try to write anything."

Blinking back tears, Mrs. Howell fled from the canteen and left Dixon alone at the table with a seething Janet Jones.

"You probably kick cats, too," she said fiercely.

"I didn't mean to hurt her feelings," Dixon said. "Look, Bob Reed told me you were his most level-headed officer. Doesn't that nonsense she spouts get under your skin?"

"She's a neat lady doing what she has to to get by," said Janet, her blue eyes snapping.

"What's that supposed to mean?"

"Forget it," she said and crushed her foam cup into a ball. "You wouldn't understand."

She strode from the canteen, and Dixon sprinted after her.

"That sounded suspiciously like a chauvinistic remark, Officer Jones."

The policewoman paused. "Yes," she admitted.

"Chauvinistic, male-directed anger with a feeling of sisterhood toward Mrs. Howell," Dixon said thoughtfully. "Does her husband beat her or run around on her?"

"Captain Reed said you were good," said Janet Jones, impressed in spite of herself. "Mr. Howell owns Lockton's second-largest bank, so I know his car."

"And?"

"It's parked at a motel out on the bypass several times a week. The woman's one of his tellers."

"Does Mrs. Howell know?"

"I don't think so. Anyhow, you've heard her. She's so pre-ERA she'd probably think it was her fault. He's the reason she's here, though. He told her she writes rotten poetry, and she wanted to impress him with something better. Now you've shot her down, too."

"I'm sorry about that. Look, if I tell Mrs. Howell I think her luminol and Clorox plot has possibilities, will you have dinner with me tonight?"

Janet Jones smiled and a small dimple appeared in each freckled cheek. "What else did Captain Reed tell you?" she temporized.

"That you're brilliant and beautiful and that if he weren't happily married, he'd ask you out himself except that you're too sensible to see anyone in the department. What did he say about me?"

Her smile became a laugh, and her blue eyes danced impishly.

"That you were the best investigator the SBI ever had, that you went into teaching because you were so exasperated with the level of incompetence on most police forces, that you'd probably ask me to dinner, and that I should say yes."

"A good officer never questions her captain's judgment," Dixon said.

"Okay, but you have to give Marie some encouragement."

They returned to the classroom, but Mrs. Howell had not

come back after the coffee break. "Next time," Dixon promised.

Unfortunately, there was no next time for Mrs. Howell.

Classes were cancelled for a week when a severe wind and lightning storm hit the area, uprooting trees and knocking out power lines. Some parts of the county were without electricity for two days.

Like others in her department, Janet Jones had worked double shifts, directing traffic around fallen power lines, assisting in medical emergencies, and patrolling business areas where store windows had been broken by flying debris.

There were still dark circles under her eyes when the class finally met again. Everyone had tales of damage the summer storm had wrought, and it was several minutes before Dixon could call the class to order. Even then, Janet interrupted him. "Did anybody hear about Marie Howell?"

The others looked around, suddenly realizing that Mrs. Howell was missing. "Was she hurt?" someone asked.

"Not her; her husband," said Janet. "A fallen limb broke one of their storm doors—left glass all over their brick patio. He was picking up the pieces when he slipped on some wet leaves and fell on a jagged edge." Janet's fingers touched her neck. "Marie found him too late."

"He bled to death?" asked one of the SBI women, shocked.

Janet nodded. "The funeral was two days ago." She pulled out a sympathy card she had bought. "I thought we could send this to her as a class."

The card went around, and everyone signed it. Dixon added a note expressing their hope that she would soon rejoin them.

A few days later, a black-bordered envelope appeared in his mailbox at Colleton Tech. He showed it to Janet at dinner that night.

"Mrs. Howell isn't coming back," he said and handed her the letter.

Dear Fellow Classmates and especially Mr. Dixon,

Thank you so much for your sympathy upon my recent bereavement. You'll never know how much the class has meant to me and how much I learned. You are a good teacher, Mr. Dixon. Most of all, you helped me see that I have no talent for complicated murders. Poetry is my first and deepest love, and I shall not wander from my field again.

> Kind friends who helped,
> I thank you so.
> Sorrow's cares are gone
> Since you I know.

Marie Howell

Janet's blue eyes were misty in the candlelight. "Poor dear," she said.

"'Poor dear,' my Aunt Fanny!" Dixon said. "Your department must have handled Howell's death. Are you sure it was an accident?"

"According to the autopsy report, he fell on a piece of glass and it pierced his jugular. Why?"

"Did anyone print the glass?"

"Of course we did, and it was just his fingerprints and hers."

"Hers?"

"She pulled it out of his neck. He was her husband, Jeff. She tried to save him. You can't possibly think—"

"Can't I? Read her letter again: how much the class meant, how much she learned! She's thumbing her nose at me. Look at that poem, dammit!"

Puzzled, Janet scanned the letter again. "Those are things people say at a time like this," she said helplessly. "You can't read double meanings into a thank-you note."

Her smile was rueful as she reread Marie Howell's poem.

"I'm afraid her husband was right, though. She's certainly not a very good poet. 'Sorrow's cares are gone/Since you I know.' Awkward."

"Awkward but accurate," Dixon said. "Since knowing us, she's managed to get rid of a wealthy, cheating bully of a husband. I told her to keep it simple, and she did."

"Oh, honestly, Jeff! It's just bad poetry."

"But good acrostics," he said bitterly. "It wouldn't stand up in court, but read the first letter of each line, dear Janet, and tell me she shouldn't get an A in the course."

THE ORCHARD WALLS

==

by Ruth Rendell

I have never told anyone this before.

The worst was long over, of course. Intense shame had faded and the knowledge of having made the greatest possible fool of myself. Forty years and more had done their work there. The feeling I had been left with, that I was precocious in a foul and dirty way, that I was unclean, was washed away. I had done my best never to think about it, to blot it all out, never to permit to ring on my inward ear Mrs. Thorn's words: "How dare you say such a thing! How dare you be so disgusting! At your age, a child, you must be sick in your mind."

Things would bring it back—the scent of honeysuckle, a brace of bloodied pigeons hanging in a butcher's window, the first cherries of the season. I winced at these things, I grew hot with a shadow of that blush that had set me on fire with shame under the tree, Daniel's hard hand gripping my shoulder, Mrs. Thorn trembling with indignant rage. The memory, never completely exorcised, still had the power to punish the adult for the child's mistake.

Until today.

Having one's childhood trauma cured by an analyst must be like this. Only a newspaper has cured mine. The newspaper came through my door and told me I hadn't been disgusting or sick in my mind, I had been right. In the broad facts at least I had been right. All day I have been asking myself what I should do—what action, if any, I should take. At last I have been able to think about it all quite calmly—in tranquility, to think of Ella and Dennis Clifton without growing hot and ashamed, of Mrs. Thorn with pity, and of that lovely lost place with something like nostalgia.

It was a long time ago. I was fourteen. Is that to be a child? They thought so. I thought so myself at the time. But the truth was I was a child and not a child, at one and the same time a paddler in streams, a climber of trees, an expert at cartwheels—and with an imagination full of romantic love. I was in a stage of transition, a pupa, a chrysalis.

Bombs were falling on London. Plymouth had been devastated and Coventry burned. I had already once been evacuated with my school and come back again to the suburb we lived in that sometimes seemed safe and sometimes not. My parents were afraid for me and that was why they sent me to Inchfield, to the Thorns. I could see the fear in my mother's eyes and it made me uncomfortable.

"Just till the end of August," she said, pleading with me. "It's beautiful there. You could think of it as an extra long summer holiday."

I remembered Hereford and my previous "billet," the strange people, the alien food.

"This will be different. Ella is your own aunt."

She was my mother's sister, her junior by twelve years. There were a brother and sister in between, both living in the north. Ella's husband was a farmer in Suffolk, or had been. He was in the army, and his elder brother ran the farm. Later, when Ella was dead and Philip Thorn married again and all I kept of them was that shameful thing I did my best to forget, I discovered that Ella had married Philip when she was seventeen because she was pregnant, and in the thirties any alternative to marriage in those circumstances was unthinkable. She had married him and six months later given birth to a dead child. When I went to Inchfield she was still only twenty-five, still childless, living with a brother-in-law and mother-in-law in the depths of the country, her husband fighting in North Africa.

I didn't want to go. At fourteen one isn't afraid; one knows one is immortal. After an air raid, we used to go about the streets collecting pieces of shrapnel, fragments of shell. The worst thing to me was having to sleep under a Morrison shelter instead of in my bedroom. Having a room of my own again, a place to be private in, was an inducement. I yielded. To this day I don't know if I was invited or if my mother had simply written to say that I was coming, that I must come, that they must give me refuge.

It was the second week of June when I went. Daniel Thorn met me at the station at Ipswich. I was wildly romantic, far too romantic, my head full of fantasies and dreams. Knowing I should be met, I expected a pony carriage or even a man on a black stallion leading a chestnut mare for me, though I had never in my life been on a horse. He came in an old Ford van.

We drove to Inchfield through deep green silent lanes— silent, that is, but for the occasional sound of a shot. I thought it must be something to do with the war, without specifying to myself what.

"The war?" said Daniel as if this were something happening ten thousand miles away. He laughed the age-old laugh of the country-man scoring off the townee. "You'll find no war here. That's some chap out after rabbits."

Rabbit was what we were to live on—stewed, roasted, in pies—relieved by wood pigeon. It was a change from London sausages, but I have never eaten rabbit since, not once. The characteristic smell of it cooking, experienced once in a friend's kitchen, brought me violent nausea. What a devil's menu that would have been for me, stewed rabbit and cherry pie!

The first sight of the farm enchanted me. The place where I lived in Hereford had been a late Victorian brick cottage, red and raw and ugly as poverty. I had scarcely seen a house like Cherry Tree Farm except on a calendar. It was long and low and thatched, and its two great barns were thatched, too. The low green hills and the dark clustering woods hung behind it. And scattered all over the wide slopes of grass were the cherry trees, one so close up to the house as to rub its branches against a windowpane.

They came out of the front door to meet us, Ella and Mrs. Thorn, and Ella gave me a white, rather cold cheek to kiss. She didn't smile. She looked bored. It was better, therefore, than I had expected, and worse. Ella was worse and Mrs. Thorn was better. The place was ten times better. Tea was like something I hadn't had since before the war. My bedroom was not only nicer than the Morrison shelter, it was nicer than my bedroom at home. Mrs. Thorn took me up there when we had eaten the scones and currant bread and walnut cake.

It was low-ceilinged, with the stone-colored studs showing through the plaster. A patchwork quilt was on the bed and the walls were hung with a paper patterned all over with bundles of cherries. I looked out of the window.

"You can't see the cherry trees from here," I said. "Is that why they put cherries on the walls?"

The idea seemed to puzzle her. She was a simple, conservative woman. "I don't know about that. That would be rather whimsical."

I was at the back of the house. My window overlooked a trim dull garden of rosebuds cut out in segments of a circle. Mrs. Thorn's own garden, I was later to learn, and tended by herself.

"Who sleeps in the room with the cherry tree?" I said.

"Your auntie." Mrs. Thorn was always to refer to Ella in

this way. She was a stickler for respect. "That has always been my son Philip's room."

Always. I envied the absent soldier. A tree with branches against one's bedroom window represented to me something down which one could climb and make one's escape, perhaps even without the aid of knotted sheets. I said as much, toning it down for my companion, who I guess would see it in a different light.

"I'm sure he did no such thing," said Mrs. Thorn. "He wasn't that kind of boy."

Those words stamped Philip for me as dull. I wondered why Ella had married him. What had she seen in this unromantic chap, five years her senior, who hadn't been the kind of boy to climb down trees out of his bedroom window? Or climb up them, come to that.

She was beautiful. For the first Christmas of the war I had been given *Picturegoer Annual*, in which was a full-page photograph of Hedy Lamarr. Ella looked just like her. She had the same perfect features, dark hair, other-worldly eyes fixed on far horizons. I can see her now—I can *permit* myself to see her—as she was then, thin, long-legged, in the floral cotton dress with collar and cuffs and narrow belt that would be fashionable again today. Her hair was pinned up in a roll off her forehead, the rest left hanging to her shoulders in loose curls, mouth painted like raspberry jam, eyes as nature made them, large, dark, alight with some emotion I was years from analyzing. I think now it was compounded of rebellion and longing and desire.

Sometimes in the early evenings she would disappear upstairs and then Mrs. Thorn would say in a respectful voice that she had gone to write to Philip. We used to listen to the wireless. Of course, no one knew exactly where Philip was, but we all had a good idea he was somehow involved in the attempts to relieve Tobruk. At news times, Mrs. Thorn became very tense. Once, to my embarrassment, she made a choking sound and left the room, covering her eyes with her hand. Ella switched off the set.

"You ought to be in bed," she said to me. "When I was your age I was always in bed by eight."

I envied and admired her, even though she was never particularly nice to me and seldom spoke except to say I "ought" to be doing something or other. Did she look at this niece, not much more than ten years younger than herself, and see what she herself had thrown away—a future of hope, a chance of living?

I spent very little time with her. It was Mrs. Thorn who took me shopping with her to Ipswich, who talked to me while she did the baking, who knitted and taught me to knit. There was no wool to be had so we picked old jumpers and washed the wool and carded it and started again. I was with her most of the time. It was either that or being on my own. No doubt there were children of my own age in the village I might have got to know but the village was two miles away. I was allowed to go out for walks but not to ride the only bicycle they had.

"It's too large for you. It's a twenty-eight inch," Mrs. Thorn said. "Besides, it's got a crossbar."

I said I could easily swing my leg behind the saddle like a man.

"Not while you're staying with me."

I didn't understand. "I wouldn't hurt myself." I said what I said to my mother. "I wouldn't come to any harm."

"It isn't ladylike," said Mrs. Thorn, and that was that.

Those things mattered a lot to her. She stopped me turning cartwheels on the lawn when Daniel was about, even though I wore shorts. Then she made me wear a skirt. But she was kind, she paid me a lot of attention. If I had had to depend on Ella or the occasional word from Daniel, I might have looked forward more eagerly to my parents' fortnightly visits than I did.

After I had been there two or three weeks, the cherries began to turn color. Daniel, coming upon me looking at them, said they were an old variety called Inchfield White Heart.

"There used to be a cherry festival here," he said. "The first Sunday after July the twelfth it was. There'd be dancing and a supper. You'd have enjoyed yourself. Still, we never had one last year and we're not this and somehow I don't reckon there'll ever be a cherry festival again what with this old war."

He was a yellow-haired, red-complexioned Suffolk man, big and thickset. His wide mouth, sickle-shaped, had its corners permanently turned upward. It wasn't a smile, though, and he was seldom cheerful. I never heard him laugh. He used to watch people in a rather disconcerting way, Ella especially. And when guests came to the house, Dennis Clifton or Mrs. Leithman or some of the farming people they knew, he would sit and watch them, seldom contributing a word.

One evening when I was coming back from a walk, I saw Ella and Dennis Clifton kissing in the wood.

Dennis Clifton wasn't a farmer. He had been in the R.A.F., had been a fighter pilot in the Battle of Britain, but had received some sort of head injury, been in hospital and was now on leave at home recuperating. He must have been very young, no more than twenty-two or -three. While he was ill, his mother, with whom he had lived and who had been a friend of Mrs. Thorn's, had died and left him her pretty little Georgian house in Inchfield. He was often at the farm, ostensibly to see his mother's old friend.

After these visits, Daniel used to say, "He'll soon be back in the thick of it," or "It won't be long before he's up there in his Spitfire. He can't wait."

This made me watch him, too, looking for signs of impatience to return to the R.A.F. His hands shook sometimes; they trembled like an old man's. He, too, was fair-haired and blue-eyed, yet there was all the difference in the world between his appearance and Daniel's. Film stars set my standard of beauty, and I thought he looked like Leslie Howard playing Ashley Wilkes. He was tall and thin and sensitive and his eyes were sad. Daniel watched him and Ella sat and I read my book while he talked very kindly and encouragingly to Mrs. Thorn about her son Philip, about how confident he was Philip would be all right, would survive, and while he talked his eyes grew sadder and more veiled.

No—I imagined that, not remembered it. It is in the light of what I came to know that I have imagined it. He was simply considerate and kind, like the well brought up young man he was.

I had been in the river. There was a place about a mile upstream they called the weir, where for a few yards the banks were built up with concrete below a shallow falls. A pool about four feet deep had formed there and on hot days I went bathing in it. Mrs. Thorn would have stopped me if she had known, but she didn't know. She didn't even know I had a bathing costume with me.

The shortest way was back through the wood. I heard a shot and then another from up in the meadows. Daniel was out after pigeons. The wood was dim and cool, full of soft twitterings, feathers rustling against dry leaves. The bluebells were long past, but dog's mercury was in flower, a white powdering, and the air was scented with honeysuckle. Another shot came, farther off but enough to shatter peace, and there was a rush of wings as pigeons took flight. Through the black trunks of trees and the lacework of their branches, I could see the yellow sky and the sun burning in it, still an hour off setting.

Ella was leaning against the trunk of a chestnut, looking up into Dennis Clifton's face. He had his hands pressed against the trunk, on either side of her head. If she had ever been nice to me, if he had ever said more than hello, I think I might have called out to them. I didn't call and in a moment I realized the last thing they would want was to be seen.

I stayed where I was. I watched them. Oh, I was in no way a voyeur. There was nothing lubricious in it, nothing of curiosity, still less a wish to catch them out. I was overwhelmed rather by the romance of it, ravished by wonder. I watched him kiss her. He took his hands down and put his arms round her and kissed her so that their faces were no longer visible, only his fair head and her dark hair and their locked straining shoulders. I caught my breath and shivered in the warm half-light, in the honeysuckle air.

They left the place before I did, walking slowly away in the direction of the road, arms about each other's waists.

In the room at Cherry Tree Farm they still called the parlor, Mrs. Thorn and Daniel were sitting, listening to the wireless, drinking tea. No more than five minutes afterward, Ella came in. I had seen what I had seen, but if I hadn't, wouldn't I still have thought her looks extraordinary, her shining eyes and the flush on her white cheek, the willow leaf in her hair and the bramble clinging to her skirt?

Daniel looked at her. There was blood in his fingernails, though he had scrubbed his hands. It brought me a flicker of nausea. Ella put her fingers through her hair, plucked out the leaf, and went upstairs.

"She is going up to write to Philip," said Mrs. Thorn.

Why wasn't I shocked? Why wasn't I horrified? I was only fourteen and I came from a conventional background. Adultery was something committed by people in the Bible. I suppose I could say I had seen no more than a kiss and adultery didn't enter into it. Yet I knew it did. With no experience, with only the scantiest knowledge, I sensed that this love had its full consummation. I knew Ella was married to a soldier who was away fighting for his country. I even knew that my parents would think behavior such as hers despicable, if not downright wicked. But I cared for none of that. To me it was romance, it was Lancelot and Guinevere, it was a splendid and beautiful adventure that was happening to two handsome young people—as one day it might happen to me.

I was no go-between. For them I scarcely existed. I

received no words or smiles, still less messages to be carried. They had the phone, anyway. They had cars. But though I took no part in their love affair and wasn't even with accuracy able to calculate the times when it was conducted, it filled my thoughts. Outwardly, I followed the routine of days I had arranged for myself and Mrs. Thorn had arranged for me, but my mind was occupied with Dennis and Ella, assessing what meeting places they would use, imagining their conversations—their vows of undying love—and recreating with cinematic variations that kiss.

My greatest enjoyment, my finest hours of empathy, were when he called. I watched the two of them as intently then as Daniel did. Sometimes I fancied I caught between them a glance of longing, and once I actually witnessed something more—an encounter between them in the passage when Ella came from the kitchen with the tea tray and Dennis had gone to fetch something from his car for Mrs. Thorn. Unseen by them, I stood in the shadow between the grandfather clock and the foot of the stairs. I heard him whisper:

"Tonight? Same place?" She nodded, her eyes wide. I saw him put his hand on her shoulder in a slow caress as he went past her.

I slept badly those nights. It had become very hot. Mrs. Thorn made sure I was in bed by nine and there was no way of escaping from the house after that without being seen by her. I envied Ella with a tree outside her window down which it would be easy to climb and escape. I imagined going down to the river in the moonlight, walking in the wood, perhaps seeing my lovers in some trysting place. My lovers, whose breathy words and laden glances exalted me and rarefied the overheated air.

The cherries were turning pale yellow, with a blush coming to their cheeks. It was the first week of July, the week the war came to Inchfield and a German bomber, lost and off-course, unloaded a stick of bombs in one of the Thorns' fields.

No one was hurt, though a cow got killed. We went to look at the mess in the meadow, the crater and the uprooted tree. Daniel shook his fist at the sky. The explosions had made a tremendous noise, and we were all sensitive after that to any sudden sound. Even the crack of Daniel's shotgun made his mother jump.

The heat had turned sultry and clouds obscured our blue skies, though no rain fell. Mrs. Leithman, coming to tea as she usually did once a week, told us she fancied each roll of thunder was another bomb. We hardly saw Ella, she was always up in her room or out somewhere—out with Dennis, of course. I speculated about them, wove fantasies around them, imagined Philip Thorn killed in battle and thereby setting them free. So innocent was I, living in more innocent or at least more puritanical times, that the possibility of this childless couple being divorced never struck me. Nor did I envisage Dennis and Ella married to each other but only continuing forever their perilous enchanting idyll. I even found Juliet's lines for them—Juliet, who was my own age—and whispered to myself that "the orchard walls are high and hard to climb; and the place death, considering who thou art . . ." Once, late at night when I couldn't sleep and sat in my window, I saw the shadowy figure of Dennis Clifton emerge from the deep darkness at the side of the house and leave by the gate out of the rose garden.

But the destruction of it all and any humiliation were drawing nearer. I had settled down there, I had begun to be happy. The truth is, I suppose, that I identified with Ella and in my complex fantasies it was I, compounded with Juliet, that Dennis met and embraced and touched and loved. My involvement was much deeper than that of any observer.

When it came, the shot sounded very near. It woke me up as such a sound might not have done before the bombs. I wondered what prey Daniel could go in search of at this hour, for the darkness was deep, velvety, and still. The crack which had split the night and jarred the silence wasn't repeated. I went back to sleep and slept till past dawn.

I got up early as I did most mornings, came downstairs in the quiet of the house, the hush of a fine summer morning, and went outdoors. Mrs. Thorn was in the kitchen, frying fat bacon and duck eggs for the men. I didn't know if it was all right for me to do this or if all the cherries were reserved for some mysterious purpose, but as I went toward the gate I reached up and picked a ripe one from a dipping branch. It was the crispest, sweetest cherry I had ever tasted, though I must admit I have eaten few since then. I pushed the stone into the earth just inside the gates. Perhaps it germinated and grew. Perhaps quite an old tree that has borne many summer loads of fruit now stands at the entrance to Cherry Tree.

As it happened, of all their big harvest, that was the only cherry I was ever to eat there. Coming back half an hour later, I pushed open the gate and stood for a moment looking at the farmhouse over whose sunny walls and roof the shadows of the trees lay in a slanted leafy pattern. I looked at the big tree, laden with red-gold fruit, that rubbed its branches against Ella's window. In its boughs, halfway up, in a fork a yard or two from the glass, hung the body of a man.

In the hot sunshine I felt icy cold. I remember the feeling to this day, the sensation of being frozen by a cold that came from within while outside me the sun shone and a thrush sang and the swallows dipped in and out under the eaves. My eyes seemed fixed, staring in the hypnosis of shock and fear at the fair-haired dangling man, his head thrown back in the agony of death there outside Ella's bedroom window.

At least I wasn't hysterical. I resolved I must be calm and adult. My teeth were chattering. I walked stiffly into the kitchen, and there they all were, around the table, Daniel and the two men and Ella and, at the head of it, Mrs. Thorn pouring tea.

I meant to go quietly up to her and whisper it. I couldn't. To get myself there without running, stumbling, shouting had used up all the control I had. The words rushed out in a loud ragged bray and I remember holding up my hands, my fists clenched.

"Mr. Clifton's been shot. He's been shot, he's dead. His body's in the cherry tree outside Ella's window!"

There was silence. But first a clatter as of knives and forks dropped, of cups rattled into saucers, of chairs scraped. Then this utter stricken silence. I have never—not in all the years since then—seen anyone go as white as Ella went. She was as white as paper, and her eyes were black holes. A brick color suffused Daniel's face. He swore. He used words that made me shrink and draw back and shiver and stare from one to the other of the horrible, horrified faces. Mrs. Thorn was the first to speak, her voice cold with anger. "How dare you say such a thing! How dare you be so disgusting! At your age—you must be sick in your mind!"

Daniel had jumped up. He took me roughly by the arm. But his grasp wasn't firm—the hand was shaking the way Dennis's shook. He manhandled me out there, his mother scuttling behind us. We were still five or six yards from the tree when I saw. The hot blood came into my face and throbbed under my skin. I looked at the cloth face, the yellow wool hair—our own unpicked, carded wool—the stuffed sacking body, the cracked boots. Icy with indignation, Mrs. Thorn said, "Haven't you ever seen a scarecrow before?"

I cried out desperately, as if, even in the face of this evidence, I could still prove them wrong. "But scarecrows are in fields!"

"Not in this part of the world." Daniel's voice was thin and hoarse. He couldn't have looked more gaunt, more shocked, if it had really been Dennis Clifton in that tree. "In this part of the world we put them on cherry trees. I put it there last night. I put *them* there." And he pointed at what I had passed but never seen, the man in the tree by the wall, the man in the tree in the middle of the green lawn.

I went back to the house and up to my room and lay on the bed, prone and silent with shame. The next day was Saturday, and my parents were coming. They would tell them, and I should be taken home in disgrace. In the middle of the day Mrs. Thorn came to the door and said to come to lunch. She was a changed woman, hard and dour. I had never heard the expression "to draw aside one's skirts" but later on when I did I recognized that this was what she had done to me. Her attitude to me was as if I were some sort of psychopath.

We had lunch alone, only I didn't really have any. I couldn't eat. Just as we were finishing and I was pushing aside my laden plate, Daniel came in and sat down and said they had all talked about it and they thought it would be best if I went home with my parents the following day. "Of course I shall tell them exactly what you said and what you inferred," said Mrs. Thorn. "I shall tell them how you insulted your auntie."

Daniel, who wasn't trembling any more or any redder in the face than usual, considered this for a moment in silence. Then he said unexpectedly—or unexpectedly to me, "No, we won't, Mother, we won't do that. No point in that. The fewer know the better. You've got to think of Ella's reputation."

"I won't have her here," his mother said.

"No, I agree with that. She can tell them she's homesick or I'll say it's too much for you, having her here."

Ella hid herself away all that day.

"She has her letter to write to Philip," said Mrs. Thorn.

In the morning she was at the table with the others. Daniel made an announcement. He had been down to the village and heard that Dennis Clifton was back in the Air Force. He had rejoined his squadron. "He'll soon be back in the thick of it," he said.

Ella sat with bowed head, working with restless fingers a slice of bread into a heap of crumbs. Her face was colorless, lacking her usual makeup. I don't remember ever hearing another word from her. I packed my things. My parents made no demur about taking me back with them. Starved of love, sickened by the love of others, I clung to my father. The scarecrows grinned at us as we got into the van behind Daniel. I can see them now—I can permit myself to see them now—spread-eagled in the trees, protecting the reddening fruit, so lifelike that even the swallows swooped in wider arcs around them.

In the following spring Ella died giving birth to another dead child. My mother cried, for Ella had been her little sister. But she was shy about giving open expression to her grief. She and my father were anxious to keep from me, or for that matter anyone else, that it was a good fifteen months since Philip Thorn was home on leave. What became of Daniel and his mother I never knew, I didn't want to know. I couldn't avoid hearing that Philip had married again and his new wife was a niece of Mrs. Leithman's.

Only a meticulous reader of newspapers would have spotted this paragraph. I am in the habit of reading every line, with the exception of the sports news, and I spotted this item tucked away between an account of sharp practice in local government and the suicide of a financier. I read it. The years fell away, and the facts exonerated me. I knew I must do something and wondered what. I have been thinking of it all day, but now I know I must tell this story to the coroner. My story, my mistake, Daniel's rage.

An agricultural worker had come upon an unexploded bomb on farmland near Inchfield in Suffolk. It was thought to be one of a stick of bombs dropped there in 1941. Excavations in the area had brought to light a skeleton thought to be that of a young man who had met his death at

about the same time. A curious fact was that shotgun pellets
had been found in the cavity of the skull.

"The orchard walls are high and hard to climb; and the
place death, considering who thou art, if any of my kinsmen
find thee here . . ."

MURDER & MYSTERY